THE FOUR HORSEMEN

THE FOUR HORSEMEN

Rupert Stanbury

Rupert Stanbury

This book is dedicated to the brave people of Ukraine.

The Four Horsemen was largely written during the war between Russia and Ukraine. Like many Europeans I have been passionately supportive of the brave Ukrainians who have had their lives turned upside down, if not destroyed, by the imperialistic ambitions of yet another tyrant. Unfortunately, our continent has a habit of throwing up these megalomaniacs every so often. It is for this reason that *The Four Horsemen* is dedicated to these brave people who are fighting to maintain their country as a free and independent nation. Since actions count louder than words, **I have also decided to give all the royalties I receive from the sale of the book to support the people of Ukraine**. This could be to charitable organizations, or for the country's eventual reconstruction, or even to provide support for the war effort. Being practical, I am making this commitment for a period of five years from the date of publication. However, let me assure readers that if I receive significant sums after that date, I will ensure they are redirected towards supporting Ukraine and its people.

(Copy of the first paragraph of the Introduction.)

Contents

Principal Characters

Principal Characters

Hades' Realm

Mrs Aggycraggywoggynog ('Aggy') – Head Cook in charge of
     the Kitchens
Botty – A painter / decorator
Budiwati – A builder
Carlos – A builder
Cerberus – A three-headed dog
Sir Christopher Wren – Chief Architect
Death – A 'being' who transports people to the Underworld;
     one of The Four Horsemen
Gigliola – Works in the Kitchens
Hades – God; King of the Underworld
Lennie – A painter / decorator
Mason Bonko – Head Builder
Micky – A painter / decorator
Ming – Vesta's friend; works in the Kitchens
Persephone – Goddess; Hades' wife
Sanjay – A builder
Satan – Director of the Torturing Department
Sisyphus – A former king who used to push a boulder up a
     hill; now works in the Quarry
Smiley – A builder
Vesta – A recently arrived girl in the Underworld
Yousef – A builder

Poseidon's Realm

Amphitrite – Goddess; Poseidon's wife
Bettina – A small whale; Moby's partner
Dolores – Head housekeeper to Poseidon
Fuad – A whale
Hashimoto – Poseidon's butler
Kinky, Linky, Minky and Pinky – Mermaids living in the Sea
     Cavern
Moby – A large white whale
Poseidon – God; King of the Seas and Oceans

Suki – A small whale; friend of Moby's and Bettina's
Totty Turniptoes – Hair stylist, beautician and fitness
      instructor; used to live in Romford, Essex

Lilliput

Archimelock – Professor; Chief Scientist
Chertassle – Empress
Einstella ('Rach') – Head of Special Projects
Golroblin – General; Defense Minister
Listrongle – First Minister
MacBeetle (Private), MacHebe (Private), MacLeonard
      (Corporal) – Recent recruits to the Argyll &
      Sutherland Highlanders Regiment from Olympus
MacGobo – Sergeant in Argyll & Sutherland Highlanders
      Regiment
MacPonsibl – Colonel in Argyll & Sutherland Highlanders
      Regiment
Mandoselin – Interior Minister
Redrelok – Finance Minister
Shefrap – Mayor of Mildendo

Tyrantland

Big Dik – Ruler of Diktatorland
Captain of the Fishy Tyrant – A fisherman
Cho-ak – A guard
Famine – One of The Four Horsemen
First Mate of the Fishy Tyrant – A fisherman
First Officer – A Naval officer
Flogzum – A young scientist
Little Dik – Deputy Ruler of Diktatorland
Ob – Nephew of Stevie's
Pestilence – One of The Four Horsemen
Plonker – Admiral of the Fleet
Segolongsunugolywalgonisumcholbultyasfogquerlogmun-
      pong ('Stevie') – Head of the Tyrant's household; the

oldest person on the world
The Tyrant – Ruler of Tyrantland

Horses

Antoinette and Arabella – Athene's mares
Bonk, Donk, Tonk and Zonk – Hebe's stallions
Dolly, Holly, Molly and Polly – Poseidon's and Amphitrite's
	mares
Tomato Face ('The Red Horse') – Mars's stallion

Introduction

*T*he *Four Horsemen* was largely written during the war between Russia and Ukraine. Like many Europeans I have been passionately supportive of the brave Ukrainians who have had their lives turned upside down, if not destroyed, by the imperialistic ambitions of yet another tyrant. Unfortunately, our continent has a habit of throwing up these megalomaniacs every so often. It is for this reason that *The Four Horsemen* is dedicated to these brave people who are fighting to maintain their country as a free and independent nation. Since actions count louder than words, I have also decided to give all the royalties I receive from the sale of the book to support the people of Ukraine. This could be to charitable organizations, or for the country's eventual reconstruction, or even to provide support for the war effort. Being practical, I am making this commitment for a period of five years from the date of publication. However, let me assure readers that if I receive significant sums after that date, I will ensure they are redirected towards supporting Ukraine and its people.

The Four Horsemen is the second book in the *Gods Galore* series, which is a mixture of fantasy and comedy about the classical gods in the 21st Century AD. While many of the characters in the original *Gods Galore* novel reappear in this second book, it is very much written on a stand-alone basis. Put simply, it isn't necessary to have read the original *Gods Galore* before reading *The Four Horsemen*. However, for those readers who requested a follow-up after my first effort, I hope they will appreciate how some of the 'open' issues have now been addressed.

The title of the book comes from The Four Horsemen of The Apocalypse, being figures in Christian religion. The Four Horsemen are War, Death, Famine and Pestilence. Classical writings certainly recognized the first two: Mars being the God of War, and Death playing a central role in transferring the deceased to the Underworld. While famines and diseases existed in the ancient world, there were no specific figures to reflect these two scourges. However, in later years Famine and Pestilence became defined figures, and both now represent a further challenge for the classical gods as they try to cope with modern life.

The events in the book take place over many locations. However, one of them is very much at the heart of proceedings. This is the island of Lilliput which was first identified in Jonathan Swift's *Gulliver's Travels* written in the early 18th century. The Lilliputians are a small people, being no more than six inches tall, but they are both resourceful and intelligent and very much able to assist the gods in meeting their many challenges.

After *Gods Galore* was published various readers made a number of helpful observations. There were two, in particular, that I feel it is appropriate to address in this Introduction.

The first one was that the book lacked an underlying plot. This was fair comment since it was written very much as a soap opera, focusing on characters and numerous small incidents and adventures that they were involved in. However, there was a feeling that there were perhaps too many unresolved issues at the end, although this did result in a widespread desire for a sequel! *The Four Horsemen* is that sequel and I can assure readers that it contains a most definite plot. I have, though, also included a few soap opera scenes, since I felt it was important to let readers know what some of the principal characters in *Gods Galore* were up to, if they were not involved in the main storyline.

The second observation was a concern that while I generally used Greek names for the gods, there were two exceptions where I used the Roman names. These were Mars, the God of War, and Bacchus, the God of Wine, since I believed, whether rightly or wrongly, that these names were more generally recognized than their Greek equivalents of Ares and Dionysus. I decided to consult the gods on this matter. Artemis, who was a great believer in democracy, managed to get Zeus, who was not democratically inclined, to agree to a referendum of the gods on the alternatives. This turned out to be evenly split, so Athene suggested that Mars / Ares and Bacchus / Dionysus should be consulted on what they wanted to be called. The God of War was adamant he should go by the name of Ares, while the God of Wine didn't mind. With this extra knowledge, a second referendum was held and everyone, with the exception of Mars / Ares, voted for the name of Mars, since it involved giving him the middle finger; as far as the Bacchus / Dionysus decision was concerned the vote remained evenly split. At that stage, Zeus decided he'd had enough of democracy and instructed me to continue using Mars and Bacchus. I hope readers will accept I did my best to resolve this matter, but for those of you who still prefer the Greek names, please understand that I am following the wishes of the gods.

As with *Gods Galore*, I accept that there could be some classical scholars who may not fully appreciate the portrayal of various gods and goddesses in the book. All I can do is repeat what I wrote in the Introduction to my first novel. Like its forerunner, *The Four Horsemen*, has been written with the purpose of being an entertaining read; if its readers end up agreeing, then it has achieved all it set out to do. If it also generates some money for the Ukrainian people, so much the better!

Rupert Stanbury

1
KBO

Death was in a pensive mood. He had already seen Hades earlier that day when he escorted the new arrivals to the Underworld and had asked for a private chat a few hours later. He was now walking slowly towards the royal palace for this second meeting, still deep in thought about what he was going to say to the god.

Cerberus was behind a boulder watching the skeletal figure in his black cloak and carrying a scythe. Despite Death always looking the same, the Underworld's three-headed guard dog, also known as the Head of Internal Security, sensed something was amiss.

"Woof, woof," Cerberus barked as he bounded out from behind the boulder. "You look very thoughtful today, Death."

"Shut it, Cerberus. I'm not in the mood," was the stern reply.

"I'm trying to be friendly, Death. You should reciprocate occasionally."

"Haven't you got a job to do?"

"That's just what I'm coming on to now. Please tell me, Mr Death, what you are in the process of doing at this moment in time?"

"I'm going to see Hades, but what's it to do with you, Cerberus?"

"I'm information gathering. Very important from a security point of view. You can't have too much information."

Death stopped walking and looked at Cerberus. "Why is knowing that I'm going to see Hades relevant to the Underworld's security?" he asked.

"You need to take some lessons from my good friend, Sun Tzu, then you'd understand," Cerberus replied.

"And who is Sun Tzu?"

"You've obviously forgotten. It was a long time ago that you brought him here. Sun Tzu was a very famous Chinese general and military strategist. He wrote a book called *The Art of War*, you should read it."

"Have you read it, Cerberus?" Death asked.

"There's no need to. Sun Tzu has become a friend of mine and is advising me on all aspects of military strategy. I only have the very best people on my team, you know."

"And this Sun Tzu has told you to ask me where I'm walking to, has he?"

"Not just you, Death, but anyone I might be suspicious of."

"And why are you suspicious of me, Cerberus?" Death asked testily.

"I said 'might be suspicious of,' " Cerberus responded calmly. "That's why I'm gathering information. You never know where fifth columnists are to be found."

"What are they?"

"Spies; people working for the other side; that sort of thing."

"Nonsense!" Death exclaimed and started to walk away from Cerberus.

"Don't go, Death," the three-headed dog said as he trotted by the side of the black-cloaked skeleton. "I don't actually think you are a fifth columnist. I'm really just showing an interest in your welfare. I'd like to talk to you again about the two of us becoming friends."

"No," said Death as he continued to march onwards.

"Don't say that," Cerberus persevered. "Let me tell you how I'm getting on in the friendship stakes. At the end of it, I'll make you a win-win proposal."

"Not interested," was Death's response.

"Well, I'll just walk along with you anyway and talk away. It won't do you any harm to listen."

Death didn't respond, but the two figures continued to walk side by side towards Hades' palace.

"My very best friend is Vesta," Cerberus continued after a few seconds. "She is the cleverest and most charming person there is."

"That figures; opposites attract," Death muttered.

"I heard that Death, but I won't respond accordingly. You should hear me out. As I've said, we're looking at a win-win situation here."

Death didn't say anything, so Cerberus continued. "After Vesta, I have the following full friends – the two librarians, Homer and Virgil, Sisyphus, General Sun Tzu whom I've already mentioned and, finally Nelson. You will have noticed that we now have new, more professional signs at the jetty. These were done by Nelson in collaboration with me. I think they're a great improvement; don't you agree?"

"Some of the spelling's improved," Death commented. "But the piranha fish are still written as BANANA FISHES."

"Quite deliberate," Cerberus replied. "That's precisely what Nelson queried at first, so I had to explain that banana fishes were a subspecies of piranha fishes. Also, I was most insistent on referring to them as fishes, not just fish, which might imply that there was only one such creature in the water. People need to know there are lots of the little beasts ready to bite all their flesh off."

Death snorted. "I suppose it's some sort of improvement," he muttered.

"After my full friends," Cerberus ploughed on, "there are a series of people with whom I'm developing a closer relationship. I won't list them all, but the one I'm most pleased with is Aggy. Some time ago we agreed to be 'temporary, associate friends, on probation'. I'm pleased to tell you that we have now progressed to becoming 'temporary, associate friends.' I gather from Aggy that the next step will be to become 'associate friends', although I'm unsure if the probation bit will come back again. Anyway, the ultimate prize will be to become full 'friends.' What do you think?"

"I don't think anything," Death replied. "It's nothing to do with me."

"Woof, woof," Cerberus went. "That's where you're so wrong. My win-win proposal to you is that you and I should start off as Aggy and I did – we should agree today to become 'temporary, associate friends, on probation' and see how it goes."

The two of them had now arrived at the steps to the palace entrance. Cerberus ran ahead of Death and stood in his way.

"Woof, woof. Go on, Death, just say yes."

The hooded skeleton gave a deep sigh. He wanted a few minutes to himself before he saw Hades, which meant getting rid of Cerberus; in particular, he didn't want the three-headed dog to follow him into the throne room.

"Whatever you like Cerberus, provided you get out of my way and leave me in peace," he said with another sigh.

"Deal done!" Cerberus replied moving out of the way. "Win-win for both of us, Death. Win-win. Have a good meeting. Bye," and he bounded away giving the occasional woof, woof as he ran.

Hades had spent much of the afternoon sitting on his throne, contemplating matters. He had a lot on his mind. His most immediate concern was the need for more accommodation in the Underworld. For more than a year now, there had been a plague ravaging through all the continents up above. It meant that Death was bringing a lot more people than usual to his kingdom and the building work was struggling to keep up. He had met with the construction team to try to improve their efficiency, but with little success. He was now thinking of what to do next – perhaps he should contact Hephaestus, the Builder God on Olympus, and ask him to pay the Underworld a visit. Another idea was to speak to Vesta and ask her if she could identify any way to make the Building Department more productive, as she had done with the Torturing area. He would think more about it, but he knew he needed to find a solution soon.

Satan was another problem. He resented the changes introduced by Vesta into the Torturing Department. He also wanted to change his team, questioning their loyalty to him. As far as Hades was concerned, that was a good reason to keep them in place; they kept watch on Satan and would tip Hades off if he got up to any mischief. Relations between Satan and Sisyphus were also very poor ever since the latter had crushed the fiend underneath his large boulder. Revenge was what Satan wanted, but he hadn't yet found a way to achieve it. Hades would keep a close eye on affairs but was reasonably confident that Sisyphus could look after himself.

Hades' wife, Persephone, was expected to return to the Underworld soon. He was both eagerly looking forward to her visit, but also apprehensive. It wasn't a particularly happy marriage, and the god was only too well aware that he was to blame for this state of affairs. She never knew what to do with herself when she was in the Underworld and only ever spent time with Aggy in the Kitchens. Hebe had suggested that he should get Persephone more involved in running the Underworld and he was already developing some ideas on how to do that. Hopefully, she would be pleased about the greater variety of food that was now on offer as well as the fine wines that Bacchus had sent him. What she would make of the changes Vesta had brought about in Cerberus would be interesting to see. He was already determined to introduce Vesta to Persephone as soon as she arrived and hoped that some sort of relationship could develop between the two of them. Perhaps they could work together on bringing more change to the Underworld?

Then there was Death. He had been in a strange mood recently and Hades suspected that Death's request for a meeting today might explain why. The god had been pondering what it could be about. He knew Death was still frustrated about the Totty Turniptoes situation, but he thought it was more likely to be something else. Perhaps it was his workload due to the pandemic, or the ferryman often keeping him waiting; maybe even a complaint about Sisyphus being released from pushing the boulder up the hill. After all, Death had once been tricked and imprisoned by Sisyphus, so there was no love lost between the two of them.

As Hades was pondering these matters, Death walked into the throne room. He stared at Hades, who nodded to him to come forward.

"Good day for the second time, Death," the god said.

"May I sit down on the stool?" the cloaked skeleton asked.

"Yes, of course," Hades replied, thinking to himself that Death had never sat down beforehand.

Death sat on the small wooden stool and looked up at Hades on his golden throne. Neither said anything for a while until Hades asked Death what he wanted to discuss.

Death began nervously. "Lord Hades," he said. "Perhaps I should start by saying that I view the conversation we are about to have as being the most important one ever held between the two of us."

"I understand," Hades answered, feeling somewhat puzzled. "Please continue."

"I have not been entirely settled for some time. I'm unsure how to describe my feelings because I don't fully understand them myself. They are new, you see. Perhaps if I asked you some questions, things might become clearer."

Hades nodded his assent.

"I am trying to find out who I am, so let me first ask if I am a god?"

Hades shook his head. "No, Death," he said. "You are not a god."

"Then am I human or was I ever human?"

"I'm afraid you're not and you never were human."

"Then what sort of animal am I, Hades?"

"I'm not sure if you are an animal. You're just Death, a unique being."

"A unique being you say. But how did I get here? Where did I come from?"

"You were a creation of the older gods, possibly even before the Titans. You were made with the sole function of terminating lives on earth and escorting them to the Underworld."

"Why?" Death asked in a slightly insistent tone.

"It was a long time ago, Death," the god replied. "But the reason then remains the same today. Only by ending lives would there be space for new ones to emerge. You provide a critical role in allowing the human race to advance and not become stale or stagnant. Let's call it 'population renewal', for want of a better description."

"So, what is my future, Hades?"

"What do you mean, Death?"

"I've been doing this job for ever. Is there no way I can advance, possibly do something else?"

"I don't understand what you're driving at, Death. You are special, unique, as I've already said, specifically created to carry out a vital function. That is what you do; there is no other role."

"Does that mean for ever and ever?"

"Yes," Hades replied.

"So, what if I went on strike, Hades?"

"What!" Hades responded angrily as he slammed his hands down on the arms of his throne. "You can't do that! Don't be absurd!"

Death was now feeling more confident, so he pressed the point. "Let me ask again, Hades, what would happen if I went on strike? You'd have to create another Death, wouldn't you?"

Hades did not reply for a while as he and Death continued to outstare each other. Now it's very difficult to outstare a skeleton, even if you are a god, so eventually Hades spoke.

"It is a ridiculous question which I've never considered. But yes, I should think the gods would want people to continue dying, so perhaps there would need to be another Death created. However, have you given any consideration to what would happen to you?"

"That's what I'm here to discuss," Death replied.

7

"Let me help you. I should think it highly likely that you would be banished to Tartarus. How would you feel about that?"

Death looked shocked. That was certainly not what he had in mind. Tartarus was a place of pure hell, deep inside the bowels of the earth. It's where the current gods' worst enemies were sent, including the Titans. That meant Cronus was there. Death remembered Cronus, who happened to be the father of Hades, Poseidon and Zeus. The biggest bastard Death had ever met – he certainly didn't want to spend eternity with him.

Hades watched Death's reaction to the Tartarus suggestion and decided to bring the conversation back to a less confrontational tone. He continued in a calmer tone. "Let's take a step back here, Death. No more talk about strikes and Tartarus; can you please explain what precisely you're looking for?"

"I'm looking for a future, Hades; something to aim at. Also, have you ever thought that I might get lonely on occasions? Being unique is all very well at the beginning, but everyone needs someone to talk to from time to time."

"I don't mean to sound unfeeling, Death, but no I've never considered you would be lonely. After all, you have a very active life, meeting new people every day."

"But that's the point. I only get to meet them once. There's no opportunity to develop longer term relationships."

Hades thought this was not surprising but decided it wouldn't be helpful to say so. Instead, he felt it was better to make a few suggestions. "I'm always very happy for you to call into the palace and have a chat with me," he said. "Also, what about the ferryman, Charon? I know he's not the most talkative of souls, but you do see him every day."

"I don't think the ferryman is a person who is likely to become a friend," Death responded.

"Well, if it's friends you're after, Death, why not have a chat with Cerberus? He seems to have a special project on at the moment, focused on making friends."

"We've already spoken. Apparently, he has decided that we should start off by becoming 'temporary, associate friends on probation'."

"Excellent!" Hades exclaimed. "You're already well on the way. 'Mighty oaks from little acorns grow', as the saying goes."

Death blinked, unsure what to make of the god's comment about acorns and mighty oaks. He needed to bring the conversation back to himself.

"I'm thinking along slightly different lines, Lord Hades," the skeleton responded. "The fundamental problem as I see it is that I am a unique creature, which means I do not meet others like me. You asked me earlier what I'm looking for; let me tell you. I have a dream that one day there will be a Mrs Death and that in due course a young Master Death will come along, followed shortly afterwards by a young Miss Death. During all this time, I would keep fulfilling my role of population renewal as you describe it. Mrs Death would look after the household and bring up the two children. As they got older, I would start to use young Master Death to assist me with the aim of him eventually taking over the family business. At that stage, I would retire and live peacefully with Mrs Death and young Miss Death who could look after the two of us."

"And where would this household be located, Death?" the god asked.

"I don't know if you've heard of a place called Eastbourne, Hades. It's a town on England's south coast. It's a popular location for people who retire, which means I visit it quite frequently because it has a large elderly population. There's an attractive bungalow overlooking the English Channel which I've had my eye on for some time. I've recently brought Mrs Smithers, the elderly lady who lived there, to the Underworld so it's now on the market with the local estate agents."

"And how do you propose to buy it, Death?" Hades asked. "You don't have any money."

"That is true, Lord Hades and is a problem to which I don't have a solution. I was thinking that perhaps the gods could buy it as an investment and let me live there."

Hades shook his head. "Very sorry, Death," he said firmly. "Property investment in Eastbourne is not something that the gods are prepared to indulge in."

"Have you any ideas then how I might raise the money for the property? Quite often, when I collect people for the Underworld, they have money in their pockets. Perhaps I ......"

Hades interrupted Death. "Certainly not," the god said in a sharp tone. "That would be most inappropriate and would reflect very badly on both you personally as well as us gods. You wouldn't want that, would you?"

"Put like that, I would have to agree. But what should I do, Hades?"

"The property issue would seem to be an insolvable one, since I agree the Death family would have to live somewhere. They couldn't do what you do at present, which I gather is to curl up under a tree for a short rest."

"Or against a stone wall if I'm in a city," Death added.

"Quite so," agreed Hades. "But as well as the property complication, there's an even bigger one, which is the assumption that the gods would be prepared to create a Mrs Death as well as both a Master Death and a Miss Death. I'm not sure if my fellow gods would agree."

"Isn't that something that you could do by yourself, Hades?"

Again, the god shook his head. "No, it's certainly something which both my brothers would have to agree to. It would then have to go to a full Gods' Council. I can already see objections from some of the younger gods because you're proposing a very traditional family. I gather the trend these days is to have single-, bi- or trans- families. I'm not really sure of all the details, but you might find that instead of a Mrs Death you have a younger Mr Death as a partner. That would mean he would be the one out and about involved in all the population renewal and you would be bringing up the younger generation. Also, it's just as likely that Miss Death would end up taking over the family business with young Master Death staying at home. Hebe was telling me all about these new trends last time she was here. She's apparently on some sort of Equalities Committee which is looking into all these matters."

Death sat on his stool looking dejected at everything Hades had said. "There seem to be great difficulties everywhere," he eventually said in a quiet, depressed voice. "What should we do?"

By now Hades was feeling a bit sorry for Death. He hadn't realized that the skeleton had all these feelings. He also noted that Death had used the word 'we' which probably meant that he considered his problem was also the god's. Hades decided to offer to speak to Zeus and Poseidon on the matter next time the three brothers got together. He knew, as did Death, this would probably be many centuries in the future by which time he hoped the whole issue would be forgotten. Anyway, at least it avoided an outright rejection of Death's wishes at this stage.

"So, that's what I'll do for you, Death; I'll speak to Zeus and Poseidon," Hades confirmed after the two of them had discussed his offer. "As far as you are concerned, my best advice to you is KBO. Yes, KBO is what you should do."

"KBO," Death repeated uncertainly. "I'm not sure I know what that means."

"KBO stands for Keep Buggering On. Yes, Keep Buggering On is your best bet for now. After all, you're good at your job Death, so KBO is the way forward."

"KBO. Keep Buggering On," Death murmured despondently. "Yes, I suppose so – Keep Buggering On."

2
Daughters – Old and New

Z eus was sitting in his study reading an old copy of the Financial Times which Hebe had brought him from her last trip to Yorkgate. He enjoyed the political commentary and the economic analysis but could never fully understand how stock markets worked. It was just incredible to him that the value of things could change from one day to the next, let alone every minute or even second of the day. He was totally confused by all these references to 'shares' because he didn't really understand what a company was and how shares worked.

In truth, Zeus only felt comfortable with physical things. As far as he was concerned, you either owned something like a factory or you didn't; perhaps you would own half and your brother the other half, with both of you going in each day. But how could thousands of people own a factory together, as seemed to be the case these days? Somehow this thing termed a company was involved, which issued so-called shares. Even more perplexing was the fact that these shares could be bought and sold in a place called a stock market. Zeus could understand this happening with gold bars, which were physically there, and you could take them away. However, if you bought a share all that seemed to happen was that you would be given a piece of paper at best. Sometimes you got nothing, just an acknowledgment that what you'd bought was recorded somewhere on a thing called the internet, which he thought might be located in a cloud. Being the God of the Sky, Zeus was pretty sure that this couldn't be correct. He'd never found a cloud with this internet thing in it, so he suspected it could all be some great big 'con'.

As the Top God was considering these weighty matters, Athene walked in wearing a white cloak over a smart red dress which came from Doreen's Fashion and Sportswear for Ladies shop, also in Yorkgate. She rested the spear she was carrying against a table in a corner of the room and then went and sat down on a chair opposite Zeus's desk.

"I was expecting you," Zeus said looking up. "I'm just having a read of this paper called the Financial Times. Have you ever looked at it?"

"Quite frequently, Father," Athene replied.

"It's got a lot of stuff in it about companies and shares, which I don't understand. Do you know how they work?"

Athene nodded her head.

"And have you ever come across this thing called the internet?"

"It's been around for some time. It was approved at a Gods' Council more than thirty years ago."

"I've forgotten; it can't have been very important, or I would have remembered it. Anyway, let's say no more about these matters, Athene. You asked to see me, but before we get onto your agenda, tell me what you've been doing in recent weeks. I've seen so little of you."

"That's because I've been spending much of my time with humanity. There are a lot of problems in the world at present."

"There always are," Zeus commented.

"I agree," Athene said. "But this time, I'm not sure we gods have much control over them."

"Meaning?"

"The world has this pandemic that's been going on more than a year and there are famines in lots of different places all at the same time. Aunt Demeter, as Goddess of the Harvest, is overwhelmed. I'm spending much of my time behind the scenes trying to encourage appropriate responses by governments and aid organizations. As usual, it's an uphill battle."

"With your involvement, Athene, I'm sure we have a reasonable level of control over the situation," Zeus said.

"No, Father, we don't!" Athene replied firmly. "The problem is that two of the Four Horsemen are on the rampage.

We've never really been able to establish complete authority over all the Horsemen because, except for Mars, the others were created before our time. Death's okay – he just works diligently and probably looks to Hades as his boss. Mars, as War, is a god and, while he's a problem, it's one we should be able to handle. Whether we're doing so is a different matter, but I'll come on to that later. But you tell me, who actually controls Pestilence and Famine? They've slipped whatever leash you were meant to keep them on."

"I wouldn't put it quite like that," Zeus responded defensively. "I may not know precisely what they're up to every minute of the day, but they understand they have to get approval from me for their major activities."

"Rubbish, Father! Did you approve this pandemic of Pestilence's which has already killed ten million people and is still going strong? Did you agree to Famine destroying the harvests throughout East Africa, South-East Asia, South America and many other places which will result in many millions more dying of starvation? Of course, you didn't; it's just happened without you knowing anything about it. What's more, such matters should have been put to the Gods' Council. Not even you, with your Top God hat on, would have dared unleash these forces without a full debate involving the other gods."

Zeus sighed. He loved Athene very much and knew the important role she played in Olympian affairs, but she did have this habit of beating him around the head every so often. As well as the pressures and responsibilities of being Top God, being a father was often even more difficult.

"I think you're being somewhat harsh in your criticisms, Athene," Zeus eventually replied. "What I'm sure you know is that I rely on Mars to assist me with the other Horsemen. I'm confident your half-brother has a good idea where Pestilence and Famine are and what they're up to."

"He doesn't!" Athene flashed back. "I've asked him where they are, and he claims not to know. Not that I entirely believe him. Mars likes to see those two create havoc in the

14

world. It results in people becoming desperate, they fight for survival and that gives the God of War an opening to start conflicts. As far as what they're up to, that's obvious for all to see."

"Isn't it likely that Pestilence is to be found where the plague is at its worst? The same applies to Famine – surely, he'll be where the crop failures are most severe?"

Athene shook her head. "It used to be like that," she replied, "but now they tend to start their problems and then move on. That's particularly the case with Pestilence; once an infectious disease takes hold, it spreads like wildfire due to modern communications. Famine will stay in one location longer, but if he poisons the soil or causes a draught, the year's harvest inevitably fails."

"I don't entirely disagree with you, Athene. You've clearly given a lot of consideration to this, which is why you've come to see me. No doubt you've got a proposal as to how we should respond?"

"Actually, Father, I haven't come to see you on Pestilence and Famine, but where they are is important. If I were you, I'd have a very challenging meeting with Mars and, if you get nowhere with him, which I suspect will be the case, I'd call an urgent God's Council Meeting and enlist the support of the other gods."

"Hmm," responded Zeus, not entirely sure he wanted to admit to the other gods that he had no idea where the two Horsemen were. "I'll think about it."

"Action not words is what's needed, Father. Please don't think too long."

"Hmm," was all Zeus said.

Athene looked firmly at her father before continuing. "Which leads neatly on to what I really came to discuss with you. Some months ago, you raised the idea of a meeting between you and your two brothers. You said you'd like me to broker such a gathering but wanted to reflect further on how to present it to them. I've been waiting all this time for you to speak to me again on the matter, but not having heard anything, I thought it was time to suggest a bit of action."

Zeus felt on somewhat stronger ground on this matter since he had actually given some consideration to meeting Poseidon and Hades.

"I was about to contact you on the very subject, Athene," he said, exaggerating somewhat on his intentions. "Let's discuss things now."

"Good. What's the brief?"

"I think we should meet here on Olympus. Invite the two of them, suggest it's a much-needed social between us brothers."

"Will wives be included?"

"No; no; no," Zeus responded shaking his head. "We want it to be more like a boys get-together; a bit of a reunion after all the years of hard work running our respective kingdoms."

Athene looked at her father sceptically. "So, I'm to present it as a bit of a piss-up in the Dog and Duck, am I? You'll all sit around drinking pints of beer, telling each other what wonderful chaps you are, slapping each other on the back and swearing eternal love – is that what you envisage?"

"That's a rather cynical way of describing it, Athene, but 'social' should be at the heart of our get-together."

Athene sighed very audibly. "Really, Father, you can't be serious. When I heard about the idea of the three of you getting together, my reaction, other than 'about time to', was that this was a chance for you to share your problems, get each other's advice, that sort of thing. It was certainly not a boozy social in the pub."

"Well, I'd be more than happy to give some advice to Poseidon and Hades, if they ask for it. You can let them know that when you see them if you think it will help."

Athene sighed again before responding. "And what about you asking them for their advice, Father?"

Zeus coughed. "I don't really see that I've anything I want advice on," he said. "No; things are pretty well under control in my kingdom."

"You're deluded, Father!" Athene spoke angrily. "We've just been talking about Pestilence and Famine on the loose, killing millions of people, and you claim things are under control!"

"Well, I suppose there is that," Zeus replied sheepishly. "Not that I think either of my brothers could help to locate them."

"You don't know unless you ask. For all anyone knows, Pestilence and Poseidon could have become best buddies in the last hundred years with Pestilence taking regular long weekends in the Sea Cavern."

Zeus blinked and looked perplexed. "Do you really think so?" he enquired.

"No, of course I don't!" the goddess flashed back. "But at least ask the question. One of them might have heard something which gives us a clue about their location."

"Hmm," was all the response that was given.

"Let me ask another question." Athene continued after seeing that her father was not going to give a more meaningful response than 'hmm'. "Why should the meeting be on Mount Olympus? Why not have it in the Underworld or the Sea Cavern?"

"Oh, I don't think that's a good idea," Zeus replied. "Olympus is a much nicer place – the Underworld's so gloomy and full of dead people, while the Sea Cavern's not very spacious. It also involves getting wet going there. No, I don't like the idea of visiting either of those places."

"Don't you really mean, Father, that if your two brothers come to you on Olympus, that implies you're the senior brother? It's as if you're summoning them to your presence."

"Not at all, Athene," Zeus blustered in reply, his face beginning to colour up as if he were a schoolboy caught out for fibbing – which, in truth, he had been. "Nothing could have

17

been further from my mind. Having said that, it is generally accepted, I believe, that I am the senior brother, as you say."

"I don't think my two uncles would agree with you, but I won't debate the point. However, I really think you should have a different location for this meet-up than Olympus."

"Why?"

"Let me tell you ….."

Athene then spent the next half an hour in a lengthy argument with her father about the location and purpose of the rendezvous between the three brothers. Eventually, she tired Zeus out with her logic and debating skills. The result was that they reached a shaky compromise, which the Goddess of Wisdom summarized as follows:

"Alright, Father. I'll go and see Uncle Poseidon and Uncle Hades. I will put forward your idea of a social meet-up on Olympus, but unless I get an immediate acceptance from both of them, I'll change tack. The line I'll probably take is that your proposal is only an initial idea; what you'd really like is to get their views on the matter. Depending on what they say, I'll try and get to the stage of suggesting that you all leave it to me to work out an agenda. I'll also propose coming up with an appropriate location which would be viewed by all as 'neutral territory'."

"Fine," Zeus said with a sigh. "I'll leave it to you to sort out. Is that all?"

"No," Athene replied. "That was only topic number one."

"How many have you got?" Zeus asked alarmed.

"Only one other."

"Which is?"

"The performance and behaviour of some of the other gods."

Zeus inwardly sighed. He had a good idea of what was likely to come up, so all he could manage to say was "carry on."

"Let's talk about Apollo first. He has many responsibilities but isn't performing most of them. He's just lazing around, playing practical jokes much of the time. My principal concern is that he's stopped communicating with the Oracle at Delphi, which is------- "

"Who is the Oracle now?" Zeus interrupted.

"She's called Simona; originally from Romania, she also doubles up as a hairdresser in the town. For many years, Apollo would visit her every few weeks for a shampoo and set; he'd suggest what might happen in the future which she'd then pass on to all the mediums. She hasn't seen him for the last five years, so has been making her own predictions which invariably go disastrously wrong. All her clients have been going ballistic because they're losing all their best customers who no longer have any confidence in their abilities."

"Presumably, Simona's been in touch with you about this?"

"She does my hair every so often. I saw her a couple of months ago and heard all about it. She showed me some of the letters of complaint she'd received. The few I remember are from Hollie's Horoscope in Canada, Fleur's Foresight in New Zealand, Missus Confucius Say in Shanghai, Octavia's Oracle in St Petersburgh, Princess Primrose's Prophecies in the Philippines, Michaela's Musings in Nigeria and so it goes on. Many of them are cancelling their subscriptions to 'Delphi's Deliberations', which Simona's been editing and selling for $10,000 a year over the last couple of decades."

"That's a lot of money!" Zeus exclaimed.

"That's what the market is. Hollie's Horoscope's been in one of Canada's national newspapers for years, earning Hollie an income ten times the amount she's been paying to Simona. At least that's the current position; she's on warning from the paper that unless her horoscope starts becoming a lot more accurate in the next six months, she'll be replaced by some bawdy cartoons."

"I'm not sure it's for the gods to be saving Hollie's job, but I agree that Apollo's got an important role in prophecy, especially as far as Delphi is concerned. I'll speak to him on the matter. I take it you've already done so and got nowhere?"

"Not quite. He's told me he'll only start visiting Delphi again if you tell him to. I suspect he thinks I'm either too busy to raise it with you or you won't speak to him. He's become very arrogant over the last couple of centuries."

"Yes, he has," Zeus agreed, nodding his head. "Who's the next problem child?"

"Hermes, but I think he's going to be alright now."

"Meaning?"

"Meaning that for the last few years he's not been pulling his weight. He's been spending all his time studying Nuclear Thermodynamics for no good reason other than it's a challenge. He is actually a messenger god, but you've been using Iris a lot in recent years. Also, he used to escort some of the dead to the Underworld, but that got handed over to Death ages ago. Anyway, we need him to carry more of the load. Hebe and Artemis are planning on spending a lot of time in the next few months with humanity; it's all to do with progressing matters for the Equalities Committee. The result is that a fair amount of Hebe's work of carrying provisions around will have to be done by others. Iris will assist and I've agreed with Hermes that he'll get involved as well. It would help if you could reinforce the point and begin using him again as your messenger."

"What about his work on Nuclear Thermodynamics? Is he going to abandon it?"

"He's been stuck on one particular point for two and a half years. I wish he'd asked me beforehand because I explained it to him in twenty minutes, so he's now pretty well got a full understanding of the subject. There's not a lot more for him to study."

"So, Hermes is a problem solved?" Zeus asked hopefully.

"In the main, but as I've said, you need to both speak to him and start using him again."

Zeus nodded. "Right; I'll do that," he replied.

"Finally, there's Mars," Athene continued.

"I knew he'd come up," Zeus commented wearily.
"What's he done now?"

"Nothing new as far as I know. I've just come to suggest something to you."

"You mean to tell me what to do?"

"Not at all, Father. When have I ever done that?"

Zeus wanted to say, 'all the time', but decided to hear his daughter out. After all, most of the Goddess of Wisdom's so-called suggestions made a lot of sense.

"Go on. What's your proposal?"

"It's very simple. You've told Mars that the next time he misbehaves, you'll banish him to an asteroid for a thousand years."

"Yes, I will," Zeus stated firmly.

"The problem with that is two-fold. Firstly, Mars and half the gods don't believe you'll dare----"

"I certainly will," Zeus interrupted.

"Fine, because that comes onto the second point. The other half do believe you will, so they're reluctant to say anything if Mars does misbehave. They tend to think, for example, that Mars thumping someone on Olympus, doesn't deserve such a lengthy punishment."

"So, the deity has two points of view, does it? I can't help that. 'Watch this space' is all I'll say."

"You've not heard my suggestion yet, Father."

"Alright; what is it?"

"Focus on what Mars believes which is that you wouldn't dare banish him for a thousand years. What he really thinks is that you wouldn't banish him at all. Show him how wrong he is. Next time he creates some trouble for us, banish him for a short period of time like a month. You'll demonstrate decisive action, while Mars will be both humiliated and shocked. He might start behaving himself a bit more after that. If not, the punishment's six months next time, then a year and so on."

Zeus didn't reply for some time as he was deep in thought. Eventually, all he said was: "Hmm. I'll think about it."

"Action not words, Father," Athene repeated for the second time.

Shortly afterwards, the Goddess of Wisdom stood up, kissed Zeus on the cheek, picked up her spear and took her leave. Her father continued to sit in his chair thinking about all the things his daughter had raised with him.

•

Later that day Mr Bumble walked into Zeus's study and handed him a letter. A postal system between the world and Olympus had been established many years ago. Anyone who wanted to write to one of the gods would send a letter to a post box address near Piccadilly Circus in London, which either Iris or Hebe would visit about once a month. When first set up quite a lot of letters were written, but since the gods usually didn't reply, the numbers tailed off considerably over time.

Zeus looked at the envelope. The handwriting looked familiar, and the Texas postmark rang another bell – quite an ominous bell as far as Zeus was concerned. He opened the envelope and read the following letter:

Dolly's Diner,
By the Big Oak Tree,
2 Miles West of Texasville,
Texasville,
Texas, USA.

Hiya Lord Zeus,

This here's Debbie-Louise. I've written to you a few times recently, but ain't got no replies so I is a tryin again.

There's great news for us two. When I did become 16 a few months ago, my Ma, Dolly Hamburger, she told me that you was my Pa. She runs Dolly's Diner outside Texasville where you did once visit her for a few days during your trip around the US of A. You and she got friendly like, if you remember, and then I got to be born.

Ma and me we live together in the back rooms of the diner with Uncle Hank. He's not a real uncle cos he's been Ma's fella for the last few years, but I do call him uncle, if you see what I do mean. We three run the diner together and have a good lot of customers. One of them, Tucker, he's become my first real fella, but I don't be seeing him all the time as he's a trucker from Colorado. Tucker the Trucker geddit? Anyways, me and Tucker we seem to be swell together and both Ma and Uncle Hank, they dig him a lot. I'm sure you will too when you be getting to say howdy to him.

Ma wouldn't tell me who my Pa was till I were 16, but now I know I'm a mighty proud gal to be your daughter. That's why I is writing to you. Firstly, to tell you the great news about you and me and second to suggest that you and me do be getting to meet up sometime soon. Ma says Uncle Hank don't mind if you want to be visiting us at the diner, provided you behave good and proper this time. But you must be a real busy person, so I would be mighty pleased instead to come and visit you on Mount Olympus. I've been a lookin on the internet for flights to Olympus, but sure can't find none. Anyways, perhaps you could sort of tell me how I'm to get to you and what dates be good for me to visit.

I should tell you, I'd really like to meet the Love Goddess, who I is told is called Affrodity. I'm only a young gal and I been thinking she could give me some ideas as to how to please my Hank, so he thinks I'm even more sweller than he thinks now. Also, I'd be mighty pleased if you could teach me how to use a thunderbolt and if you had a spare one for me to bring back to Texasville, that sure would be fine and dandy. Most of the diner's customers are real gents, but some ain't and if I had one of them thunderbolt things, I'd be able to chuck it at them if they do be misbehaving like.

Last thing, cos I do be thinking there be a problem in you getting my letters, I've written too today to your proper wife, who I is told is called Lady Hera. I'd be sure pleased to meet her as well, she being my step ma and all.

Cheerio and lots of love from

Debbie-Louise - your daughter aged 16

Zeus normally read every letter twice before reacting. However, this policy didn't apply to Debbie-Louise's letter once he read about her also writing to Hera. Instead, he jumped up, raced across his study and opened the door. He saw Mr Bumble walking down the stairs, so without saying a word, he frantically beckoned the butler to come into the study.

"Was there also a letter for Lady Hera this morning, Mr Bumble?" he asked in an anxious but quiet voice despite having closed the door.

"Yes, My Lord. I've just delivered it to her."

"Did you hand it to her directly or just leave it in her room so you could quickly retrieve it without her knowing?"

"I handed it to her. I suspect she's -------"

Mr Bumble didn't complete his sentence since he was interrupted by loud screaming and banging of doors on the first floor.

Zeus looked apprehensively at the butler. "I have to go out immediately on urgent business."

"When will you be back, My Lord?" Mr Bumble enquired.

"Probably never," the Top God said as he hurried towards the French windows. "Or at least not until her ladyship calms down." With that final comment, Zeus walked out of the study into the garden and disappeared in a flash of smoke.

"I understand, My Lord," the butler said as Zeus suddenly became a flash. He then turned round and hurried back to the kitchen before Hera came down the stairs.

"What's all that screaming and banging about?" Mrs Bumble asked on seeing her husband walk in.

"I suspect we have another addition to the family, who's suddenly appeared," was the reply.

"Then I suggest you and I should leave Lady Hera to Marie-Antoinette for the rest of the day."

"I agree," Mr Bumble said. "I think I'll go down to the cellar straight away and carry out a stock-take of the wine."

"I'll come and join you: I need to sort out all the fruit and vegetables down there," his wife replied as she followed her husband down the back stairs.

3
The First Day Back

Persephone took some time getting to sleep as she lay in bed, reflecting on all the extraordinary things she'd witnessed on her first day back in the Underworld.

Persephone was the daughter of Zeus and his sister Demeter. She was red-haired, her face was freckled, and she was of medium build and height. There was really nothing special about her until she smiled; she was blessed with an absolutely gorgeous smile. Not that she smiled much in the Underworld, which she disliked despite being its queen.

As a young maiden, Persephone had been abducted by Hades who needed a wife. This not only upset her very much since she had no wish to be the Queen of the Underworld, but also her mother who loved her daughter very dearly. Persephone was naturally shy and very much 'Mummy's Little Girl,' even when she was quite grown up. For a period, Demeter, as Goddess of the Harvest, was so distressed that she stopped making the crops grow. Zeus eventually intervened and agreed a compromise between Hades and Demeter that Persephone would remain Queen of the Underworld but would only spend a third of the year there; the rest of her time she would be based on Olympus helping her mother with the harvest.

Persephone's reflections really began the previous afternoon when she went to visit her father to say goodbye to him before leaving for the Underworld. This was only two days after the receipt of Debbie-Louise's letter and Zeus was still missing from his palace. Persephone found out what was going on from the Bumbles, making sure she avoided Hera with whom she had an uneasy relationship. As was always the case in these situations, Mr and Mrs Bumble quite truthfully claimed not to know where Zeus was. However, a little bit of pressing by Persephone resulted in a knowing look between the married couple before the words "why not ask Nell Quickly?" were quietly spoken by the Head Housekeeper.

At the Dog and Duck, Lennie the eagle, Beetle the tortoise, and Bacchus all swore blind that they hadn't seen Zeus for weeks. Mrs Quickly heard all this and sighed. "Follow me," she said and took Persephone to the end room on the first floor, opened the door, spoke the words: "one daughter duly delivered," pushed Persephone inside and then closed the door after her.

Zeus, who was sitting at a table deep in thought, looked alarmed at having been detected. "You've not brought Hera, have you?" he asked.

"No," Persephone replied. "Nor will I tell her where you are."

"Then I suppose you've come to say goodbye before returning to the Underworld? Presumably, you'll spend all your time telling me off for not protecting you from Hades when he abducted you. That's what you normally do."

"No, Father. I've just come to say goodbye and to ask how you are? I've not seen much of you recently."

Zeus gave a relieved smile and said: "Well, if that's the case, Persephone, draw up a chair and have a glass of wine. I'm not in great shape; I've lots of worries."

The Top God then proceeded to spend the next half-hour telling his daughter about his concerns. He didn't say anything about why he was hiding from Hera; the reasons were just taken as read between the two of them. Instead, he spoke about his conversation with Athene. He was clearly worried about having lost control of Famine and Pestilence and the damage they were doing. He asked Persephone if she could tactfully enquire if there was any information in the Underworld about their whereabouts. Also, he spoke about wanting a get-together with his two brothers, mentioning that Athene had agreed to try to organize a meet-up and would be visiting Hades soon on the matter. He even suggested that perhaps Persephone could help persuade her husband to respond positively, preferably agreeing to come to Olympus.

By the time, Zeus had finished speaking about the failings of Apollo, Hermes and Mars – and the suggestion that he might in part be responsible - his daughter, for the first time in her life, was starting to feel sorry for this all-powerful father of hers, with whom she'd never been particularly close.

When Persephone left Zeus, she had a slight spring in her step. It was the first time he had ever asked her to help him. Persephone was naturally shy and retiring, so people tended not to ask for her assistance, but now she had two requests from Zeus for when she returned to the Underworld.

Outside the pub, she passed Lennie who was drinking prosecco from a large bowl. "I'm surprised you hadn't seen Zeus, Lennie," she said. "I thought eagles were meant to have good eyesight. But, of course, I forgot – you're a duck!"

Lennie went mad and started squawking at Persephone as she walked away, but she just ignored him. She was aware it was only because of her conversation with Zeus that she felt confident enough to make fun of Lennie. Beetle foolishly said that he thought Persephone's comment was quite funny, which only resulted in Lennie's ire being turned away from the goddess towards the tortoise.

It was traditional that Demeter cooked a special dinner for her daughter the evening before she left for the Underworld. The Goddess of the Harvest had returned home earlier that day for this occasion, having been in the fields of South-East Asia for the past week trying to make the crops grow. It was also traditional that in the early part of the evening, friends called in to say goodbye to Persephone, always ensuring that they didn't stay too long so mother and daughter could have time together.

By the time Persephone got back to her mother's palace, the large living room was full of a select group of gods and goddesses that Athene had called together. While they were all there to see Persephone, the Goddess of Wisdom had decided to use the occasion to have a crisis meeting about The Four Horsemen since she wasn't happy waiting for Zeus to act.

As well as Demeter, Persephone and Athene, the group consisted of Hebe, Iris, Artemis, Hephaestus and Hermes.

Persephone listened to Athene describing the problem, with her mother giving a first-hand account of the widespread crop failures in the world. She didn't mention anything about her conversation with Zeus since that might lead to her giving away her father's whereabouts. Not that it would matter much with this group, but discretion seemed to be the best approach. Much of the conversation was monopolized by Hebe and Athene, but everyone agreed that they should initiate a major search for Famine and Pestilence. Hephaestus was firmly of the view, which Athene shared, that Mars must know more than he was letting on and offered to try and get some information out of him; he felt he would have a better chance than Zeus. At this stage Persephone decided to speak for the first time and suggested that someone should speak to Death. She volunteered to get Hades to do so.

"That's the best idea anyone's come up with today," Hebe immediately responded, causing Persephone to colour up as all eyes turned to her.

"I agree," Athene said. "What's more, Perse, I think it would be better if you spoke to Death. He's more likely to open up with you than Hades."

"Yes; alright," Persephone replied in a slightly nervous voice, totally bemused at all this responsibility that she was being given that day.

•

The following morning, Persephone set off with Hebe in her chariot, all her luggage having been packed the evening before. They travelled at speed and spoke about all the changes which had been taking place in the Underworld since Persephone's last visit, a subject which they'd discussed on several occasions in recent weeks and months.

They were soon galloping on top of the river leading to the Underworld. As they came out of the tunnel, Hebe's four stallions jumped onto the bank and came to a halt in front of Cerberus who was waiting for them.

"Halt! Who goes there?" the three-headed dog said in an officious tone.

"Cerberus, it's me, Persephone," the goddess called out.

"Identity papers."

Persephone looked at Hebe and whispered: "What's going on?"

Hebe was laughing. "Just play the game," she whispered back to Persephone. "Say you've got no identity papers."

"I've got no identity papers," Persephone called out, still unsure what was happening.

"Can anyone identify you then?" asked Cerberus.

"I can," Hebe called out.

"Very good," replied Cerberus. "Lady Hebe can identify you. You can pass, Persephone."

As the horses began to move, Cerberus again suddenly shouted: "Halt!"

"What's happening now?" Persephone asked even more confused.

"Who's this person with you, Persephone?"

"It's Hebe. You just spoke to her."

"Has she got identity papers?"

"No," answered Hebe still laughing.

"Can anyone identify her?"

"I can," Persephone said with a sigh.

"Very good. Lady Persephone can identify you. You can pass as well, Hebe."

Cerberus stood aside to let the chariot move off and he then ran beside the stallions as they cantered towards the palace.

"Woof, woof," went Cerberus. "I knew who you were all the time, Persephone. I was just demonstrating the new controls that have been introduced since I became Head of Internal Security. Are you impressed?"

"I think there might be a bit of a flaw in how your identification system works," Persephone answered.

"I doubt it. The best brains in the Underworld have been at work creating it. By the way, have you got a Mars bar for me, please?"

"That's from both of us," Hebe called out, throwing a bar at Cerberus's open mouth on the left.

"Thank you," the dog replied.

"You're very polite now, Cerberus," Persephone said as Cerberus was chewing away. "I heard you'd changed, but never thought you'd be saying please and thank you."

"I've been poshified. It means I've started to get friends, which I've never had before. There are lots of changes in the Underworld these days. Everything's getting better."

"So, I gather."

A short while later the chariot drew up at the King of the Underworld's palace. Hades was standing at the front with Sisyphus waiting for Persephone. The Queen of the Underworld could not help looking astonished since it was the first time her husband had ever been outside to welcome her. Hades gave his wife an affectionate hug, followed by another hug for Hebe. He and Sisyphus then picked up all the cases and led the way into the palace, followed by the two goddesses and Cerberus.

"I am so glad you are back, Persephone," Hades said as they walked into the vast hall. "We've introduced various changes which I'll explain to you in due course. There's a lot more to do and your help will be invaluable."

"Yes," was all Persephone could reply, swallowing hard. "But…. but…what about Sisyphus?"

"I'm a 'good boy' now," said the former trickster. "I've got myself a proper job; doing something useful."

"And you're doing very well at it," said Hades with a smile. "Again, I'll explain later why he's not spending all his time pushing his boulder up the hill."

Hades was speaking constantly as the party walked along. They went through the throne room and Persephone saw that there were now two thrones side by side – another first, which Hades explained was so she could participate in the decisions that had to be made when people first arrived in the Underworld. He then suggested a plan for the day which was that Persephone would need some time to unpack. He would arrange for sandwiches and refreshments to be brought to her apartment. After that, she'd probably want to rest after her journey, but in the evening, they would get together for a very special dinner which Aggy was preparing. That would give her the opportunity of telling him everything that was happening on Olympus, and he'd explain about the changes in the Underworld. Again, there was another first – having proposed his plan, Hades actually asked his wife if she agreed, or would she rather do things differently?

"Oh, er…. yes," she replied.

Once they got to Persephone's rooms, Hebe took her leave of her uncle and half-sister, who was also her aunt by marriage. She had to get back to Olympus since she was setting off for Yorkgate in the morning. Sisyphus quickly followed, but Cerberus stayed behind since there was one final matter to be resolved before Hades left his wife until the evening.

Persephone had not come with her maid from Olympus on this occasion. She shared Little Nell with Demeter and normally her mother was happy to fend for herself when her daughter was away. It also gave Little Nell an opportunity to see her grandfather in the Underworld. However, on this occasion Persephone encouraged Demeter to keep the maid with her since her mother was very tired and stressed at the constant fight against Famine's destruction. Also, Nell was not particularly keen to see her grandfather again since last time he'd got a new lady friend that his granddaughter didn't like.

Hades had learned from Hebe beforehand that Persephone was likely to come unaccompanied. On previous occasions when Persephone had come alone, Ming had been released by Aggy to look after the goddess and Hades had already set this up on a provisional basis. However, he wanted to check with his wife that this was acceptable. Again,

Persephone blinked in confusion. Normally, Hades just organized these matters without consulting her.

"Yes, that's fine," the goddess answered quietly. "I like Ming. It would be good to have her again."

"She's also the best friend of this new girl called Vesta that I'd like to tell you about over dinner," Hades said.

"Woof, woof," went Cerberus. "Ming and I are Vesta's equal best friends. Vesta is actually my best friend and my relationship with Ming is that we are temporary associate friends on probation."

Hades chuckled. "It's confusing," he said to a blinking Persephone. "But you'll get the hang of it soon enough. I'll leave you now and see you later. Cerberus, will you please let Aggy know and ask if Ming can come as soon as possible?"

"Woof, woof! Will do, Boss," Cerberus replied before bounding off to deliver his message.

Half an hour later, Ming arrived carrying a large tray with sandwiches, and a bottle of sparkling wine.

"I'm amazed," Persephone said to her. "Smoked salmon sandwiches, also avocado and prawn as well as brie cheese. Previously it was always a bowl of stew! I suggest we both sit down together, Ming, and you tell me everything that's been going on here while we tuck in. I'll pour out the wine."

"Not for me, thank you, Lady Persephone," Ming replied. "I've also brought a jug of water."

For the next half an hour Persephone listened to all the alterations which Ming told her about. She'd heard a lot from Hebe earlier, but that didn't matter. It was good to get a different perspective.

They continued to talk as they did the unpacking and arranged Persephone's bed for the night. Ming had a smaller bed in an annex off the main bedroom and that was also got ready. By the time they were finished Persephone was so excited about everything she'd heard that she wanted to start seeing some of the changes immediately. The result was that she and Ming went off to the Kitchens to say hello to Aggy and to meet Vesta who was busy that day serving fish and chips for lunch.

•

Several hours later the King and Queen of the Underworld were having their 'special' dinner together. Aggy and Ming had brought it over on large trays, which they left on the sideboard in the palace's dining room. Persephone normally didn't have a great appetite, but that evening she was feeling ravenous. Part of the reason was that Aggy had told her what was on the menu – Mediterranean vegetables as a first course, followed by paella and then strawberry tart. There were even some mint chocolates at the end, all washed down with a couple of bottles of Chablis. It was very different to a large bowl of stew and a glass of water, which had been the standard fare in the past!

Hades was keen to hear about what was happening on Mount Olympus, particularly what the other gods were up to. Persephone found that she was doing most of the talking with Hades only interrupting occasionally. This changed when she got onto talking about the two Horsemen who were on the loose.

"Mother's really struggling to create any sort of harvest at the moment," Persephone said. "I'm afraid Famine's not under control. The same's also true of Pestilence; there are plagues everywhere."

"That's very obvious," Hades replied. "On a daily basis, we're getting more people coming to the Underworld than we've ever had before. I was aware of the plagues but hadn't clocked about the famines. It's causing us a lot of problems which I'll come on to later. But first, I'd like to know why they're not under control. Isn't that Zeus's responsibility?"

"It is and I can't answer for what's happened, but suddenly two of the Four Horsemen have gone on some sort of rampage. I suppose the answer is that my father wasn't paying attention and now we don't know where they are."

There was a silence between the two before Hades said: "My brother makes me very angry at times and this is one of them. Doesn't he realise that his actions have repercussions for the other realms? Or perhaps I should say lack of action in this case."

"I think Father feels very responsible. He got beaten up over it by Athene a few days ago. She seems to have taken responsibility for leading the search for Famine and Pestilence."

"Well, that's at least something. What's she doing?"

"For a start, she's given us all tasks. I was going to discuss with you how we might help."

"It seems unlikely," Hades said dismissively.

"I'm not sure," Persephone replied, aware that she was contradicting her husband for probably the first time in their marriage. "Perhaps we might learn something from the new arrivals in the Underworld. They might have caught sight of one or the other of the Horsemen and that could give us a trail to start following."

"Yes, possibly. I suppose it's worth trying. Anything's better than doing nothing."

"Then I had the idea that we could speak to Death. He might know where they are, or he could let us know if he sees them."

Hades thought for some time before replying. "That's actually a very good idea, Persephone. I'm not sure if Death will tell us directly because The Four Horsemen act as some sort of secret brotherhood, but we might learn something. There is a problem, though, and that's that Death is not in a very good mood with me at the moment, so he's unlikely to open up."

"Oh, why?"

Hades proceeded to tell his wife about Death's wish to buy a bungalow and retire to Eastbourne and his response, which was to Keep Buggering On.

"In one way, it's really quite sad," Persephone said after hearing the tale. "But in another, it's rather funny."

"Yes, I suppose it is," Hades replied with a smile.

"Do… do… you think I should speak to Death instead of you?" Persephone asked, slightly nervously.

"Possibly yes," Hades promptly responded to his wife's relief. "But let's discuss it further over the next few days. It's a good idea, I have to say. Presumably, somebody's going to be tackling Mars as well?"

"Father and Hephaestus, but I'm not sure how much they'll get out of him."

"Probably less than we'll get out of Death."

The two ate in silence for a short while until Hades started talking about the changes in the Underworld since Persephone's last visit. Again, she had heard much of it beforehand, but she didn't want to stop her husband from speaking freely – they were having the best conversation they had ever had. He spent a lot of time explaining about the changes in the Torturing Department as well as how the Kitchens had been transformed from their previous focus of just making stew to what was now a wide variety of dishes. Hades also talked about Cerberus and how Homer and Virgil had poshified him, making Persephone laugh when she learned that for a while he was even bowing to Hades and calling him Your Gracious Majesty. Sisyphus's new role was also explained, including how Vesta had proposed it and Hades hadn't been able to find a logical argument against.

"I suppose you've heard a lot of this already?" Hades said in conclusion.

"Some, but not all and it's good to get your perspective on it. I have to admit that Ming took me off to the Kitchens this afternoon to see what was now going on. As well as a good chat with Aggy, I met the famous Vesta that you all seem to talk about. She came over as a perfectly normal girl who just uses her common sense."

"She is. But she's also brave; she's stood up to me on several occasions."

"I hope you don't mind but I'm going with Ming and Vesta tomorrow morning to the Torturing Department to look at what they do differently there."

"Not at all. In fact, you wouldn't like to wander off to the Building Department afterwards, would you? That's our biggest problem now. There are so many people coming to the Underworld because of the plague and all these famines, we're unable to build new accommodation quickly enough for them. Some are having to sleep on the floor or sharing a bed. I've spoken to the team to see if they can build faster, but they claim they can't. Perhaps you and the girls might be able to come up with some ideas."

"Yes, alright," answered Persephone. "Do you want to come with us?"

Hades shook his head. "No, I think it's best if there's a completely fresh approach. That's what happened with the Torturing Department. Vesta just asked Genghis and Attila some obvious questions which they couldn't answer."

"Does Aggy mind Vesta being taken off on these projects? Hasn't she got work to do in the Kitchens?"

"Aggy's fine. She and I have spoken on the matter, and she understands how Vesta's an important catalyst for renewal in the Underworld."

By now the King and Queen of the Underworld had finished dinner and were drinking the last of the wine. Persephone had for once had a really enjoyable evening with her husband and she felt quite relaxed. Also, she'd drunk a lot of wine and that helped! After reflecting for a short while, she decided to pluck up courage and ask the question she'd been pondering since she first heard from Hebe about the changes in the realm.

"Can I ask you, Hades," she began quite quietly, deliberately not looking at her husband. "Why you've allowed all these new things to happen? You've gone thousands and thousands of years, keeping everything the same, then suddenly it's like a revolution's taking place."

Hades looked into his wine glass as he pondered his wife's question. "It's something I've thought a lot about myself," he eventually replied. "I suppose it boils down to one simple issue. I'm a god, but I couldn't answer a few basic questions from a fourteen-year-old girl. That didn't seem right, so I just let things happen. I've no other explanation."

Another silence followed as the two reflected on Hades' answer. Eventually he asked his own question: "Do you approve?"

"Oh, yes," Persephone replied, and she looked into her husband's eyes at the same time as he looked into hers. "Oh, yes, I do!" she repeated enthusiastically, and they both smiled fondly at each other.

4
The Head Builder

Mr Mason Bonko was a singular man. People interpreted this in different ways, but most believed it meant there was only one of him. For the pro-Bonko camp, this was viewed as a negative, since this group believed that to have lots of Bonkos would simply be a good thing. For the not-so-pro-Bonko camp – a polite description for the anti-Bonko camp – this was a great relief. At the present time, the pro-Bonkos were in the minority since there was only Mason in this grouping, whereas everyone else was a not-so-pro. This had always been the case, except for a few happy months when Mr Bonko became engaged and subsequently married a young lady who became Mrs Bonko, so briefly increasing the pro-faction, before she ran off with the local ratcatcher.

Mr Bonko was the Underworld's Head Builder. He was a man of medium height, with a large stomach that stuck out at right angles. The top of his head was bald, but lower down there was a band of grey, wavy hair. He had a small grey moustache but had always avoided growing a beard. This was because he personally distrusted men with beards, so he concluded that if he had one, it would be a sign that he also could not be trusted. He was fully aware that there were times when this judgement of himself might be correct, but he didn't want to advertise the fact.

Having Bonko as a name resulted in Mason sometimes being referred to as Bonkers. Naturally, he disliked this nickname, so over a period of time he developed a way of dealing with it. To anyone more important or larger than himself, he merely smiled and said nothing if they called him Bonkers. However, everyone else was given a good thumping if they used the dreaded name. Mason himself didn't mind nicknames, so he encouraged others to call him Bonks, which he found perfectly acceptable.

Although Mr Bonko was the Head Builder, he wasn't formally Head of the Building Department. That responsibility fell to Mr Abacus who had come to the Underworld many centuries before Mason. Mr Abacus had once invented a counting machine which Hades had been very impressed with. For some reason, the King of the Underworld at that time believed that the Building Department was in need of strict financial control, so he appointed the inventor as its director. Now Mr Abacus wasn't at all sure what his role involved, so he spent his time sitting in the Building Department's storeroom playing with his machine. This meant that the Underworld's builders, who were supposedly under his control, just got on and did what they thought they should do, which often meant they made a mess of things.

Mason Bonko did know about building, and he was used to bossing people around. This meant that when he arrived in the Underworld, he took de facto control of the Department in a matter of days. He organized everyone into appropriate teams, allocated their work, sorted out the stores, created an ordering system and generally got things moving in a systematic way. Mr Abacus was very pleased with Mason for doing all of this and the two of them quickly reached a tacit agreement that Mr Bonko would run matters, leaving Mr Abacus to see if he could invent other useful gadgets. This was nearly enough for Mr Abacus to move into the pro-Bonko camp, but when Mason began to call him Beans, on account of his bean-counting machine, the inventor chose to remain in the not-so-pro faction.

While Mr Abacus, as Head of the Building Department, was ignorant of construction matters, this was not the case as far as Sir Christopher was concerned. Sir Christopher was Chief Architect and ran the Architecture Department, which meant that he and Mr Bonko had a lot of interaction on the various schemes that were in progress. Mason knew that Sir Christopher was a knowledgeable chap since the two of them had worked together to build St Paul's Cathedral in the City of London many years ago.

Mason had in fact first met Sir Christopher when he was building a house for a public servant and his family. This was Mr Bonko's first major job after completing his apprenticeship and the noble knight was the architect. The young builder was naturally keen to show a profit on this assignment, so he looked for various cost saving measures. He decided not to include two beams which Sir Christopher had included in his drawings since this would save a good deal of money. Unfortunately, he failed to discuss this matter with the architect. Even more unfortunately, the two missing beams were supporting beams, which meant that when the first bad storm came, the whole house collapsed. At that time, the only occupant was the public servant who was rapidly whisked away by Death to the Underworld.

There was a major investigation by the authorities into the collapsed house. The two missing beams were identified as the cause, but Sir Christopher was cleared of responsibility since his drawings clearly showed the need for them. The result was that the finger of blame got pointed at Mason Bonko who was hauled up in front of the judge on a potential capital offence. Now it just so happened that the public servant who had been killed was the local hangman. This undoubtedly had a considerable effect on the trial since, although everyone accepted the important role he played in society, no one was very keen on him. Half the jury either had friends or family who had been hanged at some point in time or were waiting to be hanged, while the other half knew that they'd all done things which, if found out, would result in them paying a visit to the local gallows. Even the judge, despite being very strict in his application of the law, was not a great fan of the deceased public servant due to his brother-in-law having once been one of his clients on account of a small forgery carried out some years ago.

Mason knew that he was up the creek without a paddle on this one, but he was a resourceful man as well as being an excellent liar. He found a very early unfinished draft of one of Sir Christopher's plans for the house which excluded the beams. He claimed – which meant he lied - that these were the only drawings he had received and had worked from them. The noble architect knew Mason was wrong and could clearly demonstrate that this earlier draft was superseded by a number of later ones which all included beams. However, there was an element of uncertainty as to when and how these later drawings were given to Mason, who denied ever having received them. When it was suggested that they could have got lost in the notoriously unreliable postal service of the day, the judge and jury, together with the accused, all thought this was possible. Sir Christopher privately knew this was incorrect because he was certain he had handed the final drawings over to Mason personally. However, even Sir Christopher didn't want to see Mason as a client of the newly appointed hangman, so he went along with the idea of the postal service being responsible. The result was a huge sigh of relief by everyone as Mason Bonko was found not guilty by the jury and sent off by the judge with his good name intact.

One might consider that this incident would cause Sir Christopher to avoid Mason Bonko at all costs in the future. However, this was not the case. The architect had found the quality of the builder's workmanship to be of the highest order except, of course, for the omission of the beams. He therefore collared Mason after the trial and took him to the local public house to buy him a drink, have a chat and make him a proposition. To cut a long story short, he made Mason aware that he knew he'd told a load of porkies in court about not having the final drawings and he knew why – to cut costs and make a larger profit. However, he was pleased Mason had got off; he thought he was a good builder – despite the fact that the house had fallen down! - and provided he would swear never to do the same sort of thing again, he'd like him to come and work on the construction of the big new cathedral in the City of London. And so began a fruitful partnership which lasted many years.

Mason had been a young man when he built the hangman's house, but over the coming years he learned a lot from Sir Christopher. In the main, he kept his promise to the architect never to do anything 'naughty' again. There was one very 'minor' exception, which involved him deliberately killing – a polite way of saying 'murdering' – a fellow builder. This involved leaving a broken plank on a high platform, knowing that Basher Burgess would step on it and crash to the ground. Basher was a very large, nasty thug who refused to repay Mason a sizeable sum of money he had borrowed from him two years earlier. Basher made it very clear that if Mason kept asking him for repayment, he and his three brothers, who were also very large and thuggish, would be paying him a visit to break both his arms and legs. The result was that some time ago Mason had written off the idea of ever getting repaid, but he was not averse to 'getting even' with Basher someday. The broken plank provided the ideal opportunity, and no one knew Mason's involvement in what was considered to be an unfortunate accident.

Many years later, Mason Bonko found out that he hadn't completely got away with killing Basher Burgess. Hades knew about it and when Bonko arrived in the Underworld and had his first interview with the god, he found out that his punishment was to be put in a large cauldron of boiling water from time to time, supervised by Ivan the Terrible - all because of Basher and the broken plank.

Except for Sir Christopher, the only other person whom Mason respected for his knowledge of building matters was Lord Hephaestus, the Builder God, who had advised the noble architect on an occasional basis during the construction of St Paul's. Normally, Mason and Hephaestus got on well, but at the present time the builder was in a bad mood with the god. This was because some months ago, Hephaestus had taken Norbert off to Olympus to help him on various matters. Norbert was Mason's best worker, and he was unhappy at having been deprived of his services. What's more, the rumour mill in recent months from Olympus suggested that Norbert, who had now been renamed Nobbly Butt, had shacked up with Lady Aphrodite. This caused Mason to feel particularly jealous – "Why couldn't Hephaestus have taken me instead?" he asked himself. "I wouldn't mind being Aphrodite's lover boy for a while."

Mason's team consisted of builders from all countries and all ages. He kept them in order in the traditional way by thumping each of them every so often. A few years ago, a new recruit complained. He was called Clarence Cuthbert Peregrine…. something or other. He knew nothing at all about building but had volunteered for the department when he arrived in the Underworld on the basis that his uncle was Chairman of some large construction company in the North of England. Anyway, Clarence Cuthbert Peregrine had objected to Mason thumping him, claiming it was a breach of employment law and wanting to involve something called the Human Relations Department, which Mason had never heard of. The result was that Mason thumped him again, dragged him off to Lord Hades and got him reassigned to the Sewing Department where he's remained ever since.

The Building Department had one woman in it. Mason Bonko had never come across female builders in 17th century London, so he was very reluctant to take on Budiwati when she was assigned to his team. Nevertheless, Hades had insisted, so Mason had to agree to give her a trial for a few weeks. Budiwati, or Budi for short, had started her adult life as a wrestler in Indonesia before retiring from the sport and then training to be a bricklayer. Mason was absolutely determined that she would fail her trial, but the problem was that she was the best brickie he'd ever had. He therefore agreed to keep her on, despite feeling uncomfortable about having a female in the ranks. He decided that the only way he could reconcile himself to the matter was to treat her like a man, which meant thumping her occasionally.

Mason was a fair man and only thumped people if there was a reason. Every day he watched Budi at work but couldn't find any fault with what she was doing. After getting increasingly frustrated by this, he just decided to go up to her one day and give her a good thump in the stomach to show her who was boss. She initially doubled up, recovered after about thirty seconds and, saying nothing, turned round and carried on with her work. This totally perplexed Mason as he walked away, thinking of what else to do.

A few days later, Mason Bonko was standing on the top of a ladder when Budi was walking nearby carrying a load of bricks on a hod. As she passed the ladder, she accidentally tripped and fell against it, causing Mason to topple over and break three ribs, fracture his left arm, break his nose, lose all his front teeth and be generally bruised all over. Budi was most apologetic, helped to patch him up and went off to ask Lord Hades to come along as soon as possible and mend the damage. Both the Head Builder and the female brickie knew that the matter was no accident, but the result was that from then onwards, Mason no longer felt any need to thump Budi; she, in turn, diligently continued with her work and managed never to trip against any more ladders.

•

It was midway through the day that Mason saw Persephone, together with Ming and Vesta, walking towards the site for the New Boys Dormitory that he and his team were constructing. He smiled knowingly as they approached, strongly suspecting what their visit was about. He would show them who was boss; no softy Queen of the Underworld and two little girls were going to find anything to change in Mason Bonko's empire.

As the goddess and her companions got closer to the building site, Cerberus came bounding up to them.

"Woof, woof," he barked. "I heard you were here. I'll come with you to make sure these builders behave properly. They haven't been poshified and I don't like their bad language. They're always using the "f" word."

"What's the "f" word?" Persephone asked naively.

"I don't like saying it," replied Cerberus, "so I'll give you the letters, but you'll need to rearrange them. Four letters – k, k, f and o."

Persephone blinked and looked at Vesta, who whispered the word in her ear.

"Oh, that "f" word," the goddess said, now understanding. "But it's not spelt---"

"No," Vesta agreed. "Cerberus's spelling is getting better though, but it takes time."

"What's that about?" the three-headed dog asked looking at Vesta.

"I'll tell you later."

"Okay. I'll go and announce you all and make sure no one uses the "f" word," said Cerberus before running off towards Mason Bonko.

"Woof! Woof!" be barked loudly and then called out: "All rise for Queen Persephone, Queen of the Underworld, beloved wife of King Hades, daughter of the mighty Lord Zeus, King of Olympus and the Lady Demeter, Goddess of the Harvest, sister of Lady Athene, Goddess of Wisdom, also sister of Lady Aphrodite, Goddess of Love, sister of----"

"Alright, Cerberus," interrupted the Head Builder. "We get the message; we all know Persephone."

"I haven't finished yet," was Cerberus's response before continuing: "Queen Persephone, accompanied by Lady Ming and Lady Vesta. Lady Ming, the Head of the Queen's household, former peeler of potatoes in the Kitchens, temporary, associate friend on probation of Duke Cerberus, equal best friend with Lady Vesta; the said Lady Vesta, special adviser to King Hades, also former peeler of potatoes, equal best friends with Duke Cerberus and Lady Ming, friend of---"

Vesta decided to interrupt Cerberus. "I think that will do, Cerberus," she said. "We all know each other."

"But I've not announced myself yet," Cerberus replied. "I want to tell them that I'm the Head of Internal Security; I'm to be referred to as Duke Cerberus from now onwards. I'll also list all my friends and associate friends-----."

"Persephone," Mason said in a loud voice. "Can't you tell that blasted dog to shut up? Just look at my team; they've all stopped their work and are listening to all this gibbering idiot's nonsense."

"Woof! Woof!" barked Cerberus angrily as he moved towards Mason, all three of his heads growling at the Head Builder. "I am not a gibbering idiot, Mr Bonko. I am Head of Internal Security and I'll bite yer bum if you call me that again."

"Just try it," Mason replied, picking up a hammer.

"Stop it!" Vesta shouted as she moved quickly to Cerberus and yanked him back by the tail.

"Ouch!" Audrey, the tail's head, exclaimed.

"Cerberus," Vesta said in a firm voice. "We are going to have no biting the bum today. What's more, stop all these silly titles. Ming and I are not called Lady Ming and Lady Vesta; we're just Ming and Vesta. Also, you're Cerberus, not Duke Cerberus."

"But I like being a Duke," he replied.

"Well, you're not one. The only person here who's got a title is Persephone."

After a few seconds of reflection, Cerberus answered reluctantly: "I'll stop for today, Vesta, but only because you've asked me to. But I'll need to talk to you later about how I become a Duke."

"Maybe."

Cerberus looked questioningly at his best friend, unsure why she wasn't taking his side. After giving her a frown, he turned and said with a sigh: "I'd better make sure that these builders behave themselves then."

"What do you mean by that?" Mason Bonko asked in an aggressive tone.

"Woof, woof," went Cerberus. "For a start, all your team should show a bit of respect to Queen Persephone and her companions."

"What does that mean?"

"Everyone should stand up and not sit around."

Mason looked round and observed the large group that had downed tools and gathered behind him to listen to the conversation in the last few minutes.

"They are all standing," he said, having satisfied himself on the matter.

Cerberus moved all his three heads from left to right and then back again. "Woof! Woof!" he suddenly barked as he darted between two large builders at the front. "He's not; he's not standing!"

Everyone stared as Cerberus who pushed himself into the middle of the group and was glaring at a smiling builder, wearing a bright red hat."

"Stand up! Stand up!" Cerberus shouted aggressively.

"I am standing," the smiling builder said.

"No, you're not! And why are you smiling all the time?"

"I'm smiling, Mr Cerberus," the builder said patiently, "because my name's Smiley. I happen to smile all the time; I can't help it. Furthermore, I assure you I am standing up; just look at my legs."

Cerberus looked at Smiley's legs which did look as if they were actually standing upright.

"Well, why are you only as high as everyone else's belly button?" Cerberus asked.

"Because I'm a dwarf," Smiley answered.

"What's a dwarf? Is that the name for a small man?"

"No; no," Smiley replied. "A dwarf's more like a large leprechaun."

"Is it? So, what's a leprechaun?"

"That's the name given to someone who looks like a small dwarf."

Cerberus's three brains and Audrey tried to process this information. They all felt there was something lacking by way of explanation in this circular definition of dwarves and leprechauns but couldn't work out what it was. So, after a few seconds, Cerberus thought it best to reply: "Very good. That's all clear."

"Is there anything else I can do for you. Mr Cerberus?" Smiley asked as Cerberus continued to stand in front of him

"Are there any other dwarves working here?" Cerberus enquiried.

"Only my cousin Tubby. He's standing at the back, so you won't be able to see him."

"Why's he called Tubby?"

"Because he's shaped like Mr Bonko."

"I see," Cerberus replied. "And how would you describe Mr Bonko's shape, Smiley?"

"I would say he's shaped rather like my cousin Tubby," the dwarf replied.

Again, the Head of Internal Security's three brains and Audrey were not particularly enlightened about the Tubby / Bonko shape by this explanation. However, since it appeared entirely logical, Cerberus once more said: "Very good. That's all clear as well."

"Thank you, Mr Cerberus. Is there anything else?"

"No; no. Just remember, Smiley, that I'm watching you."

"And I am watching you." The dwarf replied.

"What do you mean by that?" the three-headed dog asked, somewhat puzzled by Smiley's comment.

"Precisely what I say. I am watching you."

"Why?"

"Why? Because you are standing about two feet in front of me, Mr Cerberus. Given that I'm awake with my eyes open, I can't help but be watching you at this moment in time."

Cerberus nodded his head at this piece of wisdom. "Very good, Smiley. Carry on as you are," he said before turning round and going back to Mason.

"Are there any other behavioral matters you wish to raise, Cerberus?" the Head Builder asked in a sarcastic tone when the dog was again in front of him.

"Only one, Mr Bonko."

"What's that?"

"The "f" word is not to be used in the presence of the three ladies."

"And what "f" word would that be?"

"The one you builders use all the time because none of you are posh."

"Oh, I'm very sorry we're not posh, Cerberus," Mason said in his most sarcastic tone, "I'll just turn round and tell the lads."

Mason called out in a loud voice to the group behind him: "Did you hear that, lads? Mr Cerberus says we're not posh and we're to stop using the "f" word while Lady Persephone and her two companions are here."

There was a fair amount of laughter at Mason's statement and Cerberus was a little unsure if the group was taking his edict seriously.

Eventually a voice called out: "Is that just our normal "f" word Bonks or does it apply to all words beginning with f?"

"Thank you, Sanjay. Perhaps you could answer that question, Cerberus?"

"Just the normal "f" word; you're allowed to use other words beginning with f."

"And what will happen if we accidentally use the normal "f" word?" Sanjay continued. "Will Cerberus bite us on the bum?"

"Woof! Yes," was the barked reply.

"Remember, we've all got hammers," the Head Builder muttered quietly but loud enough for Cerberus to hear.

"I've got a question as well, Mason," another voice called out. "What do I say if I hit my thumb with a hammer if I'm not allowed to use the "f" word?"

"Let me try and answer that one, Carlos," Mason continued in his sarcastic tone. "I think it's perfectly acceptable, given what Cerberus has said, to shout out 'Oh fantastic! I've just hit my thumb with a hammer' or even to use the word 'fabulous' instead of 'fantastic'. Would that be acceptable, Cerberus?"

"Woof! Yes, very acceptable," the Head of Internal Security answered.

At this, there was widespread laughter from the group, which perplexed Cerberus.

"Why are they laughing?" he asked Mason.

"Oh, my lads are a merry group. They're always having a laugh to show they're having a good time," the Head Builder replied, trying hard to keep a straight face.

After everyone had calmed down, Mason Bonko decided it was time to move on, so he walked a few paces towards the three ladies who had been standing patiently at the side listening to Cerberus.

"What can I do for you, Persephone?" he asked in a business-like tone.

"Good morning, Mason," the goddess replied. "I only just got back to the Underworld yesterday and I'm catching up on everything that's been going on in recent months. I thought you wouldn't mind if we looked round your new building site?"

"Not at all. I'll give you a guided tour. One question though; I take it that Vesta and Ming are with you to see if they can identify any so-called efficiency improvements in our procedures?"

Persephone flushed and began to stutter at this very direct question, which had taken her off guard: "Oh…. er…no, no … What….er…made you think that?"

Before Mason had a chance to answer, Ming intervened and contradicted the goddess by saying: "Yes, we are, Mr Bonko."

There were a few seconds silence before Mason smiled and replied: "That's fine. Best to be honest and upfront about these matters. 'Honesty's the best policy'. That's always been my motto."

At this there was some laughter from the group behind the Head Builder until he spun round and called out in a stern voice: "Did I say something funny?" The laughter quickly died down, except for some muted sniggering at the back.

Turning back to Persephone, Mason said: "You do know, Persephone, that Hades has already spent a lot of time here and couldn't identify a single change in our procedures. We run a tight ship in the Building Department."

That morning, Vesta had quickly learned that Persephone was not the most confident of goddesses so, just as Ming had interrupted her earlier, she felt it was best if she jumped in to respond to Mason.

"Oh, we do know, Mr Bonko, but Lord Hades has asked us to have a second look, just in case he missed something," Vesta said. "We knew you wouldn't mind because we always get on so well with you in the Kitchens. You're one of our favourite people, which is why Ming and I always ensure we give you a second sausage for breakfast."

Mason smiled at Vesta's implied threat to his morning's breakfast. "It's a pity she and Ming aren't a few years older," he thought to himself. "I could use them in the Building Department." Then reflecting the fact that 17th century London was not the most enlightened of places, he added a final qualification: "Better if they were men though!"

After these private thoughts, the Head Builder looked directly at Persephone and the two girls. "Right," he said in a business-like manner. "Let's get started."

5
Mistaken Identity

Amphitrite, Goddess and Queen of the Seas, was sitting in her private study with Totty, both of them drinking a refreshing cranberry juice. Since the goddess had returned to the Sea Cavern after a long time away, she had been active with a number of projects. At the moment she and Totty were going through every room in the Sea Cavern's palace, noting down all the existing furniture as well as measuring the size of each room. In some instances, the two of them drew plans, especially for the more important rooms.

The palace furniture was classical, having been bought from Harrods in London more than thirty years ago. The goddess had decided it was time for a change and wanted the whole palace to be furnished in a contemporary style, especially with Italian designs. She and her companion had been working non-stop for days creating lists of what was currently in place as well as future requirements. The plan was for Amphitrite to visit Harrods again with Hebe at some point in the future and to place a series of orders. As far as Poseidon was concerned, he was happy to have his wife back home and would accept whatever she proposed.

Amphitrite had become a big sister to Totty whom she had met for the first time on her return to the cavern. Totty's arrival had been the result of a terrible accident in the Mediterranean and some dubious decision making by Moby, a large white whale, who had brought her to Poseidon's Sea Cavern. Despite this, Totty's arrival had been a force for good as she had initiated a series of changes in the lives of the palace's residents, which were very much appreciated by Amphitrite on her return.

Totty's status could best be described as 'fluid.' Most people would generally accept that if a person had drowned and been underwater for several weeks, that person would be well and truly dead. However, Hashimoto, Poseidon's butler had put forward an interesting philosophical argument which was that until someone had actually been taken to the Underworld by Death, he or she was not properly dead, which was precisely the position Totty was in. Now, Hashimoto was not a world-renowned philosopher and Poseidon didn't fully accept his argument, but since neither he nor anyone else could refute it, Totty remained in this state of limbo.

At first the Sea God accepted that he would one day have to make a decision on whether Totty should return to her hometown of Romford or be sent to the Underworld or even remain in the Sea Cavern indefinitely. By the time Amphitrite had returned, Poseidon had still not made up his mind, so his wife took charge of the matter. She decided that the choice should be left to Totty and that had remained the situation for the last few months.

This all created a dilemma for Totty since she did not know what to do. This was in large part because she had really enjoyed her time in the cavern, feeling she had achieved a lot since she had arrived. In fact, it had got even better after Amphitrite returned since they had developed a close friendship. As a result, the two of them often spoke about Totty's dilemma with the Sea Goddess trying her best to avoid encouraging Totty to choose one course of action over another.

As Amphitrite and Totty were having a well-deserved break for a few minutes, Totty raised the issue again. She had now made up her mind and wanted to tell the Sea Goddess first.

"Amphitrite," Totty said. "I've finally decided what I want to do. I want to stay here in the Sea Cavern."

Amphitrite looked at her young friend, studying her face for a while before replying: "What's made you reach that decision, Totty?"

"It was really simple, I suppose. I know I was given three options, but I don't know anything about the Underworld, so I ignored that one. Which meant it was either returning to Romford or staying here in the Sea Cavern. The more I thought about it, I realised it would be impossible to explain away where I'd been for nearly a year. I know we spoke about amnesia, but for the rest of my life I'd be being quizzed about it and I'm not sure I could keep up the lie for a long time. Then if I told the truth, no one would believe me, and I'd be spending all my time with psychiatrists and would probably end up in a mental asylum."

"What about seeing your mother and brothers?" Amphitrite asked.

"That's the only positive, but the way I look at it is that they'll all die in due course and maybe there'll be a chance to see them when that happens. I know they'll be in the Underworld, and I'll be here, but we're talking about forever and that's a long time for a meet-up to take place."

"So, it's a question of elimination, is it?" the goddess asked with a slight smile.

"No! No!" Totty replied emphatically. "I really love being in the cavern with you all. It's been the best part of my life. For once I've felt useful and that's made me happier than I've ever been."

"Thank you for saying that, Totty. We've loved having you here and I'm personally grateful for what you've done for us all, especially Poseidon." Amphitrite paused for a while before continuing. "Now, before I accept your decision, I'd like to put some of the arguments for and against and then make a compromise proposal which I think will interest you."

"Alright, but I'm not going to be talked out of my decision. I'm clear on that."

Amphitrite gave her young friend another smile. "I'm not going to try to, Totty. Let me start by agreeing with you about not returning to your life in Romford. It would just be too difficult for so many reasons which we both understand. Now, turning to the Sea Cavern, my concern is that you'll get bored. There's only Poseidon and me here, together with Hash and Dolores; that's not a lot of people to spend forever with----"

"What about the maids?" Totty interrupted. "I'm really friendly with them all, especially Kinky."

"Yes, alright, the maids as well. But you know they're living creatures. Eventually they'll pass away; they'll probably be replaced by other maids, but the cavern's still going to be a very small place."

"What happens to mermaids when they die?"

"That's a bit complicated for now. Let me continue on your position in the cavern - I suspect much of your enjoyment comes from the novelty and also the fact that everyone here needed sorting out. There'll always be sorting to be done, but it won't be the same challenge as when you first arrived. Also, Poseidon and I will be spending part of our time from now on visiting the different seas and oceans, so we won't always be here with you. I think I've already explained that the dead aren't allowed to return to the world under any circumstances, even if they're helping the gods."

Totty nodded and then said somewhat despondently: "So, what you're saying is I should go to the Underworld?"

"Not necessarily but let me say a few words about Hades' kingdom. For a start, it's a huge community with billions of people. If you spent time there, you'd make a lot of friends. You're an attractive young woman, Totty; it's not unknown for people in the Underworld to develop close relationships."

Totty blushed. "What do people do all day in the Underworld?" she asked.

"Everyone has a job; people work just like in any society. I should tell you that families don't often reunite. It's allowed, but just doesn't happen often for all sorts of reasons — that's another discussion for the future if you want it. Anyway, to continue, there are two negatives as far as you're concerned. Firstly, you won't have your own suite of rooms as you do here; most people live in dormitories. Secondly, everyone is subjected to a punishment every so often----"

"Why?" Totty interrupted. "What sort of punishment?"

"Why? Because of their misdeeds while alive. However, don't worry. While some people are boiled in hot water or impaled on a spike, someone like you is likely to receive something mild such as having to run up and down six flights of stairs. That's assuming you've not done anything very bad, which I'm sure you haven't."

Totty shuddered. "Well, you've really put me off the Underworld with all this talk about punishments, Amphitrite."

"Don't be. People get used to it…..," the goddess paused before continuing. "Now, let me come onto another option, which I've been holding back from you so as not to confuse matters. You've got to know Hebe well in recent months and she's suggested that you might like to go and live with her on Mount Olympus. Let me expand…."

Amphitrite then explained in detail what life was like on Mount Olympus as well as the personalities of the different gods. Totty had heard a lot of this from Poseidon and the goddess in recent months but hadn't realised that Hebe would like her to be her personal assistant on Olympus, as well as helping Iris, the Messenger Goddess, with whom she lived. She'd also heard about Fearless Frupert, the six-year-old boy, who was the other member of the household which Hebe hoped she would join. After lots of questions and answers, Amphitrite decided it was time to offer her advice.

"So, you've got lots of options, Totty, and will need time to think about Hebe's proposal. However, what I would do if I were you, would be to go to the Underworld for a month, then go to Olympus and stay with Hebe and Iris for another month. After that, come back here for as long as you like while you make a final decision. It may well be that you decide to split your time, say, between Olympus and here. What I do want you to know is that there will always be a home here for you at the Sea Cavern. That's a promise – Totty's room will remain Totty's room, whatever you decide."

"Thank you, Amphitrite," Totty replied with some feeling as tears began to develop in her eyes. She wiped them away, smiled and then said: "I don't need to think about it. I'll do what you suggest."

The goddess leaned over and gave her younger sister a big hug.

●

Kinky, the blonde-haired mermaid, was swimming by herself in the Sea Cavern's lagoon when suddenly there was a rush of water past her, and an auburn-haired figure emerged at the piazza edge. In one movement, the arms belonging to this figure pulled her entire body out of the lagoon as she vaulted onto the piazza. She turned round, shook the water off herself and in a matter of seconds her white smock and hair had dried completely. She looked at Kinky and smiled.

"Hello," she said. "I didn't frighten you, did I?"

"No," Kinky said. "You must be a goddess. Which one are you?"

"I'm Athene. I've not been here for a long time so I'm afraid I don't know you."

"I'm Kinky, one of the mermaids. There are four of us and we live in our own palace over there." She pointed to the far-right corner of the lagoon.

"I've heard about you all Kinky from Hebe. She says the two of you are good friends."

"I really like Hebe; we all do. We also know lots about you too, Athene. You're the Goddess of Wisdom, aren't you? But you also look so beautiful, you could be the Goddess of Love as well."

"Thank you," Athene replied with another smile. "But I'll leave love matters to Aphrodite. Have you ever met her?"

"No; we've not had many visitors for years, but we'd like her to come. We've got all these mermaid boys that live just outside the cavern and sometimes we could do with a bit of help in how to handle them."

"I'll ask her to visit you one day."

"Super!" Kinky replied and then continued: "Can I ask you a question please, Athene? Every time people talk about you, they say you carry a spear, but you haven't got it with you now."

Athene laughed. "You try swimming a long distance with a spear, Kinky. Not even a goddess would find that easy."

Kinky blushed. "Probably a silly question," she said.

"Not at all. Most people think the gods and goddesses can do everything, but even we have our limitations. Anyway, changing the subject, is Poseidon in the palace at present?"

"Yes, Old Posy's probably in his study downstairs. Amphitrite's also here; she'll be with Totty upstairs. They're doing something called a furniture stock-take, whatever that means."

"I've heard about Totty as well. I'll meet her after I've seen Old Posy as you call him. Also, I'd like to have a good chat with Amphitrite. Tell me, are the other people who live in the palace called Dolores and Hashimoto? It's so long since I've been here, I've never met them."

"That's right. In fact, I can see Hash at the main entrance now."

"I'll go and say hello to him then. I'll see you later, Kinky."

"Super," the mermaid replied.

Although dress-wear in the cavern was now informal, every so often Hashimoto had an urge to dress like a proper butler in a dinner jacket, a white shirt and a bow tie. Today was one of those days as he watched the visitor walk towards him.

"You must be Hashimoto?" Athene said as she reached the butler. "I'm----"

Hashimoto put his hands up to interrupt the visitor. "There is no need to say your name; I recognize you immediately. You are the Lady Aphrodite. Let me welcome you to the cavern, My Lady." Having said these words, Hashimoto made a low bow to the goddess.

"Well actually, Hashimoto, I'm---" Athene began to say once the butler's head had been raised, only to be interrupted again.

"Yes, My Lady Aphrodite, you are as beautiful as everyone says; songs and poems are forever being written about you. Also, it is widely known that you are as wise as you are beautiful. You outshine Lady Athene in both respects. Why we need Athene at all is beyond anyone's comprehension."

"Isn't it important to have a Goddess of Wisdom?"

"It is of course important, My Lady, but unnecessary when you can fulfil her role as well as being the Goddess of Love. Everyone has been saying that for many years."

"Have they really? Perhaps you could give me a little more detail about what you've heard, especially about Athene?"

"Indeed, I can," Hashimoto responded enthusiastically, feeling sure he was making a good impression with the goddess. "Firstly, Athene is not really wise at all; she's really quite thick. That is well known."

"Would that be as thick as two bricks?" Athene enquired with a forced smile.

"Not just two bricks, but twenty-two, a hundred and two; all the bricks in the world!"

"The sort of person who can't even add up 2 and 2 to make 4, I suppose?"

"Worse than that, My Lady. She does not even understand the word 'add'."

"Is there anything else?"

"There most certainly is. Just as you are both beautiful and wise, Athene is neither. She is very bad looking, quite ugly in fact."

"I had heard that some people consider Athene as quite attractive?"

"Definitely not!" was Hashimoto's firm response. "Or if they do, then they have defective eyesight. Should go and take an eye-test and get proper spectacles. That my view."

"So how bad-looking or ugly do you think Athene is?"

"Oh, terrible looking. I speak with great authority; I am hundred percent sure she visited Tokyo when I was there, and I actually saw her. Not a pleasant sight!"

"In what sense?"

"Face like old cow; body like back end of a bus. Totally the opposite to you, Lady Aphrodite. Beauty and brains, that's what you have."

Athene smiled as she slowly walked through the palace entrance. "I'm so pleased to have heard your views, Hashimoto. One final question on Athene, though – why do you think the rest of us gods put up with her, if she's as thick as two bricks and with a face like a cow?"

Hashimoto shrugged. "I don't know," he said. "Perhaps you feel sorry for her. Maybe you use her for simple menial tasks like washing up, cleaning the floor; that sort of thing."

"Nothing involving much of a brain?"

"Definitely not."

"And we should keep her out of sight in view of her being so ugly."

"That what I would do."

"Thank you," Athene said with another forced smile. "Look, I'd better go and see Poseidon now, much as I'd like to carry on talking to you, Hashimoto."

"I will take you to Lord P's study and announce you."

"No need at all," was the reply. "I know where it is, and I want to give him a surprise."

"Very well. Will I see you again before you leave, My Lady?"

"Oh yes; you'll definitely see me later, Hashimoto," Athene replied in a slightly sinister voice, which the butler did not notice. "That's a firm promise."

Hashimoto again bowed and, turning round, walked towards the far side of the spacious hallway. He was feeling pleased with himself, confident that he had left a strong impression with the goddess.

Athene walked slowly down the long corridor to Poseidon's study, all the time glancing back towards the butler. When she saw him move behind a marble pillar, she smiled and quickened her pace.

•

Poseidon and Athene spent more than two hours together. They hadn't seen each other for a long time and had a lot of catching up to do. However, Athene made sure that the two matters she was primarily focused on were fully covered.

"Look," Poseidon said towards the end of their discussion. "I'm not prepared to go to Olympus for this gathering because it will just put Zeus in a commanding position. I can't remember if he's ever been to the cavern, but if he has it was a very long time ago. I don't mind a neutral venue but as I said earlier, I feel it should be an island. I'd feel really uncomfortable being far away from the sea."

"To be honest, Uncle, your idea of an island is a good one and unless Uncle Hady comes up with a better suggestion, that's the one I'll try to broker. On the other issues you raise, you don't mind a bit of social, but want specific matters of concern to be addressed as well."

"Particularly all the pollution of the seas that's affecting my sea creatures. That's all coming from activities on dry land, and I want it stopped, especially all the plastic that's dumped in my oceans. I'd also like a say in whatever major wars Mars is starting which involve naval engagements. You should see the damage caused by one of those infernal battleships going down; all the oil being spilled and the like."

"To be fair to Father, he would say that major wars are normally discussed at Gods' Council meetings, to which you're invited, but you never come."

"Point taken," Poseidon said. "That's a matter we three brothers can discuss when we get together. You can put attendance at Council meetings on your agenda, Athene. Actually, I like your offer of preparing the agenda – at least we'll get one."

"Fine. What about helping to find the Horsemen?"

"I've been thinking about that as we've been talking. Famine doesn't really affect the seas much as we control our own food supply. As far as Pestilence is concerned, the fish sometimes catch diseases, but nothing out of the ordinary, at least not in recent memory. I suspect that's because Pestilence finds it a lot more rewarding devastating the human population with his plagues. Having said that, I agree it's important to have some sort of control over them, but I'm not sure how my realm can help in that regard."

"I know it's a long shot, but can you please at least put the word out? Some of your creatures might hear something of their whereabouts from sailors, for example. I'm thinking of your mermaids; also, your whales are smart - they seem to know a lot about what's going on in the world."

"Right; I'll do what I can, but most of our current problems arise from pollution and that's down to what you gods on Olympus are doing."

"I've got that one loud and clear, Uncle," Athene replied. "Now, before I leave you, please tell me how Amphitrite is?"

"All good, but I'll let her speak for herself. I'll take you to her."

"No need. I'll have a wander around the palace - I'm sure to find her. Anyway, I've another small matter I need to deal with first."

"What's that?"

"A secret," Athene said with a mischievous smile.

•

Dolores, the palace's housekeeper, was perplexed. She had just been visited in the kitchen by a small brown mouse, which did nothing but squeak. She could not understand how a mouse had got into the palace since the cavern was many hundreds of feet under water. When she moved towards the tiny animal, it ran back to the kitchen doorway and then stopped, looked at her again and squeaked once more. When it was sure Dolores was following, it ran along the corridor, frequently pausing to check the housekeeper was still coming. Eventually the two of them reached the large hallway and the mouse ran off behind a large pillar on the far side. At that point, the mouse started to squeak again until Dolores arrived.

Behind the pillar was a sight which perplexed Dolores even more. Hashimoto's butler's uniform and other clothes were lying in a confused mass on the floor with the mouse sitting on top of them. At this stage, the housekeeper felt she needed to seek some assistance to try and fathom out what all this meant. She turned round, leaving the mouse in the jumble of clothes, and started going from room to room looking for Hashimoto. She was about to go into Poseidon's study but stopped when she heard a female voice; thinking the god and goddess were having a private conversation, she moved onto the other rooms.

Having failed to find Hashimoto on the ground floor, Dolores raced onto the piazza, saw Kinky in the water and went over to ask her if she had seen the butler. Kinky couldn't help her other than mentioning that she'd last seen him with the goddess Athene who had arrived some time ago. Dolores thanked Kinky and returned to the palace, deciding to continue her search upstairs for Hashimoto.

The little mouse had remained in the palace, running along the corridors. It went round a corner and met something it really didn't want to meet. Before it had a chance of turning back and fleeing, a large paw caught it by the tail and lifted it off the ground.

"Squeak, squeak, squeak," went the frightened little mouse.

The paw turned the mouse round so the little animal's eyes could look into a big wide mouth with sharp teeth and whiskers around the sides.

"Hello," said the mouth. "Do you know what I am?"

"Squeak." This was followed by a nodding of the head.

"That's good," said the mouth, which could understand mouse language. "You don't like cats, do you?"

"Squeak, squeak," said the little mouse, shaking its head despite being upside down.

"And cats don't like mice, do they?"

"Squeak."

"No, we don't. Do you know what we do with little mice?"

"Squeak, squeak."

"We sometimes like to eat them; other times we just enjoy pulling off their arms and legs, then ripping their stomachs open. Would you like me to do those things to you?"

"Squeak, squeak," went the petrified little animal as it tried to wriggle free.

"Wouldn't you? That's very disappointing because they're the things we cats do with mice, especially naughty ones like you. You are naughty, aren't you?

"Squeak, squeak," accompanied by a vigorous shaking of the head.

"Oh, I think you are," said the cat. "But let's have a proper little chat first before I decide which of those terrible things to do to you."

"Squeak."

"I'm going to put you down on the floor now, so you can look at me the right way up. But if you try and run away, I'll hit you really hard with one of my paws. You won't like that, will you?"

"Squeak, squeak," together with a vigorous shake of the head.

When the little mouse was on the floor, it could see that the cat was black with small white stripes down the side. It had powerful leg muscles and a mouth with very sharp teeth. It gave the little mouse a nasty snarl before speaking again.

"I know what your name is," said the cat. "It's Hashimoto, isn't it?"

"Squeak," followed by a nod.

"Do you know what my name is?"

"Squeak, squeak," together with a shake of the head.

"I'm called Athene."

Hashimoto's eyes opened wide, his mouth began to tremble, and he tried to scamper away.

"No, you don't," Athene said, pulling him back with a paw. "Stay there in front of me and listen. I'm told you've been very rude about me?"

"Squeak," together with a shake of the head.

"Don't fib, you naughty little mouse," and Athene the cat gave Hashimoto the mouse a firm tap on the head. "What did you say? As thick as two bricks?"

"Squeak, squeak," and more shaking of the head.

"Fibbing again," accompanied by another tap on the head. "Face like an old cow; body like the back end of a bus?"

"Squeak, squeak." However, this time no shaking of the head. Hashimoto knew when he was beaten.

"Very rude, weren't you?"

"Squeak," now accompanied by a nodding of the head.

"Are you sorry?"

"Squeak," and yet another nod of the head.

"Are you going to ask my forgiveness by sacrificing a goat in my honour on the slopes of Mount Fuji?"

"Squeak," and a continuous nodding of the head, together with an appealing look into Athene's eyes, hoping for some sort of forgiveness. However, all Hashimoto got in return was the firmest tap on the head so far, followed by another one.

"Squeak!!!!!!"

"Well, that's not very nice," Athene answered. "I like goats. If you do that, I'll be even more annoyed!"

"Squeak, squeak, squeak, squeak," was all Hashimoto could say, unable to work out if he should be nodding or shaking his head.

"So, you won't sacrifice a goat?"

"Squeak, squeak," together with a vigorous shaking of the mouse's head.

"That's better. So, what am I going to do with you, Hashimoto? What punishment do you deserve?" And at this point Athene snarled into the mouse's face.

"Squeak, squeak, squeak, squeak," which Athene understood as being mouse for "I'm frightened."

"I know you are. That's good. I'll tell you what: I think I'll go for a little wander around for five minutes as I consider what to do with you. You stay here and don't move; if you do, I'll double your punishment. Understood?"

"Squeak," and a nod of the head.

"Good," Athene the cat answered as she walked down the corridor, turned left and then went behind another pillar, where she had left her clothes. She hopped into the middle, twitched her nose, causing a thick blue mist to suddenly appear. After a few seconds, Athene the goddess, walked out of the mist and continued into the hallway where she met Amphitrite walking down the stairs.

"Athene," said Amphitrite, giving her fellow goddess a kiss on the cheek. "I've just heard from Dolores you're here. We're all looking for a small mouse which seems to have got into the palace. Have you seen it, or do you know anything about it?"

"Oh, yes," Athene replied. "That's Hashimoto. I turned him into a mouse because he was very rude to me when I arrived."

"Hashimoto rude!" replied Amphitrite looking shocked. "What did he say?"

"Let's go to your room and I'll tell you all about it."

"But where is he? What's going to happen to him?"

"Oh, don't worry about him. He's around somewhere. I'll turn him back into a butler before I leave if you want me to. Let's go and have a good chat."

Hashimoto, being a naughty mouse, had not stayed put as instructed. Instead, he'd followed Athene the cat at a distance, so had heard the conversation between the two goddesses. When Amphitrite had called the visitor Athene and not Aphrodite, the little mouse had a 'light bulb' moment.

Now mouse language involves mixing up various words in a sentence, so this is what Hashimoto thought:

Up-cock Hashimoto bloody big he made just think.'

6
Building Matters

There were many boys' dormitories in the Underworld. However, the latest one being constructed, or just finished, was always referred to as the New Boys' Dormitory. At the time of Persephone's visit, the stone walls had been completed, the roof was on and most of the floorboards were laid. The internal work was still mainly outstanding.

Mason Bonko led the way into the building with Persephone, Vesta and Ming behind him. A few builders also decided to follow the small group, interested to see if Mason could pull the wool over the goddess's eyes as well as those of her two young helpers. They were joined by Sisyphus who had just returned from the quarry with two large boulders for the stonemasons to work on. Cerberus, however, had decided he had better things to do and went off for a wander outside, no doubt carrying out various internal security functions.

For about twenty minutes, Mason spoke non-stop, explaining the complexities of the building process with all sorts of technical terms to deliberately confuse the three female visitors. Eventually he came to the end of his lengthy speech and looked at the goddess.

"Any questions, Persephone?" he asked in a challenging tone with special emphasis on her name. He continued to stare directly at her, making it very clear that he was directing the question specifically at the Underworld's Queen and not Ming and Vesta.

Persephone had come to the building site that morning, really wanting to contribute and help her husband. However, she hadn't seen anything obvious to enquire about but realised that she was expected to take the lead as all eyes were on her. She looked at Vesta and Ming and sensed they were also aware of Mason's specific challenge to the goddess, so this time neither would intervene ahead of her. The only way out she could think of was to ask what she thought was a perfectly innocuous question and then hopefully hand the matter over to her two companions who might have something intelligent to raise.

"I... er... was just wondering what all those men were doing sitting around outside?" she asked with a blush.

Budiwati, who was in the front row, gave Persephone a quick thumbs up and smile.

The Head Builder was silent for a few seconds before replying with a touch of controlled aggression in his tone: "Isn't it obvious, Lady Persephone, after my explanation of the different stages of the building process?"

There was an audible drawing of breath from the dozen or so builders who were listening and the goddess began to blush even more.

"No," Sisyphus, who was standing behind Budi, called out. "It's not obvious to me, Mason, so I don't see why it should be obvious to Persephone."

Another audible drawing of breath occurred from the group as Mason turned round to Sisyphus and gave him an ugly stare.

"It's not obvious to me either," Ming piped up before Mason had a chance of saying anything.

"Nor me," said Vesta.

Mason spun back again to look at the three female visitors. As he was contemplating his reply, a female voice called out by his side.

"Perhaps it would be helpful, Mr Bonko, if you simply explained the role of the people sitting around in the building of the New Boys' Dormitory. Then Lady Persephone and Miss Ming and Miss Vesta will understand why they're spending all day doing what they're doing."

"Good idea, Budi," Sisyphus called out.

Mason Bonko frowned, wondering what trap Budiwati and Sisyphus were laying for him since he didn't trust either of them. However, unable to think of anything, he merely replied:

"Alright. Let's go outside and I'll point out the different teams."

At the side of the new dormitory was a large group of men who were sitting on the ground either talking in small groups, playing cards or having a snooze.

"Right," said Mason to Persephone and her two companions. "You remember what I mentioned earlier about the different stages of the building process. Firstly, we have to clear and level the ground – that's done by that group over there," and he pointed to his left. "Then the men at the back dig the foundations. After that the brickies to my far-right start building the walls either with bricks or stones. Next, the roofers, who are the group in the middle playing cards, set to work and, as you can see, they're finished – the roof is on. Afterwards, we concern ourselves with the internals, involving joiners, plasterers, plumbers, decorators and the like. That's what we're onto now, which is why you don't see any joiners outside because they're all busy laying floorboards. So, I hope that's clear, and you now understand what's going on."

Mason stared at Persephone who could only say: "Well, I suppose that's a bit clearer," before she looked in turn at Ming and Vesta for confirmation.

"No," said Vesta. "It doesn't explain why everyone's sitting around. Why aren't they doing some work?"

Mason gave a big sigh to indicate that he thought he was dealing with a bunch of thick females. However, he was aware he needed to keep his cool due to the goddess's presence.

"Because of the stage we're at in the building process," he said in a polite but firm voice. "The ground clearers, foundation team, brickies, roofing specialists have all done their jobs. They're finished; they've completed their work; they've nothing more to do. The different internal groups can't get going until the floorboards are down so they're unable to do any work at present. I trust that makes sense, Miss Vesta?"

"Well, why can't all the people who've finished on the New Boys' Dormitory start working on your next project?

You've always got masses of work to be done. Also, why can't a brickie do some joinery work, or a roofing person help with decorating?"

Mason looked at Vesta, while he worked out his reply. He was aware of her reputation of just continuing to ask questions relentlessly until she caught the other side out.

"The answer to your first question, Vesta, is management control. I don't suppose you've ever been involved in the construction industry but take it from me that building anything is a very complex process. If management isn't fully focused on the project in hand, then errors will occur and that could mean the building falls down. You wouldn't want a great big chunk of concrete landing on top of your head, would you? No, certainly not, but such occurrences take place if too many projects are being carried out at the same time."

"But...."

"No buts, Vesta," Mason said with a forced smile, but refusing to let her intervene. "Take it from me, as a professional, that's why we focus on one building at a time. Now---"

"But---"

"Let me continue," and this time Mason also put his hand up to indicate that Vesta should stop interrupting. "Continuing with the issue of complexity, it's important to appreciate that all the different functions I've explained at great length involve very different skills. My men are specialists in their own fields. For example, whoever heard of a brickie being a joiner? Or a plumber being a decorator?" Mason forced himself to laugh as he looked around; a few of the other builders listening to the conversation gave some supportive sniggers. "Believe me, it's not possible. No, it just can't be done!"

There was a long silence as no one said anything for a while. Then Sisyphus decided to intervene.

"I'd like to raise one matter, Mason ...."

71

"Shouldn't you be at the quarry, Sisyphus?" the Head Builder rasped back, since he was pretty sure the former king's intervention wouldn't be particularly helpful.

"Not for another half an hour."

"So, what's your point?" Mason asked with a touch of aggression in his voice.

"It's that Budi is both a brickie and a qualified joiner, but only ever gets used here to put up walls. Isn't that right, Budi?" and Sisyphus looked at the Building Department's only female employee.

"That's quite right, Mr Sisyphus," Budiwati replied enthusiastically. "Before I came to the Underworld, I spent most of my time doing carpentry work. I also helped out with the decorating; I liked decorating."

Mason gave Budi an angry look before saying dismissively: "There'll always be one exception."

"Oh no, Mr Bonko," Budi continued. "Tomasz who does the heavy digging for the foundations was a plumber in his native Poland. Also, Fabio told me he was a plumber as well as a brickie in Sao Paolo. There are lots of us who can multi-task."

Mason growled at Budi, but before he could say anything a voice called out: "What about the Union? The Union wouldn't accept it?"

Mason's eyes lit up. "Quite right, Yousef. Quite right. Even if we could do some limited muti-tasking as Miss Budiwati suggests, the Union wouldn't agree. Good point, my friend."

"Thanks, Mason," Yousef, a swarthy faced man in his middle years, said at being praised by his boss. This was not something that had ever happened to him beforehand.

"What's a union?" Persephone asked looking at Ming.

Ming shook her head. "I don't know," she replied. "Do you know, Vesta?"

"Yes," her friend replied. "But we don't have unions in the Underworld, so it's not relevant."

"Oh, I think that's not right, Miss," Yousef responded, emboldened by Mason's praise to participate further in the conversation. "We set one up some time ago when Karl got here. The Union represents the interests of us workers against management, you see. It ensures we get better pay, pensions, that sort of thing. Mason thought it was a good idea and we made him Union General Secretary; it was a unanimous vote of all us lads."

"But Mason is management," Vesta replied. "Also, we don't have pay and pensions here; we're dead. The whole thing doesn't make sense. It's a load of nonsense."

There was a lengthy silence as everyone looked at Mason for an explanation. The Head Builder was no longer feeling full of praise for Yousef, especially since he had volunteered the fact that Mason was Union General Secretary. That was most unhelpful! Eventually he said: "I don't think it's quite as simple as Yousef makes out, Lady Persephone. I'm also not so sure how relevant it is to our discussion."

"But you said it was a good point," Ming responded before anyone else.

"I'm rather confused," Persephone added. "I don't …."

The goddess was interrupted by Sisyphus who called out: "Oh, I understand what all this union lark is now. We had troublemakers like Karl and Yousef here when I was King of Corinth. Always trying to get the workers to combine together to make demands of me; threatened to withdraw their labour if I didn't give into them. It never worked; I just cut off their heads and said I'd do the same to anyone else who agreed with them. That's how I dealt with this union thing. We don't cut off heads in the Underworld, but we can make people sit on sharp spikes for a few weeks."

Mason was not enjoying the way this conversation was going, so he quickly intervened. "I don't think anyone's making any demands of anyone, Sisyphus. As I said before, Yousef's not quite explained the whole picture …."

"But Miss Ming's right, Mason. You did say I made a good point," a slightly aggrieved Yousef interrupted.

"Lady Persephone, may I make a suggestion?" Budi said, before pausing and looking at the goddess who nodded her head. "Thank you. Perhaps we could ignore the Union business? After all, Mr Bonko did agree after listening to Miss Vesta that it was not strictly relevant to the discussion."

"Yes, I agree, Budi. We'll say no more about the Union," Persephone replied, relieved to move on from the discussion about unions because she didn't really understand them. "But what about all this multi-tasking which you raised?"

"Perhaps I could talk further to Mr Bonko in the next few days on the matter?"

"Mason?" Persephone replied looking at the Head Builder.

"Precisely what I was going to suggest," he replied with a very false smile.

"Good. Now, what next?" the goddess asked, looking at Ming and Vesta.

"I'd like to ask about the walls," Vesta replied.

"What about them?" Mason asked.

"Why are they so thick? They must be about fifteen feet wide. It's the same in all the dormitories in the Girls' Quarters. Look." And Vesta walked over to the dormitory entrance, followed by the rest of the group.

"Yes, the walls do look rather wide," Persephone said. "I hadn't noticed it beforehand, but we don't have anything like that on Olympus."

Mason sighed and then said in a weary tone: "We have to make the walls thick so they can support the building's whole structure. If we had thin walls, the building might collapse. It's got to be resistant to all sorts of unexpected conditions."

"What does that mean?" Ming asked.

Before Mason had a chance to reply, Budiwati intervened. "Perhaps I can help on that one? When I first arrived in the Underworld, I raised precisely the same point since I had never seen such thick walls in Indonesia where I lived. However, Mr Bonko very helpfully explained to me that it was necessary to have such strong walls in case we had earthquakes and hurricanes. He is undoubtedly right because whenever my town experienced such conditions, the weaker structures were inevitably the first to fall. It's also why we dig extra deep foundations in the Underworld. Another thing we do, because of the unexpected conditions, is to ensure every roof we build has triple waterproof lining to stop the rainwater getting in."

Sisyphus was the first to respond. "Seems like a load of cobblers to me," he said.

"You don't know anything about the building trade, Sisyphus, so you're not qualified to give an opinion," Mason replied in an angry tone.

"Maybe not, Mason, but I do know we don't get earthquakes and hurricanes in the Underworld; it also doesn't rain here. These things come from the gods and Hades isn't going to allow them if they end up knocking down all his buildings."

"You have to be prepared for all eventualities," the Head Builder replied in a loud voice. "Never say never, that's what I say. Never say never!"

The goddess again looked at Vesta and Ming.

"I agree with Sisyphus," Vesta said.

"So do I," Ming added.

"No!" Mason shouted, now getting angry. "I take great exception to these ill-formed comments, Persephone. Neither Sisyphus nor these two young girls have the first idea of building matters. If you listen to them, we'll end up having buildings which collapse on top of people. Then, whom will you blame? Me and my team, that's whom. The answer's no! No! No! No!"

There was an embarrassed silence as everyone watched an angry Head Builder staring defiantly at Persephone, who was unsure how to respond.

During this brief stand-off, Ming said in a quiet voice to Vesta: "I think Mason will only be getting one sausage tomorrow."

"I was thinking of no sausages at all," Vesta replied in a similar quiet voice.

"That sounds even better."

Eventually Budiwati offered her assistance to the silent group.

"While I naturally agree with Mr Bonko, Lady Persephone," she said. "I would be very happy, if you and Mr Bonko agree, to review with him whether there might be some limited scope to take account of the issues raised by your assistants as well as Mr Sisyphus. Only, of course if you both agree."

Budi finished with a smile which Persephone acknowledged by smiling back, but Mason ignored.

"Good idea," Vesta quickly called out.

Ming immediately nudged the goddess who promptly responded before the Head Builder had a chance to erupt again: "Yes; good. That's what we'll do," without looking to get Mason's agreement this time. She then continued hopefully: "Are we finished now?"

"I'd like to ask why every roof has a dome on it?" Vesta inquired. "It must be really time-consuming to construct."

Mason sighed before replying: "Sir Christopher likes domes. Sir Christopher is the greatest architect the world has ever known. If Sir Christopher wants domes, then that's what Sir Christopher gets!"

The Head Builder finished with such force that no one felt inclined to dispute the matter. Yousef did, however, try to be helpful by suggesting that if ever it rained, it would be easier for water to drain off domes than flat rooves, but no one paid any attention to him.

"So, does that mean we're finished?" Persephone eventually asked again after a long silence.

"I can't think of anything you haven't covered," Mason said in a grumpy, but less angry tone.

"There is the decorating, Mr Bonko," Budi suddenly chirped out. "I'm sure Lady Persephone and Miss Ming and Miss Vesta would like to see the high-quality work by our decorating team."

"But we haven't done any decorating on the New Boys' Dormitory, so there's nothing to see."

"No, Mr Bonko, but we could show them the decorating in the last Men's Dormitory we finished some months ago. It's only a two minutes' walk away."

"That's the one I'm in," Sisyphus called out. "It's a sight to behold. You really need to see it, Persephone."

"Very well," the goddess replied. "Are you happy with that, Mason?"

"Delighted," he replied with a grimace, then turning round he said "Yousef, go fetch Lenny, Micky and Botty, will you? Tell them Lady Persephone is inspecting their handiwork."

Yousef went off to look for the decorating team, while the rest of the group walked towards the Men's Dormitory. Mason was walking behind Budi and couldn't resist making a V sign at her back and then raising his right hand in a fist and moving it up and down as if he were hitting her on the head. Unfortunately for him, the former King of Corinth was walking behind him and saw the hand gestures.

"Bonko," Sisyphus whispered in his ear at the same time as he tapped him on the shoulder. "I saw that. Just remember that Budi's a friend of mine."

"Piss off," Mason whispered back.

Sisyphus tapped the Head Builder's shoulder again. "Also, remember I'm bigger than you, so make sure you leave the lassie alone."

"Piss off again."

"Just remember," Sisyphus again said before moving forward to join Persephone.

The group that walked into the latest Men's Dormitory had now got a lot smaller as most of the builders had wandered off. However, Mason was still accompanied by Budiwati and Sisyphus, together with the three visitors.

They all stood in the entrance saying nothing for a full two minutes as they observed the decorating. Both the roof and walls were completely covered in classical scenes from the Renaissance period.

"I'm stunned," Persephone at last said. "It's magnificent."

Mason gave a broad smile, only to disappear once Vesta started talking.

"I'm totally stupefied," she said. "It must have taken ages to paint all this."

"What do you mean?" Persephone asked with a frown.

"It's a complete waste of time. We're in a dormitory where people come to sleep; it's not an art gallery."

"Our Girls' Dormitory doesn't have anything like this," Ming commented, unsure how to react. "All our walls are white."

"That's because it was built some time ago," Mason responded. "We've only started adding a bit of colour in recent years."

"But what about Vesta's comment about it taking ages to paint all this?" Persephone asked, now remembering that the purpose of their visit was to look for efficiency savings.

"My decorators are skilled craftsmen," Mason responded. "They work as quickly as possible, but you can't rush high quality work. What's more, the men living here really appreciate this environment. Happy men are productive men when they go off to their jobs each day."

"No, we don't appreciate it," Sisyphus said. "I sleep here, and I can tell you that no one here wants all this rubbish on the walls. As Vesta says, it's a complete waste."

"I suggest you can only speak for yourself, Sisyphus," the Head Builder replied. "Everyone knows you're a philistine."

"Come outside and say that!" an irate Sisyphus shouted.

"Stop, gentlemen, please," Persephone intervened as the two men were about to square up to each other.

At that moment, Yousef returned with the decorating team. They were all in what were originally white overalls but were now multi-coloured as different paints had splashed over them during the years. Both Persephone and Ming knew the decorators, but Vesta didn't since she'd only been in the Underworld a relatively short time, so introductions were made. After that, everyone stood around waiting for Persephone to suggest the way forward. Realising she was unsure what to suggest, Budi again came to her rescue.

"Perhaps, Mr Bonko, it would be helpful if you ask each of the decorators to briefly explain their work?" she suggested.

"Yes, alright," Mason replied, now prepared to agree to almost anything since he wanted the goddess's review to come to a quick end. "Okay with you, Persephone?"

The goddess nodded and mumbled "yes."

"Why don't you start, Micky?" the Head Builder suggested, looking at the man on his left.

Micky walked over to the group and stood in front of them. He was very thin with short curly hair and a grey beard. He looked up at the ceiling, which consisted of the same painting repeated dozens of times.

"That," he said in a loud voice, pointing at the image directly underneath the group, is "The Creation of Adam." The painting was of a naked young man lying on the ground with his hand outstretched to that of a bearded older "male" clothed in white.

Everyone waited for Micky to continue, but he clearly believed his explanation was sufficient.

"Who is Adam?" Ming asked after contemplating the painting for a while.

"Adam is Adam!" Micky replied in an arrogant tone and then said no more.

"The first human ever created," Vesta said to her friend.

Now Ming had come to the Underworld from China about eight hundred years ago. Since then, she had heard about the different religions in the world, so she quickly realised what the picture was referring to.

"Oh, that Adam," she said. "But it doesn't look like him at all. He's the Adam who does the washing up and I can't believe he ever looked as he does in the painting."

"I know him," Vesta said. "Are you sure he's the original Adam?"

"He is," Sisyphus chirped in. "Everyone knows Old Addy's the first person who came to the Underworld. I agree he now looks very different to the painting. Being in the Underworld might have had an effect, but I don't see how he could have changed from white skin to brown skin."

"My Adam is the original Adam!" Micky now spoke again with considerable force. "He was revealed to me. To me alone!"

"How's that, then?" Sisyphus asked.

"He was revealed!"

"I suspect it doesn't matter," Vesta quickly said. "I've got another question though; why is the same scene repeated over the entire ceiling?"

Micky was standing aloof with his arms folded and refusing to say any more, so Mason said he thought Sir Christopher had suggested it. The same was true of the wall paintings by Lenny and Botty.

"Let's look at them now," Persephone said.

The group walked over to the nearest wall, leaving Micky to himself. Lenny and Botty joined them; both turned out to be more talkative than Micky.

Lenny had long wavy hair which merged into his beard. He explained that the Mona Lisa, which he'd painted, was of an Italian lady called Lisa Gherardini who now ran the Housekeeping Department in the Underworld. Both Vesta and Ming knew her well because she often came to clean their dormitory.

Unlike his fellow painters, Botty was clean shaven with curly fair hair. His contribution to the décor was to paint The Birth of Venus. The central figure was a beautiful naked young female with long auburn hair standing in a large shell from which she had emerged as part of the birth process.

"Of course," Botty said as he was explaining his work. "This was all my imagination at the time. Venus is just another name for Aphrodite and I'm fully aware she didn't suddenly appear from a shell."

"She's actually my half-sister," Persephone said. "And she's got blonde hair and is much fuller on top."

"That I accept," Botty laughed. "As I said, the painting was purely my imagination at the time. Well, not quite my imagination; I used a young woman called Lucrezia to model for me. She's someone I knew from a house where you would visit if you wanted to meet girls who would be nice to you."

"You mean a brothel?" Sisyphus asked.

"Possibly," Botty replied with a large smile.

After they'd finished talking to Lenny and Botty, Persephone decided to be a bit more assertive and again asked the Head Builder about Vesta's point relating to the time taken to do all this intricate artwork. Mason now decided to lay all the responsibility at Sir Christopher's door, while of course adding that he agreed entirely with him. After all, who could possibly argue with the finest architect the world had ever known?

"But they're dormitories that are being built," Vesta again raised. "They're not churches and cathedrals."

Mason smiled back and said: "It's what Sir Christopher wants." At the same time, he opened his arms as if to say: 'what can I do about it?'

"Vesta's right of course," Botty responded more constructively. "It's a total nonsense doing all this. None of us actually enjoy it. It's bloody hard work and we did all that when we were alive. Now we're in the Underworld, we want an easier time. We're prepared to work, but not do all this creative stuff."

"It's really difficult getting the paint mix right here," Lenny added. "Something to do with the air, I'm sure. It was much better when Mr Whitewash was our team-leader."

"That's right," Botty added. "Mr Whitewash was a really good guy. All we did when he was in charge was paint all the walls white. Got through the work in no time and no problems with the paint mix."

"I liked using that Dulux brand," Lenny said.

"I agree."

Suddenly Micky joined the group. "That's what you should do," he said, now becoming communicative. "Get Mr Whitewash back. I'm sick and tired of painting Adam being created all the time. Nice white walls and ceilings, that's what I like."

Mason was becoming alarmed at the suggestions of the decorating team. "It's not so easy as that," he quickly responded. "There are many considerations to---"

"No, there aren't, Mason," Sisyphus interrupted. "I know Whitey well; he works with me in the quarries. He tries hard, but he's not really suited to the work. He'd come back in an instant if he could. Anyway, I've got to go now. I suspect you're finished as well, Persephone. No doubt you and the lassies will be reflecting on what you've seen today and will speak to Hades. Don't forget to mention the Union and that proposal of mine for dealing with it. Put the entire Building Department on a sharp spike for ten days if there's any trouble, except for Budi, of course. Bye everyone."

Sisyphus turned round and walked out of the building, leaving the entire group lost for words, including Mason for once.

7
The Great Wave

The Top God was sitting by himself on his throne in the Council Chamber. He was wearing his normal white cloak and crown of oak leaves on his head. He had forgotten to bring one of his thunderbolts, but was unconcerned as he felt it was unlikely he would need it at this meeting. No, he had other matters to worry about and, making it worse, was the uncertainty of just not knowing. He had been waiting for news all day, spending the last two hours sitting here in the chamber tapping his fingers on his throne's elegant, gilded arms.

The other gods and goddesses who were on Olympus that day were also in the chamber, congregated in small groups. A few were sitting on their thrones in front of Zeus, while most were standing up. Fortunately, there was an adequate supply of wine which Hebe and Bacchus were pouring out whenever glasses needed topping up.

The Council Meeting had been called at short notice in the early evening without much explanation. However, after multiple conversations in the chamber while waiting for Zeus to start the meeting, everyone was now sure of the subject matter.

Early on that day there appeared to have been a massive disturbance in the Pacific and Indian oceans, which none of the gods and goddesses knew anything about. Zeus had dispatched Iris, the Messenger Goddess, to go and investigate and then report back. He suspected that Poseidon might have been the cause and specifically asked her to go to the Sea Cavern to see what she could ascertain. Iris had still not returned which was why Zeus was reluctant to start the meeting since no one knew what was really going on.

There was one other matter which Zeus was aware of but was not generally known. This was that Athene suspected that Mars might have something to do with the events in the two oceans. She had gone to tackle Mars on the matter, but he had just got angry and denied any involvement. Athene was not convinced that her half-brother was as innocent as he made out and expressed this view to her father in forceful terms. Zeus, himself, was sceptical about the God of War's role in the events of the day. Instead, he felt it was far more likely to be a result of Poseidon's activities, although he had to accept that his brother had been very docile for a long time and there was no good reason for him to suddenly initiate chaos which impacted on both their realms.

Athene harbored her doubts about Mars during the day and decided to share them with Hephaestus. He was the God of War's full brother and was the only person who could exercise any sort of control over him. Hephaestus thought that Athene might well be correct in her suspicions about Mars, so the two of them went to collect him before the Council Meeting. It was just as well that they did since he had every intention of not attending, claiming he was about to leave for South America where he had urgent business concerning one of the many guerrilla wars he was sponsoring. What then followed was a fifteen-minute shouting match between the three members of the deity before Mars very reluctantly agreed to accompany Athene and Hephaestus to the meeting.

Zeus continued to tap his fingers on the arms of his throne when his eldest sister approached him. Hestia was the Goddess of the Hearth and generally kept a low profile on Olympus, unlike her two female siblings, Hera, and to a lesser extent, Demeter. She did, however, always dress immaculately and today was wearing a beautiful salmon pink dress, covered by a cloak, which had alternate silver and gold stripes.

"I think it's time for you to start the meeting, Zeus," Hestia said. "We all know that you're waiting for Iris, but the rumour mill's about to go into overtime."

"You're probably right," Zeus replied with a sigh. "Would you mind please tapping Hera on the shoulder and letting her know."

Hestia nodded but before she could turn round, there was a loud bang as the two grey doors at the chamber entrance were violently pushed open, crashing against the wall. They were followed by Poseidon with a flustered Mr Bumble in his wake who had been deprived of the opportunity of announcing the Sea God formally to the wider assembly.

Poseidon was wearing a long mail shirt covered with a cloak latticed with emeralds and diamonds. He was wearing a crown made entirely of small seashells and carried his trident in his left hand which he proceeded to bang loudly on the floor as he marched across the Council Chamber towards a small group of gods at the far end.

"Evening Zeus," he said with a slight nod of his head by way of acknowledgment as he strode past the Top God's throne on its raised platform.

Zeus stood up looking at his brother in surprise. "Poseidon," he replied in a muted voice.

The Sea God had now reached the group consisting of Hera, Athene, Mars and Hephaestus who were having an animated conversation in the far corner of the chamber. Mars had his back to Poseidon as the others suddenly stopped talking and looked at the figure behind him. He turned round and saw his uncle.

"Poseidon, what a-----" Mars said before being suddenly silenced by the Sea God's right fist smashing into his face. It was such a powerful blow that his nose immediately broke, his front teeth were knocked out and he crumpled onto the floor completely unconscious.

The chamber became totally silent with no one saying anything as they watched Poseidon turn round and march back towards the open doors. As he passed Zeus on his return journey, he merely said: "Goodbye Zeus," before exiting the room. Once outside, he stepped onto his chariot and sped away.

•

Earlier that day, life had begun normally for the occupants of the Sea Cavern. They were all on the piazza having their early morning exercise session, supervised by Totty in her usual professional manner. The four maids were also in the lagoon dancing to Abba's "Dancing Queen", which was playing on the much-loved CD recorder. They had decided some weeks ago that it was their favourite Abba song, so it tended to get played incessantly when all the maids were together in the water.

Just as the Dancing Queen was about to come to an end, there was a tremendous roar from the tunnel which connected to the outside ocean. This was immediately followed by an immense wave of water which rushed into the cavern. It swept the maids onto the piazza and, together with the group carrying out their morning exercise, they were thrown against the palace walls at the far end, everyone screaming in terror. The only exception was Poseidon who managed to stand his ground as the waters rose around him. They were soon pouring through the palace's windows and doors as more and more water continued to race into the cavern.

Poseidon let himself be lifted by the rising waters although he managed to stay in the same spot about thirty metres in front of the palace. Once he had steadied himself, he let out a mighty roar of "Back!" At the same time, he thrust his right hand in front of him as if he were pushing the wave back into the cave entrance. He repeated his roar of "Back!" again and again. Slowly, the cavern stopped filling up as the water levels stabilized about half-way up the palace wall. Amphitrite, who had now recovered from being crashed against the wall, joined her husband with her own loud shouts of "Back! Back! Back!" as she thrust both her arms forward. Between the two of them, they managed to start pushing the excess water away; this continued for about fifteen minutes until the piazza floor was cleared and the lagoon was at its normal height. The two gods had stopped shouting "Back!" after a while but continued to hold their arms up in front of them as they could sense there was still pressure for more water to come into the cavern.

"How are you?" Poseidon asked Amphitrite without looking at her as he maintained his focus on resisting the waters.

"Badly bruised and cut, but nothing broken," the Sea Goddess replied. She had by now limped to her husband's side, but like him, continued to focus in front of her with arms outstretched. "It won't be the same for all the others."

"No," Poseidon growled. "I can hear them. Look, I can hold the water back myself now; you'd better go and look at them."

"I suspect you'll have to heal them, though. I can only deal with superficial injuries."

"Yes," the Sea God nodded. "There are also the mares at the back."

Amphitrite sighed. "Of course; they'll be petrified."

"We need to focus on the piazza initially."

"Yes. There's also the damage to the palace."

"That's secondary. This has changed all our plans."

"It was a tsunami, wasn't it?

Poseidon nodded again. "It must have been," he said.

"But how? Why? You're the god that creates tidal waves, earthquakes and everything associated with them."

"I don't know, but we're damned well going to find out," he replied with aggression in his voice.

"Yes," Amphitrite agreed. "As you say, all our plans will have to change, but first I'll go and look after the others. You're sure you can hold it back without me?"

"Yes; it's much weaker now. I won't need to do anything after a few more minutes unless there's a second wave."

"I'll go then."

Amphitrite lowered her arms and turned towards the carnage by the palace wall. She was limping badly because of a damaged left knee and hip. Both her arms were badly cut, and she had a bruise on her right eye as well as suffering from a headache after hitting her head against the palace wall.

There were a lot of whimpers and groans from the wall. Amphitrite went from one to the other to carry out a quick assessment. Both Totty and Kinky were unconscious with the latter's left arm clearly broken. Hashimoto was in a similar position to the goddess with nothing broken, as were Minky and Linky. Dolores was in a very bad way with both her right arm and left leg broken as well as many of her teeth knocked out. Pinky had a dislocated left shoulder and a broken nose. Everyone had multiple cuts and bruises.

Amphitrite brought Totty and Kinky round to consciousness and told them to lie still. She hobbled back to her husband to appraise him of the situation.

"I'll hold the waters back while you go and heal them," she said.

"There's no need anymore," the Sea God replied. "They've settled." He put his arm down and studied Amphitrite in detail for the first time since the giant wave had come crashing into the cavern. "You look in a bad way."

"I'm not great."

"I'll get you sorted first but tell me all your symptoms before I begin."

After the Sea Goddess had listed everything, Poseidon lifted his arms above his head and suddenly he and Amphitrite were covered by a thick purple fog. Two minutes later the air cleared to show the Sea God holding his wife's shoulders.

"Better now?" Poseidon inquired, letting go of Amphitrite after a brief hug and kiss.

"Totally," she replied with a smile. "Thank you. Let's see to the others."

The two of them walked over to the palace wall and jointly raised their arms, resulting in a massive expanse of purple fog covering everyone. For half an hour the god and goddess worked together as they healed all the injured, although most of the power came from Poseidon. He then went round to the back of the palace and found all the mares had multiple broken legs, which he healed in a similar fashion.

In the time that Poseidon was looking after the mares, Hashimoto carried the mermaids back to the lagoon and Amphitrite, Dolores and Totty went and assessed the damage in the palace. The bad news was that the ground floor had been completely devastated, but the waters had not reached the first floor which remained intact. The piazza was a mess as all the gym equipment had been thrown against the wall, having been a significant contributor to the injuries incurred. The CD recorder was completely smashed so that was the end of Abba in the cavern for the time being.

Everyone was asking questions about what had happened. All Amphitrite could say was that it was a tidal wave, but she had to admit that she didn't know what the cause was. When Poseidon returned, he looked very tired as he had spent so much power both pushing back the waters as well as healing all the injured.

"I can't add anything to what Amphitrite's said," Poseidon said wearily. "What she and I need to do now is go upstairs and have a discussion. We'll then come down and tell you all we know and what we're going to do about it."

"We'll start clearing up," Dolores said.

"If I were you, Dol, I'd just leave everything for the time being. Much better for everyone to go upstairs, get changed and have a short rest if possible. We'll all meet up here in an hour."

"What about us?" Kinky called from the water's edge where all the mermaids were listening.

"Do the same," Poseidon replied.

"We've just looked, and our palace is a complete disaster zone."

"Try and find a place to rest. We'll meet in the piazza, so you're included."

"Super," Kinky murmured without much enthusiasm.

An hour later everyone met by the edge of the pool so the four mermaids could participate. Both Poseidon and Amphitrite were wearing mail shirts covered with their cloaks and wearing crowns. The Sea God held his trident which had remained in his study unused for the last few months, while the Sea Goddess carried a silver sword. Hashimoto, Dolores and Totty were all wearing warm clothing which had been suggested by Amphitrite who popped out to see them towards the end of her discussion with Poseidon.

All eyes were on the Sea God who had recovered his strength and now looked very angry.

"Our Kingdom has been attacked!" he boomed in a loud voice and then banged his trident on the piazza floor. "We don't know by whom or why, but when we do, there will be a bloody reckoning!"

The Sea God continued in this vein for a full five minutes before becoming calmer and moving onto practical matters. There then followed a long debate on the way forward. The god and goddess had decided that the Sea Cavern had to be evacuated by everyone since it was no longer safe. This caused huge consternation amongst the maids who viewed it as their home. They got very upset and tearful and wanted to know where they were to go and for how long, to which it was only possible to give the vaguest of answers.

"Can I please try to understand what you're suggesting, Lord Poseidon?" Totty intervened after several minutes of everyone talking at the same time. "Is it that we all travel in your chariot to find out what has happened and only then decide on the way forward?"

"Precisely," Poseidon replied.

"That may be okay for the maids, but---"

"No, it's not!" Kinky interrupted.

"Let Totty continue, Kinky," Amphitrite said in a gentle tone and put a finger to her lips to suggest silence.

"Sorry," the maid murmured, looking at her friend on the piazza to continue.

"What I wanted to say is that whereas the mermaids are alive and can go out into the world, I thought that dead people such as Hash, Dol and myself were forbidden to ever return to the land of the living?"

"You're quite right, Totty," the Sea God replied. "But these laws or rules were made by the gods and so can be undone by the gods. As far as Amphitrite and I are concerned, this is one of those exceptional situations where the rules can be set aside. Everyone here in the Sea Cavern is part of our family and we have a responsibility to protect you all. That is the basis of our decision."

"I understand that, and I will leave, but could I suggest that those who want to stay in the cavern are allowed to do so? There may be a risk, but there's also the risk of going into the oceans and seas. We just don't know what's happening out there."

Before anyone else could say anything, Hashimoto piped up: "I, Hashimoto, am bravest of the brave. I have already fought as fireman in one war. I will leave cavern to fight in second one with Lord Poseidon and Lady Amphitrite. I will do many karate chops on the enemy."

He then proceeded to swing his arms up and down, making chopping movements. Normally, everyone would laugh at these antics, but not today. Instead, Dolores said in a sombre but determined tone: "I too wish to remain in the cavern. I have only ever resided in two places. When I was in South Carolina I was well treated for what I was, but I was always a slave. We slaves did not have a home, only a place where we existed. In the Sea Cavern I am not a slave and that is why it is a real home. It is the only one I have ever known, and I do not want to leave it. I also believe that one day the rest of you will return here. I will get this place ready for that day."

There was a silence before Amphitrite replied: "You will be all alone with the maids, Dol - no one knows how long for. What if you need help? What if Hebe is unable to come with food, for instance? How will you cope?"

"We'll look after her," Kinky called out followed by support from the other maids.

"I will cope," was all Dolores would say.

Poseidon was reluctant to agree to anyone staying in the cavern, but a mixture of Amphitrite and Totty eventually persuaded him to let Dolores and the mermaids remain. It was agreed that, depending on what the others found outside the cavern, they would seek to create a support network for the five remaining inhabitants.

Half an hour later, the mares were assembled on the piazza with the chariot behind. Amphitrite had spent time with them explaining what was going to happen and they were all ready for what they viewed as a new adventure. They were also keen on some revenge following their battering earlier in the morning.

Both Hashimoto and Totty were provided with warm cloaks and small swords by Amphitrite, although neither knew how to use them. There were many tears as the departing group said their farewells to Dolores and the maids. Although the chariot was not as large as Hebe's, it still had plenty of room, allowing Poseidon and Amphitrite to stand up at the front with the other two sitting at the side, holding onto leather straps.

When they were ready to depart, Poseidon gave a slight pull on the reins and raised his trident in salute to those remaining. As the mares entered the water, Amphitrite called out: "Farewell! We will return!"

When the chariot had passed through the tunnel linking the cavern to the outside ocean, the mares pulled it to the surface. The water was still turbulent, and Poseidon chose to go in an easterly direction since the currents suggested that had been the source of the tidal wave. They passed various fish near the surface and the Sea God and Goddess asked them for information. It was clear that the fish, who were swimming around hoping to find calmer waters, didn't know much; they were just bewildered. After a while a blue-fin whale was seen in the distance and the chariot raced towards it.

"Whoa!" shouted Poseidon as he came up behind the mammal. "Do you know what's happened?"

The blue-fin turned round and saw the Sea God. "A great wave came from the east, Lord Poseidon," he answered.

"I got swept many miles, but I was lucky – many of us got battered against rocks; some even drowned."

"It's Fuad, isn't it?" the Sea God asked, now recognizing the whale. "Where are you headed to?"

"Yes, I'm Fuad. I'm going to look for Moby who was in the east a few weeks ago. I hope he's alright since we need our leader, especially now."

"Amphitrite and I will find Moby. We have another important task for you over the next few days and weeks. Do you know where the Sea Cavern is?"

"I know it's location, but I've never been in there."

"Right; now this is what we need you to do. It's of the utmost importance to the Sea Goddess and myself and will allow us to focus on what has caused this giant tidal wave and how we can prevent it from happening again."

Poseidon and Amphitrite then proceeded to give Fuad detailed instructions to protect the occupants of the Sea Cavern. He was to gather a group of about half a dozen whales and a number of sharks. They were to set up a rota system with two each in the cavern all the time and the others outside but no more than ten miles away. They were to provide whatever assistance necessary to the five inhabitants. This could involve security, passing messages to the outside world or even helping them to evacuate in extreme situations.

"I can organize all that," Fuad said after everything was explained. "I'll have it in place in the next few hours. How long will it be for?"

"We don't know," Poseidon replied. "But once we've found Moby, we'll set up some sort of information relay system with you. It all depends on what we find."

"And if Moby survived."

"I agree, but let's hope for the best. If not, we'll organize some way of communicating with you."

"Then I'll go now," the whale said.

"Good luck and thank you," Poseidon replied before setting the mares off on a gallop across the waters.

The next few hours involved considerable distress for both the Sea God and the Sea Goddess. The further east they travelled, the more dead fish and whales they came across. Some had survived, although a number were injured. All the survivors were in a state of confusion but were reassured by Poseidon and Amphitrite being amongst them. At times, the former would have bouts of anger as he cursed everything he saw, although his wife was far more resigned to the misery they were witnessing.

It was late afternoon, with the mares still travelling at speed, when Amphitrite called out that she could see land in the distance.

"Do you recognize it?" Poseidon asked, staring ahead.

"I think it's Lilliput," the Sea Goddess replied. "But it's still partially underwater. Head for that high point on the left."

"What are their chances of survival?" Poseidon asked.

"Considerable, I would expect. You've not been there for more than fifty years; I've been visiting every two years. They're very advanced scientifically and have all sorts of contingency plans to protect themselves."

"Even against tsunamis?"

"Even against tsunamis, but let's see if they work."

The chariot slowed down as it approached a sandy beach behind which there was a small hill. Both Hashimoto and Totty were encouraged to stand up; they were stiff after their uncomfortable journey, but neither complained given the devastation to the marine life they had witnessed.

It was Totty who saw the first signs of life on the island. "Look at the top of the hill," she said, pointing. "There's some movement up there." Just at that instant a blare of trumpets came from the hill.

"Let's take the chariot up to them," Amphitrite said. "Those trumpet sounds suggest they're waiting for somebody or something."

The mares cantered across the beach trying to avoid the large pools of water that were everywhere. Once they got on the slope, the going got easier and they reached the summit in a matter of minutes.

At the top they were greeted by a sight which amazed Hashimoto and Totty, but not the god and goddess. In front of them was a platform about five feet high on top of which was a small grey-haired man of no more than six or seven inches in height, wearing a purple robe. There were about a dozen similar sized men and women in blue uniforms who stood either side of him, all holding trumpets on which they had recently blown. They had reached the top of the platform by climbing tiny ladders along the side. At the bottom of the platform were a number of miniature horses being looked after by a couple of grooms.

"They're all so small," Totty whispered to Amphitrite.

"This is Lilliput, the land of the little people," the Sea Goddess whispered back.

At that moment, the purple robed figure walked to the front of the platform and called out: "Greetings, Lady Amphitrite and, I assume, Lord Poseidon, together with fellow travellers."

"And greetings to you too, Redrelok," Amphitrite replied. "Yes, you are quite correct, this is my husband, Lord Poseidon and these are our two friends, Hashimoto and Totty."

Redrelok bowed to them all and Hashimoto and Totty bowed back without saying anything. Poseidon looked to Amphitrite to continue.

"We have come to investigate the Great Wave that has emerged from the oceans," the Sea Goddess continued. "It is not of our making, and we hope you can perhaps enlighten us, Redrelok."

The small man gave a wry smile. "That is why I'm standing here, Amphitrite," he said in a more familiar tone. "The Empress and the Cabinet thought you might appear on our shores, so I was dispatched to watch out for you. The Empress, the First Minister and the Interior Minister are touring the island assessing what damage has been done, so I as the humble Finance Minister was sent to be the look-out."

Amphitrite laughed. "We all know that you're the most important person in Lilliput," she said. "After all, you control the purse strings and when the others return from their tour, they'll have to get your approval for all the expenditure they'll no doubt want to incur." Redrelok merely bowed back. "But tell us please how much damage and loss of life you think has been incurred on Lilliput?"

"Our first estimate is considerable damage, but no loss of life."

"How come no loss of life?" Poseidon asked, now involving himself in the discussion.

"We will show you all our precautions tomorrow, Lord Poseidon, when the Empress and the other ministers have returned. But for now, I would like to answer Amphitrite's earlier question about the cause of the Great Wave and then explain arrangements for your lodgings this evening."

"Please do."

"Our scientists have been tracking the activities of certain less than friendly countries for several years. Earlier today one of them launched an immense missile into the atmosphere which fell into the seas about three hundred miles from here. A number of such missiles have been launched in the past, but this one was far and away more devastating than any beforehand. The regrettable result was a giant tidal wave that might well have travelled round the globe."

"Which country did this?" Poseidon demanded in an angry tone.

"Tyrantland," was the reply.

The Sea God banged his trident on the chariot floor. "That Little Bastard! Mars's best friend!" he shouted continuing to bang his trident as he repeated the words: "Little Bastard! Little Bastard! Little Bastard!"

"And we know Lord Mars has been a regular visitor to Tyrantland in recent months."

"Right!" Poseidon shouted again. "Regrettably, a change in plans, Finance Minister Redrelok. I and the Sea Goddess have got to go to Olympus immediately."

"No!" Amphitrite screamed back.

The Sea God and Goddess then proceeded to have a loud argument before Amphitrite pulled her husband off the chariot and walked him down the hill. Twenty minutes later they returned and after further discussion with Redrelok, it was agreed that they would all immediately go to the capital where the mares could be fed fresh water and hay. Poseidon would then take the chariot to Olympus, leaving Amphitrite, Hashimoto and Totty to remain on Lilliput to meet the Empress and other ministers the next day if he had not yet returned.

The journey to the capital was very swift since Hashimoto and Totty lifted the Lilliputians and their horses onto the chariot. After refreshing themselves, the winged mares were soon seen galloping across wet fields before gradually rising into the skies as they carried Lord Poseidon towards his fellow gods on Mount Olympus.

8

The Land of the Little People

L illiput is a small island on the east side of the Indian Ocean. It was first discovered by 'normal sized' mankind about three hundred years ago when Lemuel Gulliver was shipwrecked off its coast. Since then, there have been occasional visits by the outside world, but these are generally discouraged by its inhabitants. The Lilliputians are known to the gods with whom they have good relations, and the gods try to keep outsiders away. They do this by numbing the memories of people who have visited the island, so no records are kept in any geography or history books nor in individuals' personal diaries. Lilliput is certainly not to be found in any travel brochures or tour operators' guides!

Lilliput's economy is largely self-sufficient with both strong agricultural and industrial sectors. Considerable attention is given to education, and this is one area where its inhabitants do have relationships with the outside world. In recent decades there has been a lot of focus on science and technology and Lilliputian scientists are often more knowledgeable in their chosen subjects than many leading Western and Chinese academics.

Historically, Lilliput was ruled by an Emperor who would appoint a cabinet of ministers to advise him. However, over 150 years ago, the then Emperor passed away without any next of kin. He spent the final years of his reign putting in place a new constitution for how the island would be governed after him. This consisted of creating a parliamentary democracy with regular elections every five years along the lines of the British system. There was considerable debate at the time about how the Head of State should be chosen and what his title would be. Lilliputians were attached to the concept of an Emperor so they eventually decided to retain that title instead of having a President, but the role should from then onwards be largely ceremonial and advisory. The Emperor would be chosen by a full vote of the adult population; he had to be over 60 years old and always retired on his 80th birthday when a new individual was chosen. Since these revised arrangements were set up, there have been twelve different Emperors, of whom six have been politicians, two farmers, three businessmen and one professor. The male to female ratio has been exactly 50:50.

Being a relatively small island populated by people of about six inches tall meant that over the years, flooding was a considerable problem. While a foot of flood water would not drown a full-sized human, this was not the case as far as Lilliputians were concerned. About 100 years ago the government decided that most of the population should relocate to the upper reaches of several hills on the island. The capital, Mildendo was largely reconstructed on the highest hill and named New Mildendo; the former capital being renamed Old Mildendo. In addition, large underground bunkers were created and, once science had progressed sufficiently, it was possible to seal them, so they were entirely waterproof. These bunkers were structured so each household had its own private compartment, with the result that the entire population had both a home at ground level and a sealed underground residence. The scientists in due course also created an early warning system for floods, so everyone was able to retreat underground to avoid incidents such as the Great Wave.

While Lilliput's agricultural land was particularly fertile, much of a year's harvest could be destroyed by flood water. The government therefore decreed that at the time of constructing underground bunkers for the population, similar bunkers should be created for the storage of crops. In a good year, the island's produce was sufficient to feed the entire population twice over, so with time several years' worth of stocks were built up allowing the people to survive any natural disasters.

Outside New Mildendo's gates were six large hut-like structures. They were about eight feet high and ten feet in both width and depth. These were shelters for any humans who, despite precautions to the contrary, managed to reach the shores of the island. They were also for the gods when they visited Lilliput with Amphitrite, Hebe and Athene being regular visitors. Zeus, as Top God, had never been to Lilliput and probably didn't know it existed.

In front of these huts was a large platform like the one on which Redrelok and the buglers had been standing the previous day. It was on this platform that the Empress Chertassle was standing with a number of her ministers early the following morning to welcome her visitors when they emerged.

Poseidon had returned from Olympus late in the night, feeling pleased with himself for having knocked Mars unconscious. He didn't for one minute believe his punch would stop the God of War's aggression towards the oceans and the seas but at least it made him feel better. The result was that he slept soundly during the rest of the night but was still up and about with the others shortly after the Empress arrived.

Amphitrite knew everyone, so she made the introductions to the Empress and the various ministers. Empress Chertassle was in her mid-70's but still physically very active with a sharp mind. Her hair was dyed jet black, and she wore a dark blue cloak. All her ministers wore purple robes; Redrelok was there together with the First Minister, Listrongle, the Interior Minister, Mandoselin and the Defence Minister, General Golroblin.

Soon Poseidon and Chertassle were dominating much of the discussion. Although the Empress's role was ceremonial and advisory, at times of national emergency she was expected to take the lead, and this was clearly one of those occasions.

"So, in summary, you're telling us there was no loss of life on the island because most people were on high ground and also because of these underground bunkers you've got, but there's been quite a lot of damage," the Sea God summarised after a lengthy discussion on the impact of the Great Wave on Lilliput.

"That's broadly correct," the Empress replied. "All the Lilliputians were able to reach their sealed underground bunkers before the waters came although it turned out to be unnecessary for many of us. However, we lost several animals in the low-lying areas, especially sheep and cattle. About half the year's crops have been destroyed, but we're fortunate in having seven years' supplies in store. Unfortunately, the few houses near the coast have been washed away, so we're having to temporarily re-house their occupants before a rebuilding process takes place. The worst situation though is that our navy has been completely destroyed, as have most of the fishing vessels in the ports."

The Empress saw Poseidon frown at the mention of fishing. "I know you disapprove of fishing, Lord Poseidon, but we are an island community. All such communities rely on fishing to sustain themselves. It's the same the world over."

Poseidon was just about to give an angry response when Amphitrite intervened by touching him on the shoulder and saying: "I feel as strongly on this matter as the Sea God does, but perhaps now is not the time to debate the issue. After all, the loss of marine life from the Great Wave is probably greater than all the fish caught by Lilliputian fishermen in the last thousand years."

The Empress gave a slight bow of her head to the Sea Goddess by way of thanks, before adding: "You are undoubtedly correct, Amphitrite. We saw a lot of dead fish on our northern shores yesterday when we inspected the island."

Poseidon looked at both his wife and the Empress before clearing his throat and continuing. "Agreed; let's leave it for now," he said. "What we need to focus on is what our response should be. I understand it was a missile sent from Tyrantland?"

"That is correct, Lord Poseidon," the Empress replied. "Our scientists have tracked a number of these devices in recent years, and they all come from the same facility hidden in Tyrantland's mountain regions."

"But how do you do this tracking?"

"We use satellites. Although we don't have our own, we have a way of borrowing a small part of those belonging to other countries without their owners knowing."

"Satellites," Poseidon repeated thoughtfully. "Are these the things which whizz around the sky?"

The Empress nodded.

"I must admit I don't know anything about them. Do you understand them?" he asked, looking at his wife.

"Not much. I'm sure Athene does and probably Hebe and now Hermes because he's been studying a lot of science in recent years. What about you two?" Amphitrite looked at Totty and Hashimoto.

"All I know is that they're involved in sending messages and things around the world, but nothing more," Totty replied. "What about you, Hash?"

"Hashimoto only knows about firefighting, butlering and karate. He knows nothing about satellites. However, I have helpful suggestion which is that if these satellites whizz around the sky, then maybe Lord Zeus knows all about them."

For the first time since the Great Wave struck, Poseidon burst out laughing. "I very much doubt it, Hash," he said with a smile. "Although I agree he ought to."

"Hashimoto only trying to help."

"And much appreciated, but you don't know my brother. Anyway, let's move on…. Empress, could you please tell us how you knew this tidal wave was coming so you had time to get all your people to safety? Have you some oracle on the island that we don't know about?"

"No oracle, Lord Poseidon. Again, this is the work of our scientists. We've established a tsunami monitoring system around the entire Indian Ocean and part of the Pacific which gives us an early warning of such events. It is why the loss of our navy is such a serious matter. It was not only responsible for setting up the individual monitors in the first place, but also visits the different locations on a regular basis to ensure they remain functional."

102

"These scientists of yours seem to play a very significant role in the affairs of Lilliput," Poseidon commented. "Could we meet them sometime please?"

"Certainly. It was my original intention that Professor Archimelock and Dr Einstella would be here on this platform to meet you. However, they are very busy developing computer programs to improve our defenses even more and I was persuaded that should be given priority. I promise to introduce them to you tomorrow as a matter of priority."

"It will have to be in a few days' time," Poseidon replied. "Amphitrite and I need to travel around our realm for a few days to assess the extent of the damage and to see what we can do for our fish and whales. We should be able to return within five days at the latest and then we can meet your professors."

"And your friends, Mr Hashimoto and Miss Totty, will they be travelling with you?"

"No, Empress. We had a quick word with them as we emerged this morning. If acceptable to you, we'd like them to stay here until our return."

"We'll be very pleased to look after your friends while you're away. In fact, your timing is excellent. You spoke earlier about what our response should be to the missile from Tyrantland. We're currently putting in place further defenses as I said, but we feel that there should be an element of offence as well. By the time you return, our military under General Golroblin will have our plans well developed to discuss with you."

"If offence means revenge on the Tyrant and his lackeys, that very much has our support. The creatures of my realm will want to be involved in punishing that Little Bastard, and Amphitrite and I will be returning with our own ideas."

"Then we will have much to discuss in five days' time, Lord Poseidon. Is there anything else we can specifically do for you while you and the Sea Goddess are away?"

"I don't think so," Poseidon replied, looking at his wife and Hashimoto and Totty.

"What if Moby turns up?" Amphitrite raised. "You know Moby, don't you Chertassle?" The Empress nodded her head. "If he comes to the island, please raise two matters with him. Firstly, let him know we'll be back within five days, and we urgently need to speak to him when we're here. Secondly, he needs to speak to Hash and Totty so they can explain about establishing some sort of messaging system between the Sea Cavern and Lilliput because we've still got members of our household in the cavern. Moby will sort out the details with the other whales once he knows what the issue is."

After the Empress had acknowledged Amphitrite's instructions, the discussion soon came to an end. Poseidon and the Sea Goddess went off to prepare the mares for their trip and Totty and Hashimoto returned to their huts for a brief rest. It had been agreed that Redrelok and Mandoselin would collect them later in the morning for a tour of Lilliput. Meanwhile, the Empress and her other ministers, having descended the platform by virtue of a mechanical lift at the back, returned to the palace and various government offices in a miniature silver Rolls Royce.

●

Totty and Hashimoto went their separate ways when the two ministers arrived to collect them. They had been given the choice of either a tour of the island or a detailed look at New Mildendo. Totty was feeling energetic and wanted to walk around the countryside, while Hash was more interested in the capital.

"I don't know why you don't want to look at the whole of Lilliput," Totty said as the two of them were discussing the matter after the Empress had left. "We live right next door to Mildendo. We can see it anytime."

"Miss Totty," Hash said formally to his young friend. "Hashimoto needs to conserve his energy after very arduous sea voyage yesterday."

"Oh, I see. That's okay then if you're tired, Hash. You should have said so at the beginning because we've just spent the last fifteen minutes arguing about the matter."

"I did not say I was tired!" the butler responded emphatically. "I said I was conserving my energy."

"Well, it's the same thing, isn't it?"

"No, Miss Totty, it's not! You have not yet understood the reason why Lord Poseidon and Lady Amphitrite have brought me here."

"It's the same reason as I'm here, Hash; we've evacuated the cavern. And stop calling me Miss Totty, will you? I'm Totty to you."

"Very well, Totty. I cannot help being polite. You will never find me discourteous. But to-----"

"Oh, what about that time you were rude to Athene?" Totty interrupted.

"I was led into a trap, but please do not raise again. I do not wish to be reminded of that unpleasant incident. No, as I was saying, I have clearly been brought on this mission because I am the one who will have to fight Mr Tyrant, otherwise known as Little Bastard. That is why Hashimoto has to conserve energy. It is for the tremendous battle ahead; the many karate chops I will apply to all parts of my adversary's body."

"I see," said Totty with a smile. "Well, you're quite right, Hash. I hadn't realized that's why you are here. I'll tell Poseidon and Amphitrite when they return just in case they don't know."

"There is no need to do that, Miss Totty," Hashimoto again spoke formally. "These matters are already known to the gods.

Totty just smiled before saying: "Then it better be a visit to Mildendo."

When the two ministers arrived on horseback, they quickly realised that despite their guests opting for a visit to Mildendo, Totty really wanted to tour the island. This resulted in the immediate proposal that Redrelok would show

Hashimoto the capital while Mandoselin and Totty would tour the island.

The Interior Minister was grey-haired with a neatly trimmed moustache and a friendly, pinkish face; he was about 50 years old, small for a Lilliputian, but well built. However, he handled his horse professionally as he and his visitor walked along together. They established that the best way of communicating was for them both to speak in a loud voice, with Totty bending her head a few inches towards him.

A small group of islanders followed them from a distance, but most of the local inhabitants were busy tidying up after the Great Wave.

"Tell me, Mandoselin, are you on horseback so we can talk together?" Totty asked as they were walking down a wide road leading out of the capital. "I'm sure you've got a car because I've seen a number in the distance."

"I've got a Jaguar motor," the Interior Minister replied proudly. "But you're right, I'm on horseback so we can converse, but also because it's easier to get around. You can't really see any damage here, but once we get near the bottom of the hill, it's a different matter. Trees strewn all over the place, large areas of flood water in the fields – a real mess and we'll be clearing it for weeks."

A few minutes later, Totty began to see what Mandoselin was talking about. The first sign was a massive tree that had fallen across the road. There was a group of about a dozen workers with axes hacking away at it to try and break it down into manageable pieces to pull away.

"You'll see this sight in hundreds of places," Mandoselin commented. "We'll have to go into the ditch on the right to get round."

"Don't they have electric saws?"

"I'm afraid not. I don't know why, but electricity only became widespread in Lilliput about fifty years ago. It's driven by the elements – the sun, wind and the sea. We've not had time to apply it to everything yet, but no doubt we'll have electric saws next time there's a great wave."

"But you've got cars which are much more complicated. Do you make them yourselves?"

"We do, but from specifications from the manufacturers. They all run on electric power."

"Very impressive. It should be a doddle to make electric saws."

"I agree. Come on, let me lead the way."

The Interior Minister began to ride his horse into the ditch, expecting Totty to follow him. Instead, she called him back.

"Hold on Mandoselin; I've a much better idea. That tree may be massive to you people, but I should be able to move it myself.... Stand back everyone," she called.

Totty walked over to the fallen tree once all the loggers had moved away. They knew she was one of the people who had arrived with Poseidon and Amphitrite; word on such matters tends to travel swiftly. The tree was about ten feet long and at its widest the trunk was no more than six inches. Totty bent down at the end where the roots had become dislodged, took hold of the trunk, lifted it and pulled it to the side before dropping it into the ditch. There was applause from both Mandoselin and the loggers.

"There are still quite a lot of small branches, leaves and things on the road," Totty said as she stood back. "But you guys ought to be able to clear them up fairly easily." She then looked at the Interior Minister and continued: "Mandoselin, let's get practical. Instead of a sightseeing tour, set me to work clearing what I can."

"There are lots more trees further along the road," one of the loggers called out. "We're meant to move onto them after we've cleared this one."

"It's the main road to Old Mildendo," the Interior Minister said. "But Totty, are you sure about this?"

"Of course, Mandy," she said with a cheeky smile. "Let's get going."

Totty marched along the road with Mandoselin's horse having to gallop to keep up with her. They soon came to another two trees which had fallen next to each other with a couple of axe men making a start on cutting them up, but in reality, waiting for the team higher up to join them. Within a quarter of an hour, Totty had moved both trunks to the side.

The whole afternoon was spent clearing fallen trees and debris wherever they went. As they got to the bottom of the Old Mildendo road, they came across a very agitated farmer looking for help with his lambs. When the Great Wave came, the animals had managed to make it to higher ground, but it was very rocky with no grass to eat. Unfortunately, all the surrounding area was now covered in water at least a foot high so they couldn't escape. The problem was that the main drainage route for the water was blocked by a mass of trees and vegetation which had fallen in its way, stopping the water from being released. The lambs would starve if they couldn't be rescued soon. Within an hour Totty had a team of about twenty locals pulling on ropes attached to the blockage as she also pulled with all her might. Slowly, the debris began to move, and the water started seeping out. Eventually, it was released in a torrent knocking Totty onto her backside. There were initially groans of concern, but she just laughed and stood up. The lambs began to see a path to escape and cautiously started to move on in search of good grazing ground.

By the time dusk was setting in, an exhausted Totty and Mandoselin arrived back at the capital. They were followed by a group of islanders who had gradually added themselves to Team Totty as the day had progressed.

"I'm going to organise the best meal for you and your friend that the gods and humans have ever eaten on Lilliput," the Interior Minister said as they arrived at the huts. "I can't thank you enough, Totty for what you've done."

"How much of the island do you think we've cleared?" Totty asked.

Mandoselin sighed. "Great as your effort's been today, probably not even one percent."

"Right," said Totty all psyched up. "Then that's what we'll do while Poseidon and Amphitrite are away. Collect me first thing in the morning and we'll get to work again. We'll have Hashimoto as well to help. You work out the areas to concentrate on and Hash and I will provide the muscle power."

"Are you really sure about this?"

"Of course, Mandy. But only if we have that wonderful evening meal you've promised us," was the reply, again said with a cheeky smile.

"I'll get onto it right away."

Just as the two were about to part, there was a loud shout from a member of the crowd: "Three cheers for Miss Totty...."

'Hip hip hooray; hip hip hooray; hip hip hooray' was shouted with gusto by a hundred voices.

•

While Totty had been making a positive impression with the Lilliputians, Hashimoto had also been making his mark with the residents of Mildendo but in a somewhat different way.

Like Mandoselin, the Finance Minister had arrived on horseback but he dismounted once he and Hashimoto got to the entrance of the city. There he introduced Hashimoto to Mayor Shefrap who had anticipated that the visitors would want a tour of Mildendo. The Mayor was bald with a stern face and very muscular, more the soldier type than the administrator. He was accompanied by a dozen members of the City Guard, six who walked ahead of the small group and the rest behind.

As they entered the city, Redrelok emphasized to their visitor that he should take great care while walking along the streets in view of his size.

"Ah; that is because everyone is a teeny weeny," Hashimoto said with a small laugh. "Even the guards who are to protect me are teeny weenies. Hashimoto perfectly capable of looking after himself!"

"I'm sure that's right," the Finance Minister replied politely. "They're also here to protect Mayor Shefrap and me as well as dealing with the crowds. You can see that there's a group of people gathered behind us and also a number in front."

"More teeny weenies," Hashimoto commented looking round.

"Perhaps we should carry on," Redrelok said ignoring Hashimoto's last remark. "Please lead the way Shefrap."

The mayor walked slightly ahead of Hashimoto and Redrelok, but let his fellow Lilliputian do most of the talking. They walked through the suburbs before coming to the centre of Mildendo where Hashimoto was shown the Empress's palace, various government building, art galleries, statues of famous leaders as well as a number of public squares and parks.

"It's a modern city, only built about a hundred years ago, so it's been laid out in quite an orderly way," Redrelok explained as they were walking along.

"A modern, titchy witchy city for teeny weeny people," Hashimoto replied. "Yes, to me it's all in miniature – titchy witchy for teeny weenies."

At this point, Shefrap gave an angry look towards Redrelok before deciding to speak.

"You seem to be very attached to this term 'teeny weeny,' Mr Hashimto," he said with a growl in his voice.

"Ah ha," Hashimoto laughed. "That's because it's good description. Everything here is teeny weeny, titchy witchy, tiny whiney."

"You mean to you?" the Mayor responded aggressively.

"Of course, to me. Tell me Mr Mayor, have you ever heard the saying 'in the land of the blind, the one-eyed man is king?'"

"No! What point are you trying to make?"

"I think," Redrelok intervened, sensing that this conversation was leading to trouble since Shefrap was clearly getting angry. "Hashimoto is---"

"I will explain," Hashimoto interrupted. "The saying means people with great power become the Boss. My reason for raising is that when a full-sized human, like me, comes to Lilliput, he could decide to become Emperor."

"What!" shouted Shefrap drawing his sword. There was also a very audible hiss from the crowd that was drawing closer to the group; at the same time the guards pointed their lances in all directions, some towards the townsfolk and some towards Hashimoto.

"Gentlemen; let's be calm," Redrelok said in a loud voice, moving between the Mayor and the visitor. "Hashimoto is merely expressing a view on the relative strength of a full-sized human and a Lilliputian."

"That is what I'm doing. All I am saying is that if I wanted to, I could stamp on all these people around us and squash them flat in a matter of minutes. Then, I could march off to the palace, trample on the Empress and make myself Emperor."

By now the crowd was getting very agitated. There were shouts of 'boo, boo' and 'arrest him, Mayor; arrest him' from half the populace while the other half, principally mothers and children, were running away fearing that Hashimoto's boot was about to squash them.

Redrelok again tried to intervene to bring some calm to the situation, but Shefrap pushed him away and, small man as he was, confronted Hashimoto.

"And is that what you intend to do, sir?" he shouted in an angry voice. "Squash half the population and make yourself Emperor?"

Hashimoto hadn't sensed the upset he was causing, not just with his two hosts, but also with the crowd, so he jokingly said: "Hashimoto will think about it. Let you know tomorrow." He then burst out laughing, looked around, saw astonished angry faces which he didn't really understand since he was only having a bit of fun. Anyway, he thought it wise to mutter in a more sober tone: "Maybe not. Just having a little joke," followed by a somewhat forced smile.

There was a lot of angry shouting by the remains of the crowd, so Redrelok quickly decided to take control. He shouted to the guards to clear the crowd; he then went over to Shefrap, who was waving his sword in fury, and ordered him to stand back and leave matters to him. This was followed by the minister looking up at Hashimoto and saying in the pleasantest voice he could muster in the circumstances: "Hashimoto, my friend. I think that's it for today. I'll walk you back to your residence."

On the return journey, accompanied by six guardsmen, Redrelok did everything possible to speak of matters other than the recent incident with Shefrap and the crowd. This was fairly easy since Hashimoto was still unaware he'd been the cause of any problem. Indeed, as they reached the huts, he said it had been an interesting conversation about the one-eyed man is king and he looked forward to continuing the discussion with the Mayor on some future occasion.

"I like these sayings," replied Redrelok. "I'm quite attached to the one that says: 'think before you speak.'"

"I agree. That is what I do. Hashimoto always thinks before he speaks. No problem there."

At that, the two parted for the rest of the day, agreeing to meet up the following morning. Hashimoto went off for a rest, while Redrelok hurried back to the capital, wondering how much damage limitation was required.

9
Operation Control

Z eus was in his library, having been 'doing his nut' for the last twenty minutes. His audience had listened to him in silence, but now that he'd largely calmed down Athene was the first to respond.

"So, what you're saying, Father, is that Mars has gone – scarpered." she said.

"That's exactly it. As you all saw yesterday evening, I patched him up about eighty percent and sent him back here with Bumble. He needed a good night's sleep before I interrogated him, and he was snoring away when Hera and I got back. Then it appears he woke up about three o'clock in the morning, pulled the Bumbles out of bed to make him breakfast, returned to his palace and twenty minutes later scarpered as you say. Mrs Bumble saw him disappearing into the sky on horseback from the dining room window,"

"I can't understand why you didn't patch him up fully at the Council Meeting," Hera said testily. "It would have been better to interrogate him there and then."

"Just accept I didn't," Zeus replied. "I thought it would be better to wait till morning, with him knowing I'd heal the rest of him once he'd given a full and honest account of matters."

"Well, it didn't work."

"I know that!" Zeus responded angrily.

"It doesn't matter now," Athene intervened. "What's done is done and there was some logic in what Father did. Iris hadn't returned at the time, so we didn't have all the facts to put to Mars."

"I'm not sure we know much more from what Iris told us," Hera responded sulkily.

"Yes, we do," Zeus retorted. "We know what the incident was – a tidal wave, and where it occurred – in the Indian Ocean."

"But we don't know what caused the tidal wave and who was responsible," Hera continued.

"That's not quite true, Hera," the Goddess of Wisdom said before Zeus could reply. "We know that some of the sea creatures thought they saw a flash and something falling from the sky; possibly an asteroid ----"

"It wasn't an asteroid," Zeus interrupted. "I'd know if it was an asteroid."

"You're probably right, Father, but at least there are enough reports of something falling from the sky to investigate. The other thing we know is that Poseidon was clearly not responsible for this tidal wave. That's obvious from him punching Mars in the face and the fact that Iris reports seeing masses of dead fish and whales. They're his creatures and he clearly blames Mars for what's happened. And guess what? Mars has disappeared."

"I agree. It looks like Mars has been up to something," the Top God said with a sigh.

Hephaestus had been sitting quietly with Hebe, Iris, Artemis and Hermes listening to his parents and Athene speaking between themselves, but now decided to get involved. He was a practical god, more interested in action than talk.

"Father," he said. "What are we actually going to do about this matter?"

"That's precisely why I called you all here," Zeus replied.

"No, you didn't," Hera contradicted her husband. "You only sent Bumble to find Athene, but she had the good sense to send him off to contact some of the others. You didn't even tell me; I only found out about this meeting from Mrs Bumble."

Zeus inwardly groaned. "It's obvious, my love, I can't do anything right for you today. While your criticisms may be fair, they're not helping with the current situation."

"We wouldn't be in this situation if you'd healed Mars entirely yesterday evening and got to the bottom of matters there and then, as I've already said. Anyway, you didn't, and you also ignored my suggestion that he should spend last night in Nurse Nightingale's care. There's no way Florence would have let your son run off in the early hours of the morning."

"She'd have stuck that big needle of hers into his backside and knocked him out," Hebe added with a smile.

"So, what's the plan, Father?" Hephaestus asked.

"We need to find Mars and bring him back here for a full-blown interrogation."

"How are we going to do that?" Iris asked.

"That's what we're going to discuss now."

"I have a proposal," the Goddess of Wisdom said. "Let me put it to you all and then you can hack it around."

"I'm glad at least one person has a plan, Athene. No one else here has," Hera commented, giving her husband a very disapproving look.

"Go on then, Athene," Zeus muttered wearily. "Let's hear it."

"We don't just need to find Mars; we must also find Poseidon. He clearly knows more than any of us about what's gone on as his realm's been affected. We could be looking at full scale conflict between two gods, which would have implications for us all. So, I suggest I take responsibility for finding Poseidon."

"Agreed," Zeus quickly said. "And as soon as you find him, get him to come to Olympus. Say the Gods' Council needs to speak to him."

"That's not my priority," Athene responded. "The most important thing is to find out what's happened and what he's planning to do about it. I don't think he'll view talking to the Council as being of great importance at this stage. If anything, he'll probably blame us, and particularly you, Father, for not controlling Mars."

"But it's important -----"

"Look, I'll ask him to come to Olympus, okay? But no promises about him agreeing."

"What else is in your proposal?" Zeus asked resignedly.

"The search for Mars. I think one of you should take responsibility for each continent. I'd propose Iris looking in Asia, Artemis in Africa, Herm in the Americas, especially the South, and Hebe in Europe. As well as trying to find Mars, we also need to assess what damage the tidal wave's done to the coastal regions. Let's not forget, that's our responsibility. It's unlikely that it's only Poseidon's realm that's been affected."

"Good point," Hephaestus commented. "But haven't you got some role for me, Athene?"

"Once we've located Mars, that's when you'll have a part to play."

"And what are we expected to do when we find Mars?" Hebe asked.

"You're to give him a message from me," Zeus said.

"What's that then, Father?"

"I'm about to tell you…" He paused before continuing: "'I am Zeus, most powerful of all the gods; I rule over Olympus, the earth, the moon, the planets, the stars and the entire universe. All other gods quiver and shake in my presence. I am great and mighty, for------'"

By now everyone else in the room was beginning to groan, but it was Iris who interrupted Zeus first.

"No, Zeus," the Rainbow Goddess said firmly. "That won't do. It sounds just like the start of that appalling message you made me deliver to Bacchus months ago. I suppose you'll go on and threaten to have his eyes torn out by giant rats, his stomach and bowels filled with flesh-eating serpents and so on?"

"I will. I'll do all of those things…. and more."

"I thought Mars was going to be sent to an asteroid for a thousand years?" Hebe inquired.

"That comes afterwards," Zeus replied.

"Well, a message like the one you're suggesting just won't work," Iris added. "Not that I know what we're actually trying to achieve, which goes back to Hebe's original question – what do we actually do when we find Mars?"

"You're to bring him back to Olympus," Zeus promptly responded.

"And what if he won't come?"

"Make him come, Iris. Tell him he'll be in a lot more trouble if he doesn't. That's why I still think I should send him my message which you wouldn't let me finish."

"Athene," Hera called out, wanting to impose herself on the discussion. "Please tell us what you think should be done once Mars has been located. It's clear that Zeus is in cloud cuckoo land if he thinks his son is just going to return to Olympus, however he's asked."

"I resent being told I'm in cloud cuckoo land!" Zeus snapped at his wife before Athene could reply. "And can I remind you, Hera, he's your son as well as mine."

"Yes, but all his bad bits come from your side of the family, not mine."

"We share precisely the same parents, or had you forgotten?"

"No, I certainly had not. However-----"

"Mother," Hephaestus interrupted Hera. "Can you and Father please have this part of the conversation in private afterwards? The rest of us would like to hear what Athene has to say."

"And so would I," Hera replied before looking at the Goddess of Wisdom.

All eyes turned to Athene. "I don't want to be too prescriptive because we don't know what Mars's mood will be and how he'll react," she said. "What's critical is to identify where he is. I think it's then important to try and have a conversation with him. I agree that he's not going to come back voluntarily to Olympus. But we need to know from him what's going on, what he's up to, why Poseidon punched him, his current intentions - that sort of thing. I suspect that's probably all that can be achieved at this stage so, after that, best to return here and we can then decide on the next step. Hopefully, I'll have tracked Poseidon down by then, which will mean we've got a full picture of matters."

"That all seems sensible," Hera was the first to respond. The others nodded their heads in approval as they all looked at Zeus.

"Alright, I agree," he said after some thought. "Everyone reports back here once they've got some useful information. Let's treat this library as being Operation Control, manned up jointly by Hera and me."

"I think you mean 'peopled up' not 'manned up'," Artemis said, speaking for the first time in the meeting.

"Do I?" Zeus asked, puzzled by Artemis's comment since he'd forgotten that she was now the equalities champion amongst the deity.

"Yes, you do," Athene replied. "But we know what you mean. One final point – although we're looking for Mars and Poseidon, let's also keep a look out for any signs of Famine and Pestilence. We've now got three of the Four Horsemen on the loose and it's starting to feel uncomfortable."

Shortly afterwards the meeting broke up with the gods leaving Zeus alone in Operation Control.

•

The Tyrant was sitting at his 17th century mahogany dining table eating breakfast. He was a short, fat man with puffed-out cheeks and a double chin. His hair was black, cut short and covered with large quantities of cream to stop it from sticking up in the air. He was dressed in military uniform with his jacket covered in medals. The Tyrant had never actually served in the armed forces, but that hadn't prevented him from awarding himself all the medals available in the different services.

Breakfast consisted of smoked salmon, caviar, sausages, bacon, chips, brie cheese and baked beans, suitably flavoured with large dollops of tomato ketchup. He was about halfway through his meal when the dining room door was thrown open, and the God of War marched in. He was also in military uniform with his heavy bronze armour, his helmet inscribed with a death's head and carrying a large mean-looking sword in his right hand.

"Good morning, Fatty," he said in a loud voice as he walked round the table to stand opposite the Tyrant. "I see you're still on your weightwatchers diet." At this he leant over the table and took a number of chips and a sausage from the Tyrant's plate which he put in his mouth.

"Hello, Mars," the Tyrant replied with an element of caution in his voice. "I didn't know you were here."

"I've just arrived, you little squirt. I've come to congratulate you. That missile of yours has created absolute chaos in the Indian Ocean; it's got my fellow gods all worked up and no doubt most of our enemies in the so-called liberal democracies."

"Thank you, Mars. I'm grateful for your support......By the way, what's happened to your face? You've got two black eyes and something's wrong with your nose."

"Don't worry about that, Fat Face. Being the God of War means being a fighter and fighters always pick up these superficial wounds. You should see what I did to the other side," Mars boasted. "Smashed them to smithereens. 'Might is right' in the world you and I inhabit. 'Might is right!'" As Mars said these final words, he smashed his fist down on the table, causing the Tyrant to intervene quickly to stop his plate from falling off the table.

"Yes," was the reply after the crockery had been immobilized. "So, what happens now?"

"Yesterday was just the beginning. What comes next----"

Mars suddenly stopped talking as a servant in a maroon frock coat shuffled into the room on his knees and made his way to the Tyrant's table. He was carrying a second plate of breakfast which consisted of the same quantity of smoked salmon, chips and all the rest as the first plate.

"Second helpings, Oh Great One," the servant said, putting the plate on the table before bowing and then turning round and shuffling out of the room, all the time remaining on his knees.

The Tyrant had ignored the servant until he was almost out of the room when he screeched "Shut the door, pleb!"

"Second helpings!' said Mars when the door was closed. "You are a greedy, little pig. I thought that was for me."

"If you want some breakfast, I'll ring the bell and order you some."

"No, not necessary," Mars replied. "If I'm hungry, I'll just help myself to your plate."

"I hope you won't take too much," the Tyrant said, alarmed at the prospect of having to share his breakfast,

"Don't worry, Mr Greedy Pig; I'll just take this second sausage and then I'm done." Mars leant over again and took another sausage with the Tyrant watching anxiously that he didn't take a couple of chips as well.

"That's good," Mars said as he was chewing his sausage. "What I don't understand is why you have all your servants shuffling around on their knees? Your father, who was as nasty a little git as you, never did."

"It's a sign of respect. Also, discipline. Anyone who forgets gets sent off to the firing range for a lesson."

"Seems bloody stupid to me, but if that's the way you want to run things, that's your business, I suppose."

The Tyrant took a large mouthful of bacon, caviar and baked beans which he munched away at. To his great consternation, Mars leant over and took another chip which he popped into his mouth.

"You were saying, Mars, that yesterday was only the beginning?" the Tyrant said once he'd finished munching his mouthful.

"When can you launch another missile?" was the sharp response.

"In a few days' time. It won't be as big and powerful as yesterday's, but it will still make an impact."

"Why can't you launch one like yesterday's?" the god growled. "Don't tell me you only had one, you stupid idiot."

"No; we've got a number more, but they take at least a week to prepare for firing. It's our latest model and yesterday was the first time we fired it."

"Huh," Mars replied unconvinced. "Then fire a different type of missile as soon as you can and hurry up and get another one like yesterday's to follow soon after. We want to send off as many missiles as possible over the next few weeks. Make sure the next one goes into the Pacific somewhere. We'll then follow up with this new model landing in the Atlantic. You can reach that far, can't you? That's what you told me a few weeks ago."

The Tyrant could only nod his head because he'd just taken another huge mouthful of breakfast, having started on his second helpings.

Mars now began walking up and down the room, watched anxiously by the Tyrant who remained concerned that his breakfast might again be raided for more sausages and chips.

"Yes, that's what we'll do," the God of War said. "A mighty explosion in the Indian Ocean, then one in the Pacific and finally one in the Atlantic. That will get all our enemies and my fellow gods so worked up, they'll be scampering around like frightened rabbits. Then, you and I will strike!" As he said this, he stopped at the dining table and again smashed his fist down. "Yes, we'll strike!" he repeated with another thump of the table.

"Good," The Tyrant replied, his mouth now again empty. He wanted to agree with Mars although he wasn't sure what he was being signed up to. "But what exactly does 'we'll strike' mean?"

Mars stared hard at the Tyrant who tried his best not to flinch. After a few seconds, the God of War gave a cruel smile, sat down on a chair directly opposite the breakfast eater, folded his arms, then unfolded them, leant over and took two chips this time which he proceeded to eat, all the time looking at his co-conspirator, without saying a word.

"I asked," The Tyrant said nervously, "What exactly does 'we'll strike' mean?"

"I heard you the first time," was the brisk response. "Look, Tyrant, it's time to put all the cards on the table. You and I have had lots of talks over the years about what we each want to achieve and now our time has come. Being blunt, you and I are taking over!"

The Tyrant gave a greedy, wicked smile back. "About time too, Mars. I've been waiting for this moment for years. What have you got in mind?"

"Tyrantland's going to subjugate all the other countries of the globe with you, Squirt, ending up running the whole world. As for me, I'm going to take over Olympus and become the most powerful god of all time. I've had enough of my father and two uncles. I'm going to depose them and become the Supreme Ruler. I've an agreement with Satan that he'll be responsible for running the Underworld. As far as Poseidon's realm is concerned, I'll offer it to my brother, Hephaestus, but only if he agrees to recognize that he's subordinate to me. How does all that sound?"

"I like it," the Tyrant replied eagerly. "So, what you're saying is that I run the World, you run Olympus, Satan runs the Underworld and your brother's in charge of the Oceans and the Seas? Does that mean I get to become a god?"

"You're almost right. While you, Satan and Hephaestus look after your kingdoms, you all defer to me as the Supreme Ruler. Understood?"

The Tyrant nodded his head. "But do I become a god?" he asked again before putting another sausage in his mouth.

"No. Humans can't be turned into gods. You should know that, you stupid fat little git."

"But that means I'll have to die sometime!"

"You will, but I'll make sure Death leaves you alone for a long time, provided you behave yourself."

"But I don't want to die," the Tyrant moaned. "Who's going to rule the World after I'm gone?"

"If you've got a son and he's any good, I'll let him take over. He'll have to be a nasty bastard like you, though. I'm not having any softie in charge of this place. Only a mean, vicious brute will do. Remember, 'might is right.'"

"But I haven't got a son and I might never have one," whined the Tyrant. "And what will happen to me once I'm dead? Will I have to go to that terrible Underworld place, run by Satan?"

"Don't worry about the Underworld. You can come and live on Olympus with me. There'll be plenty of spare palaces. It will be a life of luxury, just like here. Trust me!"

The Tyrant looked suspiciously at Mars. If there was one individual he'd never trust, it was the God of War, but he couldn't think of anything he could do about it.

"As far as not having a son's concerned, what's going on with that pretty new wife of yours?" Mars continued.

"We've been married two years and she's still not produced," the Tyrant replied.

"Leave her to me. I'll make sure you have a son," Mars said with a lecherous smile. "You'll be a father within a year."

"And what if it's a girl?"

"Then I'll just have to go and visit her again!" Mars replied with a laugh. "I'll keep spending time with her until you've got a son. He won't be a fat little git like you, I assure you."

The Tyrant didn't like the sound of any of this, so he suggested that Mars should leave it for a year or two while he and his young wife continued trying together.

"As long as you like," Mars replied with a wicked leer. "You let me know when you want me to get involved."

The Tyrant had by now cleared both his breakfast plates. He rang a bell and shortly afterwards the same servant as before came shuffling in on his knees carrying a large plate of cakes and gateaux. He again called him 'Oh Great One,' bowed and shuffled back out of the room. The Tyrant chose a Danish pastry and then watched with concern as Mars suddenly grabbed a chocolate éclair.

"What are you going to do with the other gods when you've taken control of Olympus?" The Tyrant asked before biting into his pastry.

"I'm going to send them all to Tartarus. Grandfather Cronus will love to be reunited with his three sons," Mars replied with a laugh. "Oh yes, he'll have a special treat for them. It will make the Underworld's Torturing Department appear like a holiday camp compared to what he'll do. I'd love to see it, but once I've thrown them in, I'll be sealing up Tartarus immediately. I don't want anyone in there getting out, especially my grandfather."

"But what about the female gods – your mother, Artemis, Athene and the like?"

"They're all going to Tartarus. They're not needed here anymore. I'll breed a whole family of new gods just like me."

"So, your brother's the only one who'll avoid Tartarus. He's on our side, is he?"

"I wouldn't quite say that. He doesn't know what's planned. If he won't accept it, he'll go with the rest of them."

"Which means they could all be locked away?"

"They could be," Mars replied before developing a wicked smile as he looked at the Tyrant. "Would you like me to give you a present, Fatty?"

The Tyrant flinched, unsure if this was a trick question. "What sort of present?" he asked cautiously.

"Aphrodite!" Mars said with an evil glint in his eye. "I'll give you my little half-sister as a slave girl. You can do what you like with her and when she bores you, we'll send her to join the rest of the family with Grandfather Cronus. Would you like that?"

The Tyrant now had a large piece of coffee cake in his mouth, but he nodded eagerly and eventually managed to splutter: "Yes.".

"Then she's all yours, Mr Piggy. She's not the brightest girl in the world, but that's not what you're interested in, is it?"

The Tyrant merely smiled back maliciously, finished his coffee cake, and then looked seriously at the god. "I like everything I'm hearing, Mars, but are you sure we can beat all the other gods – there are a lot of them? We've also got to defeat our enemies on the five continents. Except for Diktatorland, we don't have any friends."

"Absolutely certain," Mars snarled back. "Once we create chaos, then that's when we strike. Fire those two missiles we spoke about and then we'll start hitting enemy territory."

"They will fire back," the Tyrant said cautiously.

"I'll have taken over by then. I live on chaos. We've also got powerful friends. I'm expecting one of them to turn up here any time soon."

"Who's that?"

"You know him. Let's call him Mr F."

The Tyrant gulped. "Oh him," he said. "He always creates all sorts of problems for me, ruining my crops and turning most of the available food rotten."

"He's one of us," Mars said sternly. "Treat him well; he's a friend. At least you'll never starve; it's only the scum, the nobodies, people we don't care about. Count yourself lucky, it's Mr F and not Mr P. You wouldn't like to catch the plague, would you, Fatty?"

"No," was the muttered reply.

At that, Mars stood up. "Now get someone to show me to my suite," he barked at his host.

"How long are you going to stay?"

"Some time," replied the God of War. "Your palace is now our Operation Control."

10
Underground Matters

Aggy, the Head Chef, ran the Kitchens. Most afternoons she tried to have an hour to herself so she could relax between the hustle of lunch and the bustle of dinner. She was a large lady with rosy cheeks and this afternoon she was sitting at the table in her back room just off the central kitchen. She had a number of playing cards laid out on the table, some face upwards and some downwards. Almost mechanically she would turn over a card, place it on top of another, move small groups of cards around the table and repeat the process.

"Come in Death," she called suddenly without looking up as she continued with her cards.

A short while later, a skeleton wearing a long black cloak and carrying a scythe appeared at an open door to Aggy's right. He stood there looking uncertainly at the Head Chef.

"Sit down opposite me," Aggy said still not looking up as she concentrated on her cards.

Death nervously pulled out a wooden chair opposite the Head Chef and cautiously sat down, putting his scythe on the floor. Aggy said nothing for a while as she focused on the different patterns and sequences in front of her. Eventually she shook her head, muttering to herself that she couldn't complete the game, before looking at her visitor.

"And what can I do for you, Death?" she asked as she gave the skeleton a friendly smile.

"I was wondering what you were doing, Mrs Aggycraggywoggynog?" Death asked in an uncertain voice.

"Ah!" said Aggy, continuing to smile. "You remember my name after all these years. Most people just call me Aggy; my full name's a bit of a mouthful."

"May I call you Mrs Aggy then?"

"Just Aggy; that will do."

"Very well....... Aggy."

"So, you want to know what I'm doing, do you? It's called Patience; a card game which a person can play alone. Do you know anything about cards, Death?"

"No," the skeleton replied. "Are cards interesting? If so, would you be prepared to teach me, Mrs Aggy?"

"Aggy, not Mrs Aggy."

"I'm sorry…… Aggy"

The Head Chef looked at her visitor in a quizzical way. She didn't say anything for a while as she considered the situation, before eventually speaking.

"Before we discuss me teaching you how to play cards, Death, I'd like to ask you a few questions." Death was about to speak, but Aggy continued. "The first one is very personal to me. Normally, people only meet you once and when they do, it's so you can bring them here. Now, you turning up is a little disconcerting if you don't mind me saying so. It means I've now met you twice. So, I'd like to know if you're going to take me away somewhere else and if so, where, and why?"

"Oh no," Death responded, looking as shocked as a skeleton can. "That's not why I'm here. I just happened to be passing and looked through your window."

"Just happened to be passing," Aggy repeated sceptically. "But you didn't pass very quickly, did you? As far as I can judge you were peeping through my window for a good ten minutes before I called you in."

Death began to feel under some pressure as Aggy questioned him. If his body had consisted of more than a skeleton, he might be beginning to glow. "I suppose I became interested in what you were doing and lost track of time," was all he could think of saying.

"You're not very good at telling porkies, are you Death?" the Head Chef responded.

"What do you mean?" Death asked nervously.

"I think it's time to be entirely open about what you're up to."

"I don't know what you mean." At this stage a skeleton with flesh would be perspiring profusely.

"Let me tell you. Number one – your normal route from the ferry to Hades' palace and back again doesn't pass the Kitchens, so you must have made a deliberate detour. Number two – I've seen you outside my window on three different occasions in the last fortnight. Number three – you've also been seen by some of my staff looking through our dining room windows in recent weeks. Number four – Cerberus has mentioned that he thinks you're not quite right, whatever that means. Do all these matters start to ring a little bell in your head, Death?"

The skeleton sighed. "Mrs Aggy, I'll-------"

"Aggy," the Head Chef interrupted.

"Sorry, I mean Aggy." Death swallowed hard, at least for a skeleton, before continuing. "You're quite right on all these matters. I suppose I'm going through what you humans call a mid-life or, in my case a 'mid-death,' crisis. Is it the same thing as the menopause because that's what I think it is?"

"Good gracious," Aggy replied. "I've heard of the male menopause, but never thought you, Death, could possibly suffer from a similar condition. What are the symptoms?"

"I'm just unsettled, Aggy," Death said feeling increasingly able to open up to Aggy about his emotions.

"Can you try to be more specific? What's really troubling you?"

"I suppose I feel alone all the time. I meet lots of people as Hades says, but I only ever meet them once. I don't see them again, so I can't build any proper relationships. I don't seem to have any friends."

"Well, I don't mean to be hard on you, Death," Aggy replied. "But that's not very surprising, given your job. After all, you're not the most popular guy in the room when you arrive, especially unannounced."

"I know that, but there are some people happy to see me. If you're being tortured and in great pain, you're often pleased when I arrive and take you away."

"Granted, but that's not the case for most people. Still, I understand what you mean; sometimes you turning up can be a blessing."

"Thank you."

"But all this doesn't explain why you're looking through windows at people eating or, in my case, playing cards."

"I'm sorry to disagree with you, Mrs Aggy ------"

"Aggy!" the Head Chef firmly corrected her visitor once more.

"Sorry again. I can't help it. I suppose it must be part of the menopause."

Aggy looked unconvinced by this statement, so all she said was: "Please carry on. I think you were about to explain the reasons for you looking through our windows."

"Yes. It's all linked to what I said earlier about not developing any relationships. I thought if I could take an interest in a few people after I've brought them to the Underworld, then that would be good for me. Maybe I could have a bit of banter with them whenever we saw each other, me being here every day. Yes, that's what I think I need: a bit of banter and some fun with a few people."

Aggy looked at Death without saying anything for a while. In fact, she was trying to decide what to say since she doubted there would be many people in the Underworld wanting to indulge in a bit of banter and fun with a black cloaked skeleton carrying a large scythe. Eventually she decided it wouldn't help the situation if she told him this; let him learn it in his own way. Instead, she changed the subject.

"This is all very interesting, Death," the Head Chef answered. "Why don't I create a bit of interest for you now by teaching you to play cards?"

"You mean that game of Patience you're playing?"

"No. While that's principally a game for one person, it is possible for two to play but it gets complicated. Instead, I thought I'd teach you a simple game called Snap which we could play together."

"You mean you and me?" Death asked.

"That's what playing together normally means."

"That sounds good, Aggy. More friendly; it will start integrating me into Underworld society."

"I suppose it will," Aggy replied, although not wholly convinced.

Aggy spent the next few minutes showing Death how a pack of cards was constituted. She explained that there were four suits – Spades, Diamonds, Clubs and Hearts – and there were thirteen cards in each suit. They went through the ranking of the different cards – Aces being the highest, followed by Kings, Queens, Jacks and then 10 down to 2. Aggy then shuffled the cards to create an element of randomness. She got Death to try shuffling, but he kept dropping the cards, so it was agreed that the Head Chef would take on this responsibility until Death was able to do it properly.

"Right," said Aggy after having gone through all these matters. "Let's have a practice game of Snap."

She took hold of the pack, gave it a final shuffle, and started giving out the cards.

"The starting point is for each of us to have twenty-six cards, which I'm giving out now. They're all face downwards and once I've finished, each of us collects them in neat piles opposite each other"

Death followed Aggy and created a neat pile opposite hers.

"Now," she said: "I turn over the top card on my pile and put it in the centre of the table face upwards, like this. See, it's the 10 of Hearts." The skeleton nodded. "Now you do the same, Death. You turn over the top card of your pile, putting it on top of mine." Death did as instructed and laid the Queen of Spades on top of Aggy's card.

"Very good. We can see my card was a 10 and yours was a Queen. In Snap we're looking to see if two cards match. It doesn't matter what the suits are; the matching relates to the rank of the cards, so we're looking for two tens or two Queens, that sort of approach. Does that make sense?"

"So, if I'd put a 10 on top of your 10, that's what you call a match, is it?"

"Very good."

"What happens when we get a match?"

"We'll come onto that later. In this case, we didn't get a match."

"That's my next question – what happens now?"

"Now we repeat the process."

Aggy turned over the 6 of Diamonds, followed by Death putting down the 7 of Clubs. It went on like this until Aggy had the Jack of Hearts which matched Death's Jack of Clubs.

"We have a match," Death said looking at the Head Chef.

"We do indeed," was the reply. "And this is where the game becomes competitive. "The first person who shouts out Snap takes all the cards in the central pile and adds them to his or her existing cards. "Let's say you're the one who said Snap first, then you would take the cards in the middle." Aggy leant over the table and added the cards in the middle to the bottom of Death's pile, turning them all face downwards.

"Then what?" Death asked.

"We start again and create a new pile in the centre. We keep going like this until one of us runs out of cards. That person's the loser and the one who's still got cards left over is the winner. There are different variations we can play, but for now that's the simplest way to decide who wins. Does all that make sense?"

Death nodded his head.

"Let's carry on then," Aggy said.

Over the next few minutes, Death learned a lot about technique, much of which he had to quickly unlearn! The first thing he realized was that if he could look at his cards before he turned them over, then he'd have a real advantage in being able to shout Snap ahead of his opponent. He very quickly earned Aggy's disapproval since this was cheating and he had to be taught how to turn the cards over in a 'neutral' way so both players could see them at the same time. Secondly, Death noticed how Aggy would say Snap and almost in the same movement would lean over and pick up the central pile of cards to add to her own. This caused him to aggressively push Aggy's hands away as he grabbed the central pile next time she said Snap ahead of him, justifying this approach by the principle that 'possession is nine-tenths of the law.' Again, this earned yet more disapproval and a sharp lecture from the Head Chef on card etiquette.

Aggy and Death played five games of which she won four and Death the final one. At that point, Aggy felt it was time to draw a halt as she had to get back to work.

"Can't we play just one more game?" a disappointed Death asked. "I'm really beginning to get the hang of it now."

"Another time, Death. I should have got back to work twenty minutes ago. Haven't you also got work to do?"

"I suppose so. What about a return match tomorrow afternoon?"

"No, that's too soon," Aggy responded. "I've got a lot to do in the next few days. In five days' time, I'll play with you again."

"That's a long time off."

"I'll tell you what, Death. I've got plenty of packs of cards, so you take this one with you and keep familiarizing yourself with the cards. Also, practice how to shuffle and come back in five days' time and we'll have a proper contest together."

"Alright, Aggy," the skeleton replied as he stood up from the table, taking the cards, and picking up his scythe before moving towards the door. He then turned round and said: "And thank you, Aggy. Today's done me the world of good. I'll see you in five days' time."

"Goodbye, Death," Aggy said as her visitor walked out of the room.

●

Mason Bonko was feeling rather smug. It was several days since Persephone and her two young helpers had carried out their review of the New Boys' Dormitory and he'd heard nothing since then. It didn't really surprise him because they were ignorant about the building trade. Although they'd asked some annoying questions and made a few negative remarks, he was confident that after further reflection, they'd have realized they were just not equipped to make any intelligent recommendations about his department. Budiwati, however, had been pestering him on a regular basis for a follow up discussion, which he had been forced to concede to Persephone. However, he had always been too busy to engage with Budi and intended to keep it that way.

Accordingly, Mason was somewhat perplexed to see a group consisting of Cerberus, Sisyphus and Vlad from the Torturing Department walking towards the dormitory. He was busy inspecting a small amount of subsidence with a couple of his men when one of them touched him on the shoulder and whispered that he should look at the approaching group.

"Good morning, everyone," Mason said when the group arrived at the building site. "What can I do for you?"

"Woof!" went Cerberus who was at the front. "Hades wants you urgently, Mr Bonko. You're to come now."

Mason was now feeling less confident than a few minutes ago when he had been musing over his perceived success in dealing with Persephone's review. However, he was determined not to show any anxiety.

"What does Hades want to see me about, Cerberus?" he replied.

"I don't know," the three-headed dog replied. "I was just told to go and fetch you."

"Fetch me!" Mason said. "That's not a very polite way of requesting that the Underworld's Head Builder should attend a meeting."

"Fetch is the word Hades used, so you'd better come now."

"By now, the two builders who were with Mason had moved away but they continued to watch and listen to proceedings from about ten yards distance. They were soon joined by a larger group interested in what was going on.

Mason swallowed hard. He didn't like the sound of all of this. "Very well; I'll come now," he replied as he began to walk with Cerberus towards Hades' palace, followed by Sisyphus and Vlad.

"What are you two doing here?" he asked turning round to Cerberus's companions.

"I was told to come," Sisyphus said. "I don't know why. What about you, Vlad?"

"The same as you," the torturer replied. "Just following orders."

"And why are you carrying a long sharp wooden spike, Vlad?" Mason asked, beginning to feel increasingly anxious as they walked along.

"I was told to. Don't know why."

Mason looked at Cerberus and Sisyphus, hoping for some explanation, but all they did was shake their heads; in Cerberus's case, all three heads.

"I suppose," Sisyphus said after some further reflection, "If Hades decides you should sit on a sharp spike, there's one handy."

"Woof. That's what I think as well," Cerberus observed.

Mason stopped in his tracks and looked at the others. "Come on, chaps," he said nervously. "What's going on? What am I supposed to have done?"

"We don't know," Cerberus, as Head of Internal Security, replied for the whole group. "We're just speculating about the sharp spike. At least it's made of wood and not metal."

"Oh no; wood's worse," Vlad volunteered. "If it splinters it creates a real mess inside. Very nasty; yes, very nasty indeed."

"Woof. Let's get a move on," said Cerberus. "The sooner we get to the palace, the sooner you'll know what's going on, Mr Bonko."

"That's right, Mason," Sisyphus added putting an arm over the Head Builder's shoulder, while at the same time propelling him forward. "No need to worry unnecessarily, although I must say Vlad's presence would cause me to be bloody terrified if I were in your shoes."

"Thanks a lot," Mason replied sarcastically as they continued their walk.

On arriving at the palace, Cerberus led the way to the throne room. Both Hades and Persephone were sitting side by side on identical thrones, each wearing a crown and looking very stern. To the left of the room a distinguished looking man was standing. He had neat long curly dark hair and was wearing a frock coat down to his knees, together with long stockings. This was Sir Christopher Wren, Head of the Architectural Department. He looked ahead of himself, deliberately avoiding eye contact with Mason.

Hades put out his hand, indicating to the Head Builder that he should sit on the small stool in front of the two thrones. Hades then nodded to Mason's three companions who silently took up their pre-arranged positions. Vlad went and stood next to Hades with his sharp spike so Mason would always be aware of his presence when speaking to the god and goddess. Cerberus lay down to Mason's right, all three heads staring up at the Head Builder and giving off a continuous growl, inaudible to everyone but the person sitting on the stool, while Sisyphus positioned himself about ten feet behind the stool.

There was a silence for about thirty seconds before Hades began speaking in a formal tone.

"Mason Bonko," he said. "We've summoned you here to discuss the gross inefficiencies in the Building Department. As you are aware, Queen Persephone, together with Miss Ming and Miss Vesta, carried out a detailed review of your department many days ago and identified a number of issues which you were expected to address. We are therefore surprised and most disappointed that you have not reported back to Lady Persephone on the various matters raised. Also, there has been no evidence of any changes in your work methods. What have you got to say for yourself?"

Mason took a deep breath before replying. "Lord Hades" he said. "I was not aware that I was meant to report back at all to-----"

He was interrupted by Hades slamming both hands down on the arms of his throne, before shouting: "Nonsense, Bonko! Isn't it obvious that when the Queen of the Underworld raises serious matters with you, she expects a response? Or have we gods left you alone so long, you've forgotten the respect that is rightfully due to us?"

Hades stared aggressively at Mason, who decided that now was the time for eating humble pie; in fact, as much humble pie as he could manage.

"I'm very sorry, My Lord. No disrespect was meant. Regrettably, I misspoke; I meant to say that I was not aware I had to report back by a specific time. That is entirely my fault for not clarifying the matter. Indeed, My Lord, I found the review carried out by Her Ladyship and Miss Vesta and Miss Ming to be incredibly helpful. Not just myself, but my entire team. Yes, we are very grateful to have had all these points raised. So grateful, in fact, that huge numbers of my team have wanted to contribute with the result that our response to Lady Persephone is not as speedy as I would have liked. I took the view, and if am wrong in this respect, I take full responsibility, that we should establish the fullest and most detailed response possible, before reverting to Her Highness."

"You're rambling, Bonko," Hades said. "If you're consulting so widely, how come you've not spoken to Budiwati yet? You were specifically commissioned by Lady Persephone to discuss all these matters in detail with Budiwati, or have you forgotten?"

"Oh no, not at all, Lord Hades. Budiwati and I have had many discussions and she's been more instrumental than anyone in developing our revised approach."

"My sources tell me that you've been avoiding her ever since Lady Persephone's visit."

"If I might humbly say, My Lord, I believe your sources are mistaken. Budiwati and I only-----"

"I spoke to Budiwati myself yesterday evening and I'm not mistaken!" Hades growled angrily.

"My apologies again, Lord Hades. Again, I misspoke. I meant to say that Budiwati could have been mistaken."

"No, she wasn't. She was crystal clear. It took me some time to get it out of her because she was trying to be loyal to you, but I ordered her to speak the truth to me, reminding her that I am her god. I also ordered her not to tell you that she'd spoken to me, so no comebacks, understood?"

Mason nodded and there was then a long silence in the throne room. Eventually, Persephone spoke up.

"Perhaps we should leave the Budiwati matter for the time being. I would find it helpful if Mr Bonko could explain to us what his preliminary proposals are for changes in the Building Department."

"I agree," Hades responded. "Mr Bonko, give us whatever proposals you have."

"Certainly, My Lord and My Lady. The first thing we've decided is to make sure that everyone can do at least two different jobs, so there will be a minimum amount of sitting around."

"How will you train people in the new skills?" Hades asked. "Will you use the dwarf, Smiley? He was a trainer at a building college, wasn't he?".

"Indeed, Lord Hades. He was just the individual I was going to mention."

"Hold on," Hades said pensively. "Don't I mean his cousin Tubby? Wasn't he the trainer?"

"You're quite right. He was the trainer."

"Then why didn't you say so in the first place?"

"I didn't want to contradict you, My Lord," Mason replied.

"You don't have a clue, do you Bonko?" Hades said with a weary sigh. "Don't reply because I probably won't believe you. Carry on with your proposals."

Mason gulped following the reprimand and then continued: "The second thing is that we believe we'll be able to run two projects at the same time, as Miss Vesta suggested. It will be hard, but we'll try. Perhaps you could help us with this point, Lord Hades? If Norbert, who's currently working on Mount Olympus, could be brought back, then he would be an excellent person to supervise a second building project."

"There's no way," Hades replied, shaking his head. "For a start, Lord Hephaestus needs him. Also, my niece Aphrodite has developed a strong attachment to Norbert, and I'm not prepared to start a family quarrel."

"Very well, My Lord. We'll just have to do our best then."

"Next point?"

"Ah yes," said Mason thinking hard. "Ah yes; we all agree that we can reduce the thickness of the walls, and this will mean we don't need to dig such deep foundations."

"A significant reduction, I hope?" Persephone asked.

"Very significant, My Lady. And also, after a lot of debate, we don't believe it's necessary to put so much waterproofing when we construct a roof."

"You don't need any," Hades said.

"I agree, that's the conclusion we arrived at."

"What about domes? You said that we had domes because Sir Christopher wanted them. Is that right, Sir Christopher?" Persephone asked looking at the architect.

"No, it's not, Persephone," was the reply from the side of the room.

"But I thought you liked domes?" Mason said, looking to his left.

"I do, Mason," Sir Christopher responded with a sigh. "But in cathedrals and some churches, not in boys' dormitories! Haven't we discussed this on innumerable occasions?"

"I can't recall. I suppose there must have been some misunderstanding," Mason mumbled and then looked at the god and goddess and tried to smile.

"So, no more domes then?" Persephone said.

"No more domes," agreed the Head Builder.

"What about the decorating?" the goddess continued. "Again, you said that we've got all this fine Renaissance art because Sir Christopher wanted it."

All eyes again turned to the architect who just vigorously shook his head.

"But you said how wonderful their work was when you met Micky, Lenny and Botty and you wished we'd had them in London in our day?" Mason said pleadingly.

"Quite right, Mason. I would have loved them helping to decorate St Paul's Cathedral, but not-----"

"A boys' dormitory," Persephone interrupted, completing Sir Christopher's sentence.

"Precisely," the architect agreed. "We should get Whitewash back on the team."

"No doubt another misunderstanding," Hades commented ruefully. He then looked up at Mason and asked: "Anything else?"

The Head Builder racked his brain, trying to think if there were any other points. He looked at Persephone who confirmed that there were no other points.

"Very good," said Hades now determined to bring matters to a conclusion. "You seem to have got a lot of changes to introduce, Mason," and the god gave Bonko a smile for the first time that afternoon. "The sooner they're introduced the better. I've asked Sir Christopher to oversee the changes with you and he's suggested there should be a small team to assist the two of you. We've agreed on Budiwati from your department and Persephone has kindly volunteered the services of Ming and Vesta. Any objections?"

"None at all, My Lord. Just the people I would have chosen," Mason replied.

"Excellent. Let's call the meeting to an end then. Vlad will escort you back. I thought you might like to pop into the Torturing Department to see how your people who've been sitting on spikes all day are getting on. Vlad will be pulling them off once he gets back and I'll be along later to heal them. That's all everyone. Goodbye."

Hades and Persephone stood up in unison, turned round and walked out of the throne room without another word being said.

11
All Tied Up

Hashimoto woke up in the morning and yawned. He felt he'd had a very good night's sleep after the excellent dinner which Mandoselin had organized in recognition of Totty's great efforts the day before. In particular, he had enjoyed that final liqueur that the waiters were most insistent that he and Totty should drink at the end of the meal.

Hashimoto could see that it was going to be another hot day from all the sunshine pouring on his face. The previous evening had been so warm that he had decided to sleep outside in the open. While he was grateful to have his own hut, it was fairly basic inside, and he wanted to replicate sleeping under the stars as he had sometimes been allowed to do by his parents on hot muggy nights while growing up in Tokyo.

After another yawn the butler decided it was time to get up. He tried to push his arms and raise his head, but he couldn't move. He tried again with still no success. Hashimoto was puzzled and instead of looking up at the sky, he moved his eyes downwards to look along the length of his body. What he saw were about a dozen Lilliputian soldiers standing on his chest, all holding bows and arrows pointed at his face.

"What the…." began Hashimoto before screaming: "Help! Help! What happening? Help! Help! Totty! Totty! Help! Help!…."

This screaming continued with Hashimoto struggling hard to free himself, but with no success. However, the sound of his screams was so loud that the soldiers on his chest became petrified and they all turned round and fled, hurrying down two ladders resting at the side of his chest.

Totty had also slept very well and was still asleep when Hashimoto's loud screams woke her up. She was in her hut and came out to see what all the commotion was about. Before she could reach Hashimoto, who was lying about ten yards from her, she suddenly stopped and studied the scene that confronted her. She could see that her friend was lying on his back but unable to move because he was tied to the ground. His whole body was covered with ropes, which were more like thick string to a full-sized human, that were attached to pegs firmly driven into the ground. Hash was also unable to lift his head because he had grown a ponytail in recent months, and this too was tied to a number of pegs.

However, what amazed Totty even more was that the entire area around Hashimoto was covered with large numbers of infantry - well over a thousand in number - as well as several hundred cavalry. They all had either their swords drawn, lances at the ready or their bows with arrows fully drawn; all these weapons being pointed at Hashimoto.

The butler, who was clearly a prisoner, continued to scream out for help, but Totty could not reach him without trampling on large numbers of Lilliput's military. She did, however, call out: "Hash, I'm here. Please just be quiet for a minute. Something's going on. You'll be alright. Let me sort it!"

"Miss Totty; Hashimoto cannot move. Help! Help!" he wailed. "What happening?"

"Hash! Do as I say please," she rasped back. "Just try to be quiet, close your eyes and stop trying to move. I'll sort it."

"But I------"

"I know," Totty said. "I'm going to sort it now. It won't be long."

Hashimoto continued to struggle as he tried to get free and, despite what Totty had said, he could not stop himself from shouting and screaming. Totty decided to ignore him as she focused her attention on the raised platform on which Redrelok and Mandoselin were standing, the former holding a large parchment. They both looked uncomfortable as Totty walked over to them, looking exceptionally angry.

"Totty," Mandoselin said. "You're-----"

"Miss Totty to you, Minister Mandoselin," Totty interrupted in the most aggressive tone of voice she could manage as she moved to within a few inches of the platform to emphasize her size. "And the same to you, Minister Redrelok."

"Yes, Miss Totty," the Finance Minister replied politely. "Perhaps you would let us explain."

"You'd better! And it better be good!"

Redrelok then spent the next few minutes describing what had happened the previous afternoon. He emphasized how Hashimoto had kept referring to the Lilliputians as teeny weenies, titchy witches and tiny whinnies. This had very much annoyed Mayor Shefrap and to a certain extent himself, as well as all the townspeople and guards listening.

"Well, you are teeny weenies to us!" Totty brutally interrupted. "Perhaps it wasn't clever of Hashimoto to keep saying so; in fact, it was very rude, I agree! But that's no reason to tie him up and surround him with half your army!"

"There's more," Redrelok replied.

He then proceeded to tell Totty about how Hashimoto had suggested that he could trample all over the people of Lilliput, including the Empress, and proclaim himself the new Emperor. This was all said in front of a number of mothers and their children, resulting in them fleeing for their lives. When Shefrap challenged Hashimoto as to whether he was actually going to do this, he failed to give a definitive denial, saying he would think about it.

"You're not telling me you actually took Hashimoto seriously?" Totty said in disbelief.

"I'm afraid a number of people did," Redrelok replied.

"Then they're all idiots! And that includes you two as well if you really believed it! So, who made this mad decision to tie Hashimoto up?"

Mandelosin now picked up the narrative. Once Hashimoto had left the city, Mayor Shefrap raced off to tell First Minister Listrongle about what had happened. An emergency Cabinet meeting was called, attended by the

Empress. There was a very strong faction led by Listrongle and Shefrap, who was also in the Cabinet, that argued that Hashimoto was about to start an insurrection which would involve killing large numbers of Lilliputians, the Empress and no doubt many ministers, with the aim of making himself Emperor of the island.

"What total nonsense!" was all Totty could say before Mandoselin continued.

Not surprisingly, there was considerable debate in the Cabinet about what the response should be. Redrelok and Mandoselin argued that everything was being exaggerated and that there should be no response other than talking to Miss Totty and asking her to warn Hashimoto about his language and behavior. However, this was rejected by the majority who believed Hashimoto was going to start killing lots of people and then try and take over the country. Eventually, the Cabinet as a whole agreed this position and proclaimed the sentence of death on Hashimoto. The Empress was very uncomfortable with this but felt unable to overturn the ministers' decision. However, she did suggest that the sentence should be suspended for two years, subject to Hashimoto's good behavior and that Miss Totty should be made responsible for his conduct. The Cabinet reluctantly agreed to this suspension, but only because the Empress made a special plea on the matter since she was extremely concerned about how Lord Poseidon and Lady Amphitrite would react if sentence was carried out before their return.

"Well, you people really are stupid idiots!" Totty shouted at the two ministers when they had finished their explanation. "I suppose that parchment you're carrying, Minister Redrelok, is this proclamation or sentence as you call it?"

"It is," Redrelok replied. "I must read it out to Hashimoto in accordance with the law."

"Don't bother!" Totty again shouted. "Before I tell you what I'm going to do, answer me one question, you two. Did you drug Hashimoto last night so you could tie him up without waking him?"

"Yes," Mandoselin reluctantly replied.

"The food?"

"The final liqueur."

"Which I also drank! Was my glass drugged as well?"

The two ministers looked at each other in embarrassed silence. Eventually Redrelok said: "Only so you wouldn't wake up as we were securing Hashimoto."

"What nasty, little weasels you all are!" Totty snarled at the two of them, jerking her head further forwards, which resulted in the two ministers stepping backwards since they were concerned that she was going to bite them. "After all I did for you yesterday afternoon. Nasty, little weasels!"

"Miss Totty," Mandoselin said: "I want you to know that none of this is directed at you personally. Indeed, the Cabinet was made aware of your great assistance and is very grateful."

"Cut it, Minister. Let me tell the two of you what's going to happen now….." She took a deep breath and then continued: "I'm going into my hut to get my sharp sword and I'm then going to walk over and release Hashimoto. Understood?" The two ministers nodded. "As I go and release him, there had better be a clear pathway where your soldiers have moved aside. If any are blocking my way, I'll walk over them. Understood?" Again, heads nodded. "If any of your soldiers attempt to strike either Hashimoto or me, then that's war and you take the consequences. Do you understand what I mean by that?"

"Yes," croaked Mandoselin timidly.

"After Hashimoto's released, he and I are going for a little chat behind the huts. It will only take a few minutes and you two are to stay here. Understood?" The ministers nodded. "Good, then I'm going to return and tell you what you're going to go back and say to your Empress and Cabinet idiots. Understood?"

"Yes," Redrelok replied, not too confidently.

"Right; now clear me a pathway. Do it and do it now!"

Totty turned round and walked towards her hut. As she went along, she thought to herself about how aggressive she had been and compared herself today to the timid, young girl who had first arrived at the Sea Cavern less than a year ago. She wasn't sure where this newfound toughness had come from but was certain she'd have to keep it up for the rest of the day. This crisis certainly wasn't over yet.

Totty came out of her hut with her sword which she held in a menacing way in front of her. She saw that a pathway of at least three feet wide had been cleared by the soldiers allowing her to walk to Hashimoto. Either side of this pathway, the troops were standing with their swords, lances and bows and arrows ready for action if necessary.

Hashimoto was still shouting and struggling to break free, so Totty called to him that she was coming to release him.

"Hurry, Totty," he shouted back. "Hashimoto very unhappy. Hurry! Hurry!"

Totty bent down to Hashimoto's left ear and whispered to him that he should not say or do anything once he was freed but follow Totty to a place behind the huts because they needed to have an important private conversation.

"Hashimoto do what Totty say," was the response.

"Good. Let's cut these strings then."

In the space of two minutes, Hashimoto was completely freed. Totty had cut off his ponytail as the simplest way of releasing his hair, but the butler didn't complain; he was just pleased to be free and able to stand up. The two walked in silence along the pathway between the soldiers and then moved away behind the huts for their private discussion.

This was all watched by Redrolok and Mandoselin from their platform. Over the next few minutes, they observed a heated discussion between the two full-sized humans, but only caught a few words and actions. The first thing they saw was Totty slap Hashimoto on the side of his head and call him 'a stupid fool.'

"Ow! What Hashimoto done?" the perplexed recipient of the slap asked while rubbing his left ear.

"Fool! Fool!" the two ministers heard again, followed by Totty slapping Hashimoto once more but this time on the other ear.

Not a lot was heard for several minutes but it was clear from her gestures that Totty was giving Hashimoto a massive telling off. Every so often she would slap him again, especially when he seemed to argue back.

"I don't know what you're on about with all this stuff about some land of the blind where there's a one-eyed man who's king!" Totty shouted at one point. "Nor do I want to know!" And Totty slapped Hashimoto again.

Eventually the conversation came to an end and the two walked back to the huts. Hashimoto went into his hut, no doubt following orders, and Totty returned to the platform, still carrying her sword which made the two ministers even more anxious than they were already.

"Okay, Ministers Redrelok and Mandoselin, I've spoken to Hashimoto. Now, it's time for us to talk. Before I tell you what you're to do, I need the answers to a few questions."

"What questions?" Redrelok asked cautiously.

"Number one is how you people were intending on carrying out this sentence of death on Hashimoto?"

The two ministers looked at each other, neither willing to answer.

"Come on!" Totty shouted. "We haven't got all day!"

"We hadn't quite worked out the details," Mandoselin replied. "But I suppose we would have fired hundreds of arrows at him until he was dead."

"You suppose?" Totty responded disdainfully. "And what if the 'you suppose' idea didn't work?"

"Then we would have probably left him all tied up to starve to death."

Totty shook her head. "You don't get it, do you?"

"Get what?" Mandoselin asked.

"The fact that Hashimoto's already dead and so am I for that matter! Why do you think we're part of Lord Poseidon's household in the Sea Cavern? They don't advertise the jobs in the Vacancies Section of local newspapers or put them on the internet so anyone can apply. No, they employ people already in the Underworld. So, Mister Clever Ministers, you were looking at sentencing someone to death who's already dead. Very clever!"

Again, the two ministers looked at each other, hoping the other one would answer. Eventually Redrelok said: "We didn't consider that matter, Miss Totty. But permit me to say that it's not relevant because the Cabinet eventually decided to suspend the sentence."

"You didn't consider the matter!" Totty repeated sarcastically. "I suspect you didn't consider lots of matters as far as your proclamation's concerned. And don't try and wriggle out of answering my questions by claiming that they're not relevant because the sentence is suspended. What if Hashimoto comes out of his hut in the next few minutes, calls you all teeny weenies and tramples on a few of your soldiers? I'm sure the sentence wouldn't be suspended any longer."

"He wouldn't do that, would he?" a shocked Redrelok asked. "Surely that's what you've spoken to him about? After all, the Cabinet has made you responsible for his good behavior."

"I don't take orders from your Cabinet!" Totty retorted angrily. "And what Hashimoto and I spoke about is our business! Understood?"

The two small men on the platform both nodded once more.

"Good! Now, my next question, and I want a crisp, clear answer to this one. Put simply, while you were busy getting on with trying to execute an already dead man, what did you think I was going to do? Did you believe I was just going to sit back and let you get on with it?"

"Again, Miss Totty," Mandoselin answered. "We hadn't quite worked that out, but I suppose we would have taken precautions."

"You suppose again! All you ever do is suppose! Well, I'm not sure what precautions you would have taken, but just suppose – as you like to do – that they didn't work, which is very probable because I'm a lot bigger than you. Then start supposing how many soldiers and other people I would trample under foot, how many ministers I would squash, how much of Mildendo would be left after I'd finished with it. And that's just me; if I'd freed Hashimoto, you could double all of that. Then suppose an alternative, which is that you just accept that Hashimoto was never serious, and you people have just over-reacted big time. You've made me very angry and have really upset Hash, although I accept he was pretty stupid yesterday. But not stupid enough to be tied up and to be sentenced to death, even if it is suspended. Do I make myself clear?"

"Yes," mumbled Mandoselin.

"Good. Now I've got one final question. What were you intending to say to Poseidon and Amphitrite if you had managed to dispatch Hashimoto in some way? Did you not think that they might be so furious at you killing a member of their household that they would annihilate Lilliput? It would be easy for them to sink the island in the ocean for evermore. Did you think about that at all?"

"Miss Totty, that type of consideration was behind the Empress arguing and achieving the suspension of the sentence," Redrelok answered.

"But the Cabinet didn't think of it, did it?"

Redrelok took a deep breath and looked at Mandoselin, who nodded his head, before answering: "The two of us did try to persuade our fellow ministers but without success until the Empress intervened."

Totty glared at both of them for a full thirty seconds. "I'm not sure if I should believe anything any of you say," she eventually replied. "But I think I probably believe what you've

149

just said, Minister Redrelok. It probably explains why you're the only two who had the courage to come here today. That fat Chief Minister and the Mayor were probably too scared to take responsibility for what they'd done!"

"Thank you," Redrelok said.

"But there's still the issue of Poseidon and Amphitrite. What are you going to say to them about this whole situation, even if Hashimoto has been released? How do you think they're going to react to your sentence of death despite it being suspended? Answer me that one!"

"Again, Miss Totty, we don't yet have an answer. The Empress has said that the Cabinet must have an established response by the end of tomorrow. In part it will be determined by our discussion with you now."

"Well, I'm not telling you how to handle it," was Totty's reply. "You people got yourselves into this mess, so you get out of it. All I will say is that the god and goddess are in a very angry mood over this tidal wave, so tread carefully!"

"Yes," Redrelok responded. "Have you any more questions?"

"No!" Totty snapped. "But if I did, it would be pointless me asking them because I haven't had any meaningful answers to the ones I've already put. So, no: no more questions. Instead, I'm now going to tell you what I expect you to do, and I expect it to be done! Understood?"

The two ministers nodded.

"Good. You're to go back and immediately call your Cabinet together with the Empress and pass another motion, or whatever you call it, revoking Hashimoto's death sentence. Once you've done that, the Empress and the whole Cabinet are to come here and confirm to Hash and me it's been done. If you people want to apologize to Hashimoto for your treatment of him, that would be helpful. Similarly, if he chooses to apologize for his behavior yesterday, I'm sure that would also be a sensible thing to do. Finally, I suggest you should have worked out what you're going to say to Poseidon and

Amphitrite by the time you get back here, not wait till the end of tomorrow. Is all that clear?"

Redrelok and Mandoselin looked at each other.

"Yes, Miss Totty," the Interior Minister replied. "But we can't guarantee anything. What will you do if the Cabinet refuses to revoke the sentence?"

"I'm not going to tell you, but I suggest you both make sure they don't refuse!"

"We'll try our best," Redrelok sighed as he turned round to leave.

The two ministers descended in the lift, got into Mandoselin's Jaguar car and drove back to the city.

Once the ministers had left, Totty and Hashimoto sat in the sun behind the huts, not saying much but relaxing. The soldiers had moved away from their original positions and were now about thirty yards from the two full-sized humans; they had sheathed their swords, dismounted from their horses and removed the arrows from their bows.

It was a full three hours before Empress Chertassle arrived in her Rolls Royce. She was alone except for her chauffeur and once she got out of the car door, she immediately ascended the lift to the platform and waited for Totty and Hashimoto to arrive.

"I wish to speak first," said Hashimoto moving ahead of Totty. He bowed to Chertassle and continued: "Honorable Lady Empress, Hashimoto wishes to make great apology for calling honorable people of Lilliput teeny weenies, titchy witches and tiny whinnies. Hashimoto also very sorry for suggesting he could trample on honorable people of Lilliput and make himself Emperor. Hashimoto only having little joke because he knows he would make very bad Emperor. Hashimoto good at firefighting, butlering and karate, but no good at empering. He also now realises he not very good at joking; this very important thing he has learned today. That is what Hashimoto wishes to say." He then followed up with another bow and stepped back so he was standing next to Totty.

While Hashimoto was speaking, Chertassle was trying very hard to keep a straight face and not to laugh. Fortunately, years of experience allowed her to keep herself under control.

"Thank you, Hashimoto. I too wish to say a few things…. Firstly, to report to you and Miss Totty that the Cabinet has cancelled unconditionally the death sentence passed on you yesterday evening. Secondly, on behalf of the Lilliputians, I fully accept your apology; and I also offer an apology to the two of you who are guests in our country. On reflection, it would seem that I and my Cabinet went somewhat overboard in our reaction to the events of yesterday afternoon. Finally, I must admit that we haven't yet been able to work out what we should say to Lord Poseidon and Lady Amphitrite on their return. Perhaps you will allow us until tomorrow morning to come up with a proposal?"

Hashimoto looked to Totty to take over the discussion. As she was about to do so, a large number of horses drew up pulling two immense carts. On the first was a human sized pizza and on the second were a series of the largest jugs in Lilliput, each containing cranberry juice. This was lunch and Chertassle suggested the three of them should sit down on the ground and eat together. Before doing this, however, the Empress sent all the troops back to barracks where they would then be allocated clearance work following the Great Wave. She also checked that her chauffeur had brought his sandwiches and had his own bottle of juice and then sat down with her guests.

The next half an hour went well with Hashimoto being on his best behavior. Totty was keen to move on from the events of the morning and the three of them agreed it would be a good idea to continue with the clearance work she and Mandoselin had been carrying out the previous day. The Empress also agreed to Totty's request that the First Minister and Mayor should be involved in the heavy work and offered a platoon of soldiers specifically to work under Totty's orders.

•

The Empress was standing on the platform near the huts when Totty, Hashimoto, and their party returned midway through the evening. The Empress was with her Chief Scientist, Professor Archimelock, and Dr Einstella who was Head of Special Projects at the Science Institute. They were speaking with Athene and Iris who had arrived a couple of hours earlier in the Goddess of Wisdom's two horse chariot.

The two goddesses had set off together from Olympus the previous day. Although they were searching for different gods, they felt it made sense to combine forces for a day or two. After all, the origins of the Great Wave appeared to be in the Indian Ocean, so it was likely that Poseidon was in the general vicinity; it also meant Mars probably initiated the event from somewhere in Asia, although Africa was also a possibility.

As Athene's chariot had skimmed across the waters, she and Iris started to pick up information from the whales as well as some of the larger fish. As they travelled eastwards there were increasing reports of sightings of the Sea God and Goddess. In time the rumours suggested they had reached Lilliput, so Athene and Iris made that their destination.

Totty's clearance team had had another good day. Once they reached the platform, the soldiers were sent back to barracks and Chertassle suggested that her ministers should go and get some rest since many of them looked exhausted doing work they were not used to. This was particularly the case with the overweight First Minister Listrongle, who was perspiring and wheezing so much while at the same time complaining about chest pains, that Mandoselin and Redrelok decided to escort him to the A&E Department of the capital's largest hospital.

Introductions of the scientists and the two goddesses were quickly made, although Hashimoto was reluctant to move from behind Totty's back.

"Come forward, Hashimoto," a smiling Athene said when she saw his reluctance. "I met you and Totty a short while ago. Don't you remember?"

All Hashimoto did was bow from behind Totty.

"Come on; come and greet us. I want to introduce you to the Goddess Iris." Hashimoto still didn't move, so Athene continued: "Come over. You're not a mouse, are you?"

Athene couldn't help giving a little laugh at her last comment, much to Hashimoto's discomfort.

"Is this the mouse you were telling us all about?" Iris asked, looking at her fellow goddess. Athene nodded while trying to suppress her giggles. Iris started laughing and then looked to Hashimoto before continuing: "Oh, do come over, Hashimoto. I do want to meet Athene's little mouse."

As the two goddesses were having a good laugh, poor Hashimoto moved from behind Totty and started bowing to everyone. "Lady Athene," he said followed by a bow. "Lady Iris," then another bow, followed by the same with the Empress, the two scientists and even Totty. He then looked up and said: "Please all excuse Hashimoto. I am very tired and not feeling well. Have had an extremely difficult day with big mental health issues. I will go now and rest in my hut and hopefully be better tomorrow."

He then bowed again to everyone, turned round and slowly walked towards his hut. Totty looked at the others, indicated that she would follow him, and quickly took his arm in hers.

"Hashimoto got no friends," he whimpered.

"That's not true. I'm your friend, Hash."

"But you spend morning hitting me around the head," was the reply.

"That shows we're really good friends. Only someone who's a really good friend would hit you around the head. That's well known."

Hashimoto sniffed. "Yes, that true. You my only friend, Totty."

"Dolores is also your friend," Totty said.

"Yes, that right. Dolores is my friend."

"And Kinky's your friend."

"Yes, and Kinky."

"And Minky."

"And Minky, yes."

"And Pinky."

"Yes, and Pinky."

"And Linky."

"Yes, and Linky too."

"And what about Poseidon? He's a really good buddy of yours."

"Yes, Poseidon's a good buddy."

"And Amphitrite."

"Yes, and Amphitrite."

"What about Hebe? You and she are great friends."

"Yes, Hebe's a friend."

"And the stallions - Donk, Tonk, Bonk and Zonk."

"Yes, Donk, Tonk, Bonk and Zonk are all my friends."

"And the mares – Polly, Dolly, Holly and Molly."

"Yes, I agree. All friends."

"Then there's Kinky's special friend, Ted."

"Yes, Ted's a friend."

"And Moby. He's a number one friend."

"Yes, and Moby."

"Don't forget his partner, Bettina."

"That's right. Bettina's good friend."

"And Sidney Shark."

"Yes, and Sidney Shark."

"So, you've got so many friends, Hash, that I bet if you started counting them, you'd run out of numbers."

The two had now reached Hashimoto's hut. Totty kissed him on the cheek, reminded him to count all his friends and to tell her in the morning that he'd run out of numbers. She then turned round and went to rejoin Athene and Iris as well as Chertassle and the two scientists.

12
Girl Gods on the Go

Famine sat in the small sitting room off the Tyrant's large study. He had wild grey hair which looked as if it had never been washed or brushed. His face was pale and gaunt with large, white demonic eyes and tiny pupils. He was exceptionally thin, his whole body seeming to consist of a skeleton covered by dark grey skin, most of the colour resulting from ash and dirt picked up on his wanderings. All he wore was a dirty torn grey smock, his feet being completely bare and, like the rest of his body, covered in centuries of grime.

"So, how long is he going to stay here?" the Tyrant asked Mars, who was sitting opposite him in the study.

"As long as I need him," was the snarled reply.

"But you must have some idea. He only arrived yesterday evening and I'm already hearing reports about flooding in the north of the country which is damaging our crops. Also, I could only eat half my breakfast this morning; the bacon was too tough to chew, the chips soggy. I've sent the chefs off to the firing range and got new ones, but I'm not sure it was their fault. I suspect it's due to Mr F being here."

Mars gave the Tyrant an aggressive look, which caused him to flinch.

"Listen, Fatty," the God of War said. "You've got so much blubber on you that to go hungry for a few days won't do you any harm. Probably do you good, you fat, little git."

"But I only-----"

"I'm not interested," Mars responded firmly. "Mr F stays here as long as we need him, so stop complaining."

"He doesn't even shuffle around on his knees when he's in my presence," the Tyrant whined.

"Then go and tell him to if you dare!" Mars now shouted.

The Tyrant didn't respond. He just sat on his chair looking out of the window. He was in a bad mood. He hadn't had a proper breakfast and he didn't like being shouted at, but he wasn't able to do anything about Mars's aggression. He knew full well that the God of War could squash him in an instant.

After a few minutes of silence in the room, the Tyrant suddenly saw a beautiful rainbow in the distance. As he looked at it, it seemed to grow in size and to get nearer to the palace. He stood up and moved to the window.

"That really is magnificent," he said, mesmerized by the colours.

"What are you looking at?" Mars asked, turning round since he had his back to the window. "Ah, ha!" he exclaimed as he saw the rainbow. "So, they've found me already," he continued with a malicious smile. "Open the window," he ordered the small fat man.

"Why?"

"Just do it!" and Mars pushed the Tyrant aside and opened the French windows onto the terrace. As he swung them open, there was a flash of light and Iris appeared on the windowsill.

"Who's this?" the Tyrant asked, shocked as he looked at a slim, auburn-haired woman of medium height. She was wearing a rainbow-coloured dress and a golden cloak with wings. On her feet were matching golden-winged sandals.

"Good morning," she said to the two occupants of the room as she stepped into the study. "You must be the Tyrant," she continued, looking at Mars's companion. "I'm the Goddess Iris. Do you like my rainbow? I saw you looking at it admiringly."

"Yes," croaked the Tyrant, not sure how to treat Iris.

"I'm so pleased. I'm not sure it's entirely mutual as far as your country's concerned, Mr Tyrant. As my beloved rainbow was moving over the fields outside the city, it saw a firing range. There was quite a lot of activity going on. Four people with white hats and aprons seemed to be tied to posts and each one had a large cannon pointing at him from about ten yards away. Suddenly, there was a series of large bangs and the next instant, what were no doubt a bunch of cordon bleu chefs had become a thousand very burnt sausages. Was that your doing?"

The Tyrant looked at Mars.

"Ignore her," the God of War said. "She's lived too long with my gobby sister."

"Nasty, little man, aren't you?" Iris said, still looking at the Tyrant.

The Tyrant again looked at Mars, unsure how to respond.

"Come on," Mars said roughly, moving towards the door. "You and I had better go next door so you can deliver that message you've no doubt got for me. Oh, by the way, the Tyrant will want you to shuffle around on your knees when we return. Everyone does so in his presence, except for me."

"And me," the goddess replied, following Mars out of the door.

The two members of the deity settled down on large couches in the palace's library. All the bookshelves were full of books which the Tyrant had never read. However, the room looked impressive which was its chief purpose for whenever foreign dignitaries visited Tyrantland; an increasingly rare event these days.

"How did you find me so quickly?" Mars demanded abruptly once they were both seated.

"You know us messengers, we've all the skills of a modern detective agency," Iris responded flippantly. "Anyway, you don't seem surprised."

"No. I knew Zeus would send someone after me. You've no doubt got one of those pompous, tiresome messages from my father, so spit it out."

"I haven't actually, other than the fact that Zeus wants you to return to Olympus. What I'm really here for is to find out what's going on. We gods and goddesses are a bit lacking in the information stakes."

"What do you know so far?"

"Three things. Firstly, a huge tidal wave developed in the Indian Ocean, killing lots of sea life, and probably causing a mass of destruction in coastal areas. Secondly, Poseidon turned up at the Council Meeting and thumped you. Finally, you secretly left Olympus and have now turned up in Tyrantland."

"That's about all there is to tell."

"No, it's not Mars. There are loads of questions."

"Like what?" the God of War growled.

"Like what precisely caused this immense tidal wave for a start?"

"Have a guess."

"If you're determined to be unhelpful, I will. The fact that you're here in Tyrantland, from which a number of missiles have been fired in recent years, suggests that it was another missile. Right?"

Mars nodded.

"But this one has caused so much damage, it must have been more powerful than anything ever fired beforehand."

"Correct. It's the most powerful missile ever created. Far more powerful than any of the gods on Mount Olympus. Which means Zeus is no longer the mightiest force in the universe; instead, my missile is."

"Your missile?"

"That's what I said," Mars replied with an evil glint in his eye. "The Tyrant and I have been developing it over the last few years. Now we control a force greater than anything ever seen before."

"And what do you intend to do with this great missile you've created?"

"I could say 'wait and see', but instead let me ask you a question, Iris."

"Go on."

"Have you ever thought that Zeus, Hades and Poseidon are possibly approaching the end of their days?"

"What do you mean by that?"

"Just as they replaced the Titans, so one day new forces might take over from them."

"You mean you, don't you, Mars?"

"I'm specifically not saying that to you, Iris. If I did, you'd just race off to my father and tell him I'm plotting a coup. No; I'm a loyal son."

"Oh, pull the other one!"

"You don't understand me. All I'm saying is that over time other forces develop which can turn out to be greater than the Olympian Gods. I happen to control one now."

"Which goes back to my earlier question – what do you intend to do with it?"

"Despite being a loyal son, I feel it's now only right that since I've got this great power, I shouldn't be constrained as I've been in the past."

"Meaning?"

"Meaning that my activities should no longer be subject to the approval of the Gods' Council for a start. I expect to be allowed to create chaos wherever I want. I really hope you support me in this, Iris. Choose the future, not the past."

"So, the future is you, the Tyrant and your all-powerful new weapon, is it? Who else is involved? Have any other gods signed up to this new future of yours?"

"Until you commit, I'll keep that information to myself."

There was a lengthy silence between the two as they stared at each other.

"What are you playing at, Mars?" Iris eventually asked. "You don't honestly believe I'm going to sign up to an act of treachery, do you?"

"It isn't treachery!" Mars shouted, annoyed at the use of that word. "It's purely a reflection of where power now lies! As I said, I'm a loyal son, but I don't expect any more restraints on me!"

"So, that's your message to Zeus?"

"Have you got any other questions?" Mars growled in reply.

"I won't ask about why Poseidon thumped you because it's obvious. That super powerful missile of yours was a declaration of war on his kingdom. What I would like to know, although you probably won't tell me, is what happens next?"

"Wait and see," Mars snarled, giving a malicious smile. "And if you see Poseidon, tell him a bloody payback's coming his way."

"Fine. Tell me then, how do you think your father and the other gods are going to respond when I report this conversation to them?"

"I don't know," Mars said with a shrug. "But if they've got any sense, they'll recognize the power of my missile. 'Might is right', so make sure you remind them of that. Anything else?"

"No; I'll just take my rainbow away."

"You don't want to say goodbye to the Tyrant before you go?"

"I'll pass. Oh, by the way, that was Famine I saw in the other room, wasn't it?"

"What of it?"

"Nothing in particular. Is Pestilence here as well?"

"No," Mars grunted in reply.

"I'll be off then," Iris said, walking over to a window which she opened and then disappeared.

"Stupid cow," muttered Mars as he went back to join the Tyrant.

•

After spending the night at Lilliput, Iris and Athene decided to leave for a couple of days, planning to return when the Sea God and Goddess were back. Their plan was to then return together to Zeus's so-called Operation Control, so they could give as full a report as possible to the Top God, as well as a combined view on how Olympus should respond.

After tracking down Mars, Iris headed off to the Americas to try to find Hermes to let him know that the God of War had been found. She would then look for Hebe in Europe and Artemis in Africa. Athene wanted to take the opportunity of visiting Hades for her conversation about the three brothers getting together, as well as asking him to keep a look out for any information about the two missing Horsemen.

Before going to the Underworld, Athene called in at the Sea Cavern. The previous evening Totty had told her about what had happened when the Great Wave arrived, and that Dolores and the mermaids had chosen to remain. There was naturally concern about how they were, so Athene wanted to see if she could help in any way. When she got to the cavern, she found two whales in the lagoon and a whole mass of still wet furniture and fabrics on the piazza, which Dolores had cleared out from the ground floor. Within a short while of her arrival Athene and Dol were standing on the piazza in conversation with the maids, with the whales in attendance. Athene's two mares had been freed from the chariot and were nosing around all the palace's discarded contents looking for something to eat.

"So, Poseidon, Amphitrite, Totty and Hash are all on this island called Lilliput, are they?" Dolores said, after they had listened to Athene recount her side of events.

"Yes," replied the goddess. "Although I missed my uncle and aunt because they're still assessing the damage to their realm. However, they'll be back in a few days when I'll see them."

"And you said that Posy gave Mars a great big thump on the nose because he caused this Great Wave?" Kinky repeated.

"That's right," Athene confirmed.

"Good!" was Kinky's emphatic response, which was echoed by the other maids. "And what about this Tyrant bloke who's also responsible? Is Posy going to go and thump the Tyrant on the nose as well?"

"I sincerely hope so," the goddess replied.

"Please tell him to give an extra hard thump from us."

"Extra, extra hard," Pinky called out.

"I will," Athene said with a smile.

The discussion then moved on to how matters currently were in the cavern. On the positive side, the first floor of the palace was not damaged, so Dolores had a place to stay while she cleared out the ground floor where everything was ruined. Everything in the mermaid's palace was also ruined, so the maids were having to sleep on damp mattresses which were uncomfortable.

"I can help on that one," said Athene. "I'll come and look at it afterwards, but I've the power to create an intense amount of heat over a short period of time. I should be able to get rid of a lot of the damp on your floors and walls. I suggest you throw out all your wet mattresses and furniture and bring some things over from the main palace's bedrooms. Will that be possible?"

"Oh yes," Kinky answered. "Our two lovely whales, Fuad and Alfred can carry things on their backs which they'll keep above the water."

The two whales gave soft bellows as confirmation.

"But can you really get rid of the damp, Athene?" Kinky continued. "That's our biggest problem."

"I should be able to," which was met by many appreciative shouts of "super" and "totally top."

"What about food?" Athene now asked.

"No problems," Dolores promptly replied. "We managed to save some despite the Great Wave; also, Hebe visited us yesterday. She brought a good load of food and said she would continue calling in every two weeks with a delivery. She even left us some oats which I'll get later for your two horses."

"She's going to bring a chocolate cake next time," Pinky called out before Athene could reply.

The goddess smiled before thanking Dolores for the offer of the oats. Her two mares had heard about the oats, so they immediately gave up on their fruitless search of the palace's ground floor contents for food and came over and nuzzled the goddess.

"So, Hebe's been here. I thought she'd be somewhere else at this time. Did she say where she was going next?"

"She's gone to the Underworld," Dolores answered.

"That's my next port of call," Athene said. "Perhaps I'll catch her there, but first I need to help you all here for a while. Dolores, could you please get the oats for my two lovelies, while I swim over to the maid's palace and see if I can get rid of some of this damp. I'll then come and give you a hand getting some mattresses and things for the maids."

"Super!" Kinky shouted. "We'll race you to our palace, Athene," and she and the other maids set off at speed towards the far corner of the cavern.

"I think I'll let them go," a smiling Athene said to Dolores. "They'd probably beat me anyway."

•

As Athene's chariot entered the Underworld, she was met by Cerberus.

"Halt!" he called. "Who goes there?"

Athene pulled on the reins of the mares and her chariot came to a halt. "Hello, Cerberus," she replied, unaware that she was now speaking to the Head of Internal Security. "You know me well."

"Woof! I can't let personal relationships interfere with my job, Lady Athene."

"Well, you just said my name, Cerberus, so now you know who I am?"

"Woof! Woof! Did I? What did I say?"

"You called me Lady Athene, which we both know is my name."

"Woof! I didn't mean to," Cerberus said.

"Unfortunately for you, you did. May I proceed?"

"No. I need to see identity papers."

Athene sighed. "I haven't got any."

"Can anyone identify you?"

"Yes, you just did."

Cerberus thought hard about this before eventually saying: "I'm not sure that's good enough. You might be an imposter in disguise."

"And how do I know you're not an imposter disguised as Cerberus?" the Goddess of Wisdom fired back.

"Woof! Woof!" barked Cerberus, unsure how to reply. "Woof!"

The two stared at each other, Cerberus feeling much more uncomfortable than Athene, which meant he had to keep going "woof" at regular intervals. Eventually Athene decided to break the stalemate.

"Shall I show you a special trick which only Athene, the Goddess of Wisdom, knows how to do?"

"Woof! That seems a good idea. Then I'll know you're not an imposter, Athene. What is this trick?"

"I turn a three-headed dog into a three-headed mouse. Only I know how to do that."

"Woof! Woof!" Cerberus barked backing away in alarm. "Woof! Woof!"

"Are you ready for me to do it now?" Athene asked with a smile as she raised her right arm.

Cerberus continued to back away in alarm. "Woof! That won't be necessary," he said nervously. "All security checks have been passed. You may proceed, Lady Athene."

"Thank you," the goddess replied. "But how do I know you're not an imposter, Cerberus? You've not yet passed my security checks."

"Woof! Woof!" was the reply. Cerberus was having a difficult morning with Athene. He thought, as Head of Internal Security, it was his job to ask the questions. Now he found he was being interrogated and he didn't know how to reply. All he could think of saying after a few more 'woofs' was: "Give us a Mars bar or I'll bite yer bum."

Athene gave him a great big smile. "That's better," she said. "Now I know you're the real Cerberus. Here," and she threw him a Mars bar which he caught in his left mouth and started munching.

"Woof! Thank you."

"I'll see you later, Cerberus," Athene said, starting to move forwards in the chariot.

A few minutes later Athene drew up outside Hades' large golden palace. As she did so, she saw Hebe walking down the front steps.

"Just the person I want to see," said Athene.

"Eh up, Athy. What are you doing here? Poseidon's not in the Underworld, I promise you."

"I could ask you the same question, Hebe. I thought you were looking for Mars in Europe. Anyway, you don't need to. We think we know where he is."

"Why? What's happened?"

Athene proceeded to give Hebe a detailed account of the last few days. She admitted that although Iris hadn't yet seen Mars when the two of them had parted, they were certain that he was based in Tyrantland. It was from there that some missile seemed to have been launched into the Indian Ocean, causing the Great Wave. Similarly, she was still to speak to Poseidon, but he and Amphitrite were due back in Lilliput in a couple of days' time and she would see him then.

"So, we don't actually know what their intentions are yet?" Hebe asked.

"Not yet, but we do know that Lilliput is planning a major response to Tyrantland and that Poseidon wants revenge. If you go across the ocean, there are probably millions of dead sea creatures. Also, I looked at some of the coastal regions in Asia and they're devastated; they must have experienced a substantial loss of life."

"That's got to be right. Uncle Hady's just mentioned that Death's been bringing in a lot a drowned people in the last day or two."

"What's perplexing is the size of the tidal wave. We've never witnessed any missile doing so much damage beforehand. The Lilliputians claim that Mars has been visiting

Tyrantland a lot recently, which suggests he's been up to something for a while. I wonder if he's thought out the consequences."

"My brother's not got the biggest brain in the world," Hebe responded. "So probably not. To me it looks like war's going to happen."

"I agree," Athene replied. "Poseidon against Mars, unless we can stop it."

"Is that what you're going to try to do?"

Athene thought for a while before answering. "Probably not," she ended up saying. "Poseidon's got every right to have revenge given the devastation to his realm. Also, Mars has been angling for a big fight for a long time."

"How's Father going to react?"

"I don't know, Hebe, but I doubt Poseidon and Mars will pay much attention. I suspect war's got to happen to sort out some big issues between the gods."

"It's going to be just like Troy."

"Why?"

"Simple. All we gods are going to have to take sides."

Athene laughed. "Probably, but aren't we all going to be on one side?"

"Of course. After what you've told me, I'm off to Lilliput to sign up to Uncle Posy's army."

"I'll be there soon, but to talk to him, not sign up. After I've spoken to Poseidon, and Iris has seen Mars, she and I plan to go and let Zeus know what they've got to say for themselves."

"Alright, I'll leave you to it for a few days. I've got quite a few things to do on Olympus, even if I'm not scouring Europe for Mars. But after that I'm going to Lilliput."

"I'll let Poseidon know." She paused before continuing: "Anyway, I'd better go and see Hades now."

"Can I ask why?"

"To have the same conversation I had some time ago with Poseidon about the three brothers meeting up. I suspect it's going to have to be after this war we've been speaking about has taken place."

"He's with Persephone in the Throne Room now."

"Fine. She can join in. I'm also going to ask them both if they've heard anything about where Pestilence and Famine are. Do you know if Perse has spoken to Death yet?"

"Nah, I don't think so. From what I can gather Death's in a funny mood these days."

"What does that mean?"

"He's having some sort of mid-life crisis?"

"I don't understand that. Death's Death. He doesn't have a mid-life in which to have a crisis."

Hebe shrugged. "That's what I'm told. Apparently, he's taken up playing cards with Aggy. It's some sort of therapy I think." Hebe paused. "Do you think we gods and goddesses have mid-life crises?" she asked after a while.

"I doubt it. Why? Do you think you're experiencing one?"

"Of course not! You and I are young ones, Athy. I'm thinking about Mother and her moods."

"I suspect Hera was born with her moods. If they've got worse over time, it's probably living with Zeus."

"Then she'll always be in some mood or other," Hebe said laughing, before she and Athene went their separate ways.

13
Just Call Me Rach

The dark red miniature Vespa scooter sped along about six feet above the ground. When it got nearer to the huts just outside Mildendo, it slowed down before landing perfectly on the platform and coming to a halt. The rider pressed the horn: 'Toot, toot' it went; 'toot, toot.' There was no response from anybody, so the horn again went 'toot, toot…. toot, toot.'

"Totty!" shouted the rider. "Totty!" This was followed by another 'toot, toot.'

On this last 'toot, toot,' Totty appeared from her hut. She looked over at the platform and saw the rider on the scooter.

"Hello!" she called, walking towards the platform. "Do I know you?"

The rider by now had pulled off her helmet as well as her goggles and dismounted from the scooter. She had spiky, muti-coloured hair, which was green in the middle, purple on the left and blue on the right. She wore large golden rings on her ears as well as a smaller ring on the left side of her nose. Both her cheeks had small tattoos, a red rose on one side and a blue tulip on the other. The rider's arms were also tastefully covered with tattoos of different flowers and, although she was wearing jeans, her bare ankles could be seen to be similarly marked.

"You don't recognize me," the rider replied. "We met briefly the evening before last with Athene and Iris. I'm Einstella. I was wearing a white coat then because I'm a scientist and my father made me put a scarf over my head because he doesn't like my hair. He only makes me cover up when important people like goddesses are around."

"And your father's name is?" Totty asked.

"He's Professor Archimelock. You met him as well. He did most of the talking, being the head honcho."

"Oh yes," said Totty. "It's nice to meet you again, Einstella."

"Do you like my Vespa?"

Totty bent down to the platform and looked at the miniature scooter. "How did you get it onto the platform?" she asked.

"I drove it, or rather I flew it."

"You flew it!" Totty exclaimed. "But scooters don't fly."

"This one does. I made it myself," Einstella said proudly. "It's the only one in Lilliput; probably the world for all I know."

"That's amazing. And you say you made it yourself?"

"Don't forget, I'm a scientist. We do things like make flying scooters. It's still in the development stage and I had to get special permission from the government to fly it. I'm not allowed to fly the scooter at night and can't go over residential parts of the city, although I ignore those restrictions most of the time. Government officials can always find reasons to stop you doing things. If we always paid attention to them, we'd never make any progress."

"Gosh," said Totty. "You are brave; also, very clever. Where did you learn all this science?"

"School, university and from Mum and Dad."

"Is your mother a scientist like you and your father?"

"Sort of. She's a hospital consultant who spends a lot of her time carrying out heart operations. She was on duty when Listrongle was brought in after you tired him out doing some proper work for once. He didn't need an operation, but Mum carried out all the tests before sending him home."

"I didn't actually mean for him to end up in hospital," Totty replied slightly defensively.

"Well, I'm glad he did. Listrongle's a complete twat and if you could take him off another time and make sure he has a heart attack, Lilliput would be very grateful."

"I gather you don't like him?"

"Well, I didn't vote for him. The trouble is that a lot of stupid people did support him. It's because he makes promises about what he's going to do for them which are all lies. Anyway, we do have some sensible people in the cabinet like Uncle Mandy and-----"

"Mandoselin's your uncle?" Totty interrupted.

"Oh yea. I gather you and he are working together a lot, clearing up after all the mess caused by the Great Wave. He's incredibly grateful to you for all your help, you know."

"I like him. He's sensible as you say and works hard."

"He's one of the good guys in the Cabinet. The General's okay and also the finance guy, Redrelok. The only thing I've got against him is he won't always give me the money I need for all these special projects I want to do. Anyway, as Dad says, that's actually his job, controlling the money, and if we all got what we wanted, we'd go bankrupt. So, I do sort of get it, I suppose."

"What are all these special projects you're doing?" Totty asked.

"That's why I've come to see you," Einstella replied. "I hope you might be able to help me, especially in this fight we're going to have with the Tyrant."

"I'm all for that, but I'm not sure if I'm going to be much help. I've not had your education; I left school when I was sixteen and never managed to pass many exams."

"Don't be so modest, Totty. You went to the University of Common Sense from what people say about you. Look how you're organizing everyone to clear up after the tidal wave. You've got hundreds of the locals working away. Even more impressive was how you handled Grandma over your Japanese friend. You didn't learn that at university."

"Grandma! Your grandmother's not the Empress, is she?" a shocked Totty asked.

"Sure is. Grandma Chertassle's my Mum's mum."

"Wow. You must be part of the cleverest family in the whole of Lilliput," Totty replied. "You've obviously got really good education. Presumably you went to the best university here?"

"Not as a student, but I lecture there sometimes. I like it and it gives me the opportunity of finding new talent to join my team."

"So, where did you go to university?"

"Cambridge," Einstella replied nonchalantly. "Both as a student or undergraduate, as some people say, and then to do my PhD."

"That's amazing! But while I don't know anything about universities, I've never heard of people from Lilliput coming to England to be educated. In fact, I never knew Lilliput existed until a few days ago."

"You've never read *Gulliver's Travels*?"

Totty shook her head. "Never," she replied: "But I've heard of it and think I might have seen some film about it. I was sure it was just some fairy tale until I got here."

Einstella laughed. "Now you know it's not," she said. "We Lilliputians are to be found in lots of places. We like England, especially because the first big man we ever met was Gulliver and he came from there. We've got an embassy in London, you know. It's on a place called Duck Island in St James's Park. I've been there and it's really handy for official visits. One side of the park's just across the road from 10 Downing Street, so whenever our ambassador needs to see your Prime Minister, he can walk there. He has to be helped with the steps but normally there's a nice policeman to lift him up. On the other side of St James's is Buckingham Palace. When I visited the embassy, I was invited for tea with the old Queen and some of her family. We had to cross the lake on the back of a friendly swan and then there was a carriage to take us to the palace. I think it was sent to pick us up because we're small and there's a steep hill to get out of the park, followed by a busy road to cross. I really enjoyed that because I was helped into the carriage by a guard with a red jacket and a bearskin hat. He let me sit on his furry hat for a while."

"I don't know what to say!" an astonished Totty replied. "You've actually met the former Queen – the Queen of England?"

"Sure thing. She was a real okay cookie. She knew an awful lot about me, including some of the times I'd been naughty when young. I only found out from her that she and Grandma have been friends for ages. Apparently, they've been comparing notes on their grandchildren for a long time."

"Was this when you were at Cambridge?"

"Yea; I was given two days off to go down to London, so I could look at the city and meet the Queen. It's a big place is London. Are you from there?"

"Just outside. A place called Romford. You won't have been there."

"No," Einstella agreed. "I couldn't see everything; I had to get back to uni because I was two weeks away from exams."

There was a pause in the conversation as Totty wondered what to ask next. She was both fascinated and astonished at everything she was being told. As she remembered that she'd once been to Cambridge on a Sunday coach trip with her mum, she decided to ask about the university and what life was like there for a Lilliputian.

"There were always lots of us there at any time," the scientist replied. "We've got our own college; not surprisingly called Lilliput College. Grandma used to be its Provost, which meant she was the boss; she was also a university professor in Mathematics at the time. Father also spent some time as a lecturer in Cambridge before marrying Mum who was a graduate. Dad's now become an honorary professor at the university and I'm also an occasional lecturer during my annual visit to England. All of us, Grandma, Dad, Mum and me, we're fellows of the college."

"What's a fellow?" Totty asked.

"A senior academic or administrator, although there are lots of different types."

"So, you've got this college, but how does it fit in with the rest of the university?"

"We're no different to any of the others like King's, Trinity, St John's and the like. All our students attend the same lectures as the big students. There are always special arrangements for access and seating in the lecture halls. Our private tuition can be carried out by anyone; I tended to get a lot of six-foot male scientists for weekly reviews when I was there. Socially, we Lilliputians all had friends in the big colleges, but we couldn't always do things together."

"Like what?"

"Clubbing, for a start. We were likely to get stamped on if we were in a big people's club, especially as the night progressed. It meant we had to have our own places for some things. Having said that, there was a really nice pub called the Granta the other side of the river. It was mainly for the big people, but it had a section for us about the height of this platform. We Lilliputians could congregate there and chat with our friends from the other colleges. They also had a lot of small beer mugs for us to drink out of. There's no way any of us little people could drink out of a proper full pint mug. I once tried it and fell in; I thought I was going to drown but the nice landlady got hold of me and fished me out!" Einstella laughed as she told this story, recalling her student years.

"So, you really enjoyed university?"

"Yea, great fun. That's why I try and go back every year for a couple of weeks. Be a student again."

"But how do you travel there? Don't tell me you've got your own planes?"

"No; not yet. We've got an arrangement with British Airways which operates from several airports in the area. That's one of the reasons why the loss of our navy's so serious because we'd travel by boat to Indonesia and then go cross country to one of the airports. BA has a section on some of its planes at the back reserved for us Lilliputians. We've got our own small cabins with beds, couches and a minibar. It's total luxury. We always fly to Heathrow where we're met by embassy staff who escort us to wherever we want to go, normally Cambridge. Sometimes, it's all the way in one of those black cabs; sometimes by taxi and train."

"I'm stunned!" was Totty's response. "But what I don't understand is why none of this is ever reported in England."

"It's an arrangement we agreed with the gods. Whenever a big person meets someone from Lilliput, he or she forgets it after a few seconds. If they write anything about us, then those words disappear from the page very quickly. The one exception is Cambridge where everyone remembers us while there, but once they go a distance of more than five miles from the Market Square, it's all forgotten. We had to have that exception so we could fit properly into the community."

"Gosh! But why?"

"I'm not sure. It was all set up with Athene after Gulliver visited us. I suspect it was to protect our privacy, otherwise everyone in the world would come and look at us. We'd probably all be taken away and put in museums."

"But the book, *Gulliver's Travels* exists, so there is a record of you all."

"Yea, but it's written as a fantasy or fairy story, as you said." Einstella paused before saying: "Anyway, Totty, let's not talk any more about that for now. I want to show you the Science Institute and talk to you about how we might work together to zap the Tyrant. I know you're free this morning because Uncle Mandy's not available until the afternoon."

"Okay, that sounds good. I'll go and let Hashimoto know. I'll be back soon."

"Okey-dokes."

Einstella and Totty were soon on their way to the Lilliput Science Institute which was on the far side of Mildendo from the huts. It involved Totty walking through the city, but she was very careful about where she put her feet, so she didn't trample on anyone. All the inhabitants knew who she was and many waved and moved aside when they saw her coming.

Einstella was on her Vespa scooter, about three feet away from the side of Totty's head, so the two girls could continue chatting.

"Do you know why Uncle Mandy isn't free this morning?" Einstella asked as they went along.

"He said it was a Cabinet Meeting," Totty replied.

"Yea, that's right. They're still trying to work out what to say to Poseidon and Amphitrite about your friend Hashimoto. They should have done so by yesterday, but they're stuck."

"Yes, I know. The Empress came to see me yesterday morning to ask for another day. It's all that fool the Chief Minister's fault as well as the Mayor's. Presumably you know all about it from your grandmother and your uncle?"

"Sure do..... What do you think they should say to the two gods?"

"Honestly, Einstella, I think it's their problem and they should work it out. However, if it were down to me, I'd suggest that no one says anything – and that includes Hash and me. If somehow it comes out, then we just tell the truth. It won't reflect well on anyone involved, but it's what it is."

Einstella thought about what Totty had said for a time. "Do you mind if I tell Grandma what you suggest?" she eventually asked.

Totty shook her head. "No, if it helps. Personally, I think there are a lot more important things we should be focusing on."

"Like zapping the Tyrant?"

"Yes," Totty said with a smile. "Also, there's still a lot of clearing up to be done after the tidal wave."

A few minutes later the two of them arrived at the Science Institute. It consisted of a number of modern two-storey buildings in an open park setting. In one corner, however, there were two identical structures behind a high brick wall with the entrance controlled by a barrier and a number of guards in front of it.

"This is my Special Projects section," Einstella said, flying over the wall and landing on a similar five-foot high platform to the one near the huts. On one side of the platform was a screen about a foot high and eighteen inches wide. In front of it was a desk with what looked like a computer, and a chair.

Einstella got off her scooter and smiled at Totty who had followed her.

"We spent all day yesterday setting this up for you. If you're happy to stand behind me while I sit at the desk, Totty, I'll give you a presentation about what we do in Special Projects and then move on to how we might work together if okay with you. All this is top secret stuff, as you can see from the security around this section, but both Dad and Grandma have agreed I can disclose everything to you. Are you okey-dokes with that?"

"Yes, of course."

"Then I'll begin."

Einstella spent the next half an hour running through a presentation on her computer, which was projected onto the screen in front. The scientist did a lot of talking as she went through the individual slides, but it wasn't difficult to understand what Special Projects was all about. It had been set up seven years ago when Einstella returned to Lilliput, having got her PhD in Cybersecurity from Cambridge. She had been encouraged to specialize in the subject by the Empress, her father and the Minister of Defence because they could see tremendous advantages for Lilliput in applying those skills. Since then, many other graduates had followed Einstella's lead, and a Computer Sciences faculty had also been set up at Mildendo University for those students whose further education took place on the island. Naturally, many of them came on to join the Special Projects team, so by the time Totty was receiving her briefing, Einstella's empire consisted of more than 100 people, of which 20 were post-graduates, 30 were graduates and the rest were highly skilled technicians and support staff.

"What do you think, Totty?" the scientist asked at the end of her presentation.

"Despite the technical jargon, like 'information accumulation' and 'system refinement', your team's full of a load of hackers, isn't it?" Totty replied.

"Absolutely right," Einstella said with a laugh. "We focus on spying, but also we're able to alter other people's software. That last bit's what the whole team's been concentrating on since the Great Wave. We don't want another missile landing near us, so we hope we'll be able to divert it somewhere else."

"Have you done that before?"

"Not exactly," was the slightly defensive answer. "But there's always got to be a first time."

"I suppose so," Totty agreed. Then after a pause she continued: "I think what you're doing is brilliant Einstella, but I don't see how I can help you much. While I can use a computer, I'm no technical expert."

"No probs. All of that presentation was to give you a feel for what Special Projects is about. Now I want to get onto what you and I might do together. Have a look at this."

Einstella tapped away on her computer and a photograph of a fat face with short black hair on top appeared on the screen.

"That's the Tyrant," the scientist said.

"I don't fancy him, myself."

"I don't think anyone does. Now let's see if we can change what he looks like."

She again tapped away and suddenly the Tyrant had a large red ball on his nose. Totty laughed. She laughed even more when his ears turned bright orange and they quadrupled in size. This was followed by two large black horns growing out of the top of his head and fangs growing out of his mouth.

"All of that's brilliant," Totty said after Einstella went through a number of other profile changes.

"Now look at this."

The Tyrant's head disappeared, and a news programme came on the screen. It showed thousands of soldiers marching up and down in a square while martial music was being played and a shrill voice was screeching over a loudspeaker. The picture then switched to a balcony where the Tyrant was standing in full military attire surrounded by various high-ranking officers. They all waved as the troops turned their heads towards the balcony and saluted in unison. Einstella then changed the channel to what seemed to be a history programme consisting of older men who looked as if they were part of the Tyrant's family. The pause button was suddenly hit, and the scientist turned to Totty.

"Those are the only two television channels in Tyrantland, both controlled by the state. That's where the two of us come in."

"I think I can guess what you're about to suggest. You want to hack Tyrantland TV and take it over. Is that right?"

Einstella laughed. "Absolutely," she replied. "Grandma says we need to disrupt the Tyrant on many fronts, so when I suggested hacking into their TV programmes and giving a load of false news and showing funny faces of the Tyrant, she was all for it. Also, it was her idea I should involve you because we only have local news on Lilliput TV, but you could bring much more real-world experience to the party. We need to do everything we can to unsettle the Tyrant."

"You mean zap him?"

"That's right," and Einstella laughed again. "Are you in?"

Totty nodded. "Of course. How do we take it forward?"

"For now, we stop. I know you've got to get back for a busy afternoon clearing up with Uncle Mandy. What I'd like to do is introduce you to half a dozen members of my team now, then let's break up. If okay with you, I'll come round to your hut for dinner this evening and we can brainstorm. If you want to involve your friend, Hashimoto, that's okey-dokes with me, provided everyone understands that this is a project being run jointly by you and me. Period."

"Fine. It sounds great, Einstella."

"Let me call the team."

The scientist pulled out a miniature mobile phone, had a quick chat with someone and then put it away.

"One final thing, Tots," she said. "It's time for you to stop calling me Einstella. The name I'd like you to call me is Rachel."

"Why? I thought everyone on Lilliput only had one name, like the gods?"

"That's true, but when we go to Cambridge it doesn't work because big people like you have two or more names. So, we all choose another name for our friends when we're there and I chose Rachel. My father called himself Clarence, which was really old-fashioned and stupid. Mum was called Sarah which was okay as was Grandma who was Deborah. Anyway, the older generations don't use their Cambridge names on Lilliput, but we operate differently in Special Projects. Everyone uses their chosen first name, even people who didn't go to Cambridge; they get to decide on another name when they join us."

"Fine, so I call you Rachel?"

"Actually, Tots, just call me Rach."

14
The Fight Back Begins

Hundreds of whales were gathered in the sea close to a large rocky promontory on Lilliput's east coast. At the forefront was Moby's huge white body with two small female whales either side of him. They were all listening to Poseidon's commanding voice from the promontory. The Sea God was bare-chested from the waist upwards, his sword hanging by his side as he held a giant tripod in his right hand. His wife, Amphitrite, stood by his side, wearing a long plain white smock down to her knees, holding a spear at least a foot longer than her tall frame. Totty and Hashimoto stood next to the Sea Goddess, while the Empress, together with First Minister Listrongle as well as Redrelok, Mandoselin and General Golroblin were standing on a platform to Poseidon's left.

"I still think it would be better if I created an earthquake and a tidal wave off Tyrantland," Poseidon said.

"No," Moby replied. "The Sea Creatures held counsel all day yesterday and agreed that we had the right to lead the first attack. We are the ones who've suffered most from the Tyrant's missile."

The Empress coughed and was about to intervene, but the Sea God stretched out his hand towards her. "No, Chertassle," he said quietly so the whales could not hear. "They are right; they've probably suffered millions of deaths. Let them take the lead."

Poseidon looked back at Moby. "And you say it has been agreed that the whales will carry out the attack?"

"We have nearly five hundred already gathered here," was the reply. "By the time we reach our destination two or three times as many will have joined us. The sharks will provide an escort, but we do not envisage them having to fight."

"And will you be their leader, Moby?"

"If the others wish it, I will lead."

"And I will co-lead," the small female whale to Moby's right called out. "I will co-lead with Moby and fight until I die."

There was a long silence as all eyes were focused on the small beluga whale. Eventually, Moby said to her: "I do not like this, Suki. It is not what Gerrard would want."

"I have lost my mate, Moby," was the stern reply. "My sole duty is to avenge him and then I have no more purpose. I will fight until I die."

"You are with child, Suki," Amphitrite suddenly called out. "You cannot do this."

Suki did not reply.

"You are with child," Amphitrite called again.

Suki again said nothing for a while before eventually muttering in a hesitant voice: "I am not sure, My Lady."

"As your goddess, I tell you that you are. You must live and give birth to Gerrard's child."

"I agree," Moby stated firmly. "You should not fight."

"I will co-lead with you and fight until I die," Suki responded.

There was another long silence until Bettina, Moby's mate, who was on the other side of him, called out: "Lady Amphitrite, Suki will co-lead with Moby. She will fight, but she will live."

The Sea Goddess nodded her head and then stared directly at Suki who did not respond.

"Yes," Poseidon said. "Suki will co-lead, she will fight, and she will live. That is what the gods wish, Suki."

Suki again remained quiet, so Bettina repeated Poseidon's words in a loud voice: "Suki will co-lead, she will fight, and she will live."

Immediately afterwards, another whale shouted out the words 'Suki will co-lead, she will fight, and she will live.' This was repeated by other whales until there was a chorus of voices chanting in unison: 'Suki will co-lead, she will fight, and she will live.' This went on for some time until Poseidon raised his trident as a call for quiet.

All eyes from the shore were focused on Suki, who remained silent for many seconds as she struggled with her own feelings. Eventually she said in a quiet voice: "Suki will co-lead, she will fight, and she will live." Both Poseidon and Amphitrite nodded their heads towards her, recognizing how difficult that decision was.

"So be it," Moby said aloud. "Suki and Moby will co-lead, we will fight, and we will both live."

"Agreed!" Poseidon affirmed, slamming his trident on the ground. "It will take you some days to reach Tyrantland. Go first to Challogis Island, which is only about fifty miles away from its south coast. Lady Amphitrite and I will meet you there. Farewell."

"Farewell," Moby replied as he turned away. Suki and Bettina turned with him as did the other whales. In doing so, they opened up a passageway for Moby and Suki to move to the front as the whales' battle fleet steadily swam off to war.

Poseidon, Amphitrite and the others watched them go in silence. Eventually Totty said: "No matter what the outcome of the battle is, it will only be a victory if Suki lives."

"Wise words, Miss Totty," Hashimoto replied.

"Suki will live," Amphitrite added. "Moby and Bettina will make sure she does."

"And so will we," Poseidon muttered.

•

Sergeant MacGobo was supervising the troops as they came out of Mildendo's West Gate and marched up the ramp onto the big person's chariot. He was having a lot of trouble with one new recruit who had caused him considerable frustration the whole morning.

"Private!" he shouted. "I is going to ask you one final time – is you a man or is you a woman?"

"Well, I'm neither," was the reply.

"Don't you get smart with me, you 'orrible piece of cow's intestines! You is either a man or a woman; so what is you?"

"I keep----"

"Private!" MacGobo screeched. "You is only allowed to speak two words – man or woman. What is you?"

The private didn't answer.

"Answer me!" the sergeant shouted after a few seconds of silence. There was still no answer, so MacGobo tried a different tactic. "Is you a woman?" he demanded.

"No," was the swift reply.

"Right; that means you is a man!" was the equally swift response from MacGobo, who was now able to complete another box on his form which had to be filled in for all new recruits.

MacGobo now studied the private standing in front of him. He didn't like what he saw.

"Stand up straight!" he suddenly bawled. "Shoulders back! Stomach in! Chest in front! Face looking straight ahead! Do it…. now!!!"

The new recruit quickly made a series of body movements to comply with MacGobo's demands. Unfortunately, he was still not satisfied.

"What is you smiling about?" he shouted.

"I'm not, Sarge," was the ill-considered reply.

"What! What! You dare to argue with me, Private! You dare to disagree with me! If I say you is smiling, you is smiling. You do not argue with me, you piece of crocodile's bladder. Do I make myself clear, Private?"

"Yes, Sarge."

"What!" MacGobo screeched. "What did you say?"

"I said 'yes, Sarge.'"

"Sarge! Sarge! You do not call me Sarge! You say, either 'yes, Sergeant' or 'yes, sir.' We do not use abbreviations in the army. I do not refer to you as 'Privy'; I call you Private. Do you understand?"

"Yes, Sergeant."

"Good," MacGobo replied. "Something has at least got through into that thick skull of yours, hasn't it?" The sergeant waited for a reply which didn't come.

"Answer me!" he shouted.

"Answer what?" the confused recruit asked.

"Answer my question!"

"I'm sorry, Sarge, I don't-----"

"What! What did you call me? Did I hear you call me Sarge again? Did I, you 'orrible little man? Did I?"

By now MacGobo was seething with anger, his face having turned purple.

"Sorry, sir. My mistake, sir. Very nervous on my first day. Very sorry."

The sergeant breathed out slowly as he looked at the private. "You is a creep, isn't you, Private?" he eventually said. "A creep."

"Yes, sir," the recruit answered, thinking it best to agree with everything the sergeant said.

"That's better," MacGobo responded. "I want you to be a creep. Yes, a creep, but you is also a 'orrible little man, isn't you?"

"Yes, sir."

"Yes, sir, what?" the sergeant shouted. "What is you? Tell me, Private!"

"A 'orrible little man, sir."

"And what else?"

The private looked confused. "I'm not sure I understand, Sergeant?"

"I said, what else is you? Isn't you also a creep?"

"Yes, sir," was the swift response.

"Good! You is learning, Private. You and I both agree you is a creep and a 'orrible little man. Why is you a creep and a 'orrible little man, Private? Answer me."

"Because I am, sir."

"That's right; you definitely is. But there's more than that, isn't there?"

"Yes, sir."

"Good again. And tell me, Private, what is this 'more' we both agree on?"

"Not sure," was the reply. "I said it because I wanted to agree with you, sir."

The sergeant gave a little laugh. "You really is learning," he said. "Yes, you really is. The reason you is both a creep and a 'orrible little man is not just because you is, but also because I say you is. Is that not right, Private?"

"Yes, sir."

"Yes, sir. Even better. You is beginning to understand that you is in the army now and in the army, everything I say is right. Isn't it, Private?"

"Yes, sir."

"Even when I is wrong."

"Yes, sir."

The two looked at each other, the sergeant giving a smile, which the private reciprocated."

Suddenly, MacGobo ceased smiling and erupted. "Get that smile wiped off your face, you piece of skunk's liver!" he screamed. "And stand up straight! Shoulders back! Stomach in! Chest in front! Don't you ever smile at me again, Private! Is that understood?"

"Yes, sir," the new recruit answered, quickly straightening up.

The sergeant stared at the private for a full thirty seconds, waiting for the slightest sign of a smile. When none was forthcoming, he looked at his form and continued: "Right. We have to fill in some more information about you. Tell me your name again, Private."

"MacHebe, sir"

"That is right. That is what I has on this form. We is making progress at last, isn't we?"

"Yes, sir."

"Good, MacHebe. Very good. Now I want you to show me your driving licence for this 'ere vehicle of yours, together with its MOT and insurance documentation."

The private was perplexed. "I don't have any of those documents, sir," was the response.

"What! What!" MacGobo screeched. "Why has you not got them, you vile piece of hyena's testicle? Why has you not got them?"

"I've never required them before, sir."

"Well, you bloody well require them now, Private! Do you think I is going to let an unqualified driver transport the finest regiment in the whole of Lilliput to foreign lands in an uninsured, unsafe vehicle? Do you?"

"Not sure, sir."

"You is not sure! You is not sure. Why is you not sure?"

"Because I don't know the answer to your question, sir?"

"Why not?" the sergeant barked.

"Because you has not told it to me. I only know what you has told me, sir."

"That is because you has not a brain of your own, MacHebe. You is bloody useless, isn't you?"

"Yes, sir."

"Yes what?"

"Yes, I is bloody useless because I has not a brain of my own."

The sergeant gave Private MacHebe a mean angry look, as he contemplated what to say next.

"Permission to ask a question, Sergeant?" the private asked after a few seconds of silence.

"What?" growled MacGobo.

"Will you be telling the troops to disembark from the chariot; it being an uninsured, unsafe vehicle with an unqualified driver?" Then suddenly remembering to finish the question properly, MacHebe added "sir."

The sergeant's face turned crimson again and he was just about to scream at the private when he became aware of footsteps behind him. Colonel MacPonsibl had just climbed the ladder to the platform on which the sergeant was standing so he could eyeball MacHebe."

"Is all going well, MacGobo?" the colonel asked in an amiable voice.

"Yes, sir," Sergeant MacGobo answered at the same time as he and Private MacHebe saluted.

"Splendid. Is the new recruit shaping up well?"

"Very well, sir. I is getting this young whippersnapper into shape. I can guarantee that Private MacHebe will very soon be the pride of the regiment. Absolutely assured, I is."

"Well done, Sergeant," and then looking at MacHebe the colonel added: "Well done, Private."

"Thank you, sir," the whippersnapper answered and gave another salute.

"Will we be ready to leave within the hour, Sergeant?" the colonel asked, turning back to MacGobo.

"Definitely, Colonel."

"And is the chariot going to be alright for the journey?"

"We has got a fine vehicle for our troops, sir. I has also just confirmed that Private MacHebe is a very experienced driver."

"Talking of Private MacHebe, when you've finished with her, could you please release her for a while. There's a very important visitor just over there," and the colonel pointed to a person about fifteen yards away, "who would like to speak to her."

"You mean 'him', sir. I has ascertained that Private MacHebe is of the manly persuasion."

The colonel looked at MacHebe and gave her a knowing smile. "Is that right, Private?"

"Yes, sir," the private answered with a straight face. "That is what Sergeant MacGobo has ascertained."

"Well, I won't argue the point," Colonel MacPonsibl responded, still smiling before again looking at the sergeant. "Anyway, MacGobo, to go back to my original question about releasing Private MacHebe for a while, when do you think you will be finished?"

"The private can go now, sir. We has covered everything and MacHebe has passed with flying colours. A very fine recruit; very fine indeed."

"Good," the colonel replied. "Please go and see your visitor, Private."

"Yes, sir. Thank you, sir," Private MacHebe said before saluting the two men on the platform and starting to move away.

"And do not forget," the sergeant's loud voice shouted out after the new recruit: "Shoulders back! Stomach in! Chest in front! Face looking straight ahead! Quick march!"

Private MacHebe did as instructed and marched to a small hillock nearby on which Athene was sitting, from where she had been observing her half-sister's induction into the Lilliputian Army.

"Reporting for duty, ma'am," MacHebe said, saluting and standing to attention when she arrived at the hillock.

Athene gave her a big smile. "Come and sit down here next to me, Hebe," she said, patting the grass to her right.

"I can't, ma'am. I has not been told to stand at ease. I has to follow orders. I is in the army now."

Athene got up, walked over to the platform from which Sergeant MacGobo had just descended. She bent down and had a few words with him before she turned round and started walking back, followed by the sergeant who was marching at the double.

"Private!" he shouted when he reached the two goddesses. "Stand at ease!"

"Thank you, sir," MacHebe answered and gave him a salute.

"And can Private MacHebe please come and sit next to me, Sergeant?" Athene asked.

"Certainly, ma'am," MacGobo answered, before turning to the private and shouting: "MacHebe, go and sit next to Lady Athene! That is an order! Understand?"

"Yes, sir," Private MacHebe replied, saluting again before going to sit next to her sister. The sergeant then saluted back, followed by multiple salutes to Athene before marching back to the rest of the troops.

"So, what have you been up to the last few days?" Athene asked. "I've been back to Olympus twice since I saw you in the Underworld and there's been no sign of you."

"I did go back briefly, but then decided to visit the cavern again to help Dolores and the maids. They've got so much work still to do clearing up the mess."

"I know. It's just like here. Your friend Totty seems to have been organizing the clearance effort on Lilliput."

"She's a good girl is Totty. I only saw her yesterday for a short time because I spent much of the morning having to persuade Uncle Posy and the Empress to let me join the army. It was actually General Goblin who was all in favour because I have a chariot. It was the only way he could see how he could get his troops to Tyrantland now the navy's been destroyed. Posy and Amphy's chariot isn't large enough."

"Isn't it General Golroblin?"

"Yea, but I call him Goblin."

"So, you decided to sign up as a private. Couldn't you have been an officer?"

"I wanted to start at the bottom and be treated like everyone else. That's where the action is. Anyway, I'm now Private MacHebe of the Argyll and Sutherland Highlanders. Specifically, I'm part of the logistics team, responsible for driving the Regiment's chariot which has been commandeered for military reasons."

"Is that why you're wearing a kilt like all the other soldiers?"

"Sure is. I knew I wanted to be a Highlander, so after leaving the cavern I quickly called in at Olympus to pick up this kilt in my wardrobe as well as Lennie and Beetle."

"I saw Lennie flying around yesterday evening when I arrived. Poseidon told me you'd brought them, but he's not sure why."

"Neither am I yet, but I've got a hunch Lennie could be useful as a lookout or something."

Athene nodded her head. "How did you get them to come?"

"Bacchus wasn't keen, but Nell was all in favour when she knew we were going into battle against Mars. Once her frying pan was brought out, Bacchus quickly agreed. Lennie was persuaded by the prospect of meeting a load of new people who might sign his petition. He's already got Posy's and Amphy's signatures, as well as Totty's and Hash's plus half the Cabinet's. As you know, where Lennie goes, Beetle follows. He's actually proving very useful; he's in the chariot now making sure that all the troops are safely seated for the journey. It's a change for him to meet people of about his size."

"Are the two of them enlisted in the Regiment as well?"

"They're in the Special Forces section, but we're all ultimately under the command of Sweetie Pie."

"Who's Sweetie Pie?"

"Colonel MacPonsibl. I quite fancy him as far as little people go. It's why I was determined to become a Highlander because I knew it was his regiment. Anyway, enough about me, Athy, what have you been up to?"

Athene sighed before answering. "Trying to deal with this mess. I saw Poseidon and Amphitrite when they returned here. They and Lilliput have decided to go to war with Mars and Tyrantland. Our uncle was all in favour of sending a massive tidal wave over the whole country, but Amphy and the Empress were completely against it-----"

"Why?" Hebe asked. "It seems like a good idea. Mars would have got a good soaking."

"Too many innocent people would be killed. Also, the Sea Creatures want to have a fight because they've experienced huge losses and want revenge. Just drowning everyone with a tidal wave would be too quick."

"That's why everyone's gone to the east coast now, isn't it? There's a battle fleet of whales setting off, led by Moby."

Athene nodded. "Did Poseidon tell you yesterday?"

191

"No; but we soldiers know everything. I was sleeping in the open near the barracks last night and heard a lot of gossip. So, Tyrantland's going to be attacked from the sea and we Highlanders are about to leave for a land attack. Anything else?"

"Cyberattacks on their systems, a misinformation campaign. That sort of thing."

"Very modern. Mars won't know how to deal with that."

"No," Athene agreed.

"Talking of Mars, has Iris seen the stupid pig yet?"

"Yes. She found him in the Tyrant's palace. Apparently, the two of them have created this all-powerful missile which is what caused the Great Wave and all the devastation."

Athene had received a verbatim account from Iris of her conversation with Mars, which she proceeded to repeat to Hebe.

"Phew!" Hebe said when Athene had finished. "How did Mother and Father respond to all that."

"Firstly, Iris and I didn't go into all the details. We decided to see Zeus and Hera together and spent a whole day beforehand working out what to say and what direction we wanted them to take. In simple terms, we explained that Mars wanted more independence and wasn't prepared any longer to submit all his conflicts for approval to the Gods' Council. We specifically left out all the stuff about Zeus and his brothers being past it and it's important you don't mention it."

"Why?"

"Because Zeus would go mad and mess up the end game."

"Which is?"

"That Mars and Poseidon have to have this war. They have to settle matters between themselves. If Zeus interfered now, he would only be postponing a massive fight between them in the future, even if it's a thousand years off. The scene's set, so let them get on with it, instead of allowing matters to fester."

"You're not telling me Father agreed to that."

"I won't go through all the debate, but eventually he did, principally because Hera finally took our side. It took a whole day, but Zeus was finally persuaded not to go charging off to Tyrantland to confront Mars. Instead, it was agreed that Heph and Iris would go, which they did but got nowhere. After that it was decided that I would stay close to Poseidon and Iris would call in on Mars from time to time, although he did shout at her never to come back when she and Heph left. Anyway, she's gone off to find Artemis and Herm first before returning to Tyrantland.

"But what about the rest of us gods and goddesses, Athy? I'm on Uncle Posy's side and am going off to fight. Is Father saying we're not allowed to?"

"No; he accepts it will be like Troy with us all taking sides. He and Hera are the only ones who are likely to stay neutral. It's brother against son for them."

"We said it before; everyone else is going to be on Uncle Posy's side."

"I agree, including Iris and me, but we won't be joining the army like you."

"What about Famine? What are we going to do about him?"

"I don't know yet," Athene replied. "At least we know where he is for now."

The two goddesses suddenly became aware that Sergeant MacGobo was standing in front of them. He saluted before addressing the Goddess of Wisdom.

"Excuse me for disturbing you, Lady Athene," he said. "But has you finished yet with Private MacHebe and, if so, might I be allowed to address him?"

"Yes, of course, Sergeant. Private MacHebe is all yours."

"Thank you, My Lady," MacGobo replied, saluting her again before directing his attention at the private and shouting:

"Get off your backside, MacHebe! You is 'olding everyone up. We is ready to go, so move it you 'orrible piece of rhinoceros inner ear. Stand up straight! Shoulders back! Stomach in! Chest in front! Face looking straight ahead! Quick march!"

MacHebe quickly did as instructed, saluted Athene as well as the sergeant before setting off back to her chariot.

"And do not forget to check your 'orses has been properly fed and watered before we leave! You has ten minutes to do that and get them properly saddled up; do you 'ear?"

"I did all that earlier, Sergeant," the private responded.

"Do not answer me back, Private!" MacGobo screamed. "I do not want to 'ear what you has to say. But since I has done so, my order still stands. Do it again!"

"Yes, sir," Private MacHebe said, now moving at the double.

•

On a mountainside far away, the God of War and the Tyrant were sitting in a secret military facility. They were in a room full of screens with dozens of scientists on their knees who were working away on their computers.

"Press the button!" Mars shouted at the Tyrant who was sitting at a desk with a large red button in front of him. "We're days late with this second missile. Just do it - now!"

The Tyrant looked at the facility's three senior men who were kneeling a few feet to his right. "You scumbags are certain it's ready to go?"

The three men all nodded and said "Yes, Oh Great One," in unison. The Tyrant's fat right hand moved forward, and he hit the red button.

Back on Lilliput, all members of the Special Projects team had been at work for several hours. Shortly before the Tyrant pressed his red button, a small, young lady with multi-coloured hair, large gold earrings and tattooed arms also pressed a button on her keyboard. She then got up, smiled and called out to everyone that it was time for a break.

15
Advice on Naming Pigs

Segolongsunugolywalgonisumcholbultyasfogquerlogmun-pong was generally known as 'Stevie' for a number of reasons, principally to do with the fact that it was much shorter than her full name.

Aged 165, Stevie was the oldest living person in the world. Occasionally, people disputed this matter, but they were always stumped when asked to prove the age of anyone older. No one nowadays seemed inclined to ask Stevie to prove her age. Apparently, a few people had done so in the distant past, but they had always come unstuck when she demanded that they should first present her with full details of any alleged older person, together with clear documentary proof of their age.

There had once been a Mr Stevie, but his wife had mislaid him more than 140 years ago. She wasn't sure where she had put him and had given up looking a long time ago. She seemed to remember that he was born six months before her, so finding him alive would mean she would have to give up her crown of being the oldest person in the world. In view of this, she felt there was no real incentive to find him.

Stevie had been working for the Tyrant family from the age of sixteen. She had fulfilled just about every role for them over that time, including maid, cleaner, nanny, governess, chef, female footman, maintenance assistant and much more. However, for the last 120 years she had been the informal head of household, which meant she could get involved in anything she wanted to.

One particular role which she had been tasked with over the generations was introducing the younger members of the family, at an appropriate age, to the more physical or sensual aspects of life. This applied to both the boys and the girls. After the 'last group', she decided that she would retire from this particular responsibility and hand over the task to her niece, Olbigogupfibquugol…. (I give up - she's known as 'Nora'). Although Stevie was concerned that Nora, who was only 129, was a bit on the young side she felt that with a little tuition she would be able to handle the junior members of the family when the time came.

Although Stevie had been working for the Tyrants since she was a young girl, she didn't like the family much – to be more precise, she hated the men, but was rather fond of the female side of the family. When she was nanny to the children, she always tried to teach them things like kindness, consideration for others, even humility. This lasted until the age of about six for the boys when they were snatched from her care and their education was overseen by their fathers. They quickly learned that the only way to keep living in a great big palace with every luxury was to behave like evil, vicious bastards, which was precisely what they all became.

One final point to note about Stevie was that she did not have to shuffle around on her knees when she was in the Tyrant's presence. This had nothing to do with age or respect for a long-standing family retainer but was entirely due to the Tyrant being a bit scared of her. Like all bullies, the Tyrant lived in fear of a small group of people, in his case headed up by Stevie and Mars in that order.

Stevie was doing some dusting in the family's large living room when the telephone rang.

"Tyrantville 001," she said, picking up the receiver.

"I demand to speak to the Tyrant," said the voice on the other end of the line.

"I'm very sorry, but he's out of town at present. He should be back later today."

"He is to be found now and he must speak to me now," the officious voice said.

"He can't. As I said, he's not here. He's somewhere in the mountains."

"He is to be brought to the phone now. I insist on speaking to him now!"

Stevie sighed. The people that the Tyrant dealt with were just not her sort of people. She bet this sort of call wouldn't take place to Buckingham Palace. It was time for her to be a little more assertive.

"I don't think I'm getting through to you," Stevie said in a firm voice. "The Tyrant isn't here at present and it's not possible to communicate with him until he returns. To repeat, he should be back later in the day, so I suggest you phone again after 6 this evening."

"But I must speak to him now! I demand he be put on the phone immediately!"

"Who are you, sir?" Stevie demanded in return, becoming exasperated herself.

"I am phoning on behalf of Big Dik. I have a very important message to give to the Tyrant from Big Dik. The Tyrant must hear it immediately! Immediately, I repeat!"

"Please tell me what it is, and I'll pass it on to the Tyrant when he gets back."

"It is for me to give to the Tyrant," the voice said. "Big Dik is very, very, very angry."

"I'm very sorry to hear that," Stevie replied. "But you have a choice, Mr Messenger from Big Dik. Either you give the message to me now or you phone back after 6 when the Tyrant should have returned. You decide."

"But I must speak to him now!"

"Listen, Mr Stupid, Thick Messenger from Big Dik! I keep telling you that the Tyrant isn't here to speak to you. I've given you two options; you don't have any more. Choose both of them, if you like. Tell me why Big Dik is angry or phone back after 6 to give the Tyrant the message yourself. What's it to be?"

There was a silence for a while on the other end of the phone before the voice eventually said: "Are you sure I can't speak to the Tyrant now?"

"Quite sure," Stevie replied crisply. "Please tell me in confidence why Big Dik is very angry."

"I said very, very, very angry."

"I apologize. I did not mean to downgrade the seriousness of Big Dik's anger. However many very, verys there are, will you please tell me what the cause of this anger is?"

There was another silence before the voice said. "Very well, but you must keep it entirely confidential. You must only tell the Tyrant; no one else. Do you agree?"

"Yes."

"Then I will inform you. Yesterday, Tyrantland fired a missile which landed on Diktatorland. Not only was it a vile, ruthless attack on our country, but it hit Big Dik's private estate in the countryside. This is the estate where he breeds prize pigs and his great pride and joy, his favourite pig, who went by the name of Long Life was killed. That is why he is very, very, very angry. Long Life is gone; he is no more."

"I really am very sorry," Stevie replied. "Is there nothing left of Long Life? I know Big Dik is very partial to pork. Are you able to make pork chops or sausages out of what's left?"

"There's nothing left!" the voice said. "Long Life has been scattered into a million pieces."

"Oh dear. What about the other pigs?"

"His number two favourite pig, Long Life's partner, has also been scattered into a million pieces. As you can understand, this has added to Big Dik's great anger."

"I do understand," Stevie replied in a conciliatory voice. "Clearly, it wasn't a good day yesterday to be a pig on Big Dik's estate. Did Long Life's partner have a name by any chance?"

"She was called Lucky."

"Oh dear!" Stevie said and then put her hand over the phone, so the voice couldn't hear her giggle. When she was sufficiently under control, she continued: "What very unfortunate names Big Dik gave his pigs – Long Life and Lucky. Neither name turned out to be very appropriate."

198

The voice gave a tiny laugh, suggesting some degree of humanity. "I agree," he replied, followed by another small laugh.

"Perhaps you should suggest to Big Dik that he doesn't tempt fate from now onwards. Names like Luck of the Draw or even Future Unknown might be better."

"I agree," the voice said again.

"Anyway, getting back to the unfortunate demise of the pigs, I will certainly tell the Tyrant as soon as he gets back. However, let me assure you, it wasn't done deliberately. Something must have gone wrong with the missile. I'm certain the Tyrant is very sorry as we all are in Tyrantland."

"There is more."

"Not any more pigs, I hope?"

"No. There is more to the message from Big Dik. So very, very, very angry is he at this attack on our country that he has ordered our nuclear missiles to be aimed at Tyrantland. If he does not receive a satisfactory explanation from the Tyrant by tomorrow midday, together with a groveling apology and an offer of full reparations, then 5,127 nuclear missiles will be fired at once at your country. I do not think you will like that."

"Oh dear, I think you're right – we definitely won't like that. Is there any reason, by the way, why the number of 5,127 has been chosen?"

"It is all we have."

"That sounds logical. Right, Mr Messenger, I'll pass all that on to the Tyrant. Will you phone back after 6pm?"

"I will. One final matter, could you please give me your name?"

"Stevie."

There was silence on the end of the phone before the voice came back hesitatingly: "Stevie, you say? Are you the Stevie who has been there for many years?"

"I am. Do we know each other?"

"Um; you… um… won't remember me. I'm Number Two."

"Number Two!" Stevie exclaimed with pleasure in her voice. "You're Little Dik! Of course, I remember you, my dear. You and Big Dik came here for a holiday every summer from when you were both six or seven years old until you were teenagers. You came with your fathers, Big Dik Senior and Little Dik Senior. Now you're second in command of your great big country. You've done well."

"Yes, I am Number Two."

"Is that what I'm meant to call you – Number Two instead of Little Dik?"

"Officially, I'm called Little Dik, but I prefer to be called Number Two."

"Then, that's what I'll call you, my dear. Although you've done well as I said, I thought you were going to play football for Real Madrid."

"That is what I wanted, but my parents directed me towards being Number Two."

"But you were so good at football; much better than Big Dik Junior when you were here."

"I know, but I was not allowed to continue with my football career."

"Shame; you were always talking about being Number Nine for Real Madrid, but you've ended up as Number Two for Diktatorland."

"I agree, Stevie, a great shame, but officially I'm not allowed to say so, so please don't repeat what I said to anyone."

"I understand; we have rules about what you can and can't say in Tyrantland as well. It's best to be discreet. You can rely on me."

"Tell me, Stevie, how are you getting on? I gather that there's no sign yet of an heir for you to nanny. You always said being a nanny was the best part of your job."

"Regrettably, Number Two, there's no heir. The Tyrant's now on his third wife. He gives each one about five years to produce children; if they don't succeed, they get replaced by another one and so it goes on."

"What happens to the replaced wives?"

"They get sent off to the firing range. Poor wee mites. They're all so young when they marry. None of his wives have any say in the matter. If you're chosen, you have to become Mrs Tyrant; the alternative is for you and your whole family to be immediately put in front of the cannons. At least if they marry, they get an extra five years of life."

"Very nasty," said Number Two. "I don't know the Tyrant well, but I can believe he's a bit of a ….. I'm sorry, I'm looking for a diplomatic word."

"The word's vile bastard. I know that's two words, but that's the best description."

"I understand."

"What's even worse is that I suspect it's not their fault they can't have children. I'm pretty sure it's him. It's his reproductive system which is at fault. That's my view."

"Has he seen a doctor?"

"The first one he saw on the matter was after two years of marriage to his second wife. The doctor said it was down to him, not his young wife. As a reward for being professional and honest, he got sent to the firing range. From time to time, he checks again with new doctors and, not surprisingly, they all say he's in perfect condition. He then takes their reports to his wife and blames her."

"Not nice. Tell me, how are his sisters and his mother?"

"His mother's dead. She got sent to the salt mines with Little Sis, who's still alive we gather. Big Sis is here."

"I'm shocked!" Number Two said. "Why did they get sent to the salt mines?"

"Because we have some stupid rule that when you're in the presence of the Tyrant you have to be on your knees all the time. The family refused to comply, so the mother and Little Sis were punished. He normally sends people to the firing range, but since they were family, he decided to be generous and only send them to the salt mines, which normally finishes you off within a year. Fortunately, Little Sis survives. I think it's because Big Sis somehow ensures she gets favorable treatment."

"So, I assume Big Sis goes around on her knees if she's not in the mines?" Number Two asked. "And presumably you do as well, Stevie?"

"I don't and neither does Big Sis. It's complicated, but the Tyrant's always been a bit scared of Big Sis and me, so he decided to pick on the weaker members of the household."

"He does sound a vile bastard, between you and me. What does Big Sis do now? I remember she was a brainy kid."

"Both the girls are, whereas I'm not sure if the Tyrant has any brain cells at all. If Big Sis were running the country, it would be a much better place, but she and her brother don't see eye to eye on matters, so he keeps her out of the government. She spends all her time running charities she's set up to help the poor, but what she'd like to do long-term is return to Harvard and complete her PhD."

"I wish her well," Number Two said. "Look, Stevie, I must go now for a meeting with Big Dik. Can you please make sure the Tyrant gets the message? I'll also phone back at 6pm."

"Nice talking to you as well, Number Two. Could I ask a final question? Will Big Dik really fire 5,127 missiles at us if the Tyrant doesn't do all this groveling."

"Oh yes," was the crisp response. "If I were you, I'd get out of the country for a while, Stevie."

"I think I'll take my chances. One final thing you should know is that Lord Mars is staying with us at the moment. I don't think he'll take too kindly to having 5,127 nuclear missiles dropped on his head."

"Umm," Number Two went. "Thanks for telling me. I'll let Big Dik know. That could be a complication."

"I'll leave it to you, Number Two. Bye."

After the telephone call, Stevie wrote a long note for the Tyrant, marked 'URGENT' and left it on his desk. She then decided that she could do with a change of scenery for an hour or two, so she went into the town to visit some of her nephews.

The nephews she was visiting were aged between their mid-20's and mid-40's, so they were not strictly speaking nephews, but more like sons of sons of nephews of sons. You get the idea – they were family. She normally found a number of them at The Tyrant Public House which was run by her nephew Ob. Like everything else in Tyrantland, this pub was the property of the state, which meant the Tyrant, who had granted a lease to Ob to operate it. There was only one beer officially for sale called Tyrant Ale which was produced by the state brewery. Tyrant Ale was heavily diluted by the brewery, making it deeply unpopular as it tasted like dishwater. In view of this, Ob had set up a micro-brewery in the pub's basement where the excellent Ob Ale was produced. This entrepreneurial activity, if ever officially identified by the authorities, would undoubtedly result in Ob being sent off to the firing range to stand in front of a cannon. However, he found that giving free pints to all the city's guardsmen on their rounds resulted in no official inspections ever taking place.

The Tyrant pub was also the centre of the resistance movement in Tyrantville. In order to 'outfox' the authorities the movement was itself called the Tyrant. This apparently stood for Tyranical, Yodeling, Revolutionary, Anarchistic, Nihilistic Terrors. Stevie, who was an unofficial member of this group, had never been happy with its name, especially the relevance of 'yodeling'. Ob had admitted to his aunt that they hadn't been able to find a revolutionary type of word beginning with 'y', so yodeling had been included as a temporary measure until they could find a better word.

The Tyrants were very good at discussing resistance and revolution but were not much good at doing it. In the last five years, their only success had been letting the air out of the tyres of a plumber's bicycle, who was visiting the palace to clear a blocked drain. Since the plumber happened to be Ob's next-door neighbour and best friend, this success was not boasted about to any great extent.

Ob had recently acquired a book about the French Revolution written by a Mr Charles Dickens. He was very impressed with this book and had agreed with two of his fellow nephews, Ub and Eb, that they would start building a guillotine for use on the Tyrant and other members of the elite when the revolution came. He also noted that fellow revolutionaries in the book didn't use their real names, but instead called each other Jacques. This policy had recently been introduced in his pub, so everyone who was a Tyrant was called Jacques. Ob was convinced that this was another scheme to outfox the authorities. Stevie was not entirely sure about this; she found that whenever she was inquiring about various family members, she now had to call them all Jacques since every one of them was enlisted as a Tyrant. This meant that valuable time was spent identifying which Jacques they were talking about. Hints such as 'the one who lives down Cauliflower Street' or 'the mother-in-law of the Jacques we were last talking about' formed the basis of this identification.

Stevie was sipping her half pint of Ob Ale, talking to three Jacques about various other family members - all called Jacques - when there was a sudden blaring of trumpets. Everyone stopped talking and looked at the television screen in the far corner of the room. This television was permanently on to allow all the Tyrants who were called Jacques to monitor the news about the Tyrant.

The screen had turned blank when the trumpets sounded, but soon afterwards the following words were seen:

MESSAGE FROM THE TYRANT

After a few seconds a new set of words appeared:

LISTEN SCUMBAGS

These words were then replaced on the screen with a cartoon figure of the Tyrant. He was a grossly overweight, little, fat man, wearing a golden cloak and sitting on a throne made of diamonds, emeralds and rubies. The throne was surrounded by large stacks of dollar notes and gold bars. The

Tyrant's head had a large crown on top and his face was as shown by Rach to Totty: a big red nose, huge orange ears, fangs coming out of his mouth and horns protruding from the top of his head. He was smoking a large cigar and smiling maliciously.

The Tyrant suddenly disappeared and was replaced by the following words:

YOU WORK – I PLAY

The cartoon figure then returned to the sound of Abba playing "Money, Money, Money." About every fifteen seconds, it was replaced momentarily by:

I PLAY – YOU PAY

and then the Tyrant would return. This went on for the entire duration of the song at which point:

YOU WORK – I PLAY

was flashed across the screen, followed by:

I PLAY – YOU PAY

These two messages 'You Work – I Play' and 'I Play – You Pay' kept alternating every few seconds before the Tyrant's cartoon image reappeared. It then disappeared and was replaced by a new message:

MORE FOOL YOU

HA HA

Shortly afterwards, the Tyrant reappeared, making a large V sign directly to the audience. About ten seconds later, 'More Fool You – Ha Ha' reappeared before the screen went momentarily blank and then returned to the original news programme.

Everyone in the pub had watched the Tyrant's message in absolute silence. However, once it finished pandemonium broke out as people started shouting and waving their fists at the TV screen. Stevie, who had been standing next to Ob, looked at her nephew and said: "Oh dear; this means trouble. I'd better be getting back to the palace." She then left without waiting for a reply from her nephew.

16
The Bridge over the River Kwag

"Keep your blinkin 'ead down, Private," hissed Sergeant MacGobo. "It's the size of a bloody elephant's backside."

"Yes, Sergeant," Private MacHebe whispered back. "Permission to ask a question, sir?"

"What is it?"

"Would that be a Lilliput size or a big people's size elephant's backside?"

"You trying to be funny, Private?" growled MacGobo.

"No, sir."

"Then shut up."

"Yes, sir."

Colonel MacPonsibl, Sergeant MacGobo and Private MacHebe were lying on the ground at the top of the gorge, staring at the river several hundred feet below as well as the bridge to their right. Lennie and Beetle were also with the group; everyone trying to remain hidden.

"What do we see here?" the Colonel asked while looking through his binoculars.

"If the plan's to blow up the bridge, I doubt we has enough dynamite," MacGobo answered.

"I agree with you," Colonel MacPonsbl said. "None of us on Lilliput realised the size of that bridge. However, that's our objective - to take it down. It's the only crossing over the River Kwag which goes from coast to coast; it's the border between Tyrantland and Diktatorland. Without that bridge all trade is stopped by land between the two countries."

"Isn't they able to cross the river some other place?" the sergeant asked? "This steep gorge can't also go from coast to coast."

"It does. That's why taking the bridge down is so critical. Without it, Tyrantland's economy is buggered."

The group at the top of the gorge continued to study the river and the bridge. Eventually, MacGobo turned to Private MacHebe.

"Do you see anything, Private?"

"Yes, sir."

"What?"

"A large worm approaching my left eye."

"What the hell is you on about, you pathetic mouse brain?" the sergeant angrily asked, while still keeping his voice quiet.

"I is answering your question, Sergeant. You asked what I could see and I is telling you."

"I don't care about the worm. You is 'ere to look at the bridge and the river."

"Yes, sir; I understand, but you told me to keep my blinkin 'ead down and if I do that, I can't see the river and the bridge, can I?"

"Well, have a very careful look and make sure you're not seen. Only the top of your 'ead."

"Would that include me eyes, Sergeant?"

"Of course, you stupid idiot! Get on with it."

MacHebe had a quick look and then lowered her head. "I agree. We has not got enough dynamite. That's because we has Lilliput size dynamite, not big people's size dynamite."

"So, what do you suggest we do about it? Do you have any ideas Corporal MacLeonard and Private Beetle?" MacGobo asked?

Before they could answer, MacHebe intervened. "Hey!" she exclaimed. "How come Lennie's a corporal and I'm only a private? I wasn't told about that. It's not fair!"

"There is no bloody reason why a ferret's gall bladder of a private like you should know about it," the sergeant hissed. "You is not to question the decisions of your commanding officers. If they judge that MacLeonard should be a corporal and you stay as a lowly useless private, that is their decision. It has nothing to do with you. Understand, Private?"

"Well, it's not right," grumbled MacHebe. "You told the colonel I was shaping up very well; I would soon be the pride of the regiment. That meant I-----"

"You didn't believe all that nonsense, did you Private?" the sergeant interrupted. "I only said it to provide you with some motivation, you six-nosed pillock."

"Well, now you've completely demotivated me," MacHebe replied. "I don't think I want to fight any more."

"What!" screeched the sergeant before MacPonsibl touched him on the arm to indicate he should lower his voice. He continued more quietly: "If you refuse to fight, Private, you will be court-martialed and then shot! That is what we does to cowards like you!"

MacHebe didn't say anything, but Beetle had now walked over to her and looked her in the eyes. "Hebe," the tortoise said. "Do you have to be a private? Can't you just go back to being a goddess? You're a really good goddess and I'm not sure why you want to stop being one."

"Thanks, Beetle, but I intend to stay as an Argyll and Sutherland Highlander. What's more, I will get myself promoted to corporal one day and then I'll aim for sergeant afterwards."

"Does that mean you is going to fight, and we don't has to shoot you, Private?" the sergeant demanded.

"Looks like it."

"Then just say yes and don't forget the sergeant afterwards, you five-eyed porcupine."

"Yes, Sergeant," Hebe replied.

Colonel MacPonsibl had heard this entire conversation but had not intervened since his policy was always to let Sergeant MacGobo handle matters as he saw fit. This was justified by the fact that MacGobo normally ended up getting things right in his own sort of way. However, the Colonel was relieved that the proposal to shoot the Goddess Hebe had been avoided because he knew he would have to get involved in those circumstances. Instead, he wanted to focus on the task at hand.

"So, how are we going to bring this bridge down?" the colonel asked his small observation team.

"Excuse me, sir; I think I can help," the recently appointed Corporal MacLeonard said in the poshest voice he could muster."

"How's that, MacLeonard?"

"As Private MacHebe was coming into land in the field behind us, I decided it would be helpful if I surveyed the surrounding area. I spent more than an hour by myself in the air and saw a military establishment about five miles to the west. It's possible that such a place would have various munitions, including sticks of dynamite. We could try raiding it at night."

"Excellent, Corporal. Very well done. That's first-class initiative by you," Colonel MacPonsibl replied with a large smile on his face.

"It was actually Hebe who told Lennie to scout the area," MacBeetle piped up.

"Private!" hissed Sergeant MacGobo. "You is not to speak unless spoken to. That is an order! Understand?"

"You have no authority over Special Forces, Sergeant," MacBeetle replied haughtily.

"Come on, chaps," the colonel quickly said before MacGobo could respond. "No more bickering. We've got a possible solution to our problem. Well done everyone. Let's return to the rest of the troops now and work out a plan for raiding this establishment."

•

The Argyll and Sutherland Highlanders had set up camp in a forest about a mile away from the bridge. It was ideal cover in a remote area with no obvious sign of people living nearby. At about midnight, with a half moon and limited cloud, Private MacHebe led her four stallions and chariot out of the trees and set off in the air towards the military establishment. They arrived a few minutes later at the security fence and MacHebe, applying her goddess's powers, immediately placed a shield over them so they couldn't be seen or heard.

Colonel MacPonsibl and Sergeant MacGobo climbed down a ladder from the chariot and ran silently over to the fence between two watch towers. They were followed by MacHebe who carried MacBeetle with MacLeonard flying low at her side. At the fence the colonel took out his night binoculars and surveyed the establishment. He, the goddess and the eagle, who were both able to see in the dark, whispered to each other for a few minutes. They then all got up and silently moved back to the chariot where they continued their conversation.

A few hours earlier, Corporal MacLeonard with Private MacBeetle sitting on his neck, had carried out a further reconnaissance of the military establishment. The latest survey by the colonel and the others confirmed the layout on which the two Special Forces operatives had reported back, and the small group was able to quickly firm up on the draft plan they had been preparing as the evening progressed.

By the time they were ready for action 200 other Highlanders had climbed down from the chariot and the entire contingent moved forward in silence. The fence was not fortified against people of Lilliputian size, so they quickly found gaps to slip through. Half the troops followed the colonel into the base and ran as quietly as possible towards the side of a large hanger-sized building to their right. MacHebe and the Special Forces pair stayed behind with the remaining Highlanders.

When the troops had reached the side of the building, MacHebe nodded to MacLeonard who picked up MacBeetle with one of his claws, flapped his wings, took off and flew over the fence to join Colonel MacPonsibl and the others. He carefully put the tortoise down on the ground and returned to the other side of the fence. Nobody said a word, but the colonel and the Special Forces private looked at each other; MacPonsibl gave a thumbs up and MacBeetle began to walk round the side to the entrance at the front of the building.

It was quite a long walk for a tortoise to the entrance, but MacBeetle went at top tortoise speed. As he got nearer to his destination, he saw the two guards that he was expecting, both having a smoke and a good moan about their rations. They were clearly not expecting any problems that evening since there had never been anything out of the ordinary in the five years they had been guarding the same building.

"Good evening," MacBeetle said to them in the politest voice he could muster.

As expected, both guards reacted in shock, grabbing hold of their rifles and trying unsuccessfully to create sentences which only got as far as "what the…", "who the… " as they looked around for the source of this mysterious voice.

"Good evening, I said," MacBeetle repeated and then added: "I'm down here."

One guard bent down, bemused at the fact that a tortoise could talk. "Who are you?" he demanded aggressively. "What are you doing here?"

"I'm lost," MacBeetle replied with a smile. "I've been roaming around for weeks, eating nothing but grass. Could you tell me where I am, please?"

"You are in a military establishment! You should not be here! You are under arrest," and the guard pointed his gun at MacBeetle.

"Oh dear. I don't mean any harm."

While MacBeetle was engaging the first guard in conversation, the other guard was standing a few feet behind listening intently to what was being said. He was therefore unaware that MacLeonard was approaching him from the rear. The eagle was flying about seven feet in the air with Private MacHebe holding onto his claws. She dropped to the ground just behind the guard and put a hand round his face in which she was holding a cloth containing a powerful anesthetic; this almost instantaneously knocked him out. All this was done in total silence with the guard not having time to make any noise. As he fell to the ground, MacHebe leaped forward to the first guard who was interrogating the tortoise. At the last second, he became aware of a slight noise and began to turn round, only for his face to meet the same cloth soaked in anesthetic. A few seconds later, he had also slumped to the ground.

MacHebe stuffed the cloth in a plastic bag she was carrying, as she did with the gloves and medical mask which she took off. The eagle picked up the bag in one claw and MacBeetle in the other and flew back over the fence.

All the Highlanders now ran forward from the side of the building. Without anyone saying a word they got on with their prearranged tasks. About half the group began to tie up the two guards with string, having stuffed cloths into their mouths. The other half waited with the colonel and watched MacHebe pick up and hold Sergeant MacGobo so he could reach the lock to the door. The hanger was an old brick-built structure with two large wooden doors and a simple key lock between them. There was no sign of an alarm, which would have caused a change to the agreed plan.

The sergeant had brought his tool kit and within no more than two minutes there was a click as he opened the lock. The goddess pulled one of the doors, opening it a few inches to allow the colonel and most of the troops waiting with him to go inside; a small number remained outside as lookouts. MacHebe, still carrying the sergeant, followed and then pulled the door to but leaving a small gap of about six inches.

"Permission to ask a question, Sergeant?" she said as she put MacGobo down on the concrete floor.

"No!" was the hissed reply. After a few seconds as the two of them were walking towards the colonel, Sergeant MacGobo then said: "What do you want to know?"

"I was wondering, sir, if you was a crack safe-breaker before you was recruited to the army?" MacHebe asked, bending down to speak.

"Right!" MacGobo exploded, in the loudest most silent voice possible. "You is on a court-martial once this mission is completed! Understood?"

"What did I say wrong? I was just asking about your previous employment, you being so expert with locks."

"Everything you say is wrong! I've never 'ad a recruit like you, Private! You is worse than a cross-eyed ferret's kidney stone, you is! Now go and do some bloody work for once! We has a war to fight!"

"Yes, sir," MacHebe said, saluting before she moved over to where she could see the colonel.

The building was a large warehouse, which is what the Lilliputians had expected. The colonel and the troops were all shining their torches at row upon row of shelves. However, being very small torches, their light didn't shine very far. MacHebe pulled out her larger, more powerful torch and walked along the various rows reading the captions on the front of each shelf. On the second row she saw the word Dynamite; she smiled, pulled a box down and found it full of dynamite sticks. She raced back to Colonel MacPonsibl and indicated he should follow her. He gave her the thumbs up when he saw what she had found, and then he indicated to his troops that they should get to work.

The system had all been agreed beforehand and worked smoothly. MacHebe pulled a load of boxes off the shelves and opened them. Four Highlanders would then pick up each dynamite stick and carry it outside the warehouse and then to the fence. The dynamite was passed through to the soldiers waiting on the outside where similar teams would carry each stick to the chariot where it was loaded under the direction of MacBeetle.

Once the goddess had opened enough boxes she went outside the warehouse and helped the soldiers who were tying up the two guards who were still out cold. After this was completed, she dragged the two bodies into the building, taped over their mouths which already had cloth stuffed into them as a bit of added security, and then went back to see how the colonel and the others were getting on.

Within another half an hour, the Highlanders were finished. Those in the camp went through the various gaps in the fence and climbed onto the chariot. Private MacHebe closed the warehouse door, silently ran over to the fence where

MacLeonard was waiting to lift her over. Once she was in the chariot she took hold of the reins, shook them, and the stallions quickly became airborne as they set off on the next leg of the journey.

Colonel MacPonsibl was standing by himself on a ledge at the front of the chariot, allowing him to speak to MacHebe.

"Well, Lady Hebe," he said looking at his watch. "We're a few minutes ahead of schedule. Let's hope the second stage of our mission is just as successful."

There was no answer from the goddess, so the colonel repeated his words. "Do you hear me?" he finished up with.

"Yes, sir, but I only respond to the name of Private MacHebe," was the reply.

The colonel smiled and then continued: "Is it necessary for you to be a private, MacHebe? Wouldn't you do exactly the same for us if you just stayed as a goddess?"

"Probably," MacHebe answered. "But I want to do things properly. What if I'm taken prisoner by the other side? At least as an enlisted soldier, I'll be a prisoner under the Geneva Convention, which gives me certain rights."

"I don't think Tyrantland will pay any attention to the Geneva Convention, do you?"

"Possibly not, especially if they listen to my big brother, Mars. Still, I prefer to do it this way. It seems right, somehow."

"Very well, but if you change your mind, just let me know."

"Yes, sir." They continued in silence for a few minutes before the goddess asked who was going to drive the chariot on the next mission?

"What do you mean?" the colonel asked alarmed. "Surely you will, won't you?"

"I'd be happy to, sir, but I might be in prison or even shot."

"I don't understand," a confused MacPonsibl replied.

"It's just that Sergeant MacGobo has told me I'm going to be court-martialed when we get back to Lilliput. Assuming I'm found guilty, then I obviously won't be able to drive the chariot if I'm shot. I suppose if I go to prison instead, I could be let out on the days there's a mission, but I might be having a sickie because of the prison food."

The colonel smiled again. "We'll cross that bridge when we come to it," he said. "Talking of which, I can see from the moonlight we're nearly there."

The plan the Highlanders were working to involved tight deadlines. Colonel MacPonsibl had decided that the theft of dynamite had to be immediately followed by blowing up the bridge. This was because once the theft was identified, it was very likely that security around the bridge would be significantly increased since it was the only credible target in the area. This could result in it being impossible to successfully attack the bridge, meaning the mission would have to be aborted.

This plan had necessitated MacHebe carrying all the troops, who were not to be involved in the raid of the military establishment, to a spot near to the bridge as soon as it had gone dark. They disembarked carrying a mass of pulleys, ropes and other equipment. Many of them were wearing night goggles and they crept along the edge of the gorge to the bridge. Fortunately, the guard house was on the road some way back from the bridge with all the guards inside. At about half hour intervals one of them would come out, look around for a short while without moving more than a few yards and then return inside.

The bridge was supported by three large pillars sunk in the riverbed, one at either end and one in the middle. There was a two-track railway line on the bridge together with a single lane road on either side. The last train of the day crossed over from Diktatorland at 6pm and no cars were allowed to cross after that time until 6am. Just as with the military base, a casual approach appeared to be taken to security because nothing untoward had occurred at the bridge for many years.

The chariot came to rest at the same spot it had earlier in the night when it had delivered the first group of Highlanders. Everyone disembarked and waited while the colonel and Sergeant MacGobo hurried forward to the bridge to assess the situation. They returned in a few minutes, whispered their orders and everyone set to work once more carrying the dynamite sticks in silence to the spot where the bridge started to go over the gorge. This was right next to the first supporting pillar and in this area a series of ropes and pulleys had been erected at the side of the bridge. Each stick was carefully lowered to a platform which had been fortuitously built around the pillar about two thirds of the way down. There were several soldiers on the platform who collected the dynamite sticks and stacked them around the platform.

MacHebe had remained at the chariot helping to offload the dynamite. MacBeetle had little to do, but MacLeonard was able to carry sticks in his beak and claws and fly them down to the platform. All the work at the bridge had been carried out under the command of a young captain who was viewed as being a rising star in the regiment. However, when it came to attaching the long fuse to the dynamite, Sergeant MacGobo insisted on doing this himself. After all, it wasn't so long ago that the captain had been a young whippersnapper like Private MacHebe and, while the sergeant showed all due respect to him now that he was an officer, MacGobo still believed he was the best man for such an important task. The captain was perfectly happy with this, as was the colonel, so once all the dynamite was in position and the troops were returning to the chariot for a swift exit, Sergeant MacGobo was lowered on a pulley to the platform. He carefully attached the wire to the dynamite, ensuring that the long end hung over the platform ready to be lit. Having done this, he tugged on the rope, indicating he was ready to be pulled back up.

Sergeant MacGobo was a large man and this particular pulley and rope had been used continuously during the night. Unfortunately, the result of all this wear and tear was that the rope had become frayed. As the sergeant was about half-way up to safety, the rope snapped, and this was followed shortly afterwards by a splash in the water. Being a professional soldier and not wanting to jeopardize the mission, there was no shout or scream by MacGobo as he was swiftly carried away by the fast current.

Most of the Highlanders were now in the chariot, so did not see the sergeant's fall. However, Hebe had been watching the whole incident. She knew she was the only person who could save him. The question of whether she should went through her mind. After all, the sergeant had called her a 'orrible little man, a piece of skunks' liver, a six-eyed pillock, a piece of crocodile's bladder, a five-eyed porcupine' and many other unattractive things. He also had her up for a court-martial which could result in her being shot or sent to prison for a long time. On the other hand, he was only doing his job and she found him amusing but had to control herself so as not to laugh, or even smile, in his presence. Above all, however, the Goddess Hebe was one of the 'good guys.' She tried to do good, even if she messed up from time to time. She wouldn't mess up on this one!

Being a goddess, she was able to process all these thoughts in under half a second. She ran to the edge of the gorge and launched herself into the air as she half flew, and half dived into the river below. The water was exceptionally cold as she swam powerfully towards the tiny figure of Sergeant MacGobo in the distance. She caught up with him and lifted him above the water with her right hand. Just as she was about to swim towards the side of the gorge, Lennie appeared above her.

"I'll take him, Hebe," the eagle spoke.

"Thanks, Lennie," the goddess replied, letting him take hold of the sergeant in one of his claws.

"Now take my other claw."

"I can make it by myself."

"No," and Lennie took hold of one of Hebe's arms, flapped his powerful wings and pulled the two Highlanders to safety at the top of the gorge.

For the next few minutes there was a tremendous amount of activity by the chariot with Colonel MacPonsibl also trying to keep everyone as quiet as possible. It was initially feared that the sergeant had drowned, but one of the medical orderlies in the regiment got to work on his chest, and within a short while he was spluttering as he regained consciousness. Hebe applied her goddess's skills to dry herself swiftly and then went back to being Private MacHebe.

Once matters had settled down, everyone got on the chariot except for MacLeonard, who was carrying a torch in his beak which had been made for him by Totty and Hashimoto the previous day out of a fallen tree on Lilliput. After a nod from the colonel, MacHebe lit the torch and MacLeonard set off into the gorge. He flew towards the platform with the dynamite, saw the end of the fuse wire and lit it with the fiery torch. As soon as the eagle was sure the fuse was lit, he dropped the torch and then flew with all speed away from the bridge.

The chariot had also set off, getting as far away as was prudent. It was airborne and MacLeonard quickly joined MacHebe at the front together with the colonel. They circled the bridge from a distance waiting for the explosion. At first there was a small pop, then a larger bang, followed by more and more bangs in succession. Suddenly there was an immense fireball at the same time as a deafening noise which even rocked the chariot more than half a mile away. This was followed by further explosions and a large amount of smoke, so no one could see what was happening. Eventually, the smoke cleared away and the colonel and the goddess could see a large supporting pillar in the river, together with half the bridge floating downstream.

"Mission accomplished, Hebe," the colonel said. "Well done."

"MacHebe, sir," was the reply.

The colonel smiled. "Could you please put me into the main body of the chariot? I'd like to see how the sergeant's getting on."

"Yes, sir," and MacHebe put her superior officer down by her feet.

Sometime later, as they were about halfway back to Lilliput, the goddess felt something prodding at her left foot. She bent down and saw Sergeant MacGobo who indicated he'd like to be lifted up to the platform, so he could speak to MacHebe.

"Private," he said once he was in front of her. "I would like to thank you for your assistance with that spot of bother back there. You did your duty, you did."

"Thank you, sir," MacHebe replied. "Permission to ask a question?"

"Permission granted."

"Do you think I'll get a medal?"

"I very much doubt it. You was only doing your duty. Anyway, the regimental rule is that if you asks for something, you does not get it. That is the rule."

"Well, will I at least be let off my court-martial?"

"I doubt that too. Your assistance might be taken into account when sentencing occurs."

"Doesn't seem fair to me," MacHebe moaned. "What about a promotion then?"

"You hasn't been listening, Private, has you? I told you the rule is if you asks for something, you does not get it, didn't I?"

"So, if that's the rule, Sergeant, can I please have another court martial?"

"A second one? I'll see what I can do for you," the sergeant replied.

"Hey! I thought you said if someone asked for something they wouldn't get it. I just asked for a court-martial, but you're not applying the rule."

"There is always exceptions."

"I can't win, can I?"

"I see you is learning, Private. You is learning."

As he said this, Sergeant MacGobo gave Private MacHebe a broad smile. She smiled back at him and for once didn't get a good bollocking for doing so.

17
Zapped

The Tyrant and Mars were both standing up in the palace's study having a row.

"He's got to go!" the Tyrant shouted.

"Listen, squirt," Mars growled. "He's staying here with us!"

"But he can't. He's causing so many problems. There are daily reports from farmers about their crops being ruined. In some parts of the country there are floods, in others no rain. Now I've just heard of a plague of locusts. It's all caused by him!"

In saying this, the Tyrant pointed into the sitting room where Famine was lying on a couch, listening impassively to the conversation of which he was the subject.

"Belt up!"

"No, I won't!"

There was a silence for a few seconds as Mars stared menacingly at the Tyrant. He then swiftly moved forward a few steps, grabbed the small man by his tie and yanked him against his chest. The tie was pulled upwards, so the Tyrant was looking into the God of War's snarling face.

"What are you doing?" the Tyrant squeaked, now looking genuinely frightened. "I…. I…. can't breathe."

"If I tell you to belt up, you belt up, you pathetic little scumbag. Do you understand?"

The Tyrant, who was still being pulled by his tie nodded. "Yes…Yes…Of course," he managed to say.

Mars continued to snarl at him, before releasing his grip. "I don't want to hear any more from you about Mr F going away," he growled. "He stays here because I want him here."

"May I ask why?" the Tyrant inquired meekly.

"Because he's safe here. A number of my fellow gods are keen to get hold of him, which is why I want him near me. Even if it means ruining all Tyrantland's crops."

"Can't he control what he's doing?"

"No, he can't. Just being in a place causes things to go wrong with the crops."

"Lots of people will starve."

"So what? I don't care and you're such an evil little bastard, I'm surprised you do."

"No; I don't care either, but it has consequences. There'll be unrest and there might be an attempted revolt."

"Then smash it!" Mars shouted. "Round up all the known troublemakers and send them off to that firing range of yours. I thought you knew how to repress people. Since I've been here, you've been acting like a useless weakling. Look at how you groveled to Big Dik over the phone. Never ever apologise, you punk! Blame someone or something else!"

"Like what?"

"You could have said it was the wind that blew it off course."

The Tyrant frowned. He didn't think that excuse would have worked but thought it best not to argue with Mars.

"I'm really wondering if I should replace you with someone stronger."

"What do you mean?" the Tyrant asked looking scared.

"Precisely what I said! You've got to perform for me, Fatty. That last rocket was a failure. There are to be no more failures! Understand?"

The Tyrant coughed. "Of course. There won't be. All the scientists involved have been disciplined and a new team put in place," he said, trying to sound more confident than he felt.

"You're too soft on your failures. Just firing a cannon at them is no real punishment. Have you ever thought of impaling?"

"No. How does that work.?"

"Go and find some pleb and I'll show you. There are some techniques you can use to keep people alive and in agony for days on end. That's real punishment."

"If the next rocket misfires, I'll bring the scientists to you for impaling," the Tyrant said with an evil glint in his eyes. "I'd like to see someone being impaled."

"If the next rocket misfires, I might impale you," Mars said maliciously.

"But…. But…." The Tyrant started to stutter. "No!" he eventually shouted out. "We're meant to be on the same side, Mars. Have you ever thought that there must be a reason everything's suddenly going wrong?"

"Like what?"

"Too many things are happening at the same time. It could be Poseidon getting revenge for that first missile attack on his kingdom."

"Poseidon!" the God of War exclaimed. "Don't be such a fool! He only knows about fish and water. How the hell could he have made your rocket hit Big Dik's pig farm, you stupid moron?"

"He might have people working for him?"

"Think of another one! Poseidon's stayed locked away in his Sea Cavern for years. He doesn't know anyone. No, you big fat oaf, your problems are all because of you being too soft with your people. That last rocket of yours is down to useless bloody scientists, whereas that cartoon thing on that…. What's it called?"

"Television," the Tyrant answered.

"Yes, well whatever. That cartoon thing that makes a fool out of you, and that bridge which has been blown up, are both signs you've got a resistance movement in Tyrantland. I've told you what to do – round up every suspected troublemaker and execute them. Do it publicly so the population can watch. Once I've shown you how impaling works, you can have rows of these troublemakers with spikes through their backsides lining every street. That will make the rest of the scum behave."

"I still think one of the other gods is involved."

"I told you, they're not! Stop looking for excuses, you pathetic little git! Anyway, tell me when the next missile's going to be fired."

"In a few days' time."

"Is it going to be a really powerful one?"

"Possibly," the Tyrant said hesitatingly. "The new team of scientists are also trying to find out why the last rocket went off course."

"I want the powerful one," Mars growled, looking aggressively at the Tyrant. "Just do it and get it right this time, or you'll regret it. Understand?"

"Yes," was the croaky reply.

"One last thing. You'd better be aware that Mr P's expected here any day."

"Mr P! Pestilence!" the Tyrant screamed. "No! No!"

The God of War walked up to the Tyrant and stood a few inches away from the small fat man.

"What are you doing?"

The next instant a large powerful knee went into the Tyrant's groin. As he doubled-up in pain, Mars grabbed his head and pushed him firmly down; The Tyrant just toppled over, banging his head against the floor. The god spent no time reviewing his handiwork; instead, he just turned away and went to see Famine.

•

Totty stood up and walked around. She was stressed. She wished she hadn't agreed to do this, but Rach had insisted and so had Amphitrite. They were joined by just about everyone else who had an opinion, including the Empress and Totty's two friends in the Cabinet, Redrelok and Mandoselin. It was her idea and people thought she should see it through to completion, even though there were perfectly good news presenters for Lilliput TV who could have read the script that she and Rach had written together. Any one of them would have got it right first-time round, but Totty had already fluffed it six times with the recording being aborted on each occasion.

Hashimoto had been watching from the side. He was near the platform on which Chertassle was standing with the whole Cabinet and a number of dignitaries, all of whom wanted to watch Totty's performance. There was also a large crowd at the front looking upwards with Amphitrite standing behind them.

"Honourable Empress," Hashimoto said in a quiet voice after moving a few feet towards the platform and looking directly at Chertassle. "Could Hashimoto please have a private word with you?"

"Certainly, Hashimoto," she replied, moving towards him. "What is it?"

"A very private word, so no one else can hear."

"Perhaps you could help me down and we can go to a quiet spot over there," the Empress said, pointing to her left.

Hashimoto carefully took hold of Chertassle and carried her to the quiet spot. He put her down gently and then lay on the ground himself, so his face was directly opposite hers. When he had picked the Empress up there were a few murmurs of concern from the platform and crowd since Hashimoto's unfortunate comments about the teeny weenies were still remembered. However, for most people he had more than wiped the slate clean as every day he had helped the Lilliputians clear the devastation from the tidal wave. Indeed, he had now taken much of that responsibility away from Totty who was increasingly working with Rach on the war effort.

"Honourable Empress," Hashimoto now repeated in a quiet voice. "Hashimoto knows Totty better than anyone on Lilliput; he even knows her better than Lord Poseidon and Lady Amphitrite."

Chertassle nodded her acceptance of this point.

"Hashimoto would like to make a suggestion because Totty finding it very difficult doing this presentation. She keeps making a fail and each time it is causing her more and more upset. I think one of her big problems is not the words themselves, but the fact so many people are watching her. She is not used to making big performances in public and I think if we all left her alone with your granddaughter Rachel and her film team, Totty would find it much easier. That is what Hashimoto thinks."

The Empress smiled before saying: "I do believe Hashimoto is right. That's what we'll do then. I'll give the instructions straight away. Thank you."

Chertassle smiled again at Hashimoto and then walked over to the crowd. She spoke to the senior guard who was present and asked him to please disperse the crowd. She then went back to the platform where Hashimoto was waiting to lift her up. Once there, she told everyone to leave and go back to their normal work. Hash helped to lift some people down while the others climbed down the ladders at the side.

Amphitrite had moved over to try to give Totty some encouragement when Hashimoto joined them.

"What's all that about?" Totty asked, her face still looking strained.

"Everyone is going away," Hashimoto replied.

"But I've not done it yet."

"No matter. We must all get on and do our own things. You'll do it maybe next time or the time after or the time after that. It will get done when you're ready; maybe we'll all be shown it on Lilliput TV."

Totty frowned, but before she could say anything more, Amphitrite, quickly realising why everyone was asked to leave, said: "I think that's quite right. I must go and join Poseidon and the Special Projects team. Will you and Rach follow later, Totty?" There was a nod of the head, so the goddess continued. "Presumably you're leaving as well Hash?"

"I am. Must go to the north of the island where we still have a lot of work."

"Right. See you both later," and Amphitrite promptly turned round and walked off.

The Sea Goddess set off to the Science Institute. Since returning to Lilliput with Poseidon, she had got increasingly involved in what Rach and Totty were doing. In fact, she'd attached herself to their team, while making it clear that although she was a goddess she was not in charge, simply one of the workers. It had all been triggered by a conversation one evening over pizza with the two project leaders when she was telling them what the whales would be doing when they arrived at Tyrantland. Totty had asked Rach a question about whether her team could do something with ships and then ideas exploded all over the place for the next two hours.

The following morning, Rach had arrived at the huts on her flying scooter before anyone was up. She kept tooting away on her horn and made so much noise that the only way to quieten her down was for Amphitrite and Totty to go with her immediately to the Special Projects Facility. There they met Abi and Zak who were twins as well as being joint-team leaders of the Marine Section. The other eighteen members of the section were also there and by late morning a draft plan had emerged with Amphitrite immediately seconded to Abi and Zak's team. They had one clear objective and that was to zap Tyrantland on the high seas.

That evening Amphitrite had told Poseidon what they were up to. Initially he didn't appear interested in what they were doing, principally because he didn't understand technology. However, the next day Totty explained to him how it could support the whale attack. Suddenly he started having his own ideas and he was roped into the project as well. He very much deferred to Amphitrite and Totty on matters, but he wanted to know everything that was being planned. It was important because he and the Sea Goddess were soon to leave for Challogis Island to meet the whales battle fleet.

As everyone was moving away, Rach jumped on her scooter and took off to the dignitaries' platform where Chertassle was still standing as she waited for everyone else to leave.

"Thanks, Grandma," Rach said, bringing the scooter to a halt.

"For what?" the Empress asked and, then looking at her granddaughter, said: "And what on earth have you done to your face, Einstella? You've got black streaks all over it."

"New trend. Please don't be like Mum and Dad. I got an earful this morning."

"I'm not surprised. Anyway, what am I supposed to have done?"

"Clearing the crowd away. That's a real smart idea; it will make things easier for Tots."

"It was actually Hashimoto's idea."

"Yea; that's great. I've got to know him over the last few days. He's an okey-dokes guy. We all think so in Special Projects."

"I agree. Look, I'm leaving because Totty looks as if she's ready to give it another go. Remember to bring me the recording once it's completed and this time, I mean the 100% finished article. You know nothing should go out without it being approved by a sub-committee of me, the Chief Minister and the General. There are to be no last-minute additions by you as happened with the cartoon."

"Yea; yea: I know. But that addition of the Tyrant making a V sign was a much better finish, don't you think?"

Chertassle smiled at her granddaughter. "Maybe so," she replied. "But rules are rules, and they apply to you as much as everyone else."

"Okey-dokes. I promise to do it right this time." Rach leant over and kissed the Empress on the cheek. "Love you, Grandma," she said before jumping on her scooter and flying back to the large table in front of Totty.

The decision that Totty should present the news programme had obviously caused considerable difficulties in view of her being a full-sized adult. Both Redrelok and Mandoselin had volunteered as Cabinet members to oversee all the logistics. This involved creating a news set for her. Fortunately, Tyrantland's news sets were pretty spartan, being totally unlike the plush designs on US networks. All that was required was a large table and chair for Totty to sit on in front of a white wall background. As far as the cameras and audio were concerned, it was possible with careful positioning to use those belonging to various Lilliput TV stations. In addition,

Totty needed to be provided with a smart new jacket to wear, so this had to be made for her.

More than 500 Lilliputians worked in shifts for 24 hours a day over three days to create the set. The largest job was creating the furniture for Totty, so a considerable number of carpenters were involved. It was also necessary to involve the best people from the leading TV channels, production teams and various design outfits. Similarly, Lilliput's largest clothing manufacturer was responsible for Totty's new jacket, and this involved over 100 textile workers and designers also working a shift system to complete it on time.

The two final matters were solved by Rach and Totty. It was the head of Special Projects who identified how to create a large wall behind Totty. Instead of building a new one which would be very time-consuming because of the height needed, the outside of Parliament's west wall was viewed as ideal. It was high enough and had no windows. Two coats of white paint on consecutive days and a very large map of Tyrantland, together with a flattering photograph of the Tyrant, either side of the presenter's head, provided a thoroughly professional finish.

Totty's contribution was to raise the obvious point that no one else had thought of, which was that she didn't look like a Tyrantlander. This resulted in a team of hairstylists and beauticians working away to give her a new identity. Her curly ginger-hair was straightened out and dyed jet black; her eyelashes were also blackened, and make-up was applied to remove all sense of colour from her cheeks.

After seeing her grandmother, Rach landed her scooter on the front of Totty's table, which was excluded from the filming. She got off, said 'hi' to her friend and then sat down and stared into space. Totty indicated to the recording team that she was ready to try again, and she began. It was going really well until she stumbled near the end. There were a few muffled groans, but Rach said nothing. This time Totty didn't stand up and walk around. Instead, she just called out: "Let's go again. Ten seconds," took a few deep breaths and the shoot was begun once more. This is how it went:

Initially there was a caption:

BREAKING NEWS

Then Totty appeared in front of her desk and started speaking:

> *"This is breaking news from the Tyrant's Palace in Tyrantville.*
>
> *The Tyrant, in his great generosity, wishes to give a One Hundred Dollar Note to every one of his subjects.*
>
> *To receive this gift, each subject – man, woman and child - whatever their age, must present themselves personally to the Tyrant's Palace by 6pm on Friday of this week. That is in three days' time.*
>
> *Each subject will have their arm stamped as evidence of their receipt. This stamp will wear off within seven days.*
>
> *All praise to our Great Leader, the Tyrant, for his generosity.*
>
> *Thank you."*

Totty now disappeared from the camera and the following caption came up:

$100 NOTE FOR EACH SUBJECT

TYRANT'S PALACE

BEFORE FRIDAY 6PM

"Great!" shouted Rach, standing up and rushing over to Totty. "You've done it, Tots! That will zap him!"

Totty was standing up relieved, aware that the film crew were applauding her. All she could do was to agree with Rach: "Yes, that will zap him," she said quietly to her enthusiastic small friend.

"Well and truly zapped!" an excited Rach shouted out to everyone listening, as she ran around the table waving her fist in the air and repeating the word "zapped" for all to hear.

18
Property Matters

Cerberus lived in an old wooden kennel which was near the jetty where the ferryboat moored with the Underworld's new arrivals. Cerberus couldn't remember when his kennel had been built, but it was a long time ago. For centuries he had been perfectly happy with it, but recently he had begun to think that it was no longer appropriate for the Head of Internal Security - especially since he now had a wide range of important friends and acquaintances. He had once asked Vesta and Aggy if they would like to come and visit him at his home, and this had caused definite problems when they subsequently took up his offer. For a start, there had not been enough room inside the kennel for both him and Vesta at the same time. As far as Aggy was concerned, she had been unable to fit through the entrance, being a large-sized lady. The result was that they had all decided to return to Aggy's back room which did at least have the advantage of being near the Mars bar cupboard.

In addition to Cerberus's sense that his increased status in the Underworld deserved a more dignified residence, he had witnessed some of the Building Department review carried out by Persephone, Vesta and Ming. This had resulted in him comparing the new structures which were currently being built with his old wooden kennel, and deciding that the quality of his existing residence was no longer suitable for these modern times.

Cerberus had spoken to Hades on the matter, and it was agreed that he should have a new kennel which would be designed by Sir Christopher. There were initially certain differences of opinion between the architect and his client on specific aspects of the design, but Sir Christopher, after consultation with Hades, had agreed to produce two designs. The first one would be a set of drawings setting out the new home that Cerberus wished to have, and the second one was a somewhat more modest structure which the God of the Underworld and his Chief Architect had informally decided would eventually be constructed.

"I would appreciate you indulging Cerberus for a while, Christopher," Hades had said. "He's changed for the better and I don't want us to come over as being too negative right at the beginning."

"I will view it as an interesting intellectual exercise," was the reply, said with a smile.

It was early afternoon and Cerberus was sitting on a large stool in Sir Christopher's office looking at the latest draft design which was on the table in front of him. He was wearing a pair of spectacles on his middle head, which Homer, the Head Librarian had lent him. Sir Christopher, wearing his smart dark brown frock coat was standing next to Cerberus pointing out various aspects of the design.

"As you can see, Cerberus," he said. "This design has all the rooms which you require, despite my concerns that not every one will be used."

"Could you please point them out to me on the drawings," Cerberus replied in a serious tone as he stared at the complex workings in front of him.

"Certainly. Let's start with the ground floor. As you can see there is a large entrance hall; you then have a lounge, a dining room, a library, a study, a second sitting room, a conservatory, a kitchen, and a pantry for storing your supply of Mars bars."

"Woof. What about the servants' quarters?"

"I haven't included them, Cerberus, because you don't have any servants."

"But I expect I will have in the future."

"Then what I suggest is that we build an annex attached to the kitchen when the time arises."

"Can you do that quickly?"

"Yes," Sir Christopher replied promptly, knowing that it would never happen.

"I'll think about it," Cerberus said after giving it some consideration.

"Continuing to the first floor," the Chief Architect continued. "I've included twelve ensuite bedrooms as you require, with the Master Bedroom at the front overlooking the river. I still don't understand why you need twelve bedrooms, Cerberus, but I've given you what you've asked for."

"I intend to have guests coming to stay on a regular basis."

"But you're the only dog in the Underworld and I'm not aware of any other dogs coming here."

"My guests won't be dogs," Cerberus answered haughtily. "They'll be my friends like Vesta and Homer and Virgil whom I'll invite to my new residence. I intend to hold a series of house parties at weekends."

Sir Christopher sighed. "Very well. There's certainly enough space for them and the rooms will be high enough to accommodate humans."

"Excellent," Cerberus commented in his poshest voice.

"Finally, we have the top floor where I've included two large rooms for storage. Again, I'm not sure what you intend to store, other than more Mars bars, but you've got a substantial area for your needs."

"I'm thinking of starting an art collection. The top floor will be a good place to display it."

"Umm," was Sir Christopher 's reply.

"Talking of art, is it agreed that the wall decorations will be carried out by Mr da Vinci, Mr Botticelli and Mr Michelangelo?"

"No, it isn't!" the Chief Architect replied forcibly. "The reason being that Renaissance art on your walls is entirely inappropriate. If you want them to give you a couple of coats of white paint, that's fine, but not paintings of the Mona Lisa all over the place."

"Woof! Woof! I disagree," Cerberus said. "I've been learning all about Renaissance art from my friend Virgil; he's been studying it for the last century. He talks a lot about Renaissance Man. Well, I've decided my image from now onwards is going to be Renaissance Dog,"

"Really?" was Sir Christopher's sceptical response. "Look, Cerberus, I don't want to spend any more time arguing with you on this. I suggest we discuss the matter with Hades when we take the drawings to him for approval."

"When will that be?"

"I'm ready to go in the next few days, unless you've got any other matters?"

"Only the name of my new residence. I suggest we call it Duke's Palace."

"But you're not a duke!" Sir Christopher exclaimed.

"Watch this space."

The Chief Architect sighed again. "Let's discuss it with Hades."

As Cerberus began to get off his stool, Sir Christopher continued: "Before you go, Cerberus, I'd like you to look at this alternative design. Let me roll up these drawings and show you this other design. …. Here we are."

"What's this?" a puzzled Cerberus asked as he looked at a sheet of white paper with a large square in the middle.

"As I said, an alternative design. This one is a one room kennel, but with two advantages over your existing one. It's twice the size, so you'll have plenty of space; also, it will be built with modern materials. That means bricks instead of the wood you've got now."

Cerberus growled. "Woof! Woof! I don't like this!" He growled again. "Why have you shown it to me? Woof! Woof! Growl! Growl!"

"I'm trying to be helpful to you, Cerberus," Sir Christopher replied, not in the least bit concerned by the more aggressive tone of his client. "I've been reviewing the Building Department's schedule with Mason Bonko. As you know, there is considerable demand for their services. Even with the new efficiencies they're introducing and moving around certain planned projects, the earliest the Department will be able to start building your new home is in 20 years' time. Such projects typically take about two years to complete, so you won't be able to move in for 22 years."

Cerberus frowned. "What's that in days?" He asked.

"Over 8,000," was the prompt response.

"What? Woof! Woof! 8,000 days! Woof!"

"I'm afraid so, Cerberus," Sir Christopher calmly confirmed.

"Woof! Woof! And how many days to complete your alternative?"

"Eight."

"Woof!... Woof!... Woof!"

Cerberus just sat there unsure how to respond other than to say 'woof' at regular intervals, so the Chief Architect suggested they should take both drawings to Hades and discuss the matter with him. After a lot more woofing, Cerberus eventually agreed and went off to his next appointment in the Kitchens.

After he left Sir Christopher, Cerberus soon became more settled about his new home. This was because he had what he viewed as a brainwave. He would speak to Persephone on the matter and ask her to get Hades to agree to the twelve-bedroom palace, as well as insisting that the Building Department's schedule should be completely revised so Cerberus's new home took priority over all other work. He was pretty confident the Goddess of the Underworld would agree to this; after all, the two of them had formally agreed to become 'associate friends' with the aim of becoming full friends once she returned after her next visit to Olympus. In fact, Persephone hadn't been interested in the 'temporary' and 'on probation' stages of friendship. This was because she'd known Cerberus for so long, she didn't believe they would contribute anything to her understanding of him.

Cerberus was also aware that Persephone and Hades were getting on very well at the present time, with the God often consulting his wife on matters and invariably agreeing with her advice. This made him confident her support for his

Duke's Palace would be accepted by Hades. One concern he did have was that Persephone was soon going to return to Olympus, which meant it was important for him to 'nobble' her as quickly as possible. He knew she was currently in the Kitchens so he would speak to her once she left.

When Cerberus walked into Aggy's back room he found a number of his different types of friends sitting around a table playing a board game. At present Cerberus was still learning the rules, so he was merely an observer. He had become particularly interested in the different games that were being played in this room. It had apparently all started with Aggy teaching Death how to play the card game Snap. This had become a regular occurrence with Death turning up most days for a game. Aggy was often busy, so she often didn't have time for a game. However, Vesta and Gigliola, who was Aggy's de facto number 2, were both happy to play Snap with Death if they were free. Cerberus knew that Vesta had also tried to get Ming to play, but she felt uncomfortable sitting down at a table with a black-cloaked skeleton.

Sometimes Death, Aggy, Gigliola and Vesta would play a foursome. It was on one of these occasions that Gigliola had suggested playing other games as a bit of variety. She said what she would really like to do is to get hold of a board game called Monopoly. This was a game she had played a lot when she was in London in her late teens working in an Italian restaurant in Bayswater. All the kitchen staff had a free period in the afternoon between lunch and dinner and many of them played Monopoly. After returning to Sicily, where she eventually opened her own Italian restaurant, she never played Monopoly again. However, she remembered it as a real fun game and wished they could have it in the Underworld. Vesta had also played the game and she agreed it would be a lot more fun than just playing Snap all the time.

It didn't take long for Aggy to speak to Hebe and for the goddess to obtain a Monopoly game while on one of her trips to Yorkshire. It was also a British edition, as opposed to a US one, very similar to the version Gigliola had played while in London. When it was opened up, it caused tremendous excitement among the group and over the next few days Gigliola patiently taught the others how to play and what the rules were. Even Ming took an interest; she told Persephone about it and very quickly the two of them joined the group, with Ming overcoming her reluctance of sitting at a table with Death.

Monopoly is a game about property. In the British version it involves buying and selling properties in Central London, receiving and paying rents, as well as the development of sites by adding houses or hotels. The players move around the board in turn by throwing dice and where they land after each throw can provide a property opportunity or penalty, such as receiving or paying rent. Players are eliminated from the game by going bankrupt and the eventual winner is the one left while all the others are bankrupt.

When Cerberus joined the players in the back room, Persephone and Vesta had already gone bankrupt. From the accumulation of monies and properties, Death looked as if he was in the strongest position against the other three. This was no surprise to the Head of Internal Security since Death had won the last two games, but he was interested in why this should be the case.

"Death's winning," Cerberus commented. "Why are you so good at Monopoly, Death?"

"Not necessarily," Aggy replied before the skeleton could answer. "There's still a lot to play for. We others aren't finished yet."

"But Cerberus is right," Vesta said. "You really are good at this game, Death."

"I think Death runs a big property business on the side," joked Gigliola. "It's why he's such an expert."

"I certainly don't!" a shocked Death responded.

"I think Gigliola's only having a bit of fun, Death," Persephone said with a smile. "I'm sure no one thinks you've got a property business in the real world."

239

"Oh!" Death said. "So, you weren't serious, Miss Gigliola?"

"Not this time, but I must say you are very clever how you play the game. You always try and buy Park Lane and Mayfair, the most expensive properties."

"I know that area well," Death replied. "It's the most expensive in this game, but also in real life. Property there can only be bought by millionaires and billionaires."

"You're right," Gigliola said. "When I was in London, I used to live and work in Bayswater, which is near Park Lane and Mayfair. Bayswater's just north of a huge park called Hyde Park and Park Lane overlooks it from the east."

"I once visited London," Vesta added. "We spent an afternoon in Hyde Park on the lake in a small boat."

"That's the Serpentine," said Gigliola. "Do you ever go into Hyde Park, Death?"

"Quite often," the skeleton replied before rolling the dice and making another move, unfortunately landing on the Go to Jail square.

"See," said Aggy to Cerberus. "Poor Death's had a bit of a set back there. The game's not over yet."

For a few minutes, the players continued to make their moves with Cerberus watching keenly from the side. He was fairly confident that after observing another couple of games, he would know enough of the rules to be able to play. He'd agreed with Vesta and Aggy that once he felt ready, the three of them would have their own game as a trial run. If that went well, he could join the wider group as a 'first reserve.' This was because they all felt that six was the ideal number of players, but often some people were too busy to play and, in those instances, Cerberus would take their place.

For a while no one was talking much, so Cerberus decided to start a conversation.

"Woof," he said. "My friends Homer and Virgil are both reading a book in which you're mentioned, Death."

"I suspect I'm in quite a lot of books," the skeleton replied. "Which one in particular?"

"It's a book called the Bible. I only mention it because they're particularly interested in you being one of The Four Horsemen of the Apocalypse. They're still trying to understand what it all means, but they're adamant that you've got a horse. I said I've never seen you with a horse, so it can't be right, but they asked me to check if you've got one."

"Yes, I have," Death replied in a matter-of-fact manner. "But I don't ride him much these days, except when I'm in London. Strange; we were only just talking about Hyde Park, which is where we ride together."

None of the other players said anything, although both Vesta and Ming looked at Persephone since she had told them both about the search for the two missing Horsemen. The goddess pretended to be studying the board, while inwardly thinking how to progress this conversation with Death. Fortunately, Cerberus unwittingly came to the rescue.

"So, what about the other Horsemen?" the three-headed dog asked. "Do they also have horses they don't ride?"

"Yes," Death replied. "Famine and Pestilence are like me; they don't ride them much. Mars, though, keeps his with him most of the time."

"Who are these Horsemen with these strange names?" Vesta asked in a naïve tone and then told a little fib: "I don't know anything about them."

"No, neither do I," Ming said, also fibbing.

"Woof," went Cerberus. "You should read the Bible. I'll ask Homer and Virgil if you can borrow it once they're finished. It's very long, but the two bits you need to look at are the Book of Revolutions and the Book about the Prophet He's a Greek Eel."

"I think you mean the Book of Revelations and the Prophet Ezekiel," Gigliola said. She had been brought up as a Catholic in Italy and knew her bible better than anyone around the table.

"Isn't that what I said?" Cerberus responded.

"Almost."

"Woof. Well, they're the parts to read about the Four Horsemen," Cerberus said.

"I will," Vesta continued. "It seems very interesting. But tell me, Death, where does your horse stay when you're not in London? Does he just live in Hyde Park? When I visited there, I saw plenty of grass for horses to eat."

Death shook his head. "No," he replied. "There are stables just north of the park, where all three of our horses live. The same family's been looking after them for centuries. They only take them out at nighttime for a ride around the park. It's the same when I'm there and the other two. We try to be discreet, only going out at night."

"I know what you're talking about," Gigliola added. "When I worked in Bayswater, there were a number of different stables down those small streets called mews."

"That's right," said Death. "It's one of those."

"Do you see your horse often?" Ming asked casually.

"It's not possible each time I'm in London because I'm normally very busy," Death replied. "But we have a rota which is that once a month one of us visits the stables and rides all three horses during the night. All the horses know us, so they're quite happy whoever rides them."

"So, the rota won't include Mars then because his horse doesn't live in London?" Ming continued.

"That's right. Only Famine, Pestilence and me."

"It's your turn to throw the dice, Death," Aggy said, having said little during the discussion about the Four Horsemen. "See if you can get out of jail."

As Death was throwing the dice, Persephone got up and said she had to leave because she was late for an important meeting with Hades. Vesta, who was also eliminated, left at the same time quickly followed by Cerberus.

"Did you hear that?" Persephone said to Vesta when they were outside. "We now know where Famine and Pestilence keep their horses."

"Presumably, if we can get someone to keep a watch on the stables, we'll be able to catch them when they next visit?"

"Precisely. I've got to tell Hades straight away. I return to Olympus fairly soon, but it may be important to get the information passed on earlier."

At that moment, Cerberus bounded up. "Persephone," he said. "Can I please speak to you about my new palace which is going to be built."

"I've got to see Hades first," the goddess replied.

"Woof! But this is important."

"So is what I've got to tell Hades. You can come with me and wait in my sitting room. Once Hades and I have spoken, we can have a separate chat about your new kennel."

"Palace," corrected Cerberus.

"Whatever," Persephone said. "Are you coming, Vesta? You can keep Cerberus entertained until I return and then we can all talk about his new home."

"Cool."

"Woof. Have either of you got a Mars bar on you by any chance?" the Head of Internal Security asked.

Vesta looked at Persephone. "I've got a small stock in my sitting room," the goddess replied. "Vesta knows the cupboard."

"Woof!" went Cerberus running to the front. "Hurry up then. Woof, woof. Come on. Woof!" And Cerberus went charging off in anticipation of accessing Persephone's stock of Mars bars.

19
A Day at Sea

The port of Tyrantville catered for three separate activities. Firstly, there was a large fishing fleet based there. Secondly, it was the major terminal for all the commercial ships which facilitated the country's import and export of goods. Finally, Tyrantland's navy operated from its own secure base next to all the commercial shipping activities.

It was early in the morning when the fishing fleet set sale for the fishing grounds about ten miles to the north of Tyrantville. There was a fair amount of discontent on board many of the vessels because it was the last day to collect the $100 notes from the Tyrant. A number of the fishermen had been waiting outside the Tyrant's palace for the last two nights, but the gates had remained shut and there was no sign of any money.

The Fishy Tyrant had deliberately set out early so it could return by mid-afternoon, allowing its crew time to attend the palace once more in the hope that the $100 notes would eventually be forthcoming.

"I think it's all a big hoax," the captain said to his first mate. "The wife says there have been various announcements on the telly saying the original broadcast was an error. Trouble is that they're always followed a few minutes later by the original broadcast again. She doesn't know what to believe."

"I dunno," the chief mate replied. "I was near the front of the crowd last night and got talking to one of the guards, didn't I? He said he thought it were real and that's what they think in the guardroom."

"Fat chance. The broadcast was three days ago, and I've not heard of anyone who's actually received any money. Also, that bastard the Tyrant's never given us anything before; why's he suddenly going to change now?"

"So, you won't be going back to the palace when we return?"

"Well, I didn't actually say that. Got to collect the wife and two daughters and the little grandkiddies. They'll have been there all day."

"Yea, same here with me other half. She were at the North Gate yesterday afternoon when that Lord Mars came out and started screaming at everyone to bugger off. Horrible looking pig, she said. He were waving his sword around, threatening to chop everyone's heads off, he were. Made the crowd back away big time until he'd finished all his screaming and shouting and went back inside the palace."

"What happened then?"

"The crowd moved forward again and after a few minutes that nice lady called Stevie came out with Big Sis. They were carrying plates full of custard pies which they gave to people. Didn't have enough, but it were appreciated. They both said there weren't any $100's for anyone, which got lots of people annoyed, so they went back again and got some more pies. Spent all afternoon coming out with them pies. Anyway, the other half wants to believe we'll get the money, and she were happy at what the guard said last night."

"That Stevie is Ob's aunt," said the captain. "You know Ob, he runs the pub."

"Yea; does good beer. Every time I go in there, I get confused though – so many people called Jacques drinking at the bar. Once his Aunt Stevie came in and she even got called Jacques, didn't she?"

"I've noticed the same." The captain paused as his attention shifted to what was going on in the distance ahead of him. "Here; here. What's all this?"

"Blimey; them boats are rocking around a lot," his companion said as he also looked ahead.

"Look at that big white thing rising!" the captain shouted. "It's a bloody whale!"

The whales had been waiting since the early hours of the morning for the fishing vessels. They had held a detailed conference with Poseidon and Amphitrite the previous day at Challogis Island and had agreed their battle plan. They also understood how the Lilliputians were going to help them, particularly the Special Projects team headed up by the Empress's granddaughter.

The attack took place just before the fishing vessels threw their nets overboard. Many of the boats were made of wood, although a few had steel hulls. It was a medium-sized wooden one which was the first target. Moby and two other whales swam side by side towards the vessel. They were below the surface and together hit the hull at an angle, so they didn't injure themselves. The three whales then dived under the boat and moved onto their next target.

The first boat was rocking violently after being hit and the crew were thrown across the deck. Just as they were getting themselves up, they were hit again by a second group of three whales. This was followed by two more attacks, by which time the lifeboat had become detached and was sliding around all over the deck; in addition, no one was at the tiller, the rudder had snapped off and the boat was leaning partially on one side letting in water.

Within a quarter of an hour more than fifty fishing vessels had been attacked. Some were turned over and began to sink, others were being tossed by the waters with their engines damaged or with their rudders broken. Because so many had lost all control, they started to hit into each other, including the undamaged boats which tried to come to their rescue.

There were many hundreds of whales under Moby's command involved in the attack which lasted for more than two hours. A few vessels, including the Fishy Tyrant, managed to escape and head back to port, but the whales had at an early stage surrounded the fishing fleet, so not too many were able to get away.

"Strewth! I don't know what happened back there," the captain of the Fishy Tyrant said once his vessel was well away from the mayhem. "But the first thing we'll do when we've docked is go to the Harbour Master and tell him to get the

Tyrant off his backside and clear the waters of those bloody whales. After that, we need to go and have a few at Ob's pub."

"Good idea," the first mate replied. "I never seen nothing like it before. Never had whales in the fishing grounds, have we?"

"There're some strange things going on at the moment. What with all these television broadcasts, that bridge being blown up and now this. We might learn something at Ob's. He seems to have his ear to the ground."

"Yea. Him and all those people called Jacques," his companion agreed.

While Moby was leading the attack on the fishing fleet, Suki was with another large body of whales waiting about a mile outside the port near the main commercial shipping lane. They were grouped into clusters of forty to fifty whales each, biding their time until late morning when activity had begun to build up with several ships queuing to either leave or enter the port.

When she felt it was time to begin, Suki nudged a fin whale next to her who launched himself out of the water. This was the signal to the various clusters to begin the attack on their nearest ship. The first vessel to feel the presence of the whales was a cargo ship coming out of the port laden with coal. The strategy for dealing with the commercial vessels was different to the one adopted for the fishing fleet. Instead of a series of hits one after the other, the cargo ship suddenly found that a large group of whales was pushing against its starboard side. There were fifteen whales along the entire length of the hull consistently pressing it sideways. This group was backed up by twice the number behind them, who were all pushing in the same direction. The effect was that the cargo ship, while moving forwards, wasn't able to follow its planned course as it was continuously forced to the port side. The coxswain on the bridge tried to compensate for this left-wards lurch by turning his wheel in the opposite direction, but it was a never-ending struggle to try and set a consistent course as the boat zigzagged in the water.

247

Near the entrance to the port, vessels are naturally closer than on the open seas since they are either trying to enter or leave a relatively small area. While the coal carrying cargo ship was the first to be intercepted by a cluster of whales, within another few minutes four other ships were similarly attacked. One of these was following the cargo ship as it tried to leave the port while the other three were moving in line to enter the harbour. Very soon a number of these vessels outside the Port of Tyrantville were zigzagging around in a relatively tight area unable to steer a straight course. Their captains were becoming increasingly panicked, shouting out contrary instructions to their coxswains several times a minute.

The scenario which developed was invariably going to lead to an accident. It happened when the first cargo ship that was leaving the port was passing a fully laden container ship which was going the other way. Both were in a constant struggle with the whales pushing them closer together. As they were about to pass each other, the two coxswains tried to maximise the turn away from each other. The problem was that just as the container ship was beginning to veer away, all the whales dived together, so removing the sideways pressure on the vessel. Since the coxswain had pulled the wheel as far as possible to avoid a collision, the container ship suddenly jarred violently to the left. Unfortunately, the containers were not bound as strongly as they should have been. The effect of this jarring was to dislodge some of the containers from their bindings, and they began to tip over the side. This in turn disturbed the balance on the ship and it began to rock. More containers became dislodged and fell into the sea. As the deck emptied, the remaining ones had room to slide around. A number got stuck on the port side, unable to go overboard. The boat started leaning over on this side as more containers slid over. This only exacerbated the problem as very slowly the container ship continued to topple over to the left. Water started coming onto the deck, more containers fell into the sea and eventually the hull began to submerge as the ship gradually disappeared below the waves.

There were now hundreds of containers which proceeded to bob around on the water. The next casualty was the first cargo ship which had left the port. The captain and coxswain tried to avoid hitting the floating containers. The same was true of the other ships in the area, all of which were being pressed by large clusters of whales. As with the container ship, the whales would from time to time remove their pressure and dive below the surface as a group, often re-emerging the other side in a minute or so to create a new challenge for the crew at the various wheels. The result was that the coxswains were finding it impossible to navigate and it was inevitable there would be collisions. This occurred with the first cargo vessel which struck a similar sized vessel trying to enter the port. Initially, there didn't appear to be any serious damage as the two sides knocked together. However, as the two ships slowly moved apart, the two groups of whales gave a massive push against their respective vessels. This time the collision was a lot harder, and the first cargo vessel developed a leak just below the surface, which caused a mass of panicked activity from the officers and crew. The other ship avoided a leak but found that its propeller had been damaged so it gradually lost all momentum.

The whales continued to work in their clusters as they systematically attacked more ships in the area. They quickly realized that all the containers floating around in the sea could be used to their advantage. While large vessels hitting a container often only experienced superficial damage, if the floating boxes struck the stern, then sometimes the propeller or the rudder would be broken. The result would be that the ship would lose all control or become completely immobilized. As the morning progressed, small groups of whales would detach themselves from the main clusters and start pushing the floating containers towards the back of the ships themselves. The effectiveness of this technique quickly became the primary tactic which the whales adopted.

Suki, who was leading the attack on the commercial vessels, was not a member of any cluster as she watched what was happening with the larger fin whale at her side. Every so often she would send messages to the different clusters by a series of signals which were enacted by her fin whale companion launching himself out of the water. The precise angle and extent of the launch indicated different pre-agreed instructions which had been decided beforehand. Each cluster had one of its members permanently on the surface as a look-out for these messages which could then be relayed to the rest of the group.

Also staying with Suki was Bettina, Moby's partner. She was Suki's best friend and had just naturally remained outside the clusters so she could provide any help necessary. In truth, she and Moby were worried about their friend after the loss of Gerrard. As everything was progressing smoothly with the fishing fleet, Moby in due course decided to come and join Suki and Bettina; he wanted to see if he could assist in the attack on the commercial vessels. For a while he couldn't see much else to do other than add his power to a couple of nearby clusters.

As the whale attack continued, ships stopped leaving the port. In addition, those wishing to land their cargo, turned away and remained about two or three miles from the clusters as they waited to see how matters would be resolved. The one exception was a giant oil tanker approaching Tyrantville with a full delivery of crude. The captain and his officers were in regular contact with the port authorities and various other ships in the vicinity, so they knew what was happening. However, the tanker continued to plough on towards its destination, its captain confident that the vessel was so large that no cluster of whales could cause it to deviate from its course. In addition, its hull was sufficiently strong that if it hit a few containers, they would just bounce off without any damage being inflicted.

A group of whales went into action against the tanker, focusing on pushing a number of containers towards the stern. Despite several attempts, they could make no impression because the ship was very low in the water due to its full cargo; this meant that the propeller and rudder were well below the surface. Moby thought there was little point in continuing, but Suki decided to go off and investigate if something could be done. The large white whale followed her at a distance, believing she was wasting her time. He was just about to turn away when he suddenly shot off at great speed. Suki was swimming towards the propeller, having realized there was a way to damage it. She was within six feet of the whirling blades when she was struck hard by a massive blow that knocked her off course and away from her target. The next instant she was glaring at a furious Moby who had stopped her from swimming directly into the propeller's blades. He continued to push her towards safety as the tanker ploughed on relentlessly towards the port.

By mid-afternoon, the Tyrantland navy set sail. Mars accepted that Poseidon had initiated the whale attack and he and the Tyrant ordered the navy to 'obliterate the enemy.'

The Admiral of the Fleet was the Tyrant's older cousin. He was an old-fashioned naval officer who believed in strict discipline. This meant that even in the 21st century, there was regular flogging on board his ships as well as the continued use of keelhauling. However, the Admiral's favourite punishment was to make people walk the plank or the 'plonk' as he pronounced it. He had a 19th century cutlass which he used to prod their backs if they were reluctant to move forward and take their punishment.

The Admiral had a very long name, but he was generally known by the punishments he meted out. Some people called him Admiral Flogger, but his most common name was Admiral Plonker. He was very proud of the Plonker name, being unaware of its slang meaning. He even encouraged the Tyrant to use it and often referred to himself as the Plonker.

The Tyrantland navy consisted of a battle cruiser, one very old destroyer and two even older frigates; all were called into action against the whales. The battle cruiser was named the Tyranto Magnifico and had been built five years ago in Diktatorland's largest shipyard, financed by a loan which had little prospect of being repaid anytime soon. The cruiser was the Admiral's pride and joy and he often insisted on taking a hands-on role captaining it himself. It was no surprise then that he was at the wheel on the Magnifico's bridge, as the navy set sail to do battle with the whales.

The four ships set off for the area where the commercial vessels had been attacked. They sailed in single file with the Magnifico in the lead, followed by the destroyer and then the two frigates. It had been agreed that once the Admiral gave the signal, all the ships would fire broadsides continuously as well as dropping depth charges.

"Fire a few shells from the forward guns," the Admiral ordered the First Officer when they were about a mile out of port. "Let those big lumbering blobs know we're coming after them."

"Yes, sir," was the response and the forward guns shortly afterwards fired a few shells.

"That's probably got a few of the buggers," the Admiral said. "They'll know now they're up against a superior force. Yes, the Plonker's after them. You don't take on a big plonker like me every day. Do you agree, First Officer?"

"I couldn't agree more, sir" the First Officer, an intelligent and serious man, replied. He knew the Admiral well and had learned to control himself in his presence.

"Yes. Today they're going to find out what it's like to be up against the biggest plonker going."

"You put it perfectly, Admiral"

"What do you two young chaps say?" the Admiral called out, looking at the far side of the bridge where two junior officers were standing.

"Totally agree," the first one said, followed by the same words from the second, before they both looked away as they tried to stop themselves from giggling.

"Well done! You'll both go far."

After a couple of minutes, the Admiral issued instructions to fire a few more shells from the forward guns.

"Are you sure, sir?" the First Officer, who was looking through his binoculars, replied. "I think-----."

"Just do it!" the Plonker interrupted.

"Yes, sir." A few seconds later, more shells were fired.

"Did you see where they went?" the Admiral asked the First Officer who was staring through his binoculars.

"One of them seems to have hit a cargo ship, sir. It's started a fire towards the stern."

"What the hell's a cargo ship doing there?"

"It looks as if it's lost all its power. It's just floating around, no doubt waiting to be salvaged."

"Bloody fools! Open that window; they're shouting something."

As the Magnifico passed the stricken cargo vessel, a number of its crew were shouting angrily at the cruiser.

"Can't understand what they're saying," the Admiral said. "Speaking some foreign lingo. I'll shout back at them. Give me that loudspeaker." The First Officer handed a loudspeaker to the Admiral who called out: "Get out of the way, you stupid idiots! Get out of the way!" He then shut the window and said: "That's told them. Bloody fools getting in the way of the Magnifico."

"Yes, sir," agreed the First Officer.

Admiral Plonker was unaware of two developments which were about to become very relevant to his mission of obliterating the enemy whales. The first one was that after attacking the fishing fleet and the commercial vessels, the whales had swum off. This was because it had been anticipated that the navy would be sent out to do battle, but Moby and his team were not to get involved with the warships. The second development was that all the movements of the four naval ships were being plotted by the Marine Section of the Special Projects team on Lilliput. Rach, Abi and Zak had been watching a large screen on a wall: Totty was also lying outside their building with Rach running backwards and forwards to tell her what was going on through an open window. The rest of the team was split into four groups, each one focused on a different ship.

"Time for action!" shouted Rach to the entire team after running back to her desk following the latest consultation with her friend, Tots.

A minute later the two frigates slowly turned round and headed back to port. No one noticed from the bridge of the Magnifico until they heard guns firing in the distance. The First Officer immediately tried to contact the frigates on the radio, but there was no communication link.

"What the hell's going on?" shouted the Admiral.

"The two frigates are firing their guns at the port and the city," a shocked First Officer said, having gone outside onto the deck to look. "They're now following each other in a circle just outside the port, firing all their guns."

The Admiral came out onto the deck, raced back into the bridge and tried the radio link himself, also with no success. He then tried to contact the destroyer, but again all communications were down.

"What the----" the Admiral started to screech before he was interrupted by shells landing just in front of the Magnifico.

"That was the destroyer!" shouted the First Officer who was still outside on the deck. "They're shelling us!" As he said this, two more shells landed in the water, sufficiently close to the port side to cause the cruiser to start swaying from side to side.

"It's begun!" Admiral Plonker shouted. "The revolution!"

He then immediately moved into action as he grabbed hold of the cruiser's wheel and took the ship in a semi-circle so it headed round to the destroyer's port side.

"First Officer!" he screamed. "All guns blazing! We're taking out the destroyer! Torpedoes at the ready! Launch when I give the order!"

"But why, sir?" the First Officer asked as he came in from the deck, totally astonished at the command.

"Do what I bloody well say, or I'll keelhaul you!" the Admiral shouted before looking at the equally stunned junior officers. "You two as well! Get everything firing! We've got a mutiny on our hands!"

As shocked as everyone on board the Magnifico was, the officers and crew on the two frigates and the destroyer were in an even worse state. All three ships seemed to have been taken over by an outside force. This was controlling their direction, their speed and also the firing of all their guns. They were unable to do anything and couldn't even access the power supply to turn it off due to the doors to all the control rooms being tightly locked shut and refusing to be opened.

The two frigates continued to sail round in a circle firing away at the port and into the city. The crew could hear the sirens sounding everywhere in the distance. This continued for some time until there was a mighty explosion with fire and smoke everywhere as the oil tanker was hit by a shell and caused a huge fireball in the port and surrounding area. The two frigates rocked but stayed afloat. At that stage, both captains gave orders to abandon ship, and head in the lifeboats to a beach about a mile away.

For thirty minutes the cruiser and destroyer had a good old fashioned naval battle with both firing broadsides at each other. The destroyer was not in control of its own destiny but just kept moving forwards with its guns firing. The cruiser, however, was still subject to the command of the Admiral and had much greater fire power. The torpedoes struck the smaller ship early on and, together with the sheer quantum of shells hitting it, the destroyer slowly began to break up and sink.

"Right!" shouted the Admiral once he was satisfied he'd dealt with the destroyer. "We're going to do the same to the frigates!"

He tried to turn the wheel, but the ship began to turn in the opposite direction. It then started to sail due south and picked up speed. However much the Admiral and his fellow officers struggled, they couldn't establish any sort of control over it. As with the destroyer and two frigates, access to the control room was denied. Men were sent down with axes and crowbars but failed miserably to break down the heavily secure door. Meanwhile, the cruiser continued on its southerly direction.

"Where have you sent the Magnifico?" Totty asked Rach when it was all over.

"The Antarctic; that's where the penguins live," her friend replied.

"Poor penguins," Totty said, and the two of them burst out laughing.

20
The Third Missile

The sequence of events that unfolded was threefold. Firstly, Rach hit the enter button on her keyboard before getting up and going off to see Totty. This was followed shortly afterwards by the Tyrant pressing down on his big red button at the secret mountaintop facility. Finally, Zeus, who was fast asleep dreaming of young water nymphs, was abruptly awakened by the sound of an immense explosion and windows breaking in the Top God's palace.

"What the hell was that?" Zeus screeched as he pulled open the curtains, being careful not to tread on the shattered glass on the floor. It was still night, but he could see a large fire in the distance. He then raced out of his bedroom suite shouting: "Hera, Mr and Mrs Bumble, Marie Antoinette! Where are you all?"

Within a short while everyone had congregated on the landing in their night attire.

"What's going on?" screamed Zeus to everyone.

"It sounds like a bomb," Hera replied. "I think all our windows are broken."

"They are downstairs, Your Ladyship," said Mr Bumble.

"But how can we have a bomb on Olympus?" Zeus demanded. "Who set it off?"

"I don't know, My Lord," replied the butler.

"Well, go and find out! And you two," Zeus retorted, waving his hand at the other domestics. "Don't get changed. Just go out as you are. Now!"

As they reached the bottom of the stairs, Iris's rainbow appeared in the night sky and the next minute, the Rainbow Goddess was climbing through a large window in the hall which had been blown in.

"Where are you going?" she said to the portly Bumble couple and the thin French maid who were now in the hallway.

"They're going to find out what's going on," Zeus shouted from the top of the stairs. "Do you know anything, Iris?"

"Stay here," Iris said to the ground floor contingent. "I'll tell you what I know."

"Come back upstairs all of you," Hera said, "and please tell us what you know, Iris. I think it's a bomb."

"I'd say that's probably right. I couldn't sleep and was just lying in bed looking out of the window at the night sky – I didn't have the curtains closed. Suddenly, there was a flash in front of me before an explosion at Mars's palace, which is near our bungalow. I raced outside and could see that it's been largely destroyed with a large fire burning."

"A flash! What does that mean?" Zeus demanded.

"Isn't it obvious? It's another one of those missiles which the Tyrant and Mars have fired."

"But that's impossible!" the Top God exclaimed. "Why would Mars fire it at his own palace?"

"I'm sure he didn't," replied Iris. "They haven't got their accuracy sorted out for all these missiles of theirs. For all we know, it could have been aimed at you and Hera."

"What!!!" screeched Zeus. "Mars would dare to attack me! I'll show him!"

The Top God then turned round without saying anything more and marched into his suite, slamming the door behind him. Before anyone could say anything, Artemis and Hephaestus were climbing in through one of the broken windows, followed by many of the other gods and some of their staff members in the next twenty minutes. Hera took responsibility for dealing with everybody. Firstly, she sent the Bumbles and Marie Antoinette to their rooms to get changed and then start clearing up the glass in the palace. She and Iris then took the others into one of the large living rooms and told them what they knew so far.

There was so much discussion in the living room with everyone trying to talk at the same time that no one was aware that Zeus had come downstairs. He was now fully dressed and walked along one of the corridors off the main hall until he reached a large cupboard with the word THUNDERBOLTS on it. He opened the cupboard, chose a particularly large thunderbolt, and then went into his study from which he gained access to the back garden.

Zeus had the unique ability, when he had a thunderbolt in his hands, to cast his eye over very long distances and see his target. In fact, the angrier he was the more distinct his vision became. Today he was in a state of almost uncontrollable fury, so when he was looking towards Tyrantland, he could clearly see the mountaintop from where the missile had been launched. He saw through the windows of a large building a small fat man with greasy hair, whom he suspected was the Tyrant. However, he couldn't see any sign of his son, Mars. He continued looking for a while until his gaze moved to Tyrantville and the Tyrant's palace. He focused his gaze through large French windows on the back of a male he thought he recognised. He watched until the figure half turned round, and Zeus saw it was indeed Mars. He quickly got into position, pulled his arm back and threw his thunderbolt towards the source of his great anger.

Mars had decided not to go with the Tyrant to the mountaintop to launch the third missile. Instead, he wanted to wait in Tyrantville for the arrival of Pestilence whom he was expecting at any time. He would then have a detailed conference with Famine and Pestilence about a coordinated effort by the three of them to create maximum chaos in the world.

At the time Zeus had gone into his back garden with his thunderbolt, Mars was standing in the sitting room off the Tyrant's study talking to Famine who was, as usual, lying casually on the couch. They had been speaking for more than an hour and Mars was feeling hungry. Just as Zeus launched his response, Mars turned round and walked out of the sitting room into the study as he was intending to look for Stevie to organize a late breakfast. He also wanted to know if there was any message from the Tyrant about the missile launch. Before he could get out of the study door there was a large bang and a flash of light behind him, followed by a loud shriek from Famine.

Mars raced back into the sitting room and saw Famine lying on the ground moaning. He was burned on his arms, legs and abdomen, from which an ugly greenish yellow liquid oozed; his face was also singed. Mars knew Famine didn't have any blood, but what was inside his body was a mystery to the God of War. He didn't move to assist his fellow Horseman, but instead watched him in fascination as he continued to moan with pain. Suddenly he was aware that Stevie was in the room.

"Oh my!" the oldest woman in the world exclaimed. "What was that?"

"A thunderbolt sent by my father," Mars answered with a sneer. "Get Mr F back on the couch and get some medical attention for him. He doesn't look as if he's broken anything, and he'll probably heal naturally with time."

"What's that coloured stuff coming out of his wounds?" Stevie asked.

"I don't know, and I don't care. He'll heal as I said. Just do as I said!" he rasped and turned round to walk into the study.

"Aren't you going to assist, Lord Mars?" Stevie asked, not at all afraid of the God of War.

"No!" he called back as he continued to walk away. "I've got urgent business with the Tyrant."

Stevie watched Mars walk out of the study, then turned round and studied Famine in greater detail. What she saw disgusted her, but at her age she'd seen lots of disgusting things, so she knew how to cope. After a while she followed Mars into the corridor and summoned several guards to lift Famine back onto the couch. She also sent one to call a doctor and a nurse. She didn't know what they'd all make of this wounded creature, but it would no doubt get around the city in no time. It would be yet one more matter to disturb an already unsettled population. Her nephew Ob would view it as providing ever more fertile ground for a revolution. Stevie only hoped he and all the others called Jacques knew what to do if the revolution did actually happen. She rather suspected they wouldn't have much of an idea, so she'd have to tell them.

•

Zeus and Iris had spent the first part of the morning having a go at each other. After he had thrown his thunderbolt, Zeus called Iris out of the meeting with all the other gods since he wanted her to go and see how Mars was. Unfortunately, he started by commenting that he was surprised she wasn't based in Tyrantland stopping all the missiles from being fired.

"Because that was never the plan!" Iris retorted. "After Heph and I got told to clear off by Mars, it was agreed that I would back away for a while and then only visit Tyrantland on an occasional basis."

"Who agreed that?" Zeus demanded.

"You did with Hera when the two of us returned! It was in this room!"

"Was it?"

"Yes!"

"So, what have you been doing with your time?"

Iris gave a deliberately loud sigh before answering. "The first thing I did was go and find Artemis and Hermes to tell them to stop looking for Mars because we'd found him."

"Where were they looking?"

"Where you'd sent them, Zeus! Africa and America! Don't you remember?"

"Couldn't someone else have found them instead?"

"Who? You, for example?"

"I'm needed here. We agreed that this is Operation Control, or had you forgotten?" Zeus answered, trying to stand up for himself.

"No, I hadn't!" was Iris's firm response. "What I don't know is what Operation Control actually does. Perhaps you could tell me, please?"

Zeus frowned. He wasn't entirely sure himself, so he waffled something about being in control of the whole operation, taking a top-down view, that sort of thing.

"It sounds to me like you don't know yourself!" Iris retorted. "Anyway, what do you want to see me about?"

A small part of Zeus wanted to keep arguing with Iris, but a much larger part felt he was on a losing wicket. He also now remembered that she and Hermes were doing some of Hebe's work ensuring the three realms were well stocked with provisions. Common sense told him it would be unwise to question further what she'd been up to; instead, it would be much better to focus on why he needed her now.

"I've just thrown a thunderbolt at Mars," Zeus announced, "I'd like you to go and see how he is and get him to come back here."

"You haven't?" a genuinely surprised Iris said.

"I have."

"I'm impressed," the Rainbow Goddess responded, for once feeling that the Top God had done something which she and many of the other gods would approve of. "Where is he in Tyrantland?"

"In the city. I suppose it must be the Tyrant's palace."

"Right," said Iris. "I'll go once I've changed and spent a couple of hours clearing up the bungalow. I don't know if I'm going to be able to get him to return to Olympus, but I'll try."

"I think it's time I sent him a message."

"Okay. What is it?"

Zeus frowned. "Precisely the same one you gave Bacchus when he didn't turn up for the Council meeting."

Iris moaned. It had been going well with Zeus for the last minute or so, but now he had ruined it. "Just give me the words," she said with a sigh.

There was a silence before Zeus responded: "I can't remember them. I thought you might recall what I said."

Iris sighed again before getting to work. She had an excellent memory and could recall practically all the words of

262

the messages she had delivered in recent years. She sat down at Zeus's desk and wrote on a piece of paper what she had delivered to Bacchus some time ago. She and Zeus then worked together to amend the words to fit with Mars's situation before ending up with the following:

'Attack on Olympus:- I am Zeus, most powerful of all the gods; I rule over Olympus, the earth, the moon, the planets, the stars and the entire universe. All other gods quiver and shake in my presence. I am great and mighty for I can bring disaster and destruction to any who oppose me. My word is law, and I will not be defied by any other, especially a rebellious, good-for-nothing, junior god such as you.

I demand that you attend me in my palace before sunset tomorrow, when you will humbly acknowledge your wicked defiance and crave my forgiveness. If you do not do this, I will deliver terrible punishments on you. Your stomach and bowels will be filled with flesh-eating serpents, your ears and nose with cockroaches and spiders, your eyes will be torn out by immense rats, vultures will tear at your arms and legs which will be visited with terrible diseases, your groin will be fed on by crocodiles and your hair will be permanently on fire.

All this will cause great pain and you will scream with agony, begging for my forgiveness, which I will never give. These punishments will continue for eternity, after which time you will be sent to the Underworld.

There, each day, you will be impaled on sharp spikes and have your legs and arms torn off while your belly will be opened up and fed to hyenas and jackals. All this, I, Zeus, will do to you, if you again defy my command to attend me, the most powerful of all the gods whose rule is absolute.'

"That will certainly show him!" Zeus said, after finally reading aloud the final version.

"It didn't work with Bacchus," Iris replied.

"It will this time," Zeus asserted confidently. "Mars and Bacchus are two entirely different gods."

Iris shrugged unconvinced. "Is there any use in me raising the two points in the message we discussed last time?" she asked.

"What were those?"

"Firstly, the fact that all the other gods don't quiver and shake in your presence. Secondly, that eternity lasts forever, so you can't talk about other punishments after eternity."

"Oh yes, I remember now. Look, Iris, let's not debate it again. Please just go with what we've crafted. I think it sounds very good."

Iris decided it was pointless trying to get Zeus to change his mind. Instead, she asked him what she was to do if Mars was so badly injured, he couldn't make the journey back to Olympus?

"You've got pretty good healing skills," the Top God replied. "I'm sure you'll be able to get him into a position so he can return."

"Probably, but I may not want to use them."

"Why not?"

"Because I think that having an incapacitated Mars is much better than having a fully functioning God of War creating trouble everywhere."

"Umm," was Zeus's response as he thought about what Iris had just said. "I take your point. Why don't I leave it to you to judge when you get there?"

Iris thought she hadn't been given a particularly helpful answer. However, on reflection, she decided that she'd prefer to rely on her own judgement than an instruction from Zeus, so she just nodded her head.

"Anything else?" asked Zeus.

"I've a final question on you calling Mars a junior god; you also called Bacchus one as well. Are all we gods graded?"

"What do you mean?"

"Well, I just wondered if I was a junior god as well?"

"Yes."

"And Hebe?"

"Yes."

"So, what sort of god are you, Zeus?"

"I'm a senior god, of course."

"I see. Are there any other senior gods?"

"I shouldn't think so," Zeus responded before thinking and adding: "I suppose Hades and Poseidon would be as well."

"What about your wife, Hera?"

"Yes; let's also call her a senior god."

"And your two sisters, Demeter and Hestia?"

Zeus coughed. "I suppose so," he muttered.

"Is Athene a senior or a junior god?"

"Junior, of course…. What's the point of all this, Iris?"

"I'm just interested in how we're all classified, Zeus. Have you ever thought of telling us all what category we're in?"

Zeus looked perplexed, thinking this was a serious suggestion. "No," he eventually replied. "Do you think it would be helpful?"

"You could run training courses so junior gods could learn how to become senior gods," Iris said flippantly. "Perhaps you could introduce a new category called 'middle gods' that we could aspire to on the way to becoming senior gods?"

"I'll have to give all of this some thought," Zeus responded, looking very pensive.

"Don't bother, Zeus," Iris said standing up to leave. "We're all gods and we all know what our specific jobs are. I'm off to do mine now, which is to give Mars your message. I'll see you on my return."

●

A few hours later Iris was sitting with Stevie in the Tyrant's dining room drinking tea and eating a piece of fruit cake which the oldest person in the world had made the previous day.

"It's over a hundred years since we last had tea together," Iris said.

"It is. You stopped bringing your rainbow here a long time ago."

"I didn't like all these tyrants. Each generation seemed to be worse than the last."

"That's a fair assessment, Iris. The current Tyrant's definitely as bad as we've ever had."

"I suppose eventually there'll be a revolution and he'll be toppled?"

"Chopping his head off is the latest plan unless he makes an escape. Having Lord Mars here, though, complicates matters."

"Yes, I can see that," replied Iris. "So, Zeus's thunderbolt missed him completely but instead hit Mr F, otherwise known as Famine. Surprising as the Top God's normally deadly accurate."

"I suspect it wasn't Lord Zeus's aim that was wrong. Mars just happened to move out of the room as it was on its way here."

"And you say he then left shortly afterwards to meet up with the Tyrant?"

"He suddenly seemed in a real rush as if he were expecting another thunderbolt anytime."

"All bullies are really cowards at heart," Iris mused. "And Mars is about the biggest bully going."

"My view entirely," Stevie replied.

"So, he's gone to this facility in the mountains from where all these missiles get launched?" Stevie nodded her head before Iris continued. "I'm supposed to go there and give Mars a message, Stevie. However, if you don't know the precise location, I won't be able to go. That, of course, will be a huge disappointment to me."

Iris yawned, looked Stevie in the eye and got a knowing smile back.

"Well, I'm very sorry to disappoint you, Iris, but I don't know the exact location. Nor does anyone else in the palace. It's very much a state secret."

"Then I'll finish off my tea and cake with you, Stevie and return to Olympus. Perhaps I could look in on Famine before I go?"

"Do you know him well?"

"Quite well, but I'm not on particularly friendly terms with him."

"No, I suspect he doesn't have many friends. Mars seems to like him though."

"And Pestilence and Death," Iris said. "How badly is Famine injured?"

"He's not in good shape. Lots of green and yellow liquid came out of him. We've got a doctor and two nurses with him now. They don't understand what sort of creature he is since he doesn't seem to have any blood."

"What did you say to them?"

"That people from far off countries don't have blood, only yellow and green liquid in their veins."

"Did they believe you?"

"No, but they just want to get away from him. They're busy bandaging him up at this moment and then hope to be off. I think they ought to stay overnight with him, though."

Iris thought about what Stevie had said and started to develop the germ of an idea. "I'd let them go," she eventually replied. "He'll probably just heal over time. Best to leave him alone overnight."

Stevie nodded and stood up. "Come and look at this before we go and see Famine." She took Iris into another room which had a large television on the wall. "It came through shortly after Mars left. This is a recording,"

Stevie pressed the remote control and the words 'Breaking News' appeared on the screen. This was followed by Totty in her newsreader capacity announcing that the Tyrant had decreed that the working day was to be immediately increased by an extra hour and the day off that everyone traditionally had in the week was to be reduced to only half a day. The words summarizing this change then appeared across the screen as Totty's image disappeared.

"A smart looking girl," Stevie commented. "Do you know her?"

"She reminds me of a friend of a friend," Iris responded.

The oldest lady in the world and the goddess smiled at each other before going off to see Famine. All Iris did was pop her head round the door before retreating downstairs once more with Stevie. She was given another large piece of fruit cake to take with her, kissed Stevie on her cheek and then set off with her rainbow in tow. She'd decided to go to Lilliput instead of Olympus. That germ of an idea was developing as each minute passed.

21
The Mount Olympus Red Cross

The ambulance came to a halt on the front drive. It was painted all in white and had large red crosses on either side. The four horses which pulled the vehicle were naturally white in colour, with red crosses on their flanks.

Four females descended from the back, carrying a large stretcher. Two were tall, one was medium sized and the fourth was small. They all wore white nurses' uniforms, suitably annotated with red crosses, each one wearing a white head-scarf and a face mask. They hurried towards the large front door and rang the doorbell, waiting impatiently for it to be opened. It took five rings and a considerable amount of banging with the door knocker before they could hear the locks on the other side being pulled back. Eventually the door opened and an elderly man in guard's uniform appeared.

"Emergency call out," one of the tall females said, pushing her way past the guard, followed by the others with the stretcher. At that moment Stevie appeared in her nightgown, walking down the stairs.

"Good evening," she said. "Can I help you?"

"Emergency call out," the same tall female repeated. "We're here from the Red Cross, Mount Olympus Section, to take your seriously injured guest to our hospital."

"And your name would be?"

"I'm Sister Athene, accompanied by Staff Nurses Amphitrite and Iris and Trainee Nurse Hebe."

"Hey," Hebe suddenly said. "Why am I only a-----"

She was cut off by Iris putting a hand over her mouth and indicating that she should shush.

"It's like the army," Hebe moaned.

"Is he upstairs?" Athene asked, trying to push past Stevie.

"One minute, please," Stevie responded, putting her arm out to prevent Athene from passing. "Since neither the

269

Tyrant nor Lord Mars are here, could you please confirm in a loud voice so Cho-ak, who opened the door to you, can hear that you have been sent by them, and this is all properly authorized?"

Athene looked at Stevie, who gave her a very knowing smile which indicated she knew what was going on and needed the goddess to give the right answer.

"Definitely," Athene lied. "It was actually Lord Mars who called us out; nothing to do with the Tyrant. This is Olympus business."

"Did you hear that, Cho-ak?" Stevie asked, looking at the guard.

"Yes, Stevie."

"And so did I," a second, younger guard added, having just walked into the hall from a passageway.

"Very good," Stevie responded. "Let me show you where the patient is."

She turned round, walked up the stairs and along a corridor, before opening one of the doors on the left and turning the light on. She then stood aside and indicated that the medical team should go into the room. As Iris passed her, Stevie gave her earlier visitor a wink which the goddess reciprocated with a thumbs up.

Famine was lying on the bed either asleep or unconscious. He was covered in bandages, but there was no sign of blood, only yellow stains. Since the bed was a large king-size, the goddesses placed the stretcher next to the patient.

"Let's lift him onto it," Athene said quietly. "Two at the side, one at the head and the other take his feet."

As they began to move Famine, he slowly regained consciousness. He made some mumbling noises about what was going on before focusing on Athene's face. He frowned and then suddenly recognized the Goddess of Wisdom. Shocked at her presence, he began to scream before Hebe, who was at his side, pushed a gobstopper into his mouth.

"That will keep you quiet," she said as she and the other three struggled to hold Famine down. This went on for a good five minutes before the goddesses managed to immobilize him by binding his limbs together with copious amounts of tape which Hebe had brought with her. They then secured him to the stretcher by taping him to it before lifting him up and carrying him out of the room.

"It's a good job you brought that gobstopper and tape," Amphitrite said as they were walking downstairs.

"Perhaps I'll get promoted from trainee nurse to staff nurse?" Hebe inquired hopefully.

"I doubt it," Sister Athene replied smiling. Hebe pulled her tongue out at her big sister, but despite wearing a mask retracted it as soon as she saw Stevie waiting for them at the bottom of the stairs.

"How is he?" the oldest person in the world asked as they all walked to the open front door together."

"Both very restless and delirious," Athene replied. "That's why we've had to tape him up so much; it's to stop him harming himself. Also, this restraint in his mouth will protect his tongue. I've seen occasions like this when patients bite their tongues off."

"Very professional of you," Stevie replied. "Did you hear that Cho-ak?" she asked looking at the guard.

"I did," Cho-ak replied.

"And so did I," the other guard added.

"Excellent," Stevie commented as they reached the front door. "Mr F is clearly in very good hands. I'll say good-bye to you all here if you don't mind. Also, very many thanks to you, Sister Athene and your excellent team. Please take great care of the patient. We hope to have him restored to us fit and healthy, but please take your time. There's no rush to get him back to us; no rush at all."

As the stretcher bearers left, Stevie again winked to Iris who once more gave her a quick thumbs up.

When the stretcher with Famine on it was in the chariot, Athene bent down to speak to Famine.

"Hello, Famine," she said, her face a few inches from his. "You know who I am, don't you?" There was a nod of his head. "That's right, I'm Athene. Lots of your other friends are here as well – Hebe, Iris and Amphitrite. We're all really concerned about you after your accident, so we've come to take you to Olympus where we've got an excellent nurse, called Florence, who'll get you better. When you're up and running, my father, Lord Zeus will want to have a little chat with you. Unfortunately, he's a bit unhappy with you because you've been ignoring him for a long time. Anyway, I'm sure the two of you will sort things out. Then, my Aunt Demeter would like to have a few words with you. I know you remember her; she's the one who tries to make crops grow, but you often turn up and upset things for her. Anyway, don't you worry just now about all these little chats planned for you in the future; relax and have a good rest while we travel to Olympus." Athene gave Famine a forced smile. She wasn't sure if he was capable of experiencing fear, but his eyes looked as if they might be doing so at that moment.

As the chariot took off into the air, Hebe asked Amphitrite if she wanted to be dropped off at Lilliput before the rest of them went to Olympus.

"How long are you staying on Olympus?" the Sea Goddess asked.

"Less than a day. I've got to get back for our next mission."

"That's fine. I'll come to Olympus and then return with you to Lilliput. What's your next mission?"

"We plan to zap the Tyrant's air force. Tuff buns if you're one of his pilots."

"How are you going to do that?"

"We're still working on it. That team of Rach's is absolutely fantastic. Just as you used them on all those sea attacks, they've got a group that's going to help us mess up all their planes. I'm glad that my chariot's not got any of this technology stuff in it or some group of computer hackers would probably send me to places I don't want to go."

"Probably Tartarus," Athene commented.

"Why do you say that, Athy?" Hebe asked.

"I've been thinking a lot about Iris's conversation with Mars. I suspect he wants a lot more than just being allowed to start wars, without any reference to the Council."

"What do you mean?"

"That he wants a repeat of the wars between the Titans and the three brothers. He wants to dispatch us all into oblivion, so he can take over. Oblivion means Tartarus."

"The bastard!" Hebe exclaimed. "Still, it would be like my big brother to want to do something like that."

"I've thought of that possibility too," Iris said, involving herself in the conversation. "But I don't believe it would have a chance of succeeding. Mars is just not clever enough or strong enough, even with this powerful new rocket of his."

"That rocket's had a couple of misfires recently," Hebe said. "So, it's not all that great, especially when Rach's team redirect it."

"While I agree with what you say about Mars," Athene replied thoughtfully after a short period of reflection. "Chance or circumstance might tip the odds in his favour, so we need to be on our guard."

"Then we'd better keep zapping the Tyrant," Hebe said. "Zap the Tyrant and we zap Mars."

"I agree," the Goddess of Wisdom concurred.

When they arrived at Olympus, Hebe brought the chariot to a halt on Zeus's front lawn. The goddesses carried the stretcher through the open front door into the hall where they found Mrs Bumble washing the floor.

"Good morning, Mrs Bumble," Athene said. "How's it going?"

"As well as can be expected, Lady Athene," the Head Housekeeper replied. "We've got Nobbly Butt upstairs, replacing the broken windows. Mr Bumble says he passed your palace yesterday afternoon and you've got the same problem. Everywhere's got broken glass, as you know, Lady Iris." The Rainbow Goddess nodded.

"I'll look later. Where's Father please?"

"In his study. If you don't mind me asking, who have you got there on the stretcher?"

"A gentleman called Famine. He's had a bad accident."

"I've heard of him. Why did you bring him here?" Mrs Bumble asked, alarmed. "We surely don't want that horrible creature on Olympus."

"Father wants to speak to him. Don't worry, once he's better, we'll find some other place to deposit him."

"Dispose of him would be a better idea."

"That's one option we'll bear in mind. See you later, Mrs Bumble."

The stretcher party turned to their left and went down a long corridor to Zeus's study. Athene knocked on the door and then just walked in without waiting for a reply. The Top God was sitting behind his desk staring into space. All the windows in the room were broken although the glass had now been cleared.

"Good morning, Father," Athene said. "We've brought Famine to see you. Here, we'll put his stretcher on your desk. As you can see, I've got Hebe, Iris and Amphitrite with me. Poor Famine's had a bad accident and he's a bit under the weather. Apparently, your thunderbolt hit him instead of Mars."

A very perplexed Zeus stood up, unable to say anything for a while as he looked at the four goddesses in Red Cross nurses' uniform. He then stared at Famine who was covered in bandages and firmly taped to the stretcher which was now resting in front of him on his desk.

"You look all agog, Zeus," Iris was the first to speak. "Shall we sit down on the sofas and tell you what's happened."

"I think you'd better," a shocked Zeus said moving to the side of his desk so he could walk towards the sofa area in the far corner.

"I'll just plug Famine's ears," Hebe volunteered, as she pulled out more tape to wrap around the sides of his head. "We don't want him hearing what our side's up to."

Hera was called to join the group and Athene then summarized what they had been up to over the last twenty-four hours.

"So, my thunderbolt hit Famine instead of Mars," Zeus said at the end, clearly disappointed. "And you didn't see my recalcitrant son at all, Iris?"

"No," the Rainbow Goddess replied. "He left for the mountains shortly after Famine was hit. He probably thought you were going to throw another thunderbolt."

"I would have done if I'd known the first had missed. But why have you all brought Famine here?"

Athene sighed. "Father," she said, sounding slightly irritated because she was: "Have you forgotten the conversation we had about finding him and Pestilence so we can bring them back under the gods' control?"

"No," Zeus replied defensively. "But I don't know what to do with him in this condition. I clearly can't speak to him until he's recovered and I'm reluctant to try healing him."

"I don't think any of us gods should try and heal Famine. We just don't know enough about the nature of either him or Pestilence," the Goddess of Wisdom said. "Don't you have some secure place in the palace we can put him for the time being? What about your cellar?"

Zeus and Hera looked at each other and then both shook their heads.

"The cellar's got all our provisions in it, but more importantly it's not really secure," Hera said. "It may have a lock on the outside, but I think you want something more like a prison. Famine's cunning and vicious; he'll try everything to escape. I know him from of old when I used to help Demeter with the crops; that was before Persephone grew up."

"I'll tell you a place which might do," Zeus said. "Bacchus has a number of cellars which are really secure. They've got thick strong doors with multiple locks and bolts. If they need strengthening at all, perhaps Heph could add some more bolts?"

"I know what you're referring to, Father," Athene responded. "That's not a bad idea." She looked at the others who nodded.

"Agreed then," said Hebe, standing up. "Let's go."

Twenty minutes later, the four stretcher bearers were carrying Famine into The Dog and Duck public house. The first person they saw was Mistress Quickly, who was the tavern's hostess. She was wearing a pink dress with a blue apron and was busy polishing the bar area as she did every morning. Bacchus was sitting on a chair in the far corner drinking a glass of red wine as he observed proceedings.

"What are you girls doing all dressed up in nurses' uniform?" Nell Quickly asked. "And what's that thing you've brought with you on the stretcher?"

Bacchus had by now walked over, wine glass in hand. He looked at the figure on the stretcher and then said: "I've met him before. It's Famine, isn't it? Something's happened to him, but whatever it is, I hope you're all going to take him away as soon as possible."

"I'd better tell you what's going on," Athene replied, as usual taking the lead.

The Goddess of Wisdom then repeated what she'd recently told Zeus and Hera. Bacchus and Nell Quickly didn't react until they heard that the plan was for Famine to be kept in one of their cellars.

"I don't like that at all, Athene!" Nell replied.

"Impossible!" Bacchus added. "He'll turn all the wine into vinegar and the beer into something you'd find in a sewer."

"Not necessarily," Athene answered, but for once without a hundred percent conviction. "I'll put a shield around him."

"I bet you've never done that before with a creature like him," Bacchus said. "I don't believe it's possible. No, I'm landlord of the Dog and Duck. He's got to go somewhere else!"

"Father's orders," Hebe said now getting involved in the discussion. "Famine's got to be kept here."

There was then a huge argument between them all for the next half hour. Eventually, a compromise was reached which was that Famine could stay under lock and key in the most secure cellar in the Dog and Duck. However, Athene, Iris and Hebe all had to apply shields to the cellar, so there was multiple protection. Amphitrite and Bacchus didn't have the power to produce effective shields. If there was any sign that Famine was compromising the tavern's liquor supply, food stores or Nell's rose garden, then he would be moved elsewhere. Precisely where was unclear, but Zeus would be forced to make a decision.

Before finalizing this compromise, the cellars were checked and the deepest one was identified as being the most suitable. It was currently empty, had a strong door with three locks, together with a number of bolts on the outside. The keys were left hanging on a peg in the outside corridor and it was agreed that no one could go in without being accompanied by Nell with her frying pan in hand.

"So, what happens now?" Nell asked when they had all returned from the cellar inspection.

"I suggest we take Famine down on his stretcher and leave him in the cellar all bound up for the present," Athene said. "We'll lock the door and then the three of us will apply our shields separately, hoping they reinforce each other. I'm going to go and get Florence to look at him; I'll be with her, and you and your frying pan will need to come as well, Nell." The hostess nodded. "After that, I'm going to go and find Artemis, Hermes and Hephaestus. I'll be staying the next couple of days on Olympus, principally because I want to monitor what's happening with Famine. However, I'll have to return to Lilliput afterwards, so we need a team to keep watch over him."

"What about them adding shields as well?" Bacchus asked. "And can't Zeus and Hera also do so?"

"Yes, I agree," Athene replied. "Leave it to me to organize."

"Alright. One other matter; I assume you've not brought Lennie and Beetle back with you?"

"They're currently in Special Forces, attached to Lilliput's Argyll and Sutherland Highlanders Regiment," Hebe answered. "Doing important undercover work for the army. We're at war with Tyrantland, you know."

"Lennie and Beetle are in the army, are they?" Nell said. "All I can say is they must be desperate!"

"Hey! I'm in the army as well!" Hebe retorted.

"I think I'll keep quiet then. I'll no doubt hear all about it when this war's over and done with."

"Shouldn't we take Famine downstairs now?" Amphitrite spoke for the first time since entering the pub. "We've all got a lot to do. You and I, Hebe, need to get back to Lilliput as soon as possible."

"Agreed," Hebe answered before looking at Mistress Quickly. "Where's my young friend, by the way?" she asked.

"In the orchard. Since he's been staying here, he's got his own deckchair next to Bacchus's. He's no doubt sitting there now with his jug of ginger beer waiting for his lordship to join him."

"I'll go and see him for a few minutes after we've locked Famine up."

"I'll come with you," Amphitrite said. "I've never met him before. But then we must return to Lilliput."

"We will, I promise," Hebe replied. "But I also need to call in at the bungalow to get some more clothes. It will take twenty minutes max. What are you going to do, Iris?"

"Go with Athene."

"Come on then," Athene said, moving over to the stretcher. "Let's get on."

22
The Challenge

The Tyrant's secret facility on the mountainside was not a happy place. All the scientists had been kept there for several days, unable to return home in the evenings. They were forced to sleep on the floor and, while food was prepared for them in the downstairs kitchen, there were few facilities for washing and none of them had had a change of clothes.

These matters were, of course, minor compared with the fact that they had all been told they were going to be impaled very soon. Mars's arrival had suggested that something had gone very wrong with the third missile, and this was confirmed in a subsequent telephone call when the Tyrant learned from Stevie that it had hit Olympus. The only reason the impalement sentence had not been carried out already was because the Tyrant wanted to know why the missile had gone off course; he had stated publicly that the scientist who found the answer would be free to leave and wouldn't be punished.

The main room at the facility was full of all the scientists on their knees feverishly working away on their computer screens. In addition, it included several guards, also on their knees, whom the Tyrant had brought with him to ensure no one escaped. The Tyrant himself sat on a comfortable chair on a platform observing proceedings; he occasionally got up, walked around, poked the nearest scientist with a pen, barked out an instruction and would then return to his chair.

Mars spent much of his time on the lower slopes of the mountainside, cutting down thin trees or branches which he would bring back to the facility and then shave with either an axe or a strong knife to create sharp points at the end. All this was done on the platform so the scientists could see what awaited them. The Tyrant believed this acted as an incentive, while Mars just enjoyed terrifying people. The scientists were inclined to think the God of War understood human nature better than their country's leader.

It was mid-morning when Mars marched into the main room carrying a pile of wood to be turned into sharp points. He flung it down on the platform.

"Any more news?" he asked in his normal aggressive tone.

The Tyrant shook his head. "All we know is that our systems were hacked, but we don't know how or by whom."

"I don't understand all these words like systems and hacked," Mars growled. "What I do understand is it's taking too long for your bloody scientists to get an answer."

The Tyrant sighed but didn't respond. Mars and he had this conversation a dozen times a day and there wasn't anything more he could say.

A young scientist called Flogzum had a workstation near the platform. He had only been at the facility for two months, having decided to move there after falling out with his girlfriend in Tyrantville. He was still in the grief stage of his broken relationship, so he wasn't too concerned about not existing anymore; he was, though, a bit alarmed at the prospect of sitting on a sharp spike as the means of reaching this state of non-existence. His more immediate concern, however, was that he thought he had found something important, but couldn't understand it. Normally, he would consult a superior, but that was useless in the current situation because he would get no credit for it and would still end up on a spike. So, he decided he had nothing to lose by addressing the Tyrant personally.

Flogzum shuffled over on his knees to the platform. "Oh, Great One," he said, "I believe I've found something relevant about the missile hack, but there is also one problem with it, so I am not entirely sure."

"Show me," the Tyrant said, getting up from his chair and walking off the platform.

Flogzum shuffled back to his workstation and was followed by the Tyrant and Mars who stood either side of him.

"This is a map of the Indian Ocean," the scientist said. "I've traced the source of the hack three different ways and all show that it came from this one point here." At this stage, Flogzum expanded the map to focus on one area which he pointed to with a pencil.

"And your problem is?" the Tyrant enquired.

"There's nothing there," Flogzum replied. "It's all water; there's no land."

There was a dead silence for a few seconds before the Tyrant erupted. "Idiot!" he screamed as he punched Flogzum hard on the side of his head. "Idiot!" Now he started kicking the scientist, who had fallen over on his side, before a large hand suddenly appeared on his shoulder and yanked him back.

"Stop!" yelled Mars.

"No!" the Tyrant shouted, his face purple with rage at being manhandled by Mars in front of everyone. "That idiot needs to----"

"Shut it, you fat slob!" Mars interrupted, looking at the Tyrant menacingly. "That idiot, as you call him, is right. He's given us the answer."

"He can't have done!" blubbered the Tyrant. "There's no land there!"

"Yes, there is," Mars growled. "Everything's clear now. That point is where Lilliput is."

"I've never heard of it," the Tyrant said.

"Maybe not," Mars continued. "But it's real despite not being on any maps. What's more, the Lilliputians are close friends of Poseidon and his wife, as well as those bitch goddesses like Athene and Hebe. They're also known for being very advanced scientifically."

"So, what do we do?"

"You stay here. I'm off to Lilliput."

"But----"

"No buts," Mars interrupted. "Just stay here until I return." He marched across the room to the door before turning round. "And let that man go," he barked, pointing at Flogzum.

•

Poseidon saw the red horse and his rider first. He had left the daily meeting at the platform between the goddesses, Totty, Hashimoto, the Empress and various members of the Cabinet and others. They were discussing how to attack Tyrantland's air force, a subject on which he felt unable to make much of a contribution. However, with the arrival of the red horse, Poseidon knew he had a central role to play; he called out to the others and then went into his hut to get his trident.

Mars brought his horse to a halt about twenty yards from the platform. He jumped off, unsheathed his sword and started running towards the gathering.

"Poseidon!" he screamed. "I've come for you. Come and fight, you doddery old man. Don't hide, you yellow-skinned bastard."

Poseidon had now come out of his hut and advanced towards Mars, holding his trident in a fighting position. "I've been expecting you, my little baby nephew!" he shouted back. "It's time you were taught a lesson, other than potty training."

As the two gods approached each other all ready for a fight, Athene was the first to intervene. She had to stop this fight and reasoned argument wasn't going to do it. She prodded Hebe on her right and Amphitrite to her left, then shouted as loud as she could: "Stop them! Stop them!"

The response hadn't been pre-planned, but it worked as if it had. Hebe raced off to Mars's left, then came in at an angle and made a flying rugby tackle on his legs. A second later, Athene and Iris both dived for his sword hand and wouldn't let go until they had dislodged the weapon. By then, they were all on the floor but Hebe, being the smallest, was on her feet first and started kicking Mars in the face. Iris was up next and grabbed hold of his balls and squeezed, a trick she'd learned from the Hebe School of Fighting. While all this was happening, Athene, who as well as being Goddess of Wisdom, was also a warrior goddess, thumped Mars several times in the solar plexus until he collapsed defeated on the ground.

Amphitrite had tried a different technique initially. She walked up to her husband and shouted at him to 'Stop.' He paid no attention but pushed her aside. This annoyed her, so she turned round and jumped on his back, while screaming to Hash and Totty to help her.

"Come on, Miss Totty," Hashimoto shouted. "Have to stop Lord P."

Totty was totally confused about what to do. She wasn't at all sure about getting into a fight with Poseidon, but Hashimoto was racing towards the Sea God and Sea Goddess, so she followed him. Amphitrite was still holding on to her husband's back when Hash arrived in front of them and gave Poseidon a sharp karate chop across the nose. This caused him to scream out as blood started pouring down his face.

"Sorry, Lord P," Hash said, before kicking away his left leg and then chopping him on the other side to force him to fall over. Amphitrite was still holding Poseidon's back, so she went over with him, but refused to let go. Totty had now decided she'd better help, so she jumped on his right arm, pulling the trident out of his hand. She then pinned the arm back and like Amphitrite, refused to let go. Meanwhile, Hashimoto decided to follow the Iris example and he kicked Poseidon between the legs a couple of times, on each occasion eliciting a painful yelp.

"Sorry, Lord P," Hash apologized again. "It best way to stop you. Working on Lady Amphitrite's orders."

The Lilliputians on the platform watched all this fighting by the gods in amazement. To them, it was like a pub brawl taking place. When it seemed to have largely calmed down, the Empress had a word with her granddaughter, Rach, who jumped on her flying scooter and sped off.

Mars was on his back with each of his arms held down by Iris and Hebe respectively. Athene was kneeling on his abdomen and pressing him down with her arms, so all he was able to do was flail around with his legs to no useful purpose. Hebe had stuffed a handkerchief in the God of War's mouth, cutting off his angry flow of expletives.

Rach's scooter landed on Mars's chest. "Grandma wants to know if she can do anything to help?" she asked Athene, while still sitting on her seat.

"Not just yet, thank you," The Goddess of Wisdom replied, while trying to regularize her breathing.

"Okey-dokes," Rach replied and flew off to the group around Poseidon. He was in a similar position to Mars with Amphitrite on his abdomen and Hash and Totty holding down his arms. Rach received a similar response from the Sea Goddess, so she set off back to the platform. Chertassle nodded when her granddaughter had reported back, spoke to a couple of her ministers and then decided that they should all stay there to await proceedings.

Athene's brain was working feverishly. She needed to speak to Mars and Poseidon together without them hitting each other. If they decided to fight afterwards, they would have at least heard the Goddess of Wisdom, and would know the risks and consequences of what they were doing. She would still do everything possible to stop them fighting, but it was essential that they both heard what she had to say.

"Mars," Athene said, looking directly into his eyes. "I need to speak to you and Poseidon together on a matter of grave importance. Will you please agree not to fight for half an hour and listen to me, if Poseidon does the same?"

Mars shook his head angrily, again unsuccessfully tried to struggle free, and was undoubtedly swearing but his words were muffled by Hebe's handkerchief. Athene tried to reason with him but got nowhere, so she decided she would have more of a chance with Poseidon. The trouble was that she couldn't move from her position pinning Mars down and Amphitrite had precisely the same issue with the Sea God.

Athene called over to the platform and shortly afterwards Rach returned on her scooter. For the next ten minutes, the Goddess of Wisdom explained to the young scientist what message she wanted her to deliver and got her to repeat it three times until she was word perfect.

Poseidon was not gagged like Mars, but he was equally angry at being constrained and was shouting at his wife as well as Hashimoto and Totty. However, when Rach's scooter landed on his chest a second time he quietened down and waited to hear what she now had to say.

"Lady Amphitrite," Rach said, getting off her scooter and looking at the Sea Goddess. "I have been asked by Lady Athene for your permission to give a message to Lord Poseidon. Have I------"

"Of course, you have!" the Sea God interrupted. "What is it?"

Rach continued to look at Amphitrite who nodded to her. "Thank you, My Lady," she replied before turning round to the Sea God. "Lord Poseidon," Rach continued, "Lady Athene is most desirous to speak to both you and Lord Mars together on a matter of grave importance to the deity. She has asked if you would please agree to a truce for at least half an hour if Lord Mars does the same."

"So, what is this matter of grave importance?" Poseidon demanded.

"I don't know, My Lord, but Lady Athene is very concerned."

"Please do it, Poseidon," Amphitrite pleaded with her husband.

Poseidon didn't answer for quite a long time. He was far more sensible than Mars and, while angry at being restrained, he knew Athene well enough to believe that what she had to say was important. The Goddess of Wisdom was someone you did not ignore lightly. After a while, he said in a more emollient tone to the young scientist: "Rach, please leave us alone for a while."

Rach looked at Amphitrite who again nodded. She got on her scooter, winked at Totty and set off back to Athene. Having told the goddess what had happened, she returned to the platform, where the Empress deliberately didn't enquire what messages had been passed between the gods.

After a few minutes more discussion, Amphitrite, Totty and Hashimoto released their hold on Poseidon, and he stood up. His wife went up to him and gave him an affectionate hug, which he accepted with good grace before walking over to where Mars was still pinned down.

Athene had by now pulled the handkerchief out of Mars's mouth. She and the other two goddesses were being subjected to considerable verbal abuse, involving being called bitches, sluts, tarts and other such words; they also learned that the God of War was going to disembowel each of them personally and feed their guts to vultures. Hebe shouted at him to 'shut his gob,' but that had no effect, so she left all further attempts at communication to Athene. It was while this rant was continuing that Poseidon walked up and looked down at his nephew. For a split second, Mars became silent giving the Sea God the opportunity to speak.

"I've agreed to the truce Mars because I want to hear what this matter of grave importance is that Athene needs to speak about. I suggest you do the same."

"It's a trap!" Mars snarled.

"Not a trap I'm involved in."

Mars spat out of his mouth but missed Poseidon.

"I'll leave you to it then," the Sea God said before turning round and walking back to his wife.

It took another twenty minutes before Mars eventually gave in. He was sure that the three goddesses would tire and then he would release himself. However, when Athene said that they would set up a rota system with Poseidon, Amphitrite, Hash and Totty to hold him down, he decided to accept the truce.

They all sat in a semi-circle except for Athene who was standing at the front. Poseidon and Mars were as far apart as possible, and the group was near the platform so the Lilliputians could hear.

Athene gave a short speech because there was only one matter of importance she needed to raise. She did, however, start by explaining to all the gods what they already knew, which was that they were not able to exercise their powers as gods on Lilliput. She did not know why, but it had always been the case. This meant that while on Lilliput the gods were effectively human beings. There was no dissent at this; even Mars had heard the matter sometime in the distant past.

The Goddess of Wisdom then moved on to explain the implications for life and death. Gods could not die; they may get older and lose some of their powers, but they could not die. However, this was not the case on Lilliput; if a god died on the island, then he would be no more and could not be resurrected. This meant that if Poseidon and Mars fought and one of them was killed, that would be the end of him. There was nothing that the other gods could do to prevent this.

There was a dead silence for a period while Athene's words were digested by her audience. Mars was the first to react.

"I don't believe this!" Mars snarled aggressively. "You're just making it up, Athene, to stop us fighting."

"I do," Poseidon replied quietly. "I've heard this said before. Lilliput is a unique place in our universe. Athene is not making the matter up."

"Rubbish!" Mars shouted. "Anyway, even if it's true, it doesn't worry me. I still challenge you to fight me here, Poseidon, unless you're too scared."

Poseidon looked at Mars for a full ten seconds before replying very sombrely: "I accept your challenge, Mars, even if it means one of us will die."

"No!" screamed Amphitrite, putting her arms around her husband whom she was sitting next to. "You cannot do this, Poseidon. Stop him; stop both of them, Athene."

"It is agreed, Amphitrite," Poseidon said in the same sombre tone. "Mars and I will fight."

At that stage, all the other goddesses tried to intervene, and everyone was talking at once. After a few minutes of conversational mayhem, the Empress spoke to her granddaughter who jumped on her flying scooter, got as close as possible to the babbling group and then pressed her horn constantly: 'Toot, toot..... toot, toot....toot, toot.' It kept going until the gods and goddesses stopped talking and looked at Rach's scooter, zooming backwards and forwards in front of them.

"Grandma wants to say something," Rach called out before going 'toot, toot' once more and then flying back to the platform.

Everyone looked to the Empress who walked to the front of the platform. She began by introducing herself to Lord Mars and welcoming him to Lilliput. His response was to growl "get on with it" and to spit on the ground, which Chertassle ignored. She then apologized that there was no spare hut for him if he should stay the night, but there would be plenty of food and drink available later in the day. Again, Mars growled "get on with it" and spat a second time.

The Empress went on to address the conflict between Poseidon and Mars. She emphasized this was very much a gods' matter, and it was not for the Lilliputians to get involved. However, she did want to confirm that in her view Athene's assertion that a god could die on Lilliput was entirely correct. It was recorded in a number of the island's ancient texts which she had studied.

Chertassle now said she wanted to make two suggestions which she was doing entirely in a personal capacity and not as Empress; this was because she felt a strong friendship towards many of the gods present. The first one was that in order to avoid the death of a god, it might be wise to leave Lilliput and for the challenge to take place at another location. The second one was that there could be some advantage in deferring the challenge, wherever it is held, until the following morning so that there could be proper reflection on the whole matter. She finished by noting that was all she had to say, bowed and moved back to the middle of the platform.

Again, there was a babble of conversation. All the goddesses agreed with the Empress on the two points, but Mars was adamant that the fight would occur on Lilliput;

Poseidon was prepared to meet his nephew anywhere and couldn't be persuaded otherwise. Athene refused to accept this, as did Amphitrite, so the debate continued well into the afternoon. On the question of deferring the fight until the following day, Mars was slightly more amenable because he could see the advantages in getting some rest after his long journey. However, he didn't want to admit it, so he argued the point for a long time before eventually being persuaded to accept it.

•

During all this time, Mars's red horse had decided to wander off and have a look at Lilliput. He was particularly keen on finding a field with plenty of grass so he could have a good munch. After a while he heard some neighing in the distance and shortly afterwards came across the other gods' horses who had undoubtedly found the most luscious field in the whole of Lilliput.

There were ten horses in total – Hebe's four white stallions, Tonk, Bonk, Donk and Zonk; Poseidon and Amphitrite's four black mares, Holly, Dolly, Molly and Polly; and finally, Athene's two brown mares, Antoinette and Arabella.

It is often said that animals reflect their owners. This is undoubtedly true in many instances, but there are exceptions. The Red Horse was one of those exceptions; he was really quite shy and just wanted an easy life with no hassles and a number of good friends. Unfortunately, belonging to Mars, he didn't get any of those things.

"Hello everyone," he said timidly as he trotted towards the others.

"Look who's here," Dolly said. "Tomato Face!"

"Ugh! What are you doing here, Tomato Face?" Molly asked. "And who said you can come into our field?"

"Yea! Clear off!" Tonk shouted, moving aggressively towards The Red Horse. "You're not wanted here!"

"Don't be like that. I'm only trying to be friendly, and I'd like to eat some grass after my long journey."

"No one wants to be friendly with Mars's horse," Molly retorted. "If you had a different god, that might be different; but you haven't!"

"Yea, Mars is a real pig," Dolly added.

"Just because I'm Mars's horse doesn't mean I agree with everything he does," The Red Horse said. "I know he's not the nicest of gods."

"That's very disloyal!" Antoinette commented in a very posh voice.

"I agree," Arabella said in an equally posh voice. "Antoinette and I agree with everything Lady Athene says and does."

"So do we," Molly added.

"That's not surprising," Arabella responded. "Everything about Athene is perfect."

"I didn't mean Athene. I meant Poseidon and Amphitrite." Molly said.

"I can't believe that!"

"Well, most of it," Molly responded.

"Except when we don't." Dolly added. "But I bet we agree with our god and goddess more than you boys agree with Hebe." She looked towards the four stallions.

"We do actually agree with Hebe on lots of things," Donk said, deciding to involve himself in the conversation. "So, I don't think you can say that, Dolly."

"Even if we don't, life's more fun with Hebe," Tonk added, laughing.

"You're all as bad as each other," Arabella said haughtily. "None of you would ever be allowed to work for Athene."

"Oh, is there a vacancy, Miss Hoity Toity? You and your toffee-nosed friend being pensioned off, are you?" Dolly called out.

"Don't answer her," Antoinette said. "She's common."

"And you're a bleedin donkey, ain't you?" Dolly shouted.

While the other horses were holding their nice friendly conversation The Red Horse was happily munching away on a high patch of grass. The friendliest of the black mares came up and joined him.

"Hello Polly," The Red Horse said. "This is a good field you've all found."

"Hello Tomato Face. Yes, it's the best in Lilliput. Have you had a long journey?"

"From Tyrantville."

"I bet you're hungry. Tell me, is it true that Mars and Poseidon are going to have a fight?"

"It looks like it."

"So, who's going to win?"

"Athene."

"Athene!" Polly exclaimed. "Is she fighting as well?"

"Not directly, but she'll still win."

"How come?"

"I don't know, but I'm sure she'll win."

"Because she's Athene."

"Yes, because she's Athene."

•

Hashimoto and Totty had been listening to the gods and goddesses for hours. He had offered to Poseidon to fight Mars in his place, but this had been declined. Eventually it was agreed that the challenge would take place the following morning, but Mars and Poseidon were still intent on fighting on Lilliput. The conversations continued in the afternoon, but just went round in circles as the same matters were discussed.

Hashimoto got up. He had been thinking hard the last twenty minutes and wanted to go and speak to the Empress. She and the other Lilliputians had returned to Mildendo some time ago, so he set off on foot in that direction. He didn't say anything to Totty, thinking it best to act alone.

As he was about to enter the city, Rach came towards him on her flying scooter, which hovered in the air as they spoke.

"Miss Rach," Hashimoto said. "Do you know where the Empress is?"

"I've just come from her. She's in her palace. She wants me to go and see if there's any news yet from the gods."

"I will tell her. I need to speak to her on an urgent matter."

"Okey-dokes. Follow me, Hash and I'll take you to her. Watch where you put your feet.

Hashimoto sighed. Everyone said that to him, but he didn't really mind – he had more important things to worry about.

When they reached the palace, Rach went in to fetch her grandmother while Hash found a place in the large back garden where he could lie down and face the Empress. She hurried out, having told Rach she couldn't listen and to go and do something else.

"Hashimoto," the Empress said when she arrived in front of him. "You wish to speak to me on an urgent matter?"

"I do," was the response. "Honourable Empress, Hashimoto is very disturbed about this challenge between Lord Mars and Lord Poseidon, and he want to stop it."

"As we all do."

"Hashimoto has an idea but needs your help."

Chertassle smiled, remembering his last idea about how to help Totty complete her news-read. If it was only half as good as that, it would be well-worth listening to.

"I am all ears," the Empress said.

So, Hashimoto spoke, and the Empress listened.

23
Nabbed

Pestilence had been lying in a meadow overlooking the Dog and Duck for several hours. He had only been to Olympus twice before, once as a guest of Mars and the other time to meet Zeus. Both occasions were long ago, and the tavern didn't exist then. However, Pestilence knew that Famine was in there. The two of them had a special bond and could sense each other's presence from short distances of a few miles.

The woman at the Tyrant's palace had been cautious in speaking to him, but he had learned enough for his purposes. Initially he thought about following Mars to the mountains but decided to look for Famine instead. His friend needed Pestilence's assistance more than the God of War, having been injured by one of Zeus's thunderbolts. It was easy to guess where Famine had been taken from The Olympic Red Cross name. He'd never heard of it, but it clearly suggested that the gods were involved. Pestilence wondered what Mars had been up to in recent days to cause the wrath of the Top God and the capture of Famine. He would need to stay alert.

The woman was pleased when Pestilence left. She clearly knew who he was and within a matter of minutes had begun sneezing and complaining of a sore throat. This always happened and often Pestilence would deliberately stay longer than necessary, getting pleasure in seeing people's symptoms worsen. He also knew that the sight of him was disconcerting with his face covered in pustules, his gums bleeding and pus exuding from his left eye. On this occasion, though, he didn't hang around since he needed to follow Famine.

Pestilence believed that fortune was currently with him. He had visited Hyde Park a fortnight ago and, on the spur of the moment, decided to ride his horse for a few weeks; something he hadn't done for many years. This made it easy to travel from Tyrantland to Olympus. On arriving, he initially kept to the lower slopes which were uninhabited. He found a large field with plenty of grass and left his mount there while he began to stealthily move higher to where the gods resided. He could sense that Famine was nearby and as he progressed the feeling grew stronger with each step he took towards the tavern.

It the last few hours Pestilence had worked out who was who in the tavern. He recognized Bacchus, who was both fatter and balder than last time he'd seen him. Then there was a young boy who had spent much of the afternoon with Bacchus drinking in the orchard over on the right. Finally, there was the tall, thin woman in a pink dress who looked as if she did the work. As the evening progressed, a few customers arrived but it was generally quiet that day. Pestilence recognized Artemis and Apollo, but not many of the others. Few stayed long and as night set in the Dog and Duck quickly emptied.

In time the tavern's lights went out as its inhabitants retired to bed, but Pestilence remained watching from the meadow. He had a new Rolex watch which he kept referring to, having adjusted it to what he thought approximated to Olympus time. He estimated it was now about 11pm. He'd wait another three hours by which time everyone should be fast asleep in bed, then he would make his move. He only hoped that his friend, Famine, was not too badly injured and could sense that Pestilence was in the near vicinity, which meant help was at hand.

When Pestilence's Rolex told him it was time to make a move, he crept quietly towards the Dog and Duck's back door. He was used to moving around in the dark and that night there was a near full moon, so he had plenty of light for his purposes. He pulled a pouch out of one of his cloak's pockets and extracted a small metal device he used for picking locks. Pestilence was an expert at entering secure properties. Every time he introduced a plague into an area, families would lock themselves away for days in their homes, refusing entry to everyone. Pestilence still managed to find a way of getting in, spreading his plague and providing continued employment for Death.

Pestilence worked away at the lock for several minutes, but to his frustration he couldn't pick it. He wondered if the gods had created some sort of shield, which he would be unable to penetrate. It was only at this stage that he pulled down on the door handle and found the door suddenly giving way. He realized he'd been trying to pick a lock which hadn't been locked in the first place; after all, why would the gods have any need to lock doors on Mount Olympus?

Pestilence was in the kitchen from which there were stairs down to the cellars. He sensed that Famine was down there somewhere, so he slowly descended them. He stopped at the bottom because he needed to adjust his eyesight to the darker conditions. After a minute or so, he could make out a long corridor to his right which he proceeded along. With every step he was getting closer to Famine and when he reached the door at the end, he knew his friend was the other side. Looking around, he saw a large bunch of keys on a peg on the wall. He took it and tried the various keys on the locks, opening each one in turn. He then pulled the bolts aside, opened the door and walked into the cellar. There was Famine lying on a bed at the far side of the room; he had clearly sensed Pestilence's presence and put a finger to his lips to indicate silence as he began to raise himself.

Upstairs on the first floor of the tavern, Fearless Frupert kept waking up during the night, the result of drinking too much ginger-beer that day. Fearless was a six-year-old boy who had been living on Olympus for the last fifty years. He normally resided with Iris and Hebe in their bungalow, but whenever they were away a lot – as they were now – he would move into the Dog and Duck. He liked Uncle Baccy and Auntie Nell, especially all the good food the hostess cooked every day.

It was during one of those periods when Fearless was awake that he heard a slight scuffling noise downstairs. He got up and listened at the door. There was definitely something going on below and he was pretty certain it wasn't caused by either Bacchus or Mistress Quickly. That meant that there were probably intruders; a serious matter as far as Fearless was concerned. He always slept with the curtains open, so he naturally got some light into the room. Very quietly, he moved over to his chair where he put his helmet on, followed by the breastplate that Hephaestus had recently made for him. He picked up his wooden sword, opened the door and crept downstairs. When he reached the kitchen, he heard more noises as well as some whispering from the cellars. He continued very quietly down the next set of stairs, peeped round the corner at the bottom and saw two figures in the corridor. One had his arm around the other, whom he was trying to support. Fortunately, both had their backs to Fearless at that moment, so they did not see him.

Now Fearless Frupert came from the Hebe School of Fighting, which could be summed up by the two words 'Fight Dirty'. He approached the pair as quietly as possible and when he was behind Pestilence, he stabbed him hard with his sword in the back of the right knee. At that point, all hell broke loose as Pestilence screamed in pain, while at the same time his knee gave way. Fearless shouted "attack" and immediately stabbed the left knee, which also gave way as the Horseman collapsed on the ground, screaming again and pulling Famine down with him. The next attack was a hard jab in the intruding Horseman's right ear. He was about to repeat this on the other side when Famine kicked out and caused the young warrior to himself fall to the ground.

At the sound of all this fighting and screaming, Nell Quickly jumped out of bed, grabbed hold of her frying pan and raced into the first-floor corridor in her nightie. She passed Bacchus's door, opened it and shouted to him to get up. She then ran down the stairs to the cellars and saw Famine and someone else grappling with Fearless on the floor. She took a massive swipe at the unknown intruder's head, knocking him out cold. Famine looked up at her and put out one of his arms to fend off the frying pan which was now aimed in his direction. However, this opened up an opportunity for Fearless to stab him in the groin. Screaming in pain, he was naturally distracted when Nell's second attempt landed on his forehead, and he joined Pestilence in dreamland.

Bacchus was now downstairs in his red and white striped pyjamas. He and Nell helped Fearless up and checked that he was uninjured.

"You did a good job there," Bacchus said to the young warrior.

"Thanks, Uncle Baccy. Is he another baddie?" Fearless said, pointing to the inert intruder.

"Do you know him?" Nell demanded before Bacchus had a chance to reply to Fearless.

"It's Pestilence, one of the other Horsemen."

"What!" exclaimed Nell, suddenly sneezing. "What's he doing here? I thought Persephone had found out he might be in London."

"It looks like he was trying to free Famine."

"So, he is a baddie," Fearless said, answering his own question. Bacchus nodded his agreement.

"This all comes of you allowing this Famine thing to be kept in our cellar, Bacchus!" the hostess said in an accusatory tone. "I'm surprised at a grown male like you being pushed around by those four female nurses. You should have stood up for yourself and said no."

Before Bacchus had a chance to reply, Fearless said, trying to be helpful: "You push Uncle Baccy around, Auntie Nell,"

"No, I don't! Where did you get that ridiculous idea from, my young man?"

Fearless looked at the god for guidance before he too sneezed and Nell gave a chesty cough.

"Don't answer!" the hostess said, deciding now was not the time to discuss the matter. "Let's pull these two into the cellar and lock the door. Will the various shields against Famine also protect us against Pestilence?"

"I'm not sure," Bacchus replied.

"Right," said Nell, now speaking with a dry throat. "Fearless, you go straight away and wake Artemis up; run as fast as you can. Tell her what's happened and that we need her here urgently. She'll probably send you to get Hephaestus and Hermes. The three of them should be able to make sufficient wards for the rest of the night. We can then get Zeus and Hera tomorrow morning to create a total seal of the room."

"Let me help you pull these two baddies into the cellar first," Fearless replied, again sneezing.

"Leave it, Fearless," Bacchus replied. "Auntie Nell and I can do that. It's important we get Artemis here as soon as possible."

"Okay," the warrior said turning round to leave.

"And take off your helmet and breast plate and put some proper shoes on," Nell called out.

"Yes, Auntie Nell," Fearless replied hurrying up the stairs.

Bacchus now started sneezing but he and Nell Quickly easily pulled the two Horsemen into the cellar.

"We both need to stay here all night on guard," the hostess said when they had locked the door. "I'll go upstairs and get a couple of chairs."

"Do you think it would be a good idea to get a jug of Headbanger as well?" Bacchus called after her, thinking that his favourite beer would help sustain them during the night.

"No, I don't!" Nell snapped with an element of finality, followed by another cough.

•

Hashimoto hadn't slept well and was pacing around outside the huts in an agitated mood. Even though the sun had only recently risen, he decided it was time to wake Totty. He went and fetched a bowl of water, knocked on her door and, getting no response as he expected, he opened it, went inside and started shaking her. She was very tired, but he kept shaking her and eventually threw the bowl of water over her face. That got more of a reaction, and he hauled her up and pulled her out of the hut. She staggered around for a while, so he sat her down and went and fetched a mug of hot black coffee from a stove nearby, knelt beside her and got her to drink it.

"What's going on, Hash?" she asked, rubbing her eyes when she'd finished the coffee. "I'm so tired. Let me sleep."

"No time to sleep, Totty. I'll get you another cup of coffee."

When he returned, there was a look of amazement on Totty's face.

"Oh my!" she exclaimed looking around. "I can't believe it! Where's everyone else?"

"They're all asleep. Everyone was drugged last night. It was in the food."

"What about you?"

"I didn't eat much. Also spent all night drinking hot coffee."

Rach's flying scooter arrived just at that moment which she parked by Hashimoto and Totty.

"You okey-dokes, Tots?" she asked.

"Yes," Totty replied. "What happens now?"

"We need to wake the others; Athene first," said Hashimoto. "You being a lady, you must go into her hut."

"No," replied Totty. "I don't know her so well. I think we should wake Hebe first and ask her to help. It's good she spent the night here instead of with her regiment because of the crisis between the gods."

"Very well; I will go and get bowl of water. You must throw it over her. It is only way for her to wake up."

They went through the same routine with Hebe that Hashimoto had used with Totty. When the goddess had drunk her black coffee and was able to stand up and look around, a large smile appeared on her face.

"Brilliant!" she said. "Totally top brilliant! This was all your idea wasn't it, Hash? That's why you went off to see the Empress yesterday afternoon."

"How did you know that?" he replied sheepishly.

"Remember, I'm a member of the Argyll and Sutherland Highlanders. We know everything about you; and I mean everything," she said winking at him.

They next woke up Iris followed by Athene. The Goddess of Wisdom said little but walked around observing the scene. While she had a slight beam on her face, her mind was working feverishly on what to do about the situation. Eventually, she came over to the others.

"We need to wake Amphitrite now," Athene said. "But we'll have to be careful. It's going to be important to keep her in her hut until she fully understands what's going on, so she doesn't mess it up."

"What does that mean?" Hebe demanded.

"I don't actually know," Athene answered. "But we've got to think through each step from now onwards and not act impulsively."

"It's a good job she and Poseidon argued so much that he came out of the hut for some peace and slept in the open," Iris said.

"Yes," Athene agreed. "Look, I think it would be best if Totty and I went into her hut. Could the rest of you please keep passing us cups of piping hot coffee."

Athene and Totty spent a good quarter of an hour with the Sea Goddess. When she did eventually come out, she was stunned at the spectacle which confronted her despite having been forewarned.

Poseidon was lying a few yards away from her, snoring peacefully. He was fully tied up with ropes attached to pegs as Hashimoto had been on that unfortunate occasion when he had upset the Lilliputians. Mars was about fifty yards away in a similar condition. The ground around both of them was covered with masses of infantry soldiers as well as cavalry behind them. It looked as if the entire Lilliput army had been called to arms.

The soldiers around Mars had their weapons drawn – swords out, lances ready for action and arrows drawn. Quite specifically, the entire Argyll and Sutherland Highlanders

Regiment, being the country's foremost fighting force, was at the forefront of guarding Mars. The military around Poseidon, while numerous, was standing to attention but weapons were not drawn.

On the platform, the Empress stood with her entire Cabinet, none of them saying anything. Rach was now also on the platform on her scooter. She would from time to time be sent off by her grandmother to enquire if the goddesses needed anything. The only thing that they did want was a lot more hot black coffee, so a small army of kitchen staff who were in attendance busied themselves with making sure that there was always a plentiful supply available.

The four goddesses, Hashimoto and Totty went off for a conference in a quiet spot behind all the huts. After a while, it was decided that Athene should go by herself to discuss matters with the Empress.

"I think Amphitrite should come as well," the Goddess of Wisdom said, changing her mind. "Poseidon's reaction is going to be critical."

"I'm happy to leave it to you," the Sea Goddess replied.

"No. I need you," Athene said.

"Alright," the Sea Goddess assented.

The conversation with the Empress lasted a good half an hour before the two goddesses returned to the others.

"Let me tell you what the plan is," Athene said, as she and Amphitrite sat down with the others. "It's broadly as we discussed earlier."

Athene set out the official Lilliput position which was that the country was not prepared to have a fight to the death between two gods on its territory, so that was the justification for tying up both Mars and Poseidon. In addition, the God of War was viewed as being an ally of Tyrantland, with whom Lilliput was at war. That meant he was an enemy, who had been captured by the opposing side. Having established that, everyone felt the best approach was for the two gods to be returned to their respective realms. As far as Mars was concerned, that would involve immediately taking him back to

Olympus for Zeus and the Gods' Council to deal with. In Poseidon's case, he would merely return to the Sea Cavern. That could be at the time of his choosing and was what he was going to do anyway.

"So, ideas of fair play aren't coming into it," Hebe said. "There's no consideration of taking Mars and Poseidon somewhere else to have a fight?"

"Are you suggesting that?" Athene asked, somewhat surprised.

"No, I think what we're doing is absolutely right. I'm just asking the question because Poseidon might."

"I agree," Amphitrite said. "He probably will, but I'm not prepared to let him. He'll stay tied up until he agrees with us."

"Spoken like a good wife," Hebe commented to muted laughter all around.

"I want to say something," Iris now said in a serious tone. "We have a very valid reason for our actions. I for one have been ordered by Zeus to return Mars to Olympus. I believe the same could be said of both you, Hebe and Athene. We were given no instructions on how to do it but get him back was what we had to do."

"That's the justification for what we're doing!" Athene agreed. "What's more, as far as Poseidon's concerned, Mars has been captured by us three Olympian goddesses with the help of the Lilliputians on Zeus's orders. He's had nothing to do with it, so his conscience should be clear."

"Yes," Amphitrite said, "That should work with Poseidon, but it may take a little time to convince him."

"You do all know this was Hash's brilliant idea," Hebe thought it was time to chirp out.

"Was it?" Iris asked, staring at an embarrassed Hashimoto who was trying to look everywhere except at the goddesses.

"Yes; the Empress told us," Athene said with a smile, before adding: "Sheer genius!"

By now, both Mars and Poseidon were beginning to show signs of waking up. Hebe raced off to her chariot which she generally kept near the huts, found the bottle of anaesthetic she'd used at the military camp near the River Kwag bridge, soaked a cloth in the liquid and held it over Mars's face until he was knocked out cold. She then ran over to the platform, asked Rach if she could please find her stallions and get them to come back pronto because they were returning to Olympus.

Amphitrite woke Poseidon up with cold water and hot black coffee. The two of them had a long conversation during much of which the Sea God argued and struggled to get free. In due course, Amphitrite called Athene over and they continued the discussion. In time, Poseidon stopped struggling, was given a second cup of coffee and then burst out laughing.

"I'll spank that Hashimoto's backside!" he called out jovially.

Poseidon agreed to remain tied up until Mars had left for Olympus, so if the God of War woke up, he could see that both he and the Sea God were being treated equally.

Mars, however, didn't wake up due to Hebe giving him a face load of anesthetic. This allowed Iris, Hebe, Hashimoto and Totty to place him on one of the doors of the huts which had been taken off its hinges to be used as a stretcher. Hebe's chariot contained an assortment of ropes and handcuffs which she and Iris were expert at using, so Mars was suitably restrained. The stretcher was then placed on the chariot just as the four stallions returned. Poseidon by now had been won round and was laughing, so Athene and Amphitrite came over to the others. Once the horses were harnessed, Hebe, Iris and Athene went over to the platform to take their leave of the Empress and the Cabinet, promising to return in the near future since there was still the Tyrant to defeat. The goddesses then jumped onto the chariot, Hebe took the reins and off they soared into the sky carrying Zeus's problem child back to him.

Later that day Totty and Hashimoto were having a walk in the countryside.

"Do you remember, Hash, telling me that you'd been brought to Lilliput so you could fight the Tyrant?"

"Yes. Still got that to do."

"Well, you've already gone one better. You've defeated Lord Mars. What's more, Athene's called you a genius. How does that feel – the Goddess of Wisdom calling Hashimoto a genius?"

Hash held his head up high before replying. "Yes," he said. "Honourable Hashimoto is genius. That sound good. Yes, Hashimoto is genius."

The two laughed and continued their walk with Hash every so often saying out loud: "Yes, Hashimoto is genius. That sound good."

Every time he did so, the two of them laughed again. After all, they were having a good day.

24
A Week Later

T he oldest lady in the world picked up the phone on the fifth ring.

"Tyrantville 001," she said in a brisk tone.

"Is that Stevie?" the voice at the other end asked.

"It is."

"Stevie, this is Big Dik here."

"Big Dik!" Stevie exclaimed with delight. "How are you, my dear? It's been such a long time since we last spoke. You've done very well I see; now President of your country!"

"I'm fine, thank you. But I'm really phoning to find out how you are and to make you a proposition. There seems to be so much turmoil in Tyrantland."

"Let's just say a lot of changes are taking place, Big Dik. You know the Tyrant has completely disappeared? No one knows where he is."

"Ummm," was Big Dik's response. "I know something about it, but I'd like to hear your side of events before I pass comment."

"Well, all we know in the palace is that the Tyrant went to the mountains to fire off another one of his missiles. He's been firing a lot recently."

"I know."

"Anyway, he was then followed by Lord Mars a couple of days later. I suppose you know Lord Mars has been here?"

"I do."

"So, the two of them were in the mountains at this top-secret facility which everyone seems to know about. Once again, the latest missile went to the wrong place. We think it was Olympus, but you're not phoning to say your pig farm has been hit again, are you?"

"Not this time."

"That's good. Well, wherever it hit was a big problem. Lord Mars and the Tyrant were very annoyed with all the scientists at this top-secret place; they were about to impale the whole lot of them when------"

"What does impaling involve?" Big Dik interrupted Stevie.

"Sticking a sharp pole up their backsides, I believe."

"Nasty!"

"That's the Tyrant and Lord Mars for you. So, where was I? Oh yes, all the impaling's about to begin when Mars suddenly shoots off somewhere leaving the Tyrant by himself. Two or three days pass and there's no sign of Lord Mars returning. All the scientists are waiting around to be impaled.... In case you didn't know, you don't recover from having something long and sharp stuck up your backside-----"

"I gathered that."

"So, all the scientists are by now beginning to think there are more of them than the Tyrant. Also, they've got friendly with the guards, who are a bit pissed off with the Tyrant themselves because he offered them all $100 which he never paid and then extended their working week for no extra money. As time passed, the Tyrant was picking up all these negative vibes towards himself. The next thing everyone knew was that he'd gone outside for some reason and never came back. He's completely disappeared; no one knows where he is."

"I do," Big Dik said.

There were a few seconds silence before Stevie responded. "What was that Big Dik? Did you say something?"

"Yes, Stevie. I said I know where the Tyrant is."

"You do!" Stevie exclaimed. "Where? Is he dead or what?"

"No, he's still alive. He's here in Diktatorland. He managed to escape by helicopter and has asked for asylum with us. Naturally, we've agreed, but he's been told he's got to work for a living."

"So, what's he doing?"

"He's Assistant Piggery Decontaminator at one of the state's large pig farms about 500 miles from the capital. It's a very responsible position."

Stevie laughed. "Is Assistant Piggery Decontaminator what I think it is?" she asked.

"I'm sure it is. He has to clean out all the pig sties every morning and evening."

"That's what I thought!" Stevie responded laughing and Big Dik joined in.

After the jollity had subsided, Big Dik continued. "As I said at the beginning, Stevie, I'm phoning to make you a proposition. We're very aware in Diktatorland that there is a revolution taking place in Tyrantland and life must be very uncertain and unsettling----"

"No, I wouldn't-----" Stevie began to interrupt before herself being cut off by Big Dik.

"Please hear me out before passing comment. As I said, this revolution is taking place and I would like to offer you the opportunity of coming to live in Diktatorland, Stevie. You have always been a good friend to me, Little Dik and our families over many generations, and we would like to say thank you. I have a small estate of about 500 acres some twenty miles or so outside Diktatorville; it has a manor house with ten bedrooms and is fully staffed. I would be greatly honoured if you would come and live there. There will be no work for you to do; it will be your home and you will be completely looked after with everything provided. That is my proposition to you, Stevie. You are now 166 years old and----"

"165!" Stevie snapped, determined to interrupt. "We ladies are very sensitive about our age."

"I apologise and stand corrected. Anyway, how does my proposition sound to you?"

Stevie swallowed hard and thought for a few seconds before replying. "It really is tremendously kind of you, Big Dik," she said, "but I'm afraid I'm going to have to decline. The reason being that it looks as if I'm needed here for quite a while. We've got----"

"But you're in the middle of a revolution," Big Dik interposed before Stevie could finish. "These things are always bloody and you're likely in a lot of danger, especially since you've been part of the Tyrant's household. I'm sure there will be a lot of scores to be settled."

"Actually, Big Dik, things are already calming down. The revolution took place very quickly and there was no bloodshed. The main revolutionary group called the Tyranical, Yodeling, Revolutionary, Anarchistic, Nihilistic Terrors seemed to have a lot of army and police in it, so once the Tyrant had fled there was no resistance to its take-over of the country."

"Is that the group which has a lot of people called Jacques in it?"

"You've heard of it then?"

"Certainly. In confidence, several of my agents have been members for a long time; they all seem to go by the name of Jacques."

"Then we're talking about the same one. Unfortunately, your agents haven't kept you fully up to date. As of now, the revolution's ended in the sense that the new team have already taken over. The new team, by the way, is the Jacques group, the army, the police, the civil service and me."

"You!" exclaimed Big Dik. "I don't understand."

"That's right. It's not just me, but Big Sis and Little Sis as well. The new team has asked the three of us to be in charge of the country for the next two years while we set up a fully functioning democracy with a parliament and elections. We're also going to change the economy; instead of everything being owned by the state, which meant the Tyrant, we're going to have capitalism instead."

"I'm shocked!" Big Dik responded. "But all this has happened so quickly, it's unbelievable. I thought Little Sis was in the salt mines."

"She was, but Big Sis got her back yesterday. Also, the Tyrant's lovely young wife has already returned to her family in the country, so you'd better tell him she won't be joining him at the piggery."

"Are you sure about all this, Stevie?" the Tyrant responded. "You're all playing around with some very dangerous ideas."

"What do you mean, Big Dik?"

"This democracy idea for a start; it simply doesn't work. We have scholars in Diktatorland who have proved scientifically that democracy always ends in failure. It is an illogical concept."

"You mean countries like America and Britain are failures?"

"Precisely. It has been proved scientifically."

Stevie rolled her eyes at the other end of the phone. "Well thank you for telling me, Big Dik. I'll pass that on to the others involved in the revolution. I'm not sure it will have much of an effect, though. They're all rather keen on the idea, as are the people generally who are glad to see the back of the Tyrant."

"Well, I hope you can persuade them to rethink the matter. I also believe you should not look to introduce capitalism. It has been------"

"Is that another idea that your scholars have scientifically proved to be a failure?"

"It is. It's a very dangerous concept, which makes people worse off."

"I can't say the people were particularly well off with the Tyrant owning everything."

"That was due to the Tyrant's mismanagement," replied Big Dik. "It was not due to the idea of state ownership of the means of production."

"Then I'll put that on the list to discuss with the other revolutionaries," a weary Stevie said. "Is there any other advice you would like to give me, Big Dik?"

"No, Stevie; but I've got a couple of questions."

"Fire away."

"The first one is to ask what your title is going to be for the next two years?"

"That's an easy one. I'm going to be President and Big Sis and Little Sis will be joint Vice Presidents."

"President!" Big Dik exclaimed. "Then you will be my equivalent! Stevie, you really must come on a state visit to Diktatorland in a few months' time. Will you do that?"

"I'd be delighted, but we've got a lot of work to do here first. By the way, Big Dik, we're going to change the country's name – Tyrantland is going to be called Freedomland. What do you think about that?"

"Ummm. I think you should decide if you really want to adopt this democracy idea first before you decide on a name change."

"Have you got another question, Big Dik?" Stevie asked, ignoring the last comment about democracy and the country's name change.

"Only to ask what you will do after two years as President? My country estate will still be available to you then."

"Once more, many thanks, Big Dik. I and the two Vice Presidents already have our futures mapped out after that time. Big Sis is going back to Harvard to complete her PhD in French Literature and then intends to become a University Professor in the States. Little Sis will go to Oxford, where she's already got a place, and will study Classics; she wants to learn a lot more about the Greek Gods. I suspect she'll also become a University Professor. As far as I'm concerned, I'll probably go and join up with my nephew Ob and help look after his pub. He thinks he might get involved in politics then, so I could well end up having to run the place. Anyway, time will tell."

"All I can say then, Stevie, is to repeat that my offer will remain open if you change your mind. Also, to wish you well in your role as President and to ask you to make a big note about a state visit to Diktatorland as soon as you feel ready."

"I'll go and make the note now, Big Dik. Good to talk to you, by the way."

"And you Stevie. Bye."

"Bye."

As soon as she put the receiver down, Stevie walked into the Tyrant's former study which she had taken over. She sat down, took a sheet of paper on the desk which was headed up 'State Visit Invites' and wrote Diktatorland down as number 14. This was on a list which already had United States as 1, United Kingdom 2, China 3, France 4 and so on.

"The next year's going to be busy," she said to herself as she went off to continue dusting the living room.

•

Hebe's chariot slowly descended onto an enormous, flat, black rock. When it came to a halt, she immediately jumped off, carrying bags of hay and a large water bottle and spent the next few minutes looking after her four stallions. While they had had a long and tiring journey, they were exhilarated. They had never visited this location beforehand, but they adored the sights of all the different stars and planets. They didn't mind remaining harnessed because they knew they would be making the return journey in a short while.

Four others had been standing next to Hebe on the chariot. Her father Zeus was there in his white robe, looking particularly stern and saying nothing during the journey. Hephaestus and Athene were next to him as was Death. The three prisoners were sitting in the main body of the chariot; Mars and Pestilence were in chains while Famine had his arms and legs tied up with rope. All had their mouths sealed with tape.

As Hebe was feeding her stallions, Hephaestus and Athene got down from the chariot and pulled Pestilence out, then carried him about ten yards away before depositing him on the ground. They did the same with Famine before returning to deal with Mars. Unlike the others, the God of War struggled as he was pulled off the chariot, but the two gods were too strong for him.

"I don't like this, Mars," Hephaestus said loud enough for his father to hear. "But I do it because it is right." Mars made all sorts of angry grunts in reply before he was placed on the ground next to his fellow prisoners.

Athene and Hephaestus went back to the chariot and took a huge bowl of fruit which they placed on the ground. Athene now pulled out a set of keys from a pocket in her dress. She held it aloft, walked about twenty paces before placing it on the ground for all to see. She then took out a knife from the same pocket and returned to Famine.

"I'm now going to cut the bonds around your arms, Famine," she said. "You can then untie your legs and get the keys to free your two fellow Horsemen."

She did precisely as she'd indicated before joining the others on the chariot.

"Hear me, Horsemen," Zeus now spoke for the first time since they had left Olympus. "Once a year, you will be visited by either me or another god from Olympus. Freedom will only come when I, Zeus, Top God, decide it is appropriate. No one else can release you. However, I give you my word that you will not remain here longer than one thousand years. Farewell!"

Zeus nodded to Hebe who started the chariot off on its return journey. She would have liked to make some Smart Alec remark or give the middle finger to her brother, Mars, but didn't do so because everyone was so deadly serious that day. Death looked particularly solemn and, if he had tears, he would have been crying. He had asked to come along out of a sense of brotherhood with the other three Horsemen. She would take him to the Underworld after she'd dropped her fellow gods off on Olympus. Death still had a game of Monopoly to finish - hopefully that would cheer him up a bit, especially if he won!

Epilogue

O nce Mars had been returned to Olympus and the Tyrant had fled, hostilities soon came to an end and life returned to normal on Lilliput. The Sea God and Goddess, together with Hashimoto and Totty, returned to the Sea Cavern where they found Dolores still clearing up the mess from the Great Wave. They all set to work and made good progress, especially once they were joined by Hephaestus and Nobbly Butt who were engaged to carry out a much-needed refurbishment of the ground floor. The Builder God's first priority, however, was to fully redecorate the mermaid's smaller palace since they had nowhere else to live; the main palace's residents were at least able to occupy the first floor which was undamaged.

Amphitrite's other main priority during this time was to resolve Totty's situation. Totty herself was now increasingly keen on the idea of splitting her time between the Sea Cavern and Olympus, having seen more of Hebe on Lilliput as well as getting to know Iris and Athene. Of course, it all depended on Hades accepting this proposed arrangement, but Poseidon and Amphitrite were both confident he would do so.

So, early one morning, Death arrived once more at the Sea Cavern. He and Totty were taken by Amphitrite in her chariot to the Underworld. They went straight to Hades' palace where they found the God of the Underworld sitting on his throne. Totty sat on the stool in front of him while Amphitrite explained the purpose of her visit to her brother-in-law. She also presented him with three letters. The first one was jointly from Poseidon and Amphitrite which, after having sent warm greetings to the recipient, requested that Totty should be allowed to return to the Sea Cavern as a valuable member of their household. In addition, the letter explained that at Hebe's request, Totty would also spend some of her time on Olympus assisting the Servant Goddess with her various tasks. The second letter was from Athene in support of Poseidon's and

Amphitrite's request. She also explained in detail the critical role Totty had played in the war against Mars and Tyrantland, reminding Hades that the result was that far fewer people were dying and so relieving pressure on his kingdom.

Hades was surprised by the third letter which came from someone called Private MacHebe of the Argyll and Sutherland Highlanders Regiment, apparently part of the Lilliput armed forces. This letter also supported the Sea God and Goddess's request, explaining to Uncle Hady that Private MacHebe's other job as a goddess would be greatly assisted by having Totty living with her for part of each year. Having made this request, Private MacHebe then went on to address a second matter. Attached to the letter was a large parchment headed up 'PETITION'. Underneath were various words explaining that the Petition was to demand that Private MacHebe should be given a medal for exceptional bravery in the face of the enemy. Uncle Hady was asked in the letter to identify as many former members of the Regiment as possible who were now in the Underworld and to collect their signatures. After that, the petition should be returned to Hebe's bungalow at 5 Carnation Drive, Mount Olympus. Hades was somewhat perplexed by this because he couldn't recall any Lilliputians in the Underworld and wondered where Death took them when their time had come. He would have to speak to the black-cloaked skeleton on the matter next time he saw him, since he had already skipped off after delivering Totty into his presence.

Hades was feeling particularly friendly towards his brother Poseidon whom he credited with Mars's capture and his banishment to the asteroid with Famine and Pestilence. This meant that after asking Totty a few questions, he readily agreed that she could return to the Sea Cavern with Amphitrite. It was decided that they should both stay overnight in his palace so Totty could spend the rest of the day seeing the Underworld. Hades arranged for Vesta and Ming to be her guides which meant that it was inevitable that Totty would meet Cerberus. He only hoped she had a Mars bar with her.

On her first visit to Mount Olympus, Totty was encouraged to focus on fitness training by Hebe. Most mornings she ran a class on the large lawn at the front of Zeus's and Hera's palace. Hebe and Iris always attended when they were on Olympus and Fearless Frupert was particularly enthusiastic. Hera, together with her two sisters, Demeter and Hestia became dedicated followers of Totty's fitness sessions which meant that Mr and Mrs Bumble, together with Marie Antoinette, felt obliged to attend. Artemis, who was the fittest person on Olympus was always present, although her twin brother Apollo preferred to spend the mornings in bed. Nell Quickly dragged Bacchus along whenever possible, with the God of Wine always standing in the back row with the Bumbles. The one person who never attended was Zeus since he felt it was inappropriate for the Top God to demonstrate his prowess in front of everyone else. However, over time he found himself looking out of a first-floor window and joining in with the exercises. Unfortunately, his prowess was not great, and he was forever injuring himself by pulling different muscles in his body, leaving his wife perplexed as to what he had been doing while getting dressed in the morning.

In the Underworld, Mason Bonko eventually embraced change in the Building Department on the basis that 'if you can't beat them, you might as well join them.' Budiwati was formally appointed Deputy Head Builder on Sir Christopher's recommendation, which meant that she took full responsibility for managing specific projects. The first one she took on was to construct Cerberus's new kennel / house / palace. The design was the one preferred by the Head Architect which meant that Cerberus didn't get his twelve ensuite bedrooms. Budiwati managed to complete the project in six days and Cerberus was delighted with his new abode. The seventh day, however, was spent arguing with Budiwati about what name to give it. Cerberus kept insisting on including words such as Palace, Duke etc, which the Deputy Head Builder resisted. The matter had still not been resolved by the eighth day when Cerberus set off on a tour of the Underworld. On his return he found a large sign above the front door with the words CERBERUS'S HOME on it. He decided he liked that, so there was no more arguing with Budiwati on the matter.

Vesta and Ming continue to look at the workings of different Underworld departments. They have recently spent time in the Laundry which has been run by Mrs Grumblewax for more than 1,000 years. Mrs Grumblewax's qualification for the job was that she did the laundry for Merlin, King Arthur's magician. Unfortunately, she refuses to adopt modern working practices such as hot water and soap powder and won't accept making any changes without Merlin's approval. The trouble is that no one knows where Merlin is, giving Hades a tricky problem to solve.

Death is still playing various games in Aggy's kitchen. He has now taken up Chess and, like Monopoly, has a great aptitude for the game. He regularly plays against the former world champions and other grandmasters in the Underworld and invariably wins. In fact, he is so busy with both his job and playing all these games that he's decided he no longer has any time for a bungalow in Eastbourne, together with a family of Mrs Death and two younger Deaths.

Finally, we must not forget Rach. She shed a lot of tears when Totty left Lilliput to return to the Sea Cavern, fearing she would never see her friend again. Amphitrite did promise to bring Totty to visit her for a week later in the year, if things worked out in the way the Sea Goddess expected. This made Rach happier, but after Totty had left, she decided on a further course of action. She would make a mini submarine so she could go and visit Totty in the Sea Cavern. Later, when she heard that Totty might be spending some of her time on Olympus, Rach thought of also making a more advanced flying scooter. Professor Archimelock, her father, expressed grave doubts on both projects, fearing that a mini submarine would just not be able to withstand the powerful sea currents; similarly, he thought it would be impossible to steer a small person's scooter so high up because of the strong winds around Olympus. Not surprisingly, Rach is determined to overcome these obstacles. Would you bet against her? I wouldn't!

●

Every so often there is a Girls Night Out which the goddesses hold at the Dog and Duck. One took place recently when the events of the last few months were discussed. There was a lot of speculation about how long Zeus would keep Mars, Famine and Pestilence on the asteroid. No one believed they would be there for a thousand years. Instead, most thought that Zeus would let them return to the world within a year. After all, while no one likes conflict, hunger and disease, they are part of what life is about – a cynic might even say that without them, life would become boring.

"So, what are we going to sort out next?" Hebe asked, after the speculation about the Horsemen and their time on the asteroid had run its course.

"Zeus," Iris replied.

"Don't we need to sort out the whole of Olympus?" Demeter inquired. She was the only one of the three elder sisters who was present as she felt the need for some company because Persephone had once more returned to the Underworld.

"I think the starting point has got to be to get Zeus, Hades and Poseidon together," Athene chipped in.

"Personally, I want to focus on the Equalities Committee," Artemis said. "Not a lot's happened in recent months, and I am meant to be running it."

"So, which one are we going to focus…." Hebe stopped in mid-sentence. She had her back to the door but saw Iris nudge Athene; at the same time Aphrodite and Demeter suddenly looked to Hebe's left. "What's up with you lot?" she continued before a loud voice bellowed in her left ear.

"Found you, you devious crossbreed between a six eyed hippopotamus and a two eared dogfish! You is under arrest!"

As Sergeant MacGobo's voice was pounding her eardrums, Hebe spluttered the beer she was drinking. She looked to her left and saw the sergeant standing in full military uniform on a table next to her.

"Sergeant!" Hebe exclaimed. "What is you doing here?"

"I is looking for you, Private MacHebe, isn't I?" he replied, before shouting: "And put that beer glass down! Stand up straight! Shoulders back! Stomach in! Chest in front! Face looking straight ahead! Now!!!"

Hebe, or MacHebe as she had suddenly become, automatically did as instructed.

"You want to know why I is here, Private? I is here because I has a warrant for your arrest---"

"What for?" MacHebe interrupted.

"Do not interrupt me, Private!" MacGobo bawled out. "Understand?"

"Yes, sir."

"I is about to tell you. The warrant for your arrest is because of your desertion."

"I hasn't deserted!"

"Do not argue with me! If I says you has deserted, you has deserted. I am here to arrest you and take you back to Lilliput where you will be tried, found guilty and shot. That is why I is here!"

There was dead silence in the room after Sergeant MacGobo had finished speaking; all the goddesses having listened intently to the conversation between him and MacHebe. However, it was broken by Nell Quickly.

"Before you take Private MacHebe away and shoot her, perhaps you'd like a thimbleful of beer," Nell said, handing him a drink she had poured out.

"Thank you very much, My Lady," the sergeant replied bowing to her. "You would be?"

"She's the goddess Nell," Iris called out, tongue in cheek.

"Delighted to meet you, Lady Nell," MacGobo said, before bowing again and then drinking the whole thimble in one go.

"Let me top you up," Nell said, filling up the thimble again from a large jug of Hanseatic Headbanger beer she was carrying.

"I won't say no," the sergeant said. "Fine beer this."

"Permission to ask a question, Sergeant?" MacHebe said while still standing to attention.

"What is it?"

"How is it you got here?"

"I was flown here on Corporal MacLeonard's back with Private MacBeetle. They has been to Lilliput for a three-day training course, which you did not attend! You was told about it by Corporal MacLeonard and you ignored the order to attend. That is desertion!"

Hebe looked over at the far corner where Lennie and Beetle were respectively enjoying a nice game pie and a fresh lettuce. She pulled her tongue out at them as the sergeant was draining his second beer.

"Let me top you up," Nell said, immediately filling the sergeant's thimble once more.

"I is not happy!" MacHebe said, deciding to stand up for herself. "I think I should have a medal and a promotion for all my bravery in the regiment. Instead, you want to shoot me!"

"Who asked for your opinion?" the sergeant shouted, having nearly finished his third thimble. "What is it to do with you?"

"Well, I is the one who-----"

"Have another beer," Nell interrupted, topping the sergeant's thimble up.

"Thank you, My Lady," the sergeant answered bowing once more.

It was at this stage that Aphrodite decided to join Nell and come to Hebe's rescue.

"Who is your gorgeous friend?" the Goddess of Love asked, pushing herself directly in front of Hebe and in full view of the sergeant.

"This is Sergeant MacGobo of the Argyll and Sutherland Highlanders," Hebe answered with a sigh.

"Delighted to meet you," Aphrodite said, giving the sergeant a beautiful smile. "I'm the Goddess Aphrodite."

"At your service, My Lady," the sergeant replied, suddenly feeling slightly warm.

"Let me top you up again," Nell said, refilling the thimble.

"I can tell you're a real lady's man," Aphrodite said. "Is that right, Sergeant?"

"Well, I've had my moments," MacGobo replied with a blush before draining his thimble full of beer, which Nell again topped up. By now the sergeant was fully focused on Aphrodite and had forgotten all about Private MacHebe.

"Many moments, I'm sure," Aphrodite purred. "And you're a real gentleman too, I can tell."

"I try to be, My Lady."

"Please call me Aphrodite," the goddess said before adding saucily: "Yes, I'm sure you always stand up straight when a lady's present."

"Indeed, I do," the sergeant replied before knocking back another beer, which Nell promptly replenished.

This love-in continued for the rest of the evening with Sergeant MacGobo getting increasingly drunk on all the beer Nell was giving him. Eventually, Aphrodite picked up the small man, put him in her cleavage and took him home where she found a shoe box for him to spend the night. The following morning, he had the most appalling hangover, was strapped onto MacLeonard's back and returned to Lilliput. Nothing more was ever heard of the arrest warrant for Private MacHebe, who in due course wrote a formal letter of resignation from the regiment to Colonel MacPonsibl. A week later she received a handwritten reply which she had to read under a microscope. In it he thanked her for her service, informed her she had been promoted to lance-corporal the day before she left the regiment and, most importantly, she was given a medal!

Printed in Great Britain
by Amazon

21281928R00193